Riley
Moon

Riley Moon

Curse of the Dragon

Joseph Falletta

the goal is to fight them, without becoming them . . .

authorHOUSE®

AuthorHouse™
1663 Liberty Drive
Bloomington, IN 47403
www.authorhouse.com
Phone: 1-800-839-8640

Published by AuthorHouse   04/30/2012

ISBN: 978-1-4685-6386-3 (sc)
ISBN: 978-1-4685-6388-7 (hc)
ISBN: 978-1-4685-6387-0 (e)

Library of Congress Control Number: 2012904864

Illustrated by Joseph Falletta

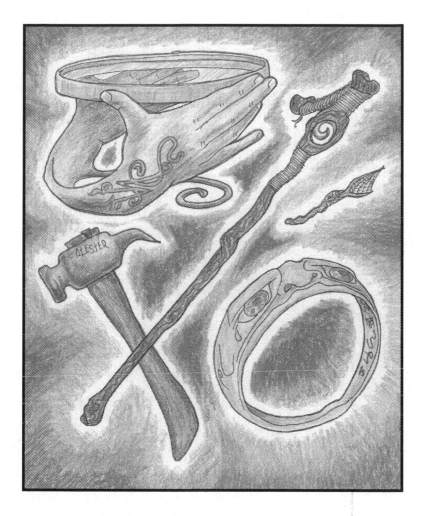

TO WRITE TO THE AUTHOR

Both the author and publisher appreciate hearing from you and learning of your enjoyment for this book. If you wish to contact the author or would like more information and free digital color copies of artwork, please contact us at josephfalletta905@gmail.com.

In loving memory of Virginia Falletta

A special thanks to Roberta Falletta and Tracee Ouville.

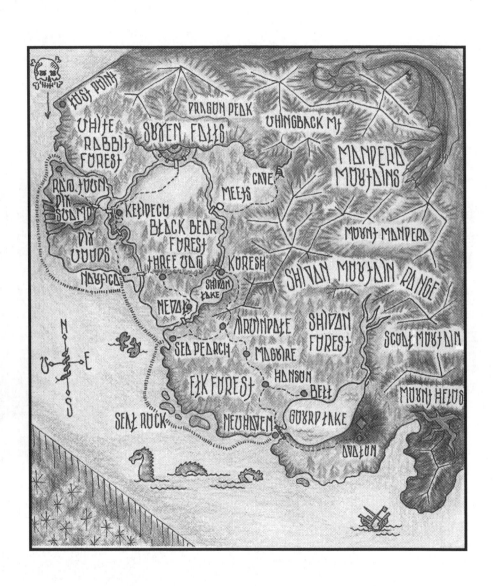

CONTENTS

Some words are understood by all

because they are spoken in a universal language,

the language of the heart.

Opening Prayer

One of the hardest things a father can do, is send his daughter off to fight a war. But this is what Avenu the Mother of all Worlds asked of me.

I know you are too young to understand. If something goes wrong it will be you that has sacrificed more than any of us. I don't even know why I am telling you this now. But you need to know the past, if you are to save our future. If you can only remember one thing, Remember, we all have to believe if the prophecy is to become true. Even with this knowledge, it is with a heavy heart I send you. I do this because I truly believe you can help them.

Let it not be said, man is his own worst enemy. Still in the end, the human race only had itself to blame. How ironic it is, that the simplest lessons are always the hardest to learn. Play with fire, you will get burned.

It was a commoner named Clarence Tipper Fergal that ultimately set in motion the chain of cataclysmic events that ended mans overindulgent way of life. Not that one person can truly be singled out. Like most sentient creatures, humans share a natural need for dominance over each other. Still it was his finger that ultimately pushed the flashing red button marked so clearly, FIRE.

The humans used a type of magic that utilized gizmos and gadgets called technology to war with each other. Amazingly enough they had no regard for the amount of energy their weapons put out. Any first year acolyte knows raw power is nothing, without control. But control was not a priority. More was. More wealth, more power, more damage and more destruction.

Knowledge and understanding are two very different things. With all the wisdom the humans had, somehow they lost respect for life, and the uncontrollable powers they wielded so carelessly in their hands. It is no wonder they were unable to truly comprehend the consequences of their actions, until it was too late . . .

Somewhere in what the humans referred to as the Twenty-third Century man unwittingly burned open a doorway that connected the elemental planes of existence to their own reality. This gateway let loose beings of fire, water, earth, and air, only dreamt of in their folklore. These beings fought with each other unleashing unimaginable destructive forces never seen before by human eyes. The humans had no idea what true power was until they were face to face with the end of days.

The enormous Elemental beings ripped through the fragile human landscape with ease. As clever as the humans were their advanced technologies could not protect them. Sadly, no one knows if the malevolent entities even realized the humans were there. The secrets of their science-magic were quickly lost, as their legendary cities of light were turned into ruble.

In time, the great elemental soldiers lost their stamina. It was inevitable. They were cut off from the endless supply of magical energy that was so abundant in their own worlds. Unable to feed, their powers weakened and the battles subsided. Ending the Great Elemental War.

The human race was devastated. For the humans this is a time of sadness, but for many others it was a celebration of deliverance. Life as the humans remembered was gone. In the aftermath of the war the humans found they now shared their home with many different creatures. Those who only needed ingenuity and fresh air to survive. These races chose to escape the elemental realms, running from their oppressors in hopes of finding a new life. To them this place was an exciting new world.

Selvains were the first to make their claim, forest folk from the realm of earth. They were followed by Gnomes, tiny creatures who floated in on living airships. Next came Killons, dark winged giants and Belenthions who looked like large humanoid insects. There were too many to count. They all had different innate magical powers that allowed them to take advantage over each other. Even our kin the Pelkins must have seemed strange to the humans. They always said our faces resembled the eloquently noble creatures they referred to as cats.

Some of these exotic races were natural enemies. Others were meeting each other for the first time. Alliances were made and broken as each fought for their place in this strange new land.

Powerless and vulnerable, striped of their technology, humans were of little consequence. Overwhelmed and easily controlled the humans had to hide in order for their race to survive.

Mans worst enemy was the strongest of these new races. A group of Red Dragons from the elemental plain of fire, they fed on the humans like cattle. Those who endured the carnage believed they had been judged. Their penance, hell on earth.

But this red horror was not shared by the humans alone. The dragons threatened the existence of all the new races. The sheer strength and size of these fire breathing goliaths was terrifying. But these obvious attributes are nothing compared to the Red Dragons superior intellect and their understanding of Arcane Magic. This combined with their innate ability to control the elements, especially the ability to create fire, is what made them so dangerous. Individually, these dragons were a force to be reckoned with. Together they were unstoppable. They dominated the other races. Their rule lasted for a thousand years.

Until a band of heroes stepped forward. Oddly they were led by a Human called Race who had befriended a Selvain Healer from the elemental realm of earth. Together they organized several of the new races including those of our kind. Fighting together we were able to win small victories over the Red dragons. We fought with promise of freedom for all. Thousands died in epic battles, but still collectively the dragons were too strong and the fighting was weighing its toll on this already unstable world.

We only had one chance. With the blessing of Avenu, Race and his group of adventures were able to divide and conquer the evil horned denizens by using a magic so powerful it separated the planet into small sections, by making a honeycomb of invisible barriers that could not be crosses.

The only way to pass safely from one area to another was to use the Sacred Temples of Avenu, these temples enabled those inside to teleport themselves to different sections of our world. These temples were deliberately designed to be too small for the dragons to use. This forced the dragons to defend their individual territories alone.

Once the Red Dragons were separated from each other, Race and the others were able to clear one location at a time and begin cleansing the earth of this red tyranny. Ending the reign of the Red Dragons.

During this time the world was given a chance to breathe again. Civilizations started to rebuild, empires were reborn. Even some pockets of humans were able to regroup and start over now that they were rid of dragons and left isolated by the invisible barriers. It was believed all the red winged demons were tracked down and killed. But we were wrong.

While the dragon warriors rejoiced in their victories, the last coven of dragons still stirred, plotting, waiting, and watching. A dragon is never completely defenseless. It was true the temples were physically too small for them to use, but not those under their influence.

The fight for earth's rule was not over. Emi the strongest of the Red Dragons still had her sights set on total domination, although trapped in her portion of this world, she was still fiendishly able to reach out and stop the dragon hunters. They paid the ultimate price for their defiance.

The fight for each area on the map has become crucial and we have recently become aware of how important the humans really are. Because they were not perceived to be any immediate threat their area has been left untouched since the days of the Dragon Wars. Because of this oversight they ultimately will become our greatest asset.

New heroes are needed to protect us from Emi the Evil Grand Dragon as she regains control and tightens her grip on this world.

All eyes are watching. So we must not be noticed as those who are needed to fight can be positioned together. With your help, there is a light at the end of the tunnel. It has been foretold that another band of heroes will be gathered.

Our last best hope for a future lies in the hands of a young human girl and a Selvain boy, who are still unaware of the evil closing in around them.

I will miss you. Avenu be with you all.

CHAPTER ONE

Passerbys

I awoke to the sound of Lou and his noisy cart. Father warned me he would be over early today. I could hear my destiny squeaking up the drive. I still was half asleep, enough to ignore my imminent fate, burying my face in a pillow, rolling over to get comfortable again. I knew Lou would first head for the main house to talk to my father, who probably had been up since sunrise. Still, this was my last chance to steal twenty more minutes of complete bliss, as they got side tracked on the weather or some other monotonous subject. Lou and Father never had a short conversation.

I can't wait in a few weeks I will be eighteen, even if I don't look a day older then twelve. I'm a Selvain boy, our kind tend not to age as fast as humans. Still father says that's when I will become a man. I don't understand the difference a few days will make, but I still am eager.

It will be wonderful, the whole town will come out to celebrate and Father says if I want, I can have a whole pie to myself. Well . . . maybe the whole town won't be there, actually no one at all. I don't have a lot of friends. Most of my kind, live in small villages deep in the forest, I grew up in a small town called Maguire here on my father's farm. Even if I don't have the birthday I always dreamed of, surrounded by all the popular kids, I can still dream of pie.

Lucky me! I think I scored at least thirty minutes of pie time, before I heard the clank of the heavy metal latch on the large barn doors. A cool updraft of cold air would be my final warning, as the barn doors slid open, shedding light on a variety of lathes, vices and other assorted tools. I pulled my blankets a little bit tighter prolonging the inevitable, cringing in expectation of what was next.

"Ring, Ring." If "Ring, Ring" could fully describe the clanging of a gaggle of old cow bells. A rope tied to a broken shovel handle, ran from below up the side of the barn, through several eyehooks into the loft. Ringing directly next to the layered blankets that had been placed on several empty fruit boxes, I used as a bed.

If the bells were not echoing through the barn they were definitely echoing in my head. Father and Lou were ringing for me. I could picture them standing there, still talking, looking up, waiting impatiently for the first signs of life.

Alester was not truly my father, yet I did call him so. He raised me more like a son than a servant. I always had free run of the place, my own space. I was encouraged to speak my mind. We always shared everything, like a family, even if there were only two of us. Father rarely even raised his voice to me. I was oblivious to punishment having never seen the crack of a whip, or the back of my father's hand.

My father also gave me books and taught me to read and write, because Selvain children are not welcome at school with the other kids. I do not see what all the fuss is about. So what my ears are a little pointier, my eyes a little bigger, my skin a little darker and green. That's no reason to treat me so differently.

Gosh, when I really think about it, I am the only Selvain that lives here in the tiny town of Maguire. The only time I see other Selvains, they're driving the fancy carriages of the more well to do as they pass by Father's farm. Heads down, eyes forward, not much to say, but an occasional polite "Good morning."

Lou Wickets was a tall, older man, who was a little overweight, sporting a well manicured beard. His silver sideburns followed his jawbone till they reached his chin, connecting to his handlebar mustache, leaving his chin as bald as his head. He spent his days in his garden, his nights harassing my father. He is our good friend.

He lives with his wife and daughter, just a stone's throw up the main road. Julia, his wife, was quiet unlike Lou who never stops talking. She also is the first to cook, clean or do any monotonous chore, while Lou is the first to sit down and theoretically talk about how to tackle the job at hand, as she gets everything done. Julia has long blonde hair with very kind eyes, the kind of eyes I pictured my mother would have, if I ever was to meet her.

Lou's daughter's name is Katinka, but we call her Kat. She is as small-town as a girl can get. Petite little thing, she can't weigh a hundred pounds, soaking wet. Her hair is beautiful, like her mother's, only she would dye the tips of her hair different colors using the juice from fruits and berries. Little Miss Prissy, if she was not fixing herself up or pretending to be in charge, her face was buried in a book. She never missed a day of school and always had an opinion on everything, especially, on what makes a person important. "Influential people go to school," quoting her teacher, "Knowledge is power." One would think that just by listening to her she was much older, but she's really more than two years younger than me.

Self-delusion is a wonderful thing. Kat would fold the ends of her dresses momentarily changing the length, then stretch or pinch the arm cuffs, always accessorizing with brightly colored scarves, anything to mimic the fashions of passing travelers she saw on the road. She would make believe she was on top of the world of fashion, parading around, pretending, she was in style. None of that mattered to me, all I ever noticed was her smile, it stretched from ear to ear, chasing away any frown I ever had.

Sometimes in the early morning hours, I would secretly watch her and the other local kids, as they waited by the roadside for the cart that would pick them up for their classes.

Kat would stand in the way on an imaginary pedestal, offering free advice, always referencing an ad from a prestigious dress shop she would probably never see. Their slogan was, "Always dress for success with . . . blah blah blah." The other kids would ignore her, but I never could. Even with all her faults, she is my best friend. In a peculiar way, she taught me it is O.K. to dream of grander things.

3

Lou and his family knew my father as long as I could remember. Kat and I were raised hand and hand. Our families spent many moons together on father's porch. Julia would help Kat and me with our studies, while Lou and my father played cards or discussed Commonwealth politics, as if the people they talked about, who are so far away, could make decisions that could actually change our lives. Considering, other than an occasional fishing trip, I can not recall any one of us traveling much farther than Airwindale or Hanson, two of the smallest towns on the long road and our only links to the big cities.

We lived along the main road that stretched the entire length of the Commonwealth. At night, after dinner and our studies, the five of us would engage in our most popular pastime. We would watch the road with anticipation, hoping for nighttime travelers. Passerbys is what we called them. They were the important people headed for the interesting places. Late night travelers who simply, passed us by?

We wondered what important messages they carried to cause them to be in such a rush. Depending on the quality of the carriage and the condition of their horses, we would speculate on their destinations. Kat and I would make up tall tales of secret packages being delivered to suspicious figures in dark alleys of far away towns. Sometimes we would pretend they were great heroes sent out on epic quests, whose noble deeds would someday save the Commonwealth. Every story we would tell would be even more fantastic than the last.

Lou would always interrupt, boasting that the city elders were always digging up old pieces of scrap metal in Avalon then quietly carting them off to private laboratories, always hiding the fact they had proof of long forgotten advanced civilization. He always told us outlandish tales of bloody wars, Kings, Queens, and of course my favorite, stories of dragons. Lou would boast the city's leaders never tell the truth, constantly preaching he would rather be here in our cozy little town than surrounded by the dreadfully deceitful characters one would meet if you traveled to the big cities. Lou always made funny faces pretending to be mean and scary to emphasize his point. He only succeeded in making us laugh.

On slow nights while we enjoyed an open fire and the starry sky. Occasionally, Lou would also do a card trick or two. It was uncanny, the way Lou always knew what card you picked, he also could make cards disappear or burst into flames and then reappear. Lou would smile and say, "It's all in the hands," as we tried to figure out how he did what he did.

Where was I? Oh ya pie, "Ring, Ring." I waited till father rang twice, first looking out, then down from between two hay bales suspended high above the floor below. Hay bales were placed on the edge of the platform making the walls of my makeshift bedroom, in the loft of my father's barn.

Shaking out the dust from my long messy hair, I threw on my cleanest clothes and grabbed for the first rungs of the ladder pole that connected my private world to the ground. I'm small, but strong and nimble, after a few steps down, I allowed myself to fall backwards, flipping out toward a pulley rope that I normally used to haul hay bales and things up to my loft. This time I used the rope to lower myself slowly down, raising a rusty old bucket to the roof of the barn. There was a loud cracking sound as the bucket got caught in the rafters stopping my decent abruptly, just before I hit the hard ground?

That's what I'd like to call a stylish landing. "You rang." I said sarcastically, as if I was unaware of what was happening. I knew I would be fixing Lou's cart, while they discussed, how to, from the comfort of the porch.

Clovis was Lou's horse, a good size stud with brown and white markings. Lou handed me Clovis's reins and an apple he had just bitten, garbling his words as he chewed, "Why don't we start by taking the old boy out to the back pasture?"

Father was grunting as he struggled to unhook the leather straps linking Clovis to the cart. Lou smiled adding, "Don't dally, I brought a bag of apples and a fresh pie Kat made." What he meant was, next I would be carrying them topside. He knew I would hurry. Kat made the best pies.

I used Lou's half-eaten apple to coerce Clovis into joining Kas in the coral outback. Kas was my father's foal, she was a little sleeker than Clovis with similar markings. Kat had braided red ribbons and white flowers into her mane. If Kat was not gussying herself up, she was helping dress up someone else. She was always saying "Only the most important people have horses with ribbons and flowers braided in their hair." She liked to pretend we were more important than we were, always hoping some day we would be one of the Passerbys.

When I returned to the barn, Lou and my father were talking about Avalon. It was a three day ride to the south and lies on the far side of Gourd Lake. Lou always told us stories about Avalon. Once he even showed Kat and I how the priests there measured time by using what he called a sun dial. All you really need is a straight stick and be able to point north. Lou knew lots of unusual things like that. He especially knew a lot about Avalon. His father was lost in the big fire there. To this day the city is still just a ghost town. I was too young to remember, it happened shortly before Kat was born and before Lou and Julia built their home here. My father told us at one time Avalon was the largest city and the capitol of the Commonwealth, before the notorious fire that left the city in ashes.

Lou was going on about the strange things he recently heard about the abandoned temple that rests in the center of the burned out abandoned city. The temple is the oldest standing building in the Commonwealth. Stone ruins where an order of priests once made offerings to the God's to protect us from dragons. Lou was reminding Father it was not so long ago.

Father was mocking Lou's frivolous suspicions of some ominous danger still lurking there. Laughing and making funny faces at the mention of real dragons, facetiously blaming the fire on the carelessness of the priests. Lou was not amused. His face was always serious when the old city was mentioned.

They didn't notice I was listening as Lou still jabbered away. He was talking about some gossip he had overheard from several of the Passerbys who had come down the road leaving Newhaven, the closest city to Avalon. They told him strange lights were seen in the forest around Gourd Lake and rumor was whole families have been reported missing in the small towns around Hanson, another stop on the way to Newhaven. And that's not all, It was said one traveler was attacked by a huge wild bear, and hunters have seen animals ten times larger than normal. Lou went on. Even stranger occurrences have been reported, like crop's, not just dying out or being eaten by bugs, the plants appear to be changing into vicious creatures then eating the livestock and attacking the farmers. Then he added, lets not mention Mount Helos started blowing smoke. Lou confirmed what he always insinuated, the Passerbys believed evil spirits from the temple were to blame.

No one could spin a yarn like Lou, and he always was overly zealous when anything was said concerning Avalon, especially when the temple was mentioned. My father laughed and blamed the tall tales on the Newhaven Brewing Company and their wicked ale. That and the healthy imaginations of sailors who spent one too many days out of dry-dock. Lou took the stories much more serious, bothered that my father was overlooking the temple's past.

Eventually they both noticed I was eavesdropping. They immediately stymied up, turning their heads, in sync. Giving me, The Look, that said, "Get movin, mister." So I grabbed the pie and the bag of apples and headed for the house. I had a regular list of things to-do. None more important right now, than having a nice big piece of pie.

Father's house was dwarfed by three cottonwood trees that hung over his little farm house, with the huge covered porch. The porch really was bigger than the inside of the house. It was where father spent most of his time relaxing. I laid the bag of apples by the front door, on one of the rocking chairs that faced the main road, placing the pie on the table next to Lou's old box of cards.

Father and I made the big table years ago. The tabletop was cut from a single slice of an old cottonwood. We had cut down the massive tree when we cleared the area on the back side of the barn for a hen house. The heavy table was nine of my feet wide and was centered on the porch just outside our front window. The window shimmered with a multitude of colors because it was fashioned out of the severed bottoms of old wine bottles. The table had five chairs, all carved out of stumps, cut from a single limb. One of the chairs around the table had a knife stuck in it. So I got comfortable and cut myself a piece of pie.

I always loved the great cottonwoods. I am very agile tree climber. Some of the largest cottonwoods stand in our village and I can climb higher than Kat ever could. It was one of the few things I did better than her and the other children around here.

The town of Mcguire is very small, there are only a couple of store fronts, so most places are used for more than one purpose. One is a bed and breakfast, which doubles as the hospital. Mister Glamchi runs the desk and his spouse is a midwife. There is also a tavern called 'The Beaten Path' that doubles as the general store. You could always tell when you were near the bar especially on a hot day when the wind was moving in your direction. The stale sent of pipe smoke and the empty barrels of ale that are neatly stacked to the roof-line leave a formidable smell in the air.

The largest building is the townhall, it doubles as the local school house. There are also several big houses; one of them has a red barn which is also the local stable. All the structures surround a small park that is more like an empty field that had been cleared for local farmers to set up shop and the occasional town celebration. Life in Maguire is pretty simple.

I was finishing my second piece of pie when Lou and father finally reached the porch carrying a basket of eggs. I just smiled my face full of pie. As Father bellowed out, expecting no less of me. "Riley, you little shit, you better have saved some for us! Now that you're done fartin around, you have chores to do." Pausing to take a deep breath, "and Lou will need the back left wheel on his cart repaired, and don't forget to feed the chickens when you feed Kas!"

Lou adding in a softer voice, "Clovis could use a good brushing too."

Content, my belly filled with pie, I shuffled down the porch steps to the path that led back to the barn to start my busy day. I did most of the work around the farm, now that Father was getting old and grey like Lou. It seems all Father does these days is just gossip with the neighbors, play cards, and plan how he going to fix his next meal.

Hustling to get my chores done, my day went by quickly. It was almost time to light lamps. I was already done fixing Lou's cart, and was brushing down Clovis when I heard the voices of Kat and Ms. Wickets, approaching the house. I whistled at Kat then waved, she was holding up a basket that meant dinner time.

I dropped what I was doing and ran to the house were everybody was gathering. Lou and my father already had a fire going, with six rabbits roasting. Kat placed her basket filled with fresh biscuits and honey on the table, next to a bowl of sliced apples and blackberries Father prepared.

I picked up a wood barrel full of hemp oil and joyfully asked Kat if she wanted to light the lamps with me. She always did. There were half a dozen lanterns on the porch, they were already lit. We started on the row of twelve large blown glass lamps that highlighted the path to the barn. The walkway curved all the way down to where it met the main road. Each light was hung on a heavy wooden post, connected by a cobblestone wall that stretched the entire length of the drive. There were four more lamps on the end, two on each side, set close under a carved sign that read, "Alester Moon and Son, Woodworkers."

The trees are so thick along this part of the road, sometimes it appears as if the road is an endless tunnel, only separated by a few small towns and a few patches of sunlight that break threw the tree tops. Wild blackberries grow along the way leaving a sweet smell in the air.

Lighting the lamps went quickly. Kat knew a trick her father taught her. She could light the wicks of the lamps without a stick of wood or a lamp that was already lit. The same way Lou could light cards on fire. A trick Lou taught her when she was young. With a simple snap of her fingers it was like sparks came out of her hand. No matter how many times I watched her do it. I could not figure it out. She sure made lamp lighting easy.

We were lighting the lamps around the sign, when we first heard horses coming from the south up the road. The trees that lined the road amplified the rumble of the oncoming carriages. Kat was excited, nights seem to go by quicker with a few Passerbys, and we could get a better look standing right by the road. I didn't mind. I was always hoping for a kiss, in the romantic lamplight. Even if I knew that it would never happen. Kat didn't want to be known as the girl who kisses Selvain boys. I still liked to try.

A single rider came first, he was dressed in dark clothes. He flew by us, continually beating his heavily panting horse with a whip, pushing it to run faster. That's when the carriage came into view, pulled by two jet black stallions, its silver lamps lit up the road. It must be someone important because the coach's bright metal fixtures and finely polished sides glimmered in the moonlight. It was moving a little fast for the dirt roads in these parts.

Then something terrible happened! When they reached the bend in the road that hugged the property by the far end of the barn, it looked like the wheels got stuck in a rut, ripping the heavy cartwheels apart, separating the axles from the cab.

The horses fell forward dropping to the ground, their harnesses were torn apart. The driver was thrown forward, followed by the cab of the carriage now separated from the wheels rolling sideways over the horses, and then over the driver, crushing his legs as the cab slid, settling on its side. It did not seem such a wreck could be possible. Carriages don't just stop when moving at full speed. Wheels don't shatter, horses don't trip.

Abruptly the door on top of the cab slammed opened, two figures climbed out. Jumping down they immediately darted away from the crash into the woods opposite the farm.

I ran to the barn to get a portable lamp. Kat moved slowly up the road, I quickly ducked through the trees to catch up with her. Calling out, "Kat wait up you can't see a thing."

As I got closer, I could hear odd shrieking sounds like I'd never heard before, dreadful sounds I thought were coming from the injured horses. The high pitched shrieks continued, followed by six of the strangest shaped mounts I'd ever seen. Riding them were cloaked figures, their eyes glowed their faces seemed to shimmer in the dim light. One of the figures pointed toward us, shouting in a tongue I'd never heard before. Two of the riders darted down the road, in our direction, passing us by. I finally got a shocking glimpse of their unique animals as they passed.

They weren't horses at all. Their mounts ran on two legs, were scaled and had a beak like a parrot. Not to mention a thick tail that stretched to the ground. The creatures lowered their heads as they ran forward grunting. They followed in the direction of the single rider who passed us very quickly.

Then the leader pointed to the forest where those who left the wreck had escaped. Two more robed figures darted into the woods after them. The creatures navigated the wild blackberries well, jumping over the large bushes disappearing into the infinite network of the dark forest.

The lead rider approached the wreck and dismounted. As strange as it seems, he reached out touching the cab. Its wood walls that shined started to lose their luster. Floors and axels seemed to bend and warp. Leaving a pile of unidentifiable wreckage, no one would know was once a carriage.

As the cab crumbled apart, it exposed a hurt passenger. His animal immediately bit into the leg of the injured man lifting him out of his would-be coffin, now a pile of rubble.

The last rider moved his mount forward, with a word I did not understand and with a yank of the reigns, the second odd beast lunged forward grabbing the man in its oversized beak by the chest. In seconds he was ripped apart by the ferocious creatures.

Not believing what I was seeing I held up my lamp. The two men caught my eye. The leader on the ground pointed and yelled. His counterpart prepared to charge, pulling out a spiked club. The ghastly creature he was riding let out a horrifying jeer, lowering its head, it was going to charge.

In anticipation we attempted to dodge the incoming threat. I don't understand how we had not noticed walking into a patch of heavy weeds. The plants by the side of the road had just reached out, entangling our feet holding us in the path of the rushing villain.

Kat in a smashing blow knocked the lantern from my hand spilling the oil on the growing plants, sparking the oil with her special talent, creating a fire charring the plants that clung to our feet.

The flash also caused the now charging beaked creature to rear back dropping its rider, who lost control falling forward loosing his heavy club. It slid on the ground toward me, as the rider took a detrimental bounce twisting his neck with a cracking sound. His startled beast took a chance at freedom running off into the woods.

Even though its spikes were almost as big as me I grabbed the club, placing myself in between Kat and the mangled figure on the ground, waiving it in a defensive motion. Everything was happening so fast. It took a moment to realize the rider was dead from his fall. I turned toward the leader, Yelling. "You will not hurt her." He just leered back with malcontent. His eyes reflecting, like an animal in the moonlight.

I could now hear familiar voices behind me. Our parents were coming up the road. Father was carrying a pitchfork in a threatening manner. The cloaked figure mounted his ride retreating back down the road from which it came.

It was not the moment I had so long waited for. Kat leaned forward and gently kissed me on the cheek. That's when we heard the driver. He was badly crushed, still alive, but not for long. There was too much blood that had stained the road. More blood than I had ever seen. Lou knelt down and comforted the dying man. There was not much he could do. All the man said was, "Tell Quinn."

Father pulled back the hood of our contorted assailant, revealing a strange snake like head covered in shiny rusty red almost orange scales. Its scaly face was tattooed with a symmetrical design that did not look natural. He could see the neck of the creature had snapped. On its cloak was a copper talisman. As if he did not want us to see Father quickly picked it up.

We tried to help the horses. They were completely engulfed in the vines that covered the area. Their legs were intertwined into tight knots completely entangled in the gripping plants. One horse was crushed by the cab as it rolled forward. The other was still alive, legs broken and bleeding from all over, not able to move other than to twist its body in agony.

Behind the mangled horses, spaced as if they were still pulling a carriage, one full wheel standing upright and three half wheels, all still held in place by growing vines. Just like the plants that grabbed us, these plants seemed to have just sprouted forward, in the middle of the road, stopping the carriage in its tracks.

The cab of the carriage itself was almost dust, as if it wrecked decades ago. Its metal pieces still shinned like new, looking like the bones of a metallic animal picked clean and left in the forest. In its stomach, lay a black leather bag. Lou looked at father and said "This is not good. There is something sinister happening down south!"

We cleared the road the best we could. Father had to put down the badly injured horse. We all walked back up to the porch in disbelief.

Our barbecue had burned out and Bauble, Kat's cat, had taken advantage of the abandoned meal, pulling a burnt piece of meat to the ground. It did not matter, no one was hungry.

Lou placed the black leather bag on the table, father opened it revealing a leather box and a letter that bore the town seal of Newhaven. Carefully wrapped inside the box were four small square clay boxes. They were a little bigger than a large egg and just like an egg they did not open. The cubicles reminded me of dice with strange symbols on all six sides. In one corner of each cube was a small air hole. If you held it to your ear you could hear hissing as if something was alive inside.

Julia said "What of the talisman." She always noticed jewelry. She liked to wear big fancy necklaces with colorful beads or large stones. Father unenthusiastically placed the piece on the table. The copper talisman was in the shape of a crest. Etched into it was a tree, behind it a circle divided into twelve pieces. The lines radiated in an outward pattern like the rays of the sun.

Father reluctantly reached behind his head and removed his gold chain placing it on the table beside the trinket. He always wore the large finely crafted jeweled gold pendant that had the identical symbol. Lou asked him if he knew what the symbol stood for. Father did not know what it meant. Saying, "I only can tell you where it came from."

Turning to me he said "I'm sorry son. You know I love you." He reached out rubbing my head, "You and that crazy long hair. I may not have been one hundred percent truthful when I told you. I bought you at an auction in Newhaven.

You were given to me by a very odd man, in the woods on the outskirts of Avalon. At the time I lived in Newhaven and only traveled to Avalon on that day to make money. People were leaving in fear, it was believed the land was now cursed. Carts were needed, so I went where the work was.

The stories are true, a few days earlier, the temple at the center of town exploded into a fire ball. Some were afraid the sect of priests who worshiped at the temple angered the gods. Other's believed that the dragons of past had returned. The only real explanation was Mount Helios must have erupted.

All anyone really ever knew was something horrific had happened, that made fire rain down reducing the entire town to ashes. Many people burned in their homes right where they stood.

I, like everybody else, was puzzled about what happened there. The few people who had survived refused to talk about it. That's why the people were running away. That's why the center of power was moved from Avalon to Suxen Falls. Nonetheless, my skills were needed making carts. I was in the nearby forest on the far side of the city gathering wood.

That's when Graziano found me, an eccentric little man, with silver streaked red hair and a beard that hung to the ground. Not that he was very tall. He only stood four foot high. Walking in very hairy bare feet wearing a green vest, tea stained silk shirt, and brown breeches. He seemed harmless. Actually he struck me as funny, other than the fact he was pointing his little cane at me in an intimidating manner. Oddly he seemed to be doing four things at once, one of which was threatening me. So I laughed out loud, "What brings you this way, my little friend."

I could tell it was not his first language but in the common tongue he asked me, if I was a priest? I answered. "No. I'm just a woodworker."

"Perfect. Perfect." he replied. Then he asked me if I lived in town. I told him, "I'm only here to make carts."

"Perfect. Perfect." he smiled like a bear with a honey pot. I don't know what was perfect. But he kept saying it. It was kind of creepy, as if he was talking to someone who was not there. He asked me if I knew how to care for a child. I said. "I never had a child."

He sighed, "Not perfect. Not perfect." I don't know why but I whispered. "I could learn."

"Perfect! That will have to do." He moved a branch and there you were, wrapped in a blanket, wearing this pendant, which was almost as big as you.

Seeing there were several large flying bugs around you. I shooed them away. One clung to my arm, purposely it bit me. I heard a little voice say. "He's not perfect." I think they were fairies or better yet pixies. Definitely not bugs! They were small people with wings like dragon flies and sharp little teeth. The strange man had better luck shooing them away.

Graziano handed me the small child, "You will take him. Care for him, you will."

I had never seen a baby like you, scrawny, dark greenish skin, pointy little ears, those round eyes that always looked too big for your head, and that crazy hair. I had never seen a Selvain before. At the time only a few people had. Lumberjacks had spotted groups of your kind living in the forests around Gourd Lake, where much of the lumber to build Avalon came from. I knew by description what you were, and suspected that's where you came from.

Holding you in my arms, I promised I would take care of you. The strange man gave me a pouch with three small rubies. He placed the bag in a box telling me, "With this, you made enough money here. You must go home now and tell no one. Hurry! Hurry! Take this child far from here."

Pixies are mean, dirty creatures. One flew up close in my face, throwing dirt in my eyes. Laughing as it said "He will do now, Graziano." Then the whole group giggled at me.

When the dust settled they were gone. You, the box and this pendant were mine. One look at those blue eyes and my heart melted. At that moment I knew I had to take you and raise you as my own.

With the rubies I bought the farm here in Maguire, we have lived here ever since. The box still sits in the front room by the window where I set it when I returned. It's the one with the mirrored sides and the keyhole that looks like a large cat biting a ring. In the box was food, honey, bread, cheese and wonderful sausages for me and a bottle of fresh milk for you that seemed to stay full for days.

It wasn't but a few years later Selvain's seemed to be caught regularly scavenging food. Eventually, the law came down on the woodland creatures stealing crops from the local farmers. At first people thought all Selvain's were savages, but as the years passed some came to believe they could be domesticated, servants forced to work for the damages they caused. The new laws made it easy to explain why I had you as you grew.

Does it really matter how I got you. I knew I loved you then, as I do today. I did what the little man said and took you home telling no one until today. I guess I thought people would think I was crazy. Stories of little men and tiny flying people. I'm not crazy. I remember it like it was yesterday.

This pendant is yours now. I've kept it safe, thinking it could answer any real questions about, who you are, or where you came from. I have been wearing it for you, till I could find the right time to tell you. But that time never came until today. I don't know how it can help, but it had to be said. It's all I know. I don't know who Quinn is."

That's when Lou interrupted. "I know of, Quinn. He is . . . He'ssssss," stalling to explain. "He is aaaaaa. He lives in Suxen Falls."

Kat who loved stories of the big city asked, "How do you know him."

Lou, frowning as if he was caught doing something wrong, "He is my grandfather. I didn't know he was even still alive. He's got to be at least one hundred years old by now. Either way, we must take what we know to him. Something sinister is brewing at the temple, we can't trust anyone. We must deliver this message to Quinn ourselves, only he has the resources to get to the bottom of whatever or whoever is behind this attack. It's no longer safe here, for any of us."

Father suggested leaving tomorrow. In a stern voice, I had never heard from Lou before. "No, these creatures will be back in numbers, we must leave tonight." No one said a word. Father just shook his head. We all knew he was right.

Father and I both filled a bag with our clothes and rolled up our beds. Lou and Kat hooked Clovis back up to the cart, leading him up to the porch. Father brought out the mirrored box, placing our stuff in it. I caged several chickens. Then set the rest free to roam, hanging the complaining chickens from the side of the cart. Kat gathered some eggs in an old jug, placing them and her basket of biscuits next to the leftover pie on the cart.

Lou gathered two barrels of ale, the bag of apples and three lanterns off the porch. There was a bar of soap, a couple of ropes, a big tarp, father's tool box, and of course, the box of cards from the table.

That's when I knew we were truly leaving, when the table was clear. I saddled up Kas and with a little nudge from Lou, we were on our way. Kat whistled for Bauble who picked up the body of the crispy critter she was eating, and jumped on the cart.

Father, Lou and Ms. Wickets sat on the bench that went across the front of the cart. Kat and I got comfortable in the back, as we entered the well traveled road.

We had not traveled ten feet before Lou stopped the cart. We were right next to the corpse of the strange creature that attacked us. In a shocking act of barbarism, pulling out the knife I used earlier that day to cut a piece of pie. Lou cut the head, hands, feet and tail off the scaly creature, placing them in an empty ale barrel, on the end of the cart. I think I swallowed my stomach and realized I will never look at Lou the same way again.

Just on the other side of the road, a couple hundred paces away we entered an obscured drive only marked by a gray boulder. The drive led to a secluded yellow two story house. The doormat read, "Welcome to the Wickets."

Kat's house was more formal looking than our farm a unique style not typically seen in these parts. Its porch had two tall fluted columns with a colored glass lamp centered above the door. Still the porch was barely big enough for two people to stand on. To the left centered in a small clearing stood an apple tree as tall as the house, on the other side was a well manicured garden. Lou asked me to gather up all the ripe fruit and vegetables I could find. Even thou it was dark, Lou knew at night I could see better than anyone else. My eyes were more like a wolf's than a man's, and as blue as a summer sky.

Looking up at the window on the second floor, I could see Kat frantically passing back and forth in front of a candle trying to decide what to take. Unlike me, she had more than just a handful of clothes to choose from. Lou entered the room attempting to make the final selections for her and an argument ensued, until Julia stepped in.

By the time I was finished in the garden, Father and Lou were lifting one very big ornate chest onto the cart. On the front were two large decorative letters, M.W. Other than that, we took a few pots and pans and Bauble's leash.

Not taking the time to arrange the cart. Lou took charge again. "We must move now!"

Father in a much calmer voice, "I think, we are doing fine."

Lou was twitching his nose. "Can't you smell it?"

He was right, we all could. It smelt like ash. As we pulled back on the road we could see flames above the trees, flames coming from my home. Pausing only for a moment, Lou yanked at the reins.

We slid away silently. It was not long before the glow of the fire was out of sight. Other than a small rumble from the Beaten Path Tavern there was no hurrah, as we passed through Maguire.

The night became a blur of sorrow and disbelief. My mind wandered, going over the evenings events, watching the countless rows of trees that lead us into darkness.

At the first sign of light we came upon Airwindale. I knew many of the people by name because this is where we shopped for things we could not find in Maguire. Grouchy Mister Kevil was sitting outside his shop reading a newspaper scratching his bald head. He was sitting on one of the rocking chairs Father had on consignment. Kat had always liked to look at the ads in the papers, until old man Kevil would shoo her away.

There was Mrs. Fullwilley setting out fresh baked goods. They always smelled as good as they looked. We even saw Kelso, a boy who went to school with Kat. He was with his father setting up a sign in front of their cart. One word, in large letters: 'CORN.' They waved as we passed them by.

To them this was a normal morning. Except that Lou did not even attempt to slow down and say Hi, Mr. Kevil was probably glad he did not have to deal with Kat messing up his newsstand or listen to one of Lou's long stories.

We were sneaking through town as if nothing had happened. With everybody watching we left without saying a word, headed to the big city, hiding our secret cargo, keeping our silence. Somehow, in the night we had become the Passerbys.

CHAPTER TWO

Keeping Secrets

Tired, scared, sad, we all had our reasons, no one said a word. Even the road was quiet, as if the wild life was aware something sinister was following us. It was like we all were keeping secrets.

The huge cottonwood trees that gave me solace for so many years, now hung over us like a weight. The Shivan Forest seemed endless. In reality it extends from the east side of the road to the far off mountains, stretching all the way down to Gourd Lake. On the other side of the road is the Elk forest, it reaches west to the ocean, where the cottonwoods are scarce and huge pine trees cut into the cliffs overlooking the sea.

If you follow the road we are on south, there are several small towns. The end of the line is the burned out city of Avalon. That's where the ancient temple is.

To get to Avalon you must go over Newhaven, by crossing the great bridge.

Father grew up in Newhaven, it's primarily a fishing village now, but at one time it was the main seaport for Avalon. Now it is the largest city to the south. We had traveled there once when I was young to meet his mother, who had fallen sick.

The seaport is situated under two crumbling old stone bridges. The tallest is an extension of the main road that stretches across a massive ravine that skirts the coast. Some call this bridge the gateway to Avalon. Facing east from the top there is a breathtaking view of Gourd Lake feeding a sequence of waterfalls. As the water passes threw large rock formations, it pours into Gull Bay, this waterway surrounds the city below.

From the other side of the bridge you can see where the river meets the ocean, where there are always groups of small boats anchored in the natural harbor, just off the coast.

The large pylons that support the superstructures come directly out of the water and loom hundreds of feet in the air, many dwellings are attached directly to these pillars, like barnacles that cover a ship's stern.

Down below, completely encircling the bases of the massive posts are a series of make-shift docks that connect to each other by many smaller wooden bridges, creating a floating city. This is the town's center and the heart of Newhaven.

A second bridge protrudes directly out of a cave situated on a steep cliff side, and abruptly ends as it passes underneath the taller structure above. This middle platform looks as if the original builders never finished it, constructing a road to nowhere.

There is a series of platforms that can be lowered and raised by a system of large pulleys. The construction certainly shows the lack of technology, compared to the much older main stone structures they are connected to. These lifts are the only way to reach the lower bridge, and the city below, from the main road that towers so high above.

The road we are on starts in Avalon. After crossing the bridge at Newhaven it winds threw the mountains eventually passing threw Hanson then Maguire. It winds far to the north, all the way to Suxen Falls. Lou said that's where Quinn lives.

We traveled almost to nightfall the next day, stopping only briefly. Clovis needed to rest. We all did. That night we made a small fire, camping by a covered wooden bridge on the outskirts of a town called Neval.

Julia started to prepare the meal. We could hear the water trickling in the creek below. Father broke the silence, "That's the sound of the Shivan River." Father pointed to the east saying, "This water flows out of Shivan Lake." We had camped and fished there many times and for a minute we had forgotten our problems, reminiscing about our old trips.

We would catch rainbow trout, catfish and the occasional sun fish, at the end of the day we always had a full pan. Even so, I think the Egrets pulled more out of the water than we ever did.

Kat had never seen an Egret before. I explained Egrets are tall skinny white birds with long black feathers on the back of their heads. They hunt in the shallow water for small fish or stand in the tall reeds looking for beetles and bugs. They nest close to the shore where they constantly walk back and forth feeding their young.

The Egrets were lightning quick, and their precision attacks were lethal, plucking bugs, fish and frogs at will from the water. If only we were as accurate with our trawling skills we could have fed our entire village.

Smaller hatchlings were fed regurgitated food, the larger chicks, feed on live prey. Father and I would watch the proud parents purposely wound their quarry, keeping them alive but incapacitated, unable to escape or be able to hurt their fragile offspring. This is how the Egrets teach their young to kill with a single blow; how to become more effective hunters.

One year I even saw a mother bird catch a baby turtle. I liked the turtles, they are green like me. Father always said the awkward looking little creatures were good luck. The only time I ever saw them was when they would come out of the water to sun on a rock. I always wanted to catch one, but they are quick, not all the stories you hear are true. Once they hit the water, they're gone; back to a secret underwater world, where we can not follow.

Father was telling us a bedtime story, "The Legend of Two Dragons." Once they fought each other, now they watch over us, providing hope and good will for lost travelers who need help along the way. Their spirits live in the mountain ranges that extend the length of the Commonwealth. If you could see the entire skyline you would say it is shaped after two dragons sleeping, their tales entwined in the middle around Shivan Lake.

One dragon faces south ending at Mount Helos, the volcano that overlooks Avalon. The other stretches all the way to Suxen Falls, the big temple there is carved into Dragon's Peak. It is said dragons had perched there overlooking Black Bear Forest at one time. They guarded a great horde of treasure. Some believe is still hidden in the mountain.

Julia interrupted with a call to dinner. She had stewed some chicken and vegetables, serving it with Kat's biscuits. Lou was tending the fire still trying to figure out just what happened, hoping to make a game plan over dinner.

Things were said like, "We won't be able to just return home," and "We should have reported this problem to the authorities in Airwindale." Lou insisted this be brought directly to Quinn, and only Quinn! Rudely stating the authorities in Airwindale would not be able to address an enemy of this sort, or even understand a problem of this magnitude. He made us all promise to talk to no one about what we knew.

After dinner Lou grabbed his large leather bound book and a small mat from his chest, then moved away from us and the fire. I saw the cover as he went by, "Arcane Symbols." Sitting on the mat he started to examine the clay cubes in secret.

Later that night, Lou told us the talisman and my pendant radiated no special qualities. But the cubes appeared to have a unique aurora around them. He also stated out of the six symbols on the cubes, he was only able to identify one, Dracoda, a symbol representing the strength of dragons. He grumbled stating. "Whatever these cubes are for, no good can come of it."

I don't think any of us really understood what Lou was going on about. We all just shook are heads in amusement like we always did when he would tell his fantastic stories. Nothing of interest was said after that and as exhausted as we were it was time to get some rest.

Not that any one of us got a full night sleep, and in the morning we all stayed busy so as not to talk. Julia was scrambling up breakfast while I brushed down the horses. Father gathered some tree limbs, bending them from corner to corner on the cart, fastening a tarp across the top. Saying, "Soon we will need shade." Kat arranged the chests and laid out blankets to soften our ride, so two people at a time, could get comfortable in the back of the newly covered wagon. We all knew we had a long bumpy road ahead.

Sometime toward the end of the day we came upon a place know as Three-keys, it was four times bigger than Airwindale. Lou said, this was the last town before we hit a really big city.

In the middle of the road there was a big wooden pole, on a raised stone pedestal. On the pole there were three separate arms made to mimic the shape of skeleton keys, each pointed out a different direction, on the end of each key were hand painted letters with different destinations.

The sign was surrounded by a circular group of shops, divided by three roads. One sign pointed east to a road that went around Shivan Lake to a town called Koresh. This small road funneled back to Airwindale. We took the road labeled 'Nautica'!

It wasn't long after passing Three-keys, we finally broke out of the thick cover of the trees. The road overlooked a vast valley, beyond that Black Bear Forrest stretched as far as we could see.

Such a beautiful day, the view was clear for miles, from the sea to the Mandera Mountains. The mountains form one of the sleeping dragons Father told us about the night before. Father pointed north-east and to each mountain separately. "That's Dragons Peak. It's the head." It was too far away to see the city of Suxen Falls where the great road starts. "Over there is Wingback Mountain and Mount Mandera, they make the back of the mythical creature." Behind us was the Shivan Mountain Range, a group of smaller peaks that divides the Commonwealth, "The dragon's tail!"

Gradually the road turned west and we could see a river down in the valley, carved deep into the forest floor. It was the Mandera River, jam-packed with barges traveling to and from Nautica, toward Suxen Falls.

We set up camp just off the road. At night we could see the bright lights of Nautica. Every now and then a small light would break off from the large speckled mass, passing underneath us, before it floated away into the night disappearing in the distance. We had hundreds of Passerbys to entertain us. But we could not think of a single adventure more secretive or extraordinary than ours.

This was my, and Kat's first experience in a big city. Tomorrow we would really be there. Our expectations helped us forget momentarily why we had left our homes. Anticipation made the morning sun rise ever so slowly, but once we were on our way, the real excitement began.

Quickly a few travelers turned into a lot of travelers, and we were lost in the mix. Somewhere along the way, without notice the dirt road became paved. The recurring clacking of the wagon wheels became a welcoming drum roll as we descended into the city.

Ahead we could see several smaller dirt roads all leading to a heavy stone block bridge. It took three arches to cover the entire span of this river. The bridge was large enough for barges twenty paces high to pass below, in both directions, on the far shore a new world pulsated with life.

Lou covered his chest with a tarp and Bauble was placed in an empty chicken cage, her ears were tufted back, she was not pleased with her situation. Bauble was not your average house cat, she was a lynx, a snub-tail wild cat. Her body was small compared to other cats of her kind, making her feet look super-sized. She had a lightly mottled reddish to yellow brown coat. Our big Kat dyed the tips of our little cat's ears purple, with blackberry juice. Needless to say, Bauble was not a happy camper. She gave us all, "The Look."

Crossing the bridge revealed a long slightly curved street full of shops and inns. All the buildings were at least two and three stories high. Some had stone entryways or cobblestone walls.

There were several cockeyed streets to turn on. They seemed to be filled with private residences, houses crammed together, built in groups of six and eight. They had orange roofs that looked like they were made of broken clay flower pots. We passed several alleys that curved into darkness even in the day. They did not look safe or inviting. All the same the town had an enticing feel and a gentle roar to it; the sounds of civilization.

The city even had its own distinct odor, the fresh smell of the open ocean was prevalent, but it was slightly tainted by the less than sanitary streets and the people living in such close quarters.

At a glance it looked to be the end of the long road. There I could see a large open market. Beyond that were docks filled with rows of fishing boats unloading their catch of the day. As we drew closer I realized the road did not end, it sharply turned north following the coastline.

Instantly the gentle ocean breeze was corrupted by the odor of fish, laid out in the sun. On the right along the marina were temporary booths, arranged with fresh fruits, vegetables, trinkets and gear, and of course the fresh catch of the day. The majority of the proprietors sold fish, fresh fish, lots of fresh fish. One fish was so big it covered the table it lay on. There were so many different kinds of sea creatures; many I had never seen before. Some simply did not look appetizing. Of course my favorite stands sold a variety of ready-to-eat, ocean delicacies, like fish cakes and steamed mussels.

We finally slowed down as we came around the sharp corner. Now we could see another section of the city. On our left the marina became more visible. Extended along the waters edge was a boardwalk, with steps leading down to private docks, painted white, to give them a touch of refinement.

Amongst the crowds of people, Kat pointed out a young couple strolling by, they stopped to kiss and stare out at the rows of fancy sailboats moored in the scenic landscape. Kat and Julia were trying to whisper softly. Pretending to talk about the lady's hat, but I overheard them giggling to themselves about how cute the boy was, as if we men didn't know what they were really talking about.

We finally stopped just past the farmers market. The intensity of city sounds grew. People were chattering, bargaining over prices or arguing over rumors. There was an occasional horn from a boat out in the harbor and seabirds squawking, hovering overhead, waiting for a merchant to turn away. We were definitely not in Maguire anymore.

Anchored off shore was an ominous looking boat, three times larger than any other boat in the harbor. Lou reached in his chest and pulled out an eyepiece. A series of glass lenses rolled in a piece of hard leather. It allowed us to see the boat closer, showing the fine detail of the carved balconies, and the finely polished captain's wheel engraved with silver.

The woodworking was of no design Lou could recognize. It looked like the ship was constructed without seams, as if its pieces were grown into the shapes they needed. Its lines were fluent and utilized soft natural arches, unlike the other boats whose structures were rigid and boxy by comparison.

The hull of the ship almost resembled a giant seed pod, if that was possible. Along the side was some form of writing Lou was not familiar with. A large stylized eye was painted on the bow. Lou stopped to copy the symbols from the strange boat onto a piece of parchment.

I asked Father if someone could cross the ocean in a ship that size. Father said, "No boats cross the ocean and return." If a vessel could, he guessed that one was big enough to. He had never heard of a boat sailing from anyplace other than up or down the coast. Some ship captains believe you will fall off the edge of the world if you sail too far from shore. Those who tried have paid with their lives.

Father was reciting a list, "Were getting low on chickens, apples," I added "Pie." Lou reminded him twice we were also low on ale. Lou and father sure can drink a lot.

Lou announced we were going to stay the night, he would need time to gather supplies for the last leg of the trip. Finding a place to settle, we purchased two rooms at The Belly of the Whale Inn. A heavy wooden sign hung where it could be seen from either direction, right on the corner where the main road turned left at the edge of the farmers market.

We found a stable for the horses not far from the inn. The cart sat in the alley outback. Empty, except for the 'barrel' containing our pickled friend who was defiantly getting a little ripe. No less odorous than the extravaganza of foreign delights coming from the alley behind the shops.

Mrs. Wickets, Kat and I went to check out the farmers market. None of the shop keepers would talk directly to me or even look me in the eye. They just kept telling Ms Wickets to keep the Selvain boy away from the merchandise.

There was a lot of gossip about the big ship in the harbor. The townsfolk were uneasy. It was obvious the dark ship was not of these waters. Everybody was talking about it. Rumor was, no humans were found aboard, and several dead Selvain's were taken off the ship, while several more were caged and discreetly ferried off to Suxen Falls.

The town's people made no qualms about letting me know I was not wanted. Making sure I was within ear shot, one man boasted the only good Selvain is a dead one.

People believed Selvain's must have stolen the ship because none aboard had the ability to navigate the large vessel. One girl pointed to a damaged part of the dock, claiming the massive vessel floated out of control, drifting into the harbor, damaging the railings and several small boats.

Kat was making a spectacle of herself removing Bauble from her cage leading her around on her leash, while strutting and flashing a bright yellow scarf, as if she was modeling a fancy outfit. Bauble was of no help, glad to be free again and curios about all the new sights and smells, she lead Kat down the rows of booths sniffing the ground looking for scraps. In many ways bauble acted more like a dog than a cat. Bauble was smart too, she always listened, it was as if she understood everything Kat said.

Like bees to honey, Kat attracted the eye of one of the locals who started to flirt with her. A young boy, who introduced himself as Alerick, was attempting to pet her kitty, using a small piece of fish to gain Bauble's trust.

Sarcastically he improvised. "Nice tail." Kat spun around showing off her assets, laughing as if he said something funny.

Alerick was dressed like most of the men, he wore a soiled green bandanna over his lousily fitting soiled shirt, he had old leather boots and dark brown leather breeches. A colorful sash made of many pieces of cloth made him stand out against the crowd. His breath smelled like the area behind The Beaten Path. His lip, ear and eyebrow had multiple piercing. There was a round ivory plug in one ear, you could see right though it, accompanied by several small silver loops, and a shark tooth earring dangling from the other side.

He didn't look safe or nice to me. Alerick was showing off his tattoo of a mermaid, flexing his muscle to make the seductive creature dance. Kat enjoyed the attention, smiling, and batting her eyes, as she felt his biceps. He was twisting the long hairs of his scruffy goatee as he thought about what to say next.

I did not like the way he looked. Especially the way he leered at Kat, she did not seem to care. She kept flirting back, till her mother gave her, The Look, "Get movin, Missy." She smiled and winked at Alerick one last time and moved on.

We were almost done getting the supplies on our list, when the lamplighters started to light the rows of large hanging oil lamps lining the main street and the nicer areas of the boardwalk, mainly the areas that were painted white.

Daylight was disappearing quickly. Taking shape in the sky was a breathtaking sunset, the kind of sunset where there is a million shades of red, layered across the horizon, reflecting glimmering streaks of color across the ocean. Long shadows highlighted the boats in the harbor. A gypsy girl tending a booth leaned forward singing, she kept repeating one verse, "Red sky's at night, sailor's delight, red sky in the morning, sailor's warning."

The streets of the city were dimly lit, the makings of a romantic setting. Julia crushed my hopes with one sentence. We should get back to the rooms and find your fathers. When we do, you kids better not go far. We are leaving early in the mourning.

When we finally caught up with Lou and my father they were drinking in the tavern nestled in the front lobby of the inn. It's been a long time since either of them traveled to a large town. They were the loudest patrons in the establishment.

There was a long haired brunette sitting on my fathers lap spilling beer on his pants, I think she was one of the barmaids. He laughed deeply as he enjoyed her company, I don't remember the last time I saw him so happy.

Julia was attempting to pull Lou up to the room. I did not get far into the bar before I was told by the bartender with a cleft lip, to stay out of the tavern. My kind was not allowed inside. Kat and I decided to walk outback into the alley. Julia reminded us again not to wander far, as she escorted a tipsy Lou to their room.

There was a sign above the door that said "No Drinking Outside", that was probably true. I could barely stop myself from gagging. I didn't think anything could smell as bad as the area behind The Beaten Path, but nothing could prepare you for the interesting bouquet of odors that was fermenting outside the backdoor of The Belly of the Whale.

I don't know what smelled worse, the large canister of trash from the kitchen, filled with fish bones and what was left of the lunch special, combined with the largest pile of empty ale barrels I had ever seen, not to mention years of customers not able to handle their drink, or our cart . . . , with the rotten concoction of inhuman body parts.

Bauble was sitting on the rancid barrel, constantly trying to get at what was inside. She and a large group of flies were intrigued by the noxious fumes. Seizing the moment Bauble settled for a flying snack.

We were close enough to the bar to hear the happy drunks telling their stories, constantly being interrupted by the clang of glasses and the whining lull of a local band of musicians playing in the tavern. Slowly we became desensitized to the stench permeating the area around the barrel but we still sat downwind.

That's when he showed up. Alerick, the dirty boy from the marketplace we had seen earlier. It was creepy the way he snuck up on us, nonchalantly asking Kat if she felt safe in the alley, all alone. Joking about how pretty girls can disappear easily. He said slurring his words, "Sometimes they are whisked off unwittingly, to a different world, waking up far from home."

Amused Kat giggled. "I am already far from home."

Alerick talked as if I was not even there. So I stood up. "She's not alone . . . pal."

He laughed and asked Kat if her Selvain does any other tricks. She laughed back, as if this witless wonder was funny. Alerick pulled out a jeweled dagger thrashing it in the air. "I can protect you," flirting back tightening his shoulder muscles flaunting a different tattoo of a big shark with sharp teeth.

Touching the tip of his little sword, Kat smugly replied, "Courage and a dagger may not be enough."

"I am Alerick of the Shark Fin Clan. My friends and I run this town. We have even been aboard the dark ship." Bragging with a crooked smile, "That's where I boosted this fine dagger." He pulled a piece of fine cloth from his belt, claiming it also came from onboard the insidious dark ship. The cloth was very soft and woven out of a special thread. It shimmered, changing colors as it turned in the light. He handed the beautiful piece of fabric to Kat, "For you, my lady."

He continued telling us about the ship. He could not believe the massive sails were made entirely out of this exquisite fabric. Alerick said the oddest thing about the fancy ship was what was held in its cargo hull, he was surprised to find nothing of significant value. His friends thought they were going to hit it big, but the ship was filled with flowers. Swearing an oath to his clan that he was telling the truth, the lower decks were filled with rows of potted plants, and dried flower petals wrapped in leather bundles. Expressing his opinion, "My clan will make a better profit off the sails."

Bragging next, about the other loot he and his friends found aboard the ship. A book, a ring, a weird shaped twisted metal sextant and a map that hinted of a distant shore, not to mention several elaborately embroidered robes and a flag made of a similar fine cloth.

Kat's eyes lit up. It was like he knew what she wanted to hear, mentioning her three favorite things. "I like flowers, pretty cloth, and books," I thought to myself, we can add boys with tattoos.

Sliding herself closer to Alerick, as if it was necessary to continue talking, Kat asked him what kind of book he found. Smiling at him, batting her eyes again, and attempting to use her girlish charms. She never looked at me like that.

Alerick's face went blank, it was the first time he didn't have a quick answer. I don't think he even knew how to read, as he replied generically, "An expensive book with a fancy cover."

Kat was curious, "Really can I see it."

Alerick was flustered as if he had already said too much. "I don't know, its worth quite a bit of coin, maybe too expensive for a young girl like you," finally making up an excuse, "Besides, it's stashed."

Changing the subject he said, "Me and my clan think the pink flower petals are some kind of new tobacco."

Alerick pulled out an ornate glass pipe, with an assortment of yellow streaks swirled into the hand blown handle. Opening a small tinder box made out of a carved whale bone, Alerick offered the pipe to Kat. She shook her head no, giggling, "I don't know how to do that."

Kat had a one track mind and it was still thinking about the book, questioning him about the name on the cover one more time. Not wanting to talk about the book anymore, preoccupied with getting a match out of the little box. Alerick snapped back, "If you like books so much, you must have some yourself."

Kat knew better than to talk about her father's books and had promised not to talk about what we were doing here. So she lied. "We don't have any books. That's silly, were just in town shopping for medicine for my mother."

An electrified look came over Alerick's face as he fiddled with the dagger at his side. "You wouldn't lie to me, would you?" He scraped a wooden matchstick across the stone wall as he talked, lighting the pipe.

Kat was offended snapping back herself. "I don't need to lie to you." Kat looked at me to confirm her story, "Riley, tell him." I just nodded my head in an affirming motion.

Alerick offered the pipe to me, stuffing a fresh pink petal into the bowl. I was hesitant to take it, until he called me a coward. Not wanting to look afraid in front of Kat, I snatched the pipe from his hands. He stood close holding the small box open so I could take a match, gloating because he got his way. Then Alerick started to ask subtle questions, like, "I think your heading for Suxen Falls, probably leaving in the morning." Kat looked at me before denying it.

Alerick twitched, and then smiled. I was still trying to light the match, like he did, against the wall. "Most people who come through here are buying or selling something." he said, taking out another match lighting it in front of me, cupping the flame with his other hand to stop it from going out. "Your cart is empty. So you're, not selling anything. Maybe you are looking to spend some coin."

Kat never got a chance to answer. "Little lady!" Startling us, Ms Wickets was yelling to Kat. She had opened a window on the second floor, and was leaning out, glaring down at us. I looked up, bellowing out a cloud of smoke, choking on the sweet tasting tobacco.

Julia could clearly see what we were doing and who we were with. She was visibly unhappy to see the boy from town. Kat was trying to shoo him away. Alerick could tell when he was not wanted, taking his pipe, he shuffled down the alley.

I was never so happy to be caught doing something I shouldn't. Thank goodness. Ms. Wickets to the rescue, I really did not like Alerick. Protectively, I walked Kat inside, and up the stairs to her door. Her mother was waiting with the door open giving us, The Look. When the door closed I could hear them start to argue. "I hope that was not the boy from the market." Julia said, as Kat did her best to defend herself, arguing with her mom was always a losing battle.

I cowardly slipped away back to my room, when I opened the door, I saw father passed out, laying on one of the beds. I was feeling a little strange myself, and somewhat nauseous, like I had eaten a bad egg. My mind was racing. I don't know what had come over me. I tried to fall asleep, but I could not sit still. The soft mattress was uncomfortable, so I pulled the blankets onto the floor.

My head was swirling. How could a little puff of smoke do so much damage? When I shut my eyes I still could see an explosion of colors.

Even though I was relaxed I did not feel tired. I sat motionless in the dark, staring out the window at the night sky. The stars were twinkling brightly, I don't know why they amused me more then normal. I noticed one of the larger stars made me feel like I was being watched over by the great eye of some benevolent creature, peeking through my window. There was a gentle breeze and for a moment I could smell wild flowers.

Wild flowers always reminded me of the old willow tree that grew in the forest just beyond Kat's house. In the summer wild flowers would grow in abundance around it, filling the air with their subtle fragrance. Kat and I would lay high in the willow's branches, day dreaming. The breeze would almost sound like singing as it passed through the branches of the old tree, lulling us to sleep as we enjoyed the intoxicating fragrance carried on the comforting mountain winds.

I was overcome with a sense of inner peace, as my mind continued to wander on the proverbial psychedelic highway I was floating down. I did not want the good feeling to stop. I don't know how long I lay awake dreaming, absorbed in the sensation of colors dancing in my mind.

For a moment I thought I was in the wrong room. I was still in a bedroom, but in this room there was a fancy four poster bed, with gauze fabric draped over thick posts. The posts looked like large corkscrews winding down turning into carved eagle claws, that gave the appearance the bed was gripping the floor. I no longer was staring out the tiny hotel window.

The brightest light in this room passed through colored glass set into a pair of large balcony doors. There was a design in the stained glass windows on the double doors, of a green tree with a yellow sun rising behind it. The sun was one color, but was evenly divided into twelve pieces, like a pie. Like my pendant. The rich colored pains of glass did not allow me to see clearly outside, but I could tell it was night, and that outside was a balcony. As the moonlight passed through the window it shimmered on the extravagant fabrics the grand bed was made up with.

The room was filled with detailed carvings and fancy chests, with several beautiful paintings of nobility. One was angled just right in the room so I could see three figures in the light. It was a wealthy Selvain family, a man and his wife holding a baby Selvain girl in a little reddish orange dress. The couple was dressed in long gowns and fancy outfits made with lavish fabrics. It was too dark to make out their faces, but they were wearing jeweled necklaces and diamond rings, I believed them to be royalty, like the King and Queen in one of Lou's outlandish stories.

In one of the corners of the large room was a tall mirror big enough to view your entire body at one time. It was held up by a silver metal frame that allowed the mirror to be tilted easily. The frame looked like wind was swirling around the mirror all frozen in time. The swirls came together at the bottom, where they were shaped into two hands holding a smaller mirror, the size of a key hole. On the ground next to the grand mirror were two carved candlesticks, fashioned to look like small figurines holding bowls above their heads. In the bowls were candles with multiple wicks, only one wick was lit, shedding just enough dim light to give hint to the subtle details in the decorative silver frame.

A cloaked figure holding a baby, wrapped in white cloth entered the room. He came through a large door I didn't see, until it was opened and highlighted by the light coming from outside the room. He quickly shut the door behind him. The figure set the child down on the bed momentarily, returning to the door he came in. He shook the knob frantically double checking to see if the mechanism had engaged, tripping over something left on the ground as he rushed across the room to lock the balcony doors in a similar manner. He seemed to be unaware I was standing there watching him.

He untied the ropes holding back the drapes, which he immediately pulled to cover the window so no light would shine through. He stepped into the candle light, opening a small chest that lay at his feet. The chest was filled with gold coins, rings, and assorted gems, a true treasure fit for a King. Reaching into the chest he pulled out an ordinary pocket mirror. He held the small mirror so he could see the larger mirror in its reflection. In the reflection of the large mirror, a key appeared to be floating in the smaller mirror. Reaching into the glass he grabbed the key, placing the tiny mirror in his pocket, kneeling down, he placed the key into the hole at the bottom of the silver frame.

The mirror no longer reflected the dark room with a single candle lit. Now the mirror brightly illuminated the cloaked figure, as if he was staring out a window, brightly lit by the sun. The cloaked figure went to the bed and gathered up the sleeping child, stepping through the mirror as if it was a doorway, into the well lit room.

I got closer to get a better look. What I saw was not a room, but more like a hallway, with twelve windows thirty feet high arched at the top like arrows. In-between the oddly shaped windows were more mirrors with similar metal frames and I was looking through one of the mirrors, out the windows, at castle towers, with tops shaped like upside down acorns, they stood against an incredible backdrop of the mourning sun, over a vast ocean.

In the hallway of mirrors and windows guarding two doors, was a menacing, masked guard holding a long spear, wearing a scary mask made with big red feathers and the jawbone of an animal with big teeth. Menacing, until the cloaked figure stood next to him. He was twice as tall as the strange guardian of the room, even with the mask, that made the little guy appear larger than he truly was. The cloaked figure turned away from the sentry who never flinched or even changed his stance.

At the other end of the hallway he was met by another man of short stature, dressed in a colorful robe. He was older and bald like a tiny Lou, only with larger ears. Immediately he reached up to take the baby from the cloaked figure, who knelt to be eye to eye with the undersized man.

Two more long haired little people approached and an argument erupted. I could hear them but they spoke in a language I did not understand. By their expressions, I could tell the tall man wanted to leave the child, as he placed a large leather pouch on the ground. The three short men spoke between themselves picking up the bag, nodding and bowing. They still disagreed as the tall figure dropped the key back into the small hand mirror he pulled from his pocket, placing it on the floor as well. The small well dressed figures were agitated and grasped at the tall mans cloak as he started to rise. They obviously did not want him to return from where he came. Shaking them off, leaving the child, he stepped back through the mirror and into the dark room lit by only one candle. Then he smashed the mirror with one of the candle sticks.

He went to the window and opened the curtains. In the light you could see tears on his cheek as he shed the dark cloak revealing the long robe of the man in the painting.

A shadow in the darkness moved and he suddenly slumped forward revealing the hilt of a finely crafted dagger in his back. The grip was made of tightly woven red leather, the end of its handle a carved dragon's claw.

In the morning it felt like someone was banging on my head. Then I realized it was the innkeeper, banging on Lou's door, yelling about the barrel of rotten, what he called, "fish." He was irate demanding it be removed immediately. It was pointless to argue, the proprietor had a point. Last night the barrel had attracted a regiment of flies, now it was attracting stray dogs to the alley. With the temperature rising it was probably just starting to ferment, and the cart was parked right by the back door of the tavern.

The bar was already filled with regular patrons having a morning drink and complaining of the smell. Lou explained we would not be staying another day. The barrel and us would be packed and gone by noon. This was not acceptable to the outraged man who was losing business. Lou was half-dressed and half-asleep. He grunted agreeing to leave immediately to retrieve his faithful steed, mumbling as he passed our door heading for the steps.

Father was fumbling around. He could not find his money pouch or remember the name of the girl who entertained him last night, desperately re-searching his pockets, then the room, then under the bed, and then his pockets again, he was still searching when Lou returned.

Lou made fun of Father's misfortune, hoping to forget his own. Lou was not very impressed with the locals in this town, generalizing them as sailor scum, gripping the colorful piece of fabric Alerick had given Kat. Using my father as another prime example of why she should not be talking to anyone especially boys, while cursing about the obnoxious, unreasonable, untrustworthy, deceitful, scum you meet when you travel to the big cities!

We shoved off before eating breakfast, with a to-go box from the bar kitchen, the agitated innkeeper offered it to persuade us to leave immediately. I was sure glad to see Nautica and Alerick behind us.

Between Lou's garbled sentences of obscenities, a single outburst said it best. "Good riddance! "Sighing as he noted "We will be in Suxen Falls, in two days." It was obvious Lou was not amused to be on this road life had chosen for him, and judging by his demeanor, I don't think he wanted to return to Suxen Falls at all.

Regardless of our Father's misfortune, it was another beautiful day, so I was riding Kas. Not far out of town we came across a huge bluff that allowed a full panoramic view of the city and the harbor.

From the top of the coastal mesa, I could feel the soft ocean breeze pressing against my face. The sound of the waves seem to wash away the city's misgivings.

During the day several carts went by, loaded with merchandise from the local farms headed for Nautica's market. I also noticed there were others on the road behind us. They never let themselves get close enough for us to recognize who they were. Even with Lou's eyepiece, they stayed illusive. The road winded as we climbed several hills making my informal inquiries to our new neighbors even harder, but there were many other sights to keep my interest. Sometimes the canal skirted the road fifty feet below us, it was the same slow moving river we crossed entering Nautica. Every now and then, down the steep embankments we could see boats heading downstream. Father yelled to me, "Stay close to the cart." Lou gathered the reigns pushing Clovis to quicken his pace.

Lou knew we were coming up on Kelideco because he grew up there. He was shouting, "It's just past another bridge, we should be coming up on it any time now." His recollection of the area was pretty good. Just as he finished his sentence, the road turned sharply, rounding a small cluster of trees, placing us at the top of a hill overlooking a small bridge.

It wasn't long before something didn't seem right. Before we knew what was happening, we had already started down the steep incline, making it hard to stop the cart until we were halfway across the bridge. We had two little problems. One, on the bridge, a couple of men were waiting with green bandannas covering their faces. Two, they had made the bridge impassible with our cart, by placing a huge log in our path.

Lou was forced to come to an abrupt stop jostling everything in the back of the wagon as we were greeted. "Howdy Governor, we are part of the Commonwealth's Roads and Bridges Department. Today there will be a small toll to cross the bridge."

The other man snickered in a sarcastic voice, "In your case there will be a toll whether you want to cross the bridge, or not." The bandits looked at each other, chuckling.

"What would that be," Lou asked.

The bandit chimed back "I don't know governor, what have you got. I can see you are traveling with two fine ladies."

The second bandit interrupted. "If you want the bridge to be safe for the ladies," pointing back at his own chest, "I'm your man for keeping pretty girls safe." He started waiving his short sword, tapping it twice on the rail of the bridge.

I turned Kas around, only to see four more bandits at the top of the hill. They were cutting off any possible route to escape, trapping us in.

"Let's be reasonable. How about five pieces of copper for your troubles," The lead bandit ending Lou's sentence with, "Each, that and maybe what's in the fancy chest."

Father palmed our pie knife. "I don't have five pieces of copper. If I did, I would not give it to the likes of you."

Lou put his arm in front of Father whispering loudly, "It's not worth it."

The men behind us on horseback slowly moved down the hill crowding the back of the cart, pulling out an assortment of bladed weapons. There was an uneasy tension as the bandits strengthened their position again.

Lou took out his money pouch, throwing it to the ground. Saying, "There's enough coin there to let us pass."

The lead scoundrel shook his head, replying, "I doubt that my friend."

Then Lou slowly reached into his chest and pulled out a small wooden stick. It looked like it had little slimy nets made of string tangled around it. "I could sweeten the pot." The leader was not amused, he ordered the other men, "Get the chest,"

Lou moved first, with a wave of his makeshift wand and a word I had never heard before. "Kebisilk" A gooey mass outstretched from the wand toward the men flanking our behind. It was as if a giant net appeared out of nowhere wrapping around our enemies, the ropes seemed animated gripping hard and pulling tight around them. Their horses reared up but could not move, covered in what looked like fishing nets covered with honey. The riders and their horses were glued to each other, and to the road. They struggled to get free but were held tightly by the stringy substance.

The thugs on the bridge advanced forward. With a yank of the reigns, I turned Kas and charged, jumping over the log. One of the bandits had to jump the rail on the bridge to avoid being trampled, falling over forty feet into the icy rushing water below. Within minutes he was flushed fifty paces downstream.

The bandit with the short sword approached the cart. Father threw the pie knife into his foot nailing him to the ground. The bandit let go of the short sword, screaming in pain. Then Father grabbed a hammer out of his toolbox and jumped to the ground. Slamming the hammer down smashing the hand of the crippled crook, stopping him as he reached for the knife that had pinning him in place. When Father pulled the knife out of the bandit's foot he sliced the man's hand. I don't think Father even realized he had cut off one of the thug's fingers. Once the tension was released the robber fell to the ground clutching his mangled hand. It all happened so quickly.

"Not so tough now," Father gloated, wiping the bloody knife on the cowering thief. Throwing both the hammer and knife away, he reached down grabbing the bandit who was trying to crawl away, pulling him to his feet, gripping his shirt so tightly it choked the whimpering scoundrel. "Whose bridge is it now?" Father pulled him to the edge, throwing him over. He peered down over the side content with his aggressive action, asking, "How exactly did you put that Lou?" Emphasizing, the words, "Good riddance!" as he looked down at the man gasping for air as he floated away struggling in the churning river.

I turned Kas around quickly. Jumping down I picked up the short sword that the gimp had dropped. Lou had reached in his chest and pulled out another staff, this one seemed to be longer and not so disgusting. Maybe he grabbed it from the back of the cart? I wasn't really watching. This staff was too big to fit in the chest. Lou stood up on the back of the cart, positioning himself above those caught in his spell struggling to move, poking at the contorting captives in an intimidating manor.

Father gathered his weapons and followed me around the cart, to the gooey mass of thieves and horses. Lou yelled at me, "Use that pig-sticker and cut this skinny one here on the end free". Knocking one of them in the head with his heavy stick, I did as I was asked. With another swift nudge from Lou's staff the skinny bandit fell from his horse.

Recognizing the configuration of earrings, Kat jumped down pulling his mask away. It was Alerick! Taking the dagger he showed her the night before, she said, "Now I can protect myself."

Father pulled him to the bridge. "Let's see if this one can swim too," as Kat added, "You better be careful, a pretty boy like you can be whisked off unwittingly to a different world waking up far from home." Giving Alerick a genial kiss on the forehead, over the side he went. One by one they were all dealt with in the same way.

When it was over Lou picked up the webbed stick and waived it, the gooey mass unraveled as quickly as it appeared. I gathered up the reigns of the horses as Kat madly searched through their saddle bags, mumbling to herself. "The book, he said a map, and a book?" They were no where to be found.

Father suggested that we might get a good price for the horses in town, so after I used them to move the log blocking our way, I tied the horse's reigns to each other with the lead horse fixed to the end of the cart.

When I went to retrieve Lou's bag of coins, I noticed the bloody finger in the dirt. On it was a ring with a green sparkly stone set into a large repeating pattern. Boldly written inside around the band were letters of a language I did not understand. They were similar in style to the letters on the bow of the strange ship.

We were almost on our way when Father gave Lou, "The look." Lou stayed silent. "The Look," was not enough, until one brow raised. "You, my friend, have some explaining to do!"

Lou grinned. "You're not the only one with secrets. I suspect all the skeletons in my closet will be free soon enough." As we traveled Lou told us his story.

CHAPTER THREE

LOU

"You are all aware I grew up just outside of Suxen Falls in a town we will soon pass, called Kelideco. What you don't know is long before I was born dressed in strange robes, what seemed to be a simple man walked out of the forest and changed all of our lives forever! This man began to sculpt the nearby mountainside without using even the smallest of tools. The structure was so big it could be seen from miles away, attracting people from the local villages.

This man went by the name Race Bliss. With a single wave of his hand he formed the entrance to the great temple, shaping it right out of the steep cliffs. A fresh water spring started to flow creating a waterfall. He was able to harness the natural energy of the earth. Somehow he was able to command the elements. Those who stood by, watched in awe. Race's story is definitely the stuff legends are made of. To those of us who believe in the impossible, he will live in our memories forever.

To understand who I am, and why I can do the things I do, you must first understand the history of where I came from, and why I chose to leave it all behind.

Race had unearthed an ancient library from deep within the rocky refuge, revealing a large collection of very old texts, a true wealth of information. His legacy was to leave this knowledge to be shared by all.

Those stories about ancient societies I told around our fire at night, the ones that made you laugh because they were to far-fetched.

They are true. I know, I have seen the proof first hand. Soon you will see things that will make you believe. Suxen Falls is no ordinary city.

Before Race, there were very few people who knew how to read and write. You kids take for granted the knowledge he has given us. It was not long ago that reading and writing was a talent only limited to a few educated elders. Books were unheard of. Our ancestors keep records on leather rolls, history lessens were handed down through generations verbally.

These books Race found were lost by an ancient society, they were always in the mountain Race just uncovered them.

How long were these books buried in the mountain before he discovered them, was unknown," Lou pondered, "Long enough for nature to have erased any trace of the great cities described in relentless detail; communities larger than the entire Commonwealth, if descriptions were accurate.

Back when I was young as you children are now, I had an unquenchable thirst for knowledge. I was drawn to the library and the endless shelves of books.

The scholars found most of the books were written in a dialect similar to the common tongue. Give or take a few variations in their lettering and a couple references of slang that conflicted with traditional interpretations, there was no denying, the language of the ancient writers was ours. To be more precise, our language was theirs. The scholars who studied the writings found detailed facts on how our language evolved, dissecting the root meaning of each word to the syllable and its origin. Origins that don't exist today, until the library had been discovered all but the language of these ancients had been forgotten.

What was so unbelievable is that these books denoted a sophisticated civilization with advanced technology, a world filled with intricate contraptions and specific parts no longer identifiable as pieces of this world. But even with all their accumulated knowledge, somehow this society did not survive.

This lost civilization collected these texts, keeping a recorded history that stretched over two thousand years. They even speculated about civilizations that came before their time. A history of this world before they even existed.

The books talked about different nations, different races, and different beliefs; there were records of great and horrifying battles to defend what ever ideology they believed true. Some men fought for honor with heroic deeds, others to acquire wealth or power. In the end all their differences seemed petty; the rise and fall of countless empires.

Not every book was helpful, they wrote about everything and anything. Down to the trivial in and outs of their everyday lives. Who's hair was hot, and who's was not, what dresses were in style that week, and who drank too much and with whom.

To our leaders these journals were just as irrelevant as the books explaining advanced technologies. The scholars found detailed schematics on how to build ships that could fly and devices that could talk. This understanding of what they called machines was so complex; the scholars are still unable to fully understand today. Even if we could comprehend their meaning, we lacked the tools to fabricate the advanced hardware and the energy sources to empower them. We had to walk before we could learn to run. Someday we will be able to unravel the mysteries of this technology, for now we must settle for the tools our forefathers considered crude.

Most of what we could use, was from their past. The books showed us how to draw power from our rivers to mill wood, and how to irrigate crops to yield a richer harvest. Followed by information on how to build better bridges, faster boats, taller buildings, how to forge stronger metals, and craft the tools we needed to make our lives easier. Race had given us the chance to rebuild their legacy. A legacy I believe we share.

What we had taken from our lessons is apparent. It was not long before craftsmen were able to mimic their architecture and their sense of style, Nautica is a replica of a city long gone, a testimony to a culture that no longer exists. So is the home I built in Maguire it is fashioned after an image I once saw in a picture book.

I believed as important as it was to learn about their science facts, it was equally important to learn about ourselves. Some of the most interesting books were about the way the mind works. The ancients tried to explore the duality of man and the destructive nature within ourselves. This seemed to explain why these men of mystery could cure almost any aliment, and still devote so much time to creating weapons of war.

The capacity these men had to love and care for one another was only matched by their capability to hate. The weapons they created were so powerful many feared they could bring on their own demise, which is probably why the subject of death was discussed in great detail.

Many books made reference to mysterious gods that watched over these men, dictating their destinies. There were literally hundreds of different religions these great nations worshipped. Many of the religious beliefs had a common denominator. Scripture based around devastating revelations, leading to the periodic destruction of their world, a day of judgment.

I had so many questions. Had these men had a hand in their own destruction, or did the Gods fulfill the prophecies and bring about their demise?

I asked one of my teachers once if he believed in fate. Do the decisions we make really give us control over our lives, or are we subject to a series of life's predetermined circumstances. I don't think he really had an answer, he just put it another way, two men choose to make a bet on a game of chance, but only one wins, science, luck, faith. Is life a gamble?

If I could have stayed in the library forever I would have. Sometimes I think I am as guilty as any of them for what happened. Would Race have left the books in our care if he knew we would fight over them? He taught us everything, we learned nothing.

No one knows why, but shortly after Race finished the Divine structure he disappeared as quickly as he came. I wish I could have seen him just once myself, but my father was not even born yet.

Originally the Great Temple Library was left in the care of a handful of local farmers. Race had spent only a short time teaching the few who were given the task of educating the masses. He entrusted his beliefs in these men hoping they would learn to walk in his path. This group called themselves the Keepers of the House of Bliss. They controlled the temple library for many years.

As I was explaining back then very few people even knew how to read and write, and even less cared what went on at the temple.

In the early days after Race had gone there were only two types of students. Some chose to take a spiritual path, taking a vow to follow in Race's footsteps. These men became priests, their mission was to spend their lives interpreting and spreading the words they believed true. They were taught one could draw strength from within by having great faith in a higher power. For this unquestionable conviction they would be vested with natural energy from within. This endowment was only bestowed on those tough enough to stay on their fundamental path. This type of commitment was not easy; it demanded a strong spiritual devotion. The rich reward was enlightenment for those who stayed true to their vows.

Many men joined the priesthood in hopes of becoming Acolytes for the House of Bliss. Some gained Spiritual Title, none became as strong as their mentor Race Bliss.

Others, students like my father researched a different set of beliefs. They learned to control the elements by studying, biology, metallurgy, mathematics, the magic called science. This knowledge was taught in the books, the laws of nature, matter, energy, force, and motion. Once a man truly mastered the rules that predetermine how elements react to each other, he could predict and learn to control the elements themselves, shape metal, build bridges and forge communities.

These engineers of science fact dreamed of rebuilding this futuristic society.

I remember being a young boy when my family left Kelideco and moved closer to the temple. Ideas from the books took form. Every week new inventions were being rediscovered. Anything the students of science could reproduce they did, from clothes to carriages everything was changing rapidly. But we still lacked the raw materials and the massive machinery to build anything of grandeur.

For years The Priests of Bliss lived in and maintained the temple, while scholars traveled from all over, some traveled from as far as Avalon to study in the massive library.

Together we formed a small city of eager students growing in the shadow of the immense architectural formation Race created. That small town, dubbed back then Suxen Falls, was the tip of the iceberg compared to the thriving metropolis that stands there today.

The city engineers had already started making previsions for the influx of people who were showing up daily planning to make the city their home. With Suxen Falls popularity and the benefits of knowledge form the books, the port of Nautica grew larger as well. It was the largest go-between for those traveling from the main city. Avalon was still the largest city, but Suxen falls was the place to be. I was just another student then. Those were good times, I was maybe twenty five, and like the two of you, my whole life was in front of me.

That all changed, almost Sixty years after race had left, behind an unnaturally altered cavern wall, a second secret stash of manuscripts was uncovered. They found many more books including a handful of even older tomes, physically larger, as if written for giant men or maybe not for men at all. These texts were also written in a language unique to the other groups of documents, with a testimonial history of their own.

It was not a popular theory, but some myself included, believed the scripts were part of a treasure horde left by the last of the winged serpents.

The hidden area was quite different from the other rooms in the temple. It was ridden with large glyphs that created luminescent fields of light. You could feel the magical energy when you were near. The few scholars that were granted access to this area believed the auroras were made to protect those inside. This part of the temple was truly a wondrous place.

These books were difficult to understand the writers used a series of symbols instead of letters. But from what little we could decipher, came a new understanding of the raw elements, they referred to them as living beings. This contradicted the other library books. These tomes contained instruction showing how to bend the laws of nature. Very few students gained the understanding of alchemy needed to break these rules that predetermine our worldly limitations. Studying this energy, this Magic, was dangerous especially with a language of symbols subject to interpretation. There were great risks, but also substantial physical rewards, for those of us that were able to command this power. Those of us who did, learned to alter the perception of truth, we were able to physically manipulate reality.

I was one of these exceptional students. We achieved these unexplainable effects by pulling energy from the living source of the true elements. We call this knowledge, this ability 'Arcane'. Those scholars, who master this art, gain the title of Wizard or Mage.

The problem is once a man gains title, Spiritual or Arcane, the power he receives can be addicting.

No one had ever questioned the leadership of the Priests of Bliss until then. The men of Science and Magic although divided on the different fundamentals formed a society called the Schools of Thought. Questions arose as to who should govern the masses. A council of six was formed, two established city engineers and four privileged members of this emerging elite institution, one mage to represent each of the four elements. My family was wealthy; they were highly respected figures in the developing hierarchy. My father served on the newly formed council in Suxen Falls with Master Quinn. This was a long time ago. They were still working on the plans to build the great walls that form the tiers of the city today.

Suxen Falls was peaceful then. The city engineers were still building things by hand. That all changed when Magic mixed with Technology. Priests and Mages joined in the construction efforts. Mages could produce and alter larger pieces of metal easier than the men of science could do with traditional methods. And first year acolytes from the House of Bliss were taught to permanently enlarge stone. The city planners were no longer held back by the sheer magnitude of the project. Roads and walls could be built much faster when stone did not need to be quarried and metal no longer needed to be forged. Working together allowed even more of the secrets of technology to be uncovered.

There was a playful competition, between the Schools of Thought, and the House of Bliss. The Schools of Thought was able to replicate a more advanced machine, a printing press. The House of Bliss gained the ability to enchant crystals, making light without fire.

Influenced by the cities of lights pictured in the books, the council focused on growth. More and more unnatural sources of energy were tapped. The city started to grow quickly. Buildings and roads, were lined with fancy lights and lampposts, constructed using a mish-mash of old school construction and the elemental forces that were not truly understood.

It only took a couple months and a thousand young Acolytes to carve out the harbor that surrounds the city. A project of that size, using pick axes and pulleys, would have taken thirty years or more to complete.

When one toys with Magic without the respect it demands, accidents happen. One day an overwhelming release of energy killed hundreds of people. Destroying a small portion of the newly built city

The tactical advantage to this destructive ability was obvious. Those on the council argued that these books from the second library, the one with the large magical texts, posed a threat if placed in the wrong hands. The House of Bliss argued that these books had no spiritual value. The information contained within was deemed dangerous and made off limits.

The City Council was made up of city planners and the leaders of the Schools of Thought. Again they questioned the authority of the House of Bliss.

Realizing the power of those who controlled the knowledge in the library the council came to terms with the House of Bliss. Together they declared Arcane Knowledge illegal to teach to those without privilege. Everyone still believed in upholding the founder's ideals to share the knowledge. They just varied on who the knowledge should be shared with.

The council was given authority over who had access to the library. This omission came at a price; officially two members of the priesthood were given seats on the council.

For the first time I could remember those who came to learn at the temple were turned away. Not just the Tomes of Magic, anything related to science was outlawed as well. The council justified this by claiming certain sciences can be used to create weapons of war.

Not all the priests agreed to relinquish this authority over the library. This decision caused dissension, forcing the House of Bliss to split into separate factions. Many joined the House of Knowledge who also demanded a seat on the council as well. Like those of the past, we were dividing ourselves with symbols and flags. Those who came to learn were now recruited, forced to summit to different ideologies to gain access to the library.

Walls built to protect were now designed to keep the populace out. Bigger became better" Lou was shaking his head as he continued.

"Race's contribution had given us the ability to build a strong government, seeing the downfalls of greed in society. Our schools had allowed us to advance mentally, physically, and technologically. From the Houses of the Holy we also grew spiritually. Our society made giant advancements in the last one hundred years; advancements that took those who came before us millenniums to master. We were still unable to learn from their mistakes. The slightest taste of power brought treachery. Tension rose, as the city was divided."

I had to interrupt, Lou was steering us off the road as he focused on his story. He was unaware we were slowly starting to move up several steep hills. Some areas of the road had deep ravines to one side or another, with only a few small clusters of trees that could be a saving grace if a sudden jerk sent you over the side.

Never missing a word, Lou smiled, looking down, continuing to recollect his repressed memories.

With the city divided anything that was helpful was kept secret, "Not many people knew that a little over twenty years ago the scholars of Suxen Falls unearthed a group of hand written leather scrolls at the foot of Wingback Mountain. They were found in an isolated cave hidden by years of overgrowth. These scrolls are the oldest writings we possess that we can physically verify, were written by those we are direct descendants of.

I was in my mid thirties when the scrolls were found. I was part of the minority who had achieved a higher level of understanding in my Arcane Studies. Older, respected, a son of privilege and with Quinn and my father's influence on the council, I became one of the few given direct access to the fragile writings.

Like the library books they were written in the same language. Most of their story spoke of foraging for food in Blackbear Forest, constantly moving, living in fear of a deadly dragon they called Cosmo. Just like the men who wrote the books from the library, these men kept records of their everyday life, large celebrations, their leaders words, marriages, those who died a natural death, and those whose lives were taken by Cosmo.

In the year 978 this tribe of hunters took note, writing about a temple they had found, inadvertently labeling it the Time Temple. They only knew it was constructed overnight and was immediately abandoned.

They were categorically referring to the temple in Avalon, Accurately described, as the temple beyond the Great Bridge, they were talking about the bridge at Newhaven its location was identified on a simple but detailed map of the area.

Some of the scrolls were destroyed by decay, but there were enough scrolls in good condition for us to paint an accurate account of the daily hardships they endured. We deciphered over two hundred years of recorded history, most of which was learning to survive in the forest and eluding Cosmo.

The scrolls we found were dated from the winter solstice of the year 788 to, 986 ending on April 18 the year they broke ground in Avalon.

There was only one other significant event recorded during this time, a testimonial, to a powerful band of travelers loosely portrayed as soldiers. They came from the abandoned Time Temple they had found almost ten years earlier.

The first of these warriors was described as a very large dark-winged creature with glass blue eyes, standing as tall as the treetops. The second was a man clad in metal armor carrying a sword and shield, his belt emitted lights and sounds. The third was a green dark skinned man of a slightly smaller stature, wearing a robe elaborately embroidered with a tree. When his war hammer swung in battle it ignited in a blue flame. The fourth was a female, as to what race, they could only describe her as covered with hair, having the facial features of a Jaguar or a great cat. She had very sharp claws and carried an assortment of specialized range weapons. Finally, a small, tiny man with excessive facial hair, wearing a colorful, exquisitely ornamented outfit made of embroidered leather. He had no visible weapons. He sat with his legs crossed on top of an unknown creature, like one would sit on a giant pillow.

They were at a loss of words to describe the alien-looking animal the little man was perched upon, noting that it floated without wings, was shaped like a wine bladder that was not full, it had no visible arms or legs, and propelled itself by passing air threw several tube like appendages that distorted its spherical shape. The animal left a distinct odor that made it easy to track in the forest.

During the day the adventurers adept for traveling through the woods, tracked Cosmo the dragon, back to his place of power. Our ancestors moved as close as believed safe to avoid being detected by the unlikely band of heroes, not to mention, Cosmo their quarry. Many were afraid to follow. Those who did, saw the group enter the mountain lair as the sun started dropping in the sky.

It was not long before they could hear fighting, and loud explosions from deep within the mountain, such that the ground rumbled. Night had fallen and still they could hear the sounds of battle. The ground shook one last time and the side of the mountain blew open, tossing rocks of all sizes into the air, deadly projectiles rained down on those who had strayed to close.

The dark winged creature now enlarged was entangled in the dragons grip. Thrown by the force of the blast into a mid air battle high above the forest floor. The dragon's distinctively red burning breath was met with blue flames as the black gladiator exhaled. Their fight lit up the sky, as the mammoth monsters clutched at each other, both struggling to stay in flight. They came crashing down, disappearing into the thick tree line. The rest of the group moved in quickly. The dragon was now vulnerable, no longer protected by its place of power within the mountain. Stunned from the fall, overwhelmed by the group of warriors, the dragon's life was ended.

The last account the woodland people made of the dragon hunters was after they tracked them back to the Time Temple, where it was said they vanished.

Weeks later, the dust from the battle was still settling, Cosmo no longer appeared in the skies.

Believing the heroes would return someday. The people decided to make a pilgrimage to the Temple leaving the safety of the forest for a home by the coast. Here the records kept by the scrolls ended, but we can piece together the rest.

For the first time in centuries the people from under Wingback Mountain fished from the sea and built free standing structures. Men flourished while dragons were forgotten. Till one day the oldest and wisest of us had never seen a real dragon, their true existence became doubted. The only memory of dragons to survive was weaved into colorful antidotes, our local lore, and the bedtime stories we were all told as children.

This information was brought before the council. The wingback scrolls very existence raised many questions. The most disconcerting was a true record of a living dragon.

This supported the theory Race had built his temple on Cosmo's place of power. Cosmo's name, still breed fear in certain circles.

News of this discovery was heard as far as Avalon. The politics in Avalon were different than those in Suxen Falls. It was a much simpler city that had never really seen the benefits of all the information found in the library. Remember Avalon was still the capital then and mostly ruled by a sect of Priests who followed the religion of those who came from under Wingback Mountain. Because they worshipped at the Temple of Time they became known as the House of Time. Back then they still made offerings in the Temple to ensure Cosmo would never return.

The elite members of the House of Time referred to themselves as Temple Guardians. They sent one of their own to Suxen Falls to examine the scrolls themselves. They were surprised to see how Suxen Falls had grown.

The House of Time claimed to be the oldest of the Spiritual Houses, and under the divine authority of the leaders in Avalon, they stated they had supreme authority over the Temple Library, the Arcane Manuscripts, the Wingback Scrolls, and the council. They believed if the scrolls were to prove the Arcane manuscripts were Cosmo's, they should be considered evil. They vowed to destroy them.

Nobody was going to relinquish control of anything, and Avalon no longer had the might to uphold its authority over those in Suxen Falls. Still a seat on the council was given to the House of Time as a gesture of good will.

With the religious houses gaining a forth seat on the council The School of Thought was lousing its influence over important decisions in Suxen Falls. Fearing the council could vote to destroy the magical manuscripts they questioned the legitimacy of the scrolls themselves. They chose to believe we were the descendants of the men who wrote the library books. They cast doubt on the beliefs of the House of Time arguing stories of dragons are not true, referencing library records that described these beings to be mythical creatures believed to have never truly existed.

This placed the scrolls under scrutiny. It was ordered that more evidence was needed to confirm the facts and the dates listed in the scrolls. But the dates on the scrolls were accurate. Even with the council's omissions, nothing could change the facts. For instance, Kodasfoemar was one of the city's oldest holidays, the House of Time pointed out it's date coincides with Cosmo death. The Temple Guardians still honored this day by planting a tree, to represent starting a new life, a life without fear, without Cosmo. The problem was most folks in Suxen Falls just light a candle and maybe say a prayer, they had never heard of these silly traditions.

Then we noticed another common holiday observed by our ancestor's that lived under Wingback Mountain, dully noted as the Day of Sorrow. We call this The Day of Souls.

On this day, each year, the scrolls date was marked differently there was a suffix, A.J. Eventually we found a reference in the scrolls to these initials. The letters represent the words After Judgment.

What is significant about this date was on May 6th, 2157, the records of those who wrote the books in the library ceased to exist. To those who were familiar with some of the more selective reading in the library there was only one explanation. It seemed the day of reckoning our ancestors foretold of, had arrived. Sealing their fate, total annihilation was the only explanation for our ancestors to return to such a primitive way of archiving like the hand written leather scrolls. The only reasonable explanation was the library had been buried over a thousand years. Their end marked our beginning.

The time line was clear to those who were not jaded to the truth. Those who wrote the books in the library came first. Our ancestors under Wing Back Mountain survived whatever catastrophe had befallen them.

Like everything else this theory only brought about more questions. What of the large magical tomes and where did they fit into the equation?

At first we thought these older tomes were not dated, it was as if the writers had no sense of time. Then we realized the writers of these books had a very different measurement of time. Their calendar year had sixty two cycles. Much like our months, each cycle having the equivalent to one hundred and twenty-four days. There was no day or night only an influx and outflow of energy similar to a high and low tide. The tomes were dated to the year 83,683. The date did not seem real.

On closer inspection we also realized there was a difference in the way the books were bound and printed. The texts from the library were bound using a superior binding method. The Magical tomes were bound utilizing a magical essence, there was no stitching or glue. They used a method of magical binding described in one of the tomes. There was nothing that gave the appearance that these books were even written by men. The size, the language, the dates, even the paper they were written on was different. Every thing pointed to the theory, these tomes belonged to Cosmo.

The representative from the House of Time came forward he had recognized this quality of workmanship in another book, The Holy Book of Time.

He explained the book was one of his faction's most prized possessions. It was found in the early days of Avalon, exactly one year after Cosmo's, death, in the year 987. It was said to commemorate the Holy Day, Kodasfoemar, his sect planted a tree in the garden in front of the temple. In the garden, in the ground, they found the Holy Book of Time. It was accepted as sent by those heroes who killed the last dragon. The same heroes mentioned in the scrolls.

The Temple Guardian pointed out more than a few cultural beliefs were centered on this book. The religious practices taught in the old text are intricate parts of our history as far back as records of Avalon exist. The Book of Time clearly stated the Temple was built to protect us from dragons. We are required to make continual offerings to honor those who constructed it, those who defeated Cosmo. It was written to dishonor them would cause the dragon's wraith to be unleashed again. He reminded the council that our ancestors made the first offerings in Avalon over two hundred years before the tomes of magic were found. He added, to that day the Priests of Time still honored this debt.

A group was officially sent by the Suxen Falls City Council to Avalon with the sole purpose of examining this Book of Time. Those who studied the Holy Manuscript established it contained nothing they could deem useful, magic or otherwise. They did confirm the book was bound the same way the as the magical tomes, only it was much smaller, the size of an average book from the library. It was also written in our language not the language of Arcane Magic.

On closer inspection they found the book had no name on its cover and no dates were found within its pages. The name, The Book of Time only references the temple where it was found. The omnipotent author left only the initials C.T., other than Cosmo the dragon no other names were mentioned within the writing.

Rumors about the council's investigation sparked a movement. The House of Sunfire was formed; a fanatic religion growing in Suxen Falls out of the newly discovered ancient lore. They respected the power of dragons and believed they would someday return.

The priests of Sunfire believed people of Suxen Falls should be allowed access to the information in the tomes. The power of this knowledge would protect them.

The fact the council hid the wingback scrolls from the public only caused a frenzy of speculation. Acolytes stood in the streets preaching the end is near. Dissension in the city was growing, as outrage over the secret deliberations leaked out.

The amount of followers the House of Sunfire was receiving put pressure on the House of Bliss who was being alienated from the other spiritual houses and slowly losing control over significant decisions concerning their temple and the library. The leaders of The House of Sunfire demanded equal representation on the council. The School of Thought agreed as long as two more seats were given to leaders representing science and the magical arts.

The truth was the leaders of the Schools of Thought liked the indecisiveness of the spiritual houses and this added three votes in favor of preserving the Magical Tomes.

The schools of thought did not care about the Wingback Scrolls or the Book of Time; to them what was said in the writings had become irrelevant. What gained their attention was the Time Temple itself, it was obvious to those with experience in the Arcane, that it was some kind of magical doorway. They wanted to harness the raw power of the Temple. Some mages unlike me had no respect for history or religion especially the old traditions of the House of Time.

The leaders of the School of Thought used the bickering on the council to gain access to the Time Temple without letting the others know of their true intentions. Our understanding of magical energy was advancing, but my teachers were influenced by their ambitions. Their vanity, their greed may have jeopardized us all.

The council elected a priest from the House of Bliss by the name of Kayal, to oversee the expedition back to Avalon he was accompanied by my father and several other Arcane Masters. They were to study the Temple and only observe the Temple Guardians who still gave contribution following the rituals described in the Book of Time.

In secret Quinn had given the mages a second agenda they were to try and activate the doorway and go through. That was the last I ever heard of my father.

Avalon went up in flames overnight, countless numbers of innocent people died. It was a catastrophe like some ancient story found in the library. The city was reduced to a blight covering the land.

The Temple Guardians who regularly preformed the daily rituals to ensure the dragons would never return were presumed to all be dead. The ancient text was gone. The priests of Time that remained in Suxen Falls were shunned by the other Spiritual houses many left the city and returned to Avalon. Their religion was lost.

The fact that the Schools of Thought wanted to tamper with the old Temple was conveniently forgotten. The people were purposely mislead by carefully crafted widespread rumors. Those who were truly responsible for causing the destruction were overlooked.

Conveniently, the blame fell upon Kayal and the House of Bliss, their leaders were disgraced. This was the opportunity the Schools of Thought needed to officially gain control over the council, the daily workings of the Library, Race's Temple and that was not all. Suxen

Falls became the official capital, its population exploded because of all the people racing to leave Avalon.

In all the commotion none of our leaders cared what the ramifications would be, now that we had forsaken the protectors described in the Book of Time. No one believed in the curse of the dragon. No one cared about what we had done. Avalon was made off limits. The council officially voted not to investigate.

The House of Time was no longer given representation on the council and the House of Bliss lost their second seat. This newly restructured Suxen Falls City Council was to take complete control over the entire area, Nautica, Newhaven, and everything in between. What was so ironic was their first order was meant to bring unity, they created the commonwealth.

What we needed was leadership. What we got was corruption, a fight for power amongst our most beloved teachers, our most respected leaders and the greatest minds of our time.

Moral ideals came second to proving who was more devout or versed in their knowledge of the Spiritual or Arcane. What you knew meant nothing compared to what you could do. The more destructive the power, the more one was feared.

This draw for control clearly divided what was left of the Spiritual Houses. Also the different Schools of Thought, who had always agreed up to now, split, forming the Disciplines of Science Fact and the Schools of Arcane Magic.

Those who had fine tuned their magical abilities thought they were supreme. But the men from the Disciplines of Science Fact had saved their deadliest invention for last. They had recreated several guns. Weapons from the past that shoot a metal bullet, With a 'Bang' the assignations began. The most powerful spell users were targeted many sat on the council.

The city became a beacon for those who wanted control and power. Strong-arm politics fed by greed are what motivated those in charge. Those who were educated or gifted in the Spiritual or Arcane were using their talents to selfishly help themselves to a piece of the pie. They all positioned themselves to protect their interests, seeking favor on crucial decisions. Deciding who would eventually be given absolute authority to control the inter-workings of the Commonwealth became a contest of wills.

The authority of the council was in question as those who spoke out for civil freedom were eliminated. In a desperate attempt to retain control of the populace an arena was created for those who wished to prove their authority with force.

Time Trials were created to test the abilities of the different factions. I myself was pressured into fighting to protect the honor of my family and my school. It was no more than a violent death match. Many did not survive.

The mob rule was the only saving grace for the Houses of Religion. The House of Sunfire became the strongest spiritual faction, emerging with a kamikaze elitist cult like movement. For every true mage there were one hundred inspiring priests ready to be made into cannon fodder, all hyped up to believe they were the one.

How could the men of science fact not realize their weapons were based on the laws of physics? There guns were made of metal and worked by the ignition of the element of fire. They were no match against spells that could easily manipulate metal and the elements.

Like in the stories of old, the bigger the bomb, the harder they fall. The few mages who had mastered truly destructive powers devastated the final games. Those who were victorious thrived in the brutality, leaving a wake of the maimed and disfigured.

The priests of the House of Sunfire did not like the disadvantage of the arena. They believed they were the chosen. Their elevated positions were empowered by their god. Declaring the knowledge contained in the library sacred, their destiny was to take total control of the temple. Their only true reason was greed.

Race's monument was taken in a show of force, as hundreds of acolytes occupied the area. These butchers referred to the killing of impartial students as, "Culling the herd." They started executing those whose only crime was to want to learn.

The Schools of Arcane Magic did not sit idle. The House of Sunfire's claim was disputed in blood."

Tears filled Lou's eyes for a moment as he regained his composure. "Many good people lost their lives that night, as the battle was taken to the streets of Suxen Falls!

Suxen Falls existed because of a noble deed. Race's dynasty was slowly being washed away. All I could see was turning red. Race's Utopian ideals were replaced with corrupted morals and mislead holy riotousness.

In the end, like in the battles of yesteryear, knowledge and communication was the key. Scrying, spying magically on others became as important as detecting and deterring Scrying on themselves. Once a leader was targeted he had little chance, the heavy handed would teleport in and fix the problem, permanently.

Only the highly protected, well informed and most brutal remained alive, taking control. Amongst the madness, alliances were formed, truces were eventually enforced. The Priests of Sunfire conceded any authority over the temple to the Schools of Arcane Magic, who retained the majority of control over the council.

When it was over they locked away what was left of the scrolls and any books of importance that were not burned or stolen especially those that denoted any sophisticated technology. It was said only three Tomes of Magic survived they were removed from the library completely, only to be used by those accepted into the Academy of the Arcane. The truth was no longer taught as the council rewrote our history excluding everything we had discovered.

As power changed from one hand to another so did the faces of the people I knew and once respected. Quinn was the only member of the original council to persevere the rest lost their lives. I could not even look him in the eye. Not after the things I had seen and done.

Very few people are privy to what really happened; even less know all of what I have told you today.

Under the new rule the inviting city became perverted by peddlers of tricks infesting the streets. Around every corner I saw the faces of the friends that I lost who were dear to me. In the shadows lurked the enemies I earned in the arena. Before these dark times fell on the city we were taught noble ideals. Knowledge should be shared by all. What knowledge we had, we destroyed, what was left was hidden away. That is why I chose to leave.

We all read the books, the warnings were there for those who looked, how could they not have understood. We were no different than those who failed before us.

I needed to find out the truth about Avalon and what happened to my father. I was ordered not to leave, but I no longer accepted the decisions of the council. In all honesty, there was no one who could have stopped me. I left never looking back.

At the time it seemed the council was right about one thing. Avalon was a dead end. Fate helped me to decide my destiny. I settled in the small town of Maguire when a tree root broke the axle on my cart. I met Alester and little Riley. You know the rest.

Sometimes I still wonder if someone or something is really out there watching over us. It had to be more than a coincidence that we were placed along that road that night. If the fears shared by the Temple Guardians are warranted and my suspicions are correct. We will need all the help we can get.

You must believe me, my story is true and I hope you can understand why I chose to live a simple life surrounded by good hearted people I love. You are all my family now. I have never regretted my decision. Always remember all the power and wealth one could have does not measure up to true happiness or true understanding. Those are found in the heart and in the mind.

But if it is power and wealth you seek. You will love the city. The population has doubled and tripled since I left. If Quinn is alive he probably runs the whole show. If there is something dark in that temple now, it's very dangerous. If it has to do with Quinn it's beyond our control."

Not that we didn't have a lot of time to pass. I was still glad Lou's history lesson had come to an end. Lou can be very long winded. Resorting to our storytellers other weakness, I asked, "Julia, What's for dinner?"

CHAPTER FOUR

Mix Pride In Your Faith,
For Getting The Truth

Lou was still a little emotional even after we had changed the subject. By now we had already entered Kelideco, Father was pointing to a friendly looking inn hoping to distract Lou with the smell of stewed potatoes that was lingering in the air.

Lou was unfamiliar with the establishment that sat just beyond an old dirt road that led to where he once lived. Lou could not believe it. Everything looked so different. Telling us, "This area was all forest when I was a child." Lou started rambling again. "Trees here have been cleared for timber, most likely to construct homes in the big city."

The wind changed suddenly and the pungent smell of a dairy farm was in the air. Purposely to disrupt Lou before he got started again. I blamed the fragrant fumes on Kat, using her as the "butt" of my joke. She pointed back at me plugging her nose. "Did not" "Did too." "Did not" "Did too." "Did not" "Did too."

Julia stepped in, asking for a moment of silence. Giving Lou, "The Look." saying, "That means everybody!" she emphasized the word "everybody."

Kelideco was just a small river town not much bigger than Airwindale or Three Keys. The river ran directly through it, not the road, it only skirted the water. Several roads broke to the north. They all lead to a string of docks that lined the river's edge, where carts were waiting to be loaded onto ferries.

The boats here were different than the sea going vessels in Nautica. father said they had flat bottoms. Some of the larger boats were propelled by huge rotating paddle wheels. Lou said they ran on spring power. The gear systems required constant winding that was done with a multitude of foot cranks.

We could see a large section of town across the water. Directly next to the shore was a raised walkway with ladders down to a lower dock, were more boats quickly handled their business and moved on. Behind that, was a row of older broken down storehouses mixed in with private residences and a few shops, all crowding the shore where the river widened.

We watched the city's lanterns being lit in prediction of the night sky, highlighting the hum-drum lives of the river folk. The people were watching us. I guess we weren't the only ones who liked to gaze at the passerbys. Like the sunset their faces slowly faded as the sun slipped behind the buildings. Until that moment I never realized how much I will always cherish the uneventful nights we shared together, back home, on father's porch. After a few more hours of travel we were able to find a place to camp not far from our final destination.

Even though I did not understand all of what Lou was saying about unique powers, I knew it explained why he could do things I could not.

That night Lou gathered the items we collected from our would-be thieves. Kneeling on the decorated mat he pulled from his chest, placing the book of symbols down by the items. We were all curious as we gathered around. Lou smiled mischievously holding his hands up making a series of elaborate hand gestures, "It's all in the hands." With a moment of seriousness, and a small sigh, then a few strange words "Desivena Nostrmoso."

It was magic, we could all see it. Kat's dagger and my sword started to glow as he held each piece. There were symbols on my sword shimmering in strange colors following the length of the blade. My ring also now had writing that was clearly highlighted, written in a magical language. The letters were similar in style to the writing on the bow of the cursed ship we believed the items came from.

A small breeze twirled the stale air. Lou's book slammed open, something out of the ordinary was turning the pages back and forth. It clearly stopped on a specific page, but only long enough for us to identify a single symbol.

Lou held the dagger first explaining the pages of the book had turned to the symbol of Divination. Then he held the sword, the luminescent ruins on the side jumbled and rearranged for a brief moment, I thought it said comprehend. The pages of the book fluttered again, as if in a windstorm, one way, then back to the same page, "Divination again." Then he held up the ring, it dimly glowed green. Then the book slammed shut. Lou said, "I can do no more here the enchantment on this ring is of a spiritual nature." Returning our items to us he declared, "I have divined all I can from these pieces."

Lou told us when an item is enchanted it gains special powers. The spells the enchanter chooses, leave a magical fingerprint. We may not know exactly what spell was used to enchant the item, but we can sense the type of magical energy from which the spell was forged.

I asked what the symbol of Divination stood for. Lou told us Divination is a type of Magic. The spells of this doctrine are meant to help one understand by divining the truth. Just like the spell he cast helped to interpret and detect magical auroras, other spells of this school help people see over long distances or to hear things not meant for their ears. Sometimes wizards can even foretell the future or the see the past. He did not know what, if anything, our items did, only that we might find them very helpful someday.

That night Lou let Kat study a book from his chest, sighing, "Soon enough, she will have her fill."

Morning came and again we awoke to the sound of traffic. It was not long before we were on the outskirts of Suxen Falls. Lou was lecturing us on street smarts, warning us that not everybody here is as they seem. "Don't trust your eyes, or your ears, only trust each other. Always hide your coin pouch, and again don't trust anyone."

Julia added, "Especially boys with tattoos." asking me if I would help, by keeping my eyes on Kat.

I responded, "I always do."

Lou kept going on and on, "Suxen falls can be a place of wonderment, but also a bed of deceit." staring directly at Kat in an attempt to gain her attention again. Kat, still mad about Alerick, was trying to ignore him, carving her name into the old cart, with her new little dagger. I don't know how she kept her eyes down, the city was grand! There were more people here than in all the little towns in the entire Commonwealth, put together.

Coming through the hills, we could see glimpses of the mountainside that overshadowed the city. There were three massive half circle walls radiating out from the remarkable temple that stood in the center. From here we could see the temple took the shape of an hourglass with a man standing in the lower half. The shape of the hourglass was carved out of the cliff side standing a thousand feet above the city.

From the base of the temple out-poured two rivers that entwined with the many roadways that stemmed from the foot of the temple, and spread throughout the city like an intricately crafted maze. The inner circle was mostly green from this distance unlike the middle ring that was a patchwork of colors and dingy brown. The outer tier from here looked like a blue ring, in reality it was a water level which served as a moat and a harbor. It was filled with boats traveling in and out of the lower tier. The outer border was a checker board of farm lands.

Groups of huts were clustered on the outskirts of the city, most likely houses for those who worked the fields. From what I could tell most of the workers were Selvain. They made their homes with hay and clay from the river bottom. Some had shingle roofs like in Nautica, but most were just layered with branches or hay. The air here smelled sweet. It caught the essence of the nearby fields. The fields were filled with strawberries, corn, cabbage and peppers all ready to be picked. Even a small orange grove added to the subtle, pleasant aroma, as we approached the outer wall.

Along the way we also passed a winery called The Peeled Grape. Lou suggested we stop to buy a light snack for our journey into town. I think he just wanted to taste the wine, he did not leave empty handed.

Next we came along side those who were working diligently on the stone pathways. The cart was detoured off the main road to a side road. Eventually we were redirected back onto pavement. We saw how the stone roads were being built. Lou pointed out the road crew was made up of priests from the temple, learning to control the element of earth. Some knowledge can only be mastered by tasks, reading books, understanding the text is not enough. Casting spells in the field especially under pressure is the best training.

First the young devotes would clear the land, magically digging out the earth shaping the road. Then the older acolytes would take turns altering small stones, turning them into huge blocks, fitting each piece tightly together creating an irregular interlocking pattern. Lou said the older and wiser the student, the larger the mass of rock they can manifest.

Race Bliss must have been very powerful to have molded the facade of the temple and the great statue, in only a few days. Lou took another swig of his grape elixir, distracted from his worries momentarily. He continued giving us the narrated tour. Mentioning, "They are always working, from sunup to sundown. Someday this road will reach all the way to Newhaven."

Giving us a final warning, "You're about to witness many wonderful spectacles of ingenuity." His only explanation, "It is the sheer will of man that allows us to witness such extraordinary things. Oh, and don't trust anyone."

The first wall was not very tall at all. Lou explained it served as a dike creating the man-made harbor. He said parts of the wall could be lowered, feeding a series of small aqueducts that watered the local farmer's crops. Along this outer wall were several small docks, strategically located by some of the larger fields.

Across the water were enormous wooden docks. They were as big as some of the small towns we passed, covered with rows of warehouses they looked like individual cities suspended above the water. The piers were lined up with many different size barges and boats, no two alike. Empty carts waited their turn, to load or unload their various cargos, as other ships remained patiently anchored off shore, for a go around at the wheel. The large docks had private gated entrances leading into the city. Only through the large doors could entry be gained from the long piers.

We started across the only bridge that led directly into the city. It was larger and wider than any other bridge we had seen on our trip so far. The architecture of the bridge was a marvel in itself. From a distance the bridge resembled a giant swan, nestled in the water, with four lanes of traffic crossing over its back. It was enough to raise even Kat's brow.

Together we stared at the enormous metal ropes draped down in a symmetrical pattern, abstractly resembling the wings of the bird. Each twisting rod was as wide as the table in front of father's house. High above our heads, they merged together as one, creating a single round pointed tip, the head of the angelic swan. As the metal wires reached down they passed directly through the stone block on each side of the bridge, giving an evenly spread support to its gracefully poised raised roadway.

The details were exquisite. There were metal hand rails and a string of metal poles that held rows of artistically shaped lanterns, all adorned with a feather motif, extending the length of the entire bridge. Like the rest of the metal construct these accents were copper in color, and turning green, similar to the tarnished patina on the handle of a older coach door. I pointed up at the fascinating lights, "Lighting them must be a chore."

Lou said, "Even though it's hard to tell in the day, they are already illuminated and always remain lit. Priests can harness the reflective qualities in the crystals by trapping a ray of sunshine inside, it permanently lights up the stones."

Lou went on telling us that the whole bridge was magically created. The metal rods were shaped much smaller, maybe the size of a horse, and then enlarged as they were merged into the stone platform through a joint effort of Arcane and Spiritual manipulation. Lou had read in one of the papers. The City Council had commissioned the project several years ago. It was completed by an old friend of his father's, Dalton Terintino. He sits on the council, a true master of the discipline of alteration.

The sweet smell of the farmlands dissipated as an unpleasant stench tainted the air. Staggered away from the piers and the bridge I could see man sized red clay pipes, partly submerged in the water. These pipes were continuously draining their murky contents through crisscrossed bars into the harbor water that was slowly being tainted by the brown liquid.

Now that we were drawing closer to the far side of the bridge the outer wall was growing more and more intimidating it jetted at least seventy-five paces out of the water and surrounded the entire city.

Finally we reached the gate; it had a raised walkway above the entrance. Soldiers leered down into the open carts passing below. None of them even batted an eye, sitting motionless, peacefully overlooking the constant stream of Passerbys. Under a long arm rail, hung more uniquely forged lanterns on crude metal poles highlighting a long banner. In big letters it read "Welcome to Suxen Falls."

Immediately, as we passed under the gate, the scent of food permeated the air. A constant roar of voices could be heard above the repetitious sounds of the carts and carriages, as their wheels spun across the uneven roads.

This tier was highly populated. There was what seemed to be a never ending row of specialized shops, especially along the main corridor, signs hung everywhere. The buildings stood several stories high topped with steep A-frame style roofs adorned with clay or cedar shingles, accented with lots of windows, each with its own style of curtain, all pulled shut.

Even though attached, no two buildings were alike. Each roof line was modified differently with multiple dormers and even more oddly shaped windows, all in a variety of colors.

There were many secluded balconies with decorative metal railings with lots of little curly-Q's, nuzzled in the shadowy corners and across the front and sides of the cramped buildings. Some only large enough for one person to stand on, others had groups of large potted plants with hidden sitting areas, tranquil getaways far above the clinging and clanging of the hectic streets below.

All the roofs had multiple chimneys, or long pipes venting upward. Pipes that came from below out of anywhere and everywhere, turning black the higher they rose curving and twisting up following the contour of elongated buildings, somehow each finding a spot to vent above the rooftops discharging steam, smoke, and soot, creating a vast unnatural expanse of cockeyed shapes polluting the air.

Where there were voids, thin walkways, dark alleys, and smaller roads were created, a demented labyrinth of intertwined paths leading to obscurity, the farther you strayed from the main road.

At some of the over congested intersections there were city guards directing traffic, repeatedly blowing their whistles.

All the major streets were made of tiled stone block, but the raised sidewalks had a bumpy texture, they were covered with small natural looking river rocks. These walkways were overcrowded with all sorts of well dressed people, showing off the latest fashions, walking on the colorful stonework. The people dressed here so differently. Not prudent at all. The clothes were tight and conforming and very well tailored. I guess this is what they mean by city clothes. Kat was in awe, pointing out the most obnoxious outfits, funky hair styles, over decorated hats, and uncomfortable looking shoes she loved best to her mom, they were chatting away like two hens.

Never have I seen so many coaches. They rushed in both directions down the busy main streets dropping people off and then wisp-ping away eventually lining up along the sidewalks parked in front of the elaborate shops. There were people riding strange contraptions, Lou referred to them as bicycles they quickly darted past the crowds. It seemed everyone was trying to pass Lou. All at once if that was possible. Lou was driving his cart cautiously, as if he was still in Maguire.

One driver yelled an obscenity as he passed noting the bottle in Lou's hand, "Wow? Even flies get drunk at the bars, in the big city."

Every now and then you could hear water flowing under the city. Lou said there was a network of pipes big enough to walk through just below our feet, pointing to the grated holes on one of the street curbs. Lou even calmed the rooms at the inn have hot and cold running water, waste drain's into the pipes below, then out of the pipes we saw in harbor. He called this underground system a sewer.

It took the rest of the day. But we finally made it to the last tier, known as the high quarter. This wall was posh, crowned with red brick. It seemed the farther we traveled the larger the walls became. Two sizable open doors adorned with large crests, called attention to the entrance. On one side the Spiritual Houses were represented the other Arcane Schools. Carved into the wall were winged creatures, Lou called them griffins. They were made to appear as if they were holding the doors open.

Through the large elaborately decorated well guarded gates, we could get a better look at the two rivers. The water sprang forth from two massive carved marble dragon heads set on either side of the great temple's steps. The rivers flowed into a series of pools and channels, redirecting the water, energizing huge fountains and small waterfalls in the elaborate private parks of the high quarter, before the water was ultimately rerouted then funneled underground feeding the lower tiers need for fresh water.

Everything was centered on what looked like a building itself, a pyramid of steps leading to the entrance of the city's focal point. We could not see the doors, but Lou assured us they were there. They are the only way into the massive landmark and the great library!

At the bottom corner of each side of the steps were two ribbed columns, as thick as a house and taller than any tree. They stretched up forever to the height of the cliff. The terrace at the top of the steps held a large round pool with a statue of the city's founder Race Bliss. He stands at least two hundred feet high, dressed in a robe wearing a decorative belt, holding both hands to the sky. A constant shower of water fell from above through his fingers draining into the pool at his feet. The water fell from a cave high above, located in the center of the cliff. The cave opening is carved to look like an open mouth. From the outer rings of the city the mouth looks like the centerpiece of an hourglass creating the illusion of sand falling from its midpoint. Up and down, arching from the mouth piece, the cliff side was tapered and polished to enhance the illusion of glass. The top of the cliff mimics the stairs below in reverse. This is where the huge ribbed columns finally connect, creating the perfect hourglass effect.

Inside the high quarter, in the shadow of the temple, there were maybe thirty much smaller, but still well sized structures, an odd assortment of uniquely designed mansions and city buildings, all with extensive landscaping, utilizing a bizarre array of colored trees and bushes. Some of the architecture was so outlandish I could not comprehend how these houses were even built. Definitely not like anything you would find in Maguire.

The whole city was surreal, with its fancy contraptions and oversized architecture. You could tell as you moved through downtown what was built by hand and where magical shortcuts were taken, but no place was that as apparent as here in the high Quarter.

I could not believe what looked so small hours ago now towered above me, especially the walls. I could only wonder what could be so important to need two heavy armored gates, that big, for protection. Who or what were they trying to keep out that could justify this overwhelming stone and metal barricade.

We waited patiently in front of the gates, while Lou was hassled by several guards wearing very formal and intimidating uniforms bearing the insignia of the Suxen Falls Elite Guard. There was practically a small army guarding the immense doors, more men than in our whole village.

Lou was finally allowed to speak with one man who seemed to be in charge. Brandishing the sealed letter, Lou only had to say one word, "Quinn." Without hesitation the leader turned then shouted orders to a group of solders. The squad of men escorted us inside the gate.

The roads inside the wall were made of small olive and tan bricks laid out in decorative patterns, separating the lush finely manicured greenbelts decorated with elegantly positioned rows of planted flowers. After passing several long driveways we were motioned to turn toward a dubious looking dark structure with no noticeable windows. Unlike all the other buildings this one had no definition. It looked like two rectangle boxes were stacked on each other, one towering straight up. The outside walls were made entirely out of a polished black stone making it reflective like glass.

As we came closer, I could see the light refracting inward into the dark stone capturing our distorted reflections. Kat said she thought it was obsidian. Lou turned and smiled, reiterating the small details of lessons past, "Which has protective properties, that can deter Scrying, deflect energy drains and repel mental attacks."

The single tower rose a little above the belt of the ominous statue, making it the tallest of all the elaborate places in the high quarter. The bridge at the city's entrance was the only other structure in the whole city able to severely alter the skyline. Two steps up placed us in the moderately sized courtyard adorned with trees that were geometrically shaped. This is where our escorts stopped, pointing to the door in a demanding motion.

Above the doorway, stretching over what seemed to be an inadequate entrance for such a large building, was a carved relief. Four words in a waiving banner, it read "Academy of Arcane Knowledge." The front doors were made completely out of silver etched with a multitude of engravings, Lou said the symbols were wards of protection, placed to keep the unwanted out. Lou took a final swig of his bottle and threw it to the ground.

Inside the small doorway we found ourselves standing in a long room. Above I could see exposed metal beams The length of the room gave the appearance the walls, floor, and the ceiling tapered in, growing smaller until the room was only the size of a hallway at the far end.

Everything was covered with overlapping symbols just like the ones on the front door. The etchings were sporadic crossing over from the walls onto the doors, onto the floors, no flat surface was left exposed. Some of the symbols illuminated as people walked by, some just glowed.

There were many metal doors covering both sides of the long room. They were all the same except for the placement of the etchings on them. Some doors were suspended in the air twenty feet high, making no sense if the door needed to be used. Randomly, the doors opened and closed, as people entered and exited the peculiar rooms.

We were immediately greeted by two very tall, intimidating, well armed, very muscular guards in plate mail. The suits they wore were made of a dull metal except for their helmets obsidian like the outside of the building. Unlike the solders outside these guards bore the insignia for the Academy of Arcane Knowledge. They politely asked us to relinquish our weapons. We all looked at Lou, who nodded yes.

Father pulled our pie knife from his boot handing it to one of the men, handle first. The leering gent took a small pouch from his side, sliding the knife in through the narrow opening of the little bag.

Kat's dagger was next. Her dagger was bigger than our old pie knife and it looked twice the size of the small pouch. Yet the strange man had no problem sliding it into the tiny little hole.

I handed him my sword, which definitely would never fit. He had no expression as he slid it into the bag, without a problem. Gesturing us to move forward, the two men immediately excused themselves, returning to their stations next to the door.

Quickly, Lou was approached again as if he was expected, this time by an older well-mannered man. The first thing that caught my eye was his bedazzling bracelet, with the two red stones that seemed to stare back at you, like they were alive.

The older gentleman was dressed in a maroon colored cape elegantly embroidered in gold and silver. He obviously knew Lou well, giving him an unwanted hug. He introduced himself as Nathan Lightbender. Shaking each one of our hands briefly, talking quickly as if he was hyped up on too much pie, informing Lou he would be at Roz's later, as if we were expected to be there. Lou was shaking his head no, trying to explain. "She does not know we are . . ."

Not waiting or not listening for Lou's reply, he apologized, insisting we not be delayed on his account. It seemed as soon as he said hello, he was saying goodbye. I wanted to get a better look at his bangle, but his hands moved so fast. I don't ever remember being fascinated by a piece of jewelry. It was mesmerizing.

Stopping himself as if he forgot something important. He spun around to face Kat, emphasizing how much a pleasure it was to finally make her acquaintance. Promising Kat he would see her tonight at Roz's. Lightbender shuffled away through the crowd, his bracelet leaving behind a slight tracer, unwittingly it kept your eye focused on him till he was no longer in sight.

Continuing forward into the room there was constant sporadic movement, tall, short, thin, heavy, people of all sizes randomly moving from what seemed like one side of the room to another and back, some carrying huge piles of paper, strange objects or stacks of boxes.

One elongated door flew open as a strange man pushed a wheeled staircase across the room to one of the raised doors. Pulling a lever, the corners of the staircase dropped to the floor. At the same time at the top of the stairwell the door swung open, another flashy well dressed person climbed down the portable set of steps. Someone else grabbed the wheeled stairway cranking the lever again before pushing it into position just below another room. I don't know who coordinated this meticulously timed chaotic dance, but they would have to be bordering on the insane!.

The crowd seemed to clear a way stepping around the path of a small figure in an immaculate white robe. She floated through the crowd chanting, holding up a wooden symbol of her faith. She was half the size of a small girl but her slightly grayed curly amber hair and pale weathered face gave the appearance she was much older.

I was caught in her gaze immediately. Her presence was calming giving momentary order to the chaos around us. Reaching out to touch each one of us she smiled, then nodded in approval, never really saying a word to anyone. Temporary incapacitated it took a moment to clear my thoughts before I was able to move on.

Suddenly it became noticeable the room no longer had high ceilings, no longer did it just appear that the room was smaller the farther we went, it was physically smaller. I was getting that claustrophobic feeling. Because we were now walking down what seemed more like a large hallway than a spacious room and it was gradually tapering smaller and smaller.

Lou seemed to know which way to go, unlike some, rudely uncoordinated gent that knocked into us, as he abruptly tried to pass us in the tight quarters. "Pardon me, excuse me." I think he patted my sides looking for pockets as we awkwardly got a little close.

Two doors slid open on either side of the narrowing room, reveling glass windows. Inside we could see men wearing colored glasses that magnified their eyes. The men started shaking their heads.

Instantaneously, two men similar in stature to the tall men who greeted us originally, popped out of nowhere cornering us. Each armed with a long staff, with ends that lit up like fireflies.

They pointed the scary end of their staffs in a threatening manner trying to intimidate Lou. They were interested in the leather bag containing the letter and the four clay boxes. Giving the distinct impression they wanted Lou to relinquish it before we went any farther.

Lou stood his ground producing the letter, with the wax seal. In what became a brief but heated argument, Lou insisted he must hand deliver the parcel directly to Quinn. Quinn must be a big shot, again upon hearing his name they reconsidering their actions, allowing us to pass.

By the time we reached the end of the hallway, Lou's head was almost touching the ceiling. A bar slid out of the wall sectioning us off from the room. Under our feet a perfect square lit up illuminating the crystal floor. The highlighted portion started to rise.

Briefly we could see into large rooms as we were lifted up past each floor. One hall was filled with live animals in cages, another hung reconstructed skeletons. We came across a room where noisy men were engaged in a furious debate, then the ultimate laboratory with glass beakers and a wall decorated with an assortment of dangerous looking tools, a living forest, a quiet library, each area more out of place than the next.

When we finally stopped we were in a very formal room. There was a well dressed older man sitting behind a large desk. His healthy, silver hair was well maintained, perfectly shaped by years of conditioning. It had an unnatural sheen making it appear unreal.

On the desk in front of him were several odd gadgets, a few books and a couple ornate little boxes next to a large stack of papers. There were two doorways behind him, one on each side of a large book shelf, which was directly behind the desk. The shelves were covered with fancy books, even more elaborately decorated boxes and a eclectic variety of chotchkies. There was one intricately detailed painting on the left wall of a red and a blue dragon battling. On the other wall, a window that allowed us to overlook the tiers of the city, from this height we could see the harbor, the bridge, and the fields we spent the greater part of the day passing.

The old man seemed to be waiting for something to happen before he began. He was steering Lou down. You could feel tension in the air. Oddly for the first time, Lou seemed speechless.

Two men dressed in dark clothes entered the room, one through each of the formal-looking doors. They stood behind him like bodyguards crossing their arms, glaring at us not saying a word.

Once in place, the aging man at the desk began to speak. In a low tone, speaking very slowly, emphasizing each syllable as if he was choosing each word with care, "Lu-scious Mir-i-am Wic-kets, I trust your have been keeping up with your studies," he said sarcastically. "At least you did not return, empty handed."

Kat and I caught eyes. "Miriam," we said in sink with each other. Lou just gave us, "The Look," holding his index finger up, as we giggled in sync unable to hold in the laughter.

The old man stood up walking across the room, cautiously reaching out taking Kat's hand. "An-'d would this be Katinka?" With the mention of her name his voice became friendly, "Wonderful, just wonderful." He was smiling, raising her hand and smelling it, as if it was a delicate rose. "My child you know understanding comes from within. Trust your instincts. Great energy is prevalent in our family. You are a shining star, in a sky of darkness." Glancing momentarily at Lou, "We have all waited patiently to meet you." Repositioning his focus on Kat, "I can sense, you will not disappoint us. I hope you will not stay a stranger when you realize you have family, here, who love you!" This said as sincerely as he could, holding Kat's hand firmly looking directly into her eyes.

Turning back to Lou shrugging his shoulders, his voice returning to a more demeaning tone, avoiding eye contact he looked at the ground and raised his voice. "She should be here studying, learning, I can feel her energy! I can see power in her eyes." having agitated himself with his own words. "What brings you here." hesitating "Now, and why do you travel with such?" Quinn glared down at me with an evil eye, smacking his lips as if he tasted something sour, turning his head abruptly away as if his demoralizing glance was not noticed, finally maneuvering back around the desk to the comfort of his chair.

Lou opened the leather bag pulling out the letter, carefully placing it and the clay boxes on the desk. "Quinn I'm not here to squabble with you over our past, my lifestyle, or ask for your approval." Lou raised his voice, "I warned you long ago, Now something evil is stirring in Avalon." Then he gave a detailed description of what occurred at the barbecue the night we were attacked.

Boldly interrupting Lou's story, "What proof do you have? Where is the head you collected?"

Lou, jabbed back, "It's still on the cart old man." Then he pointed down at the desk. "Don't believe me. But this letter is in your man's own hand. I suspect it contains verification of my accusations!"

Quinn raised his hand snapping his bony fingers, gesturing to one of the men behind him, without a word the silent figure turned leaving the room.

Quinn slowly picked up one of the cubes, reaching across his desk, he slid a huge magnifier toward him so he could examine the box without straining to lean forward. The device had a thick piece of glass held up between two pewter hands that spiraled into its ornate stand, leaving Quinn's shaky hands free to examine the cube.

Looking through the glass at the small little clay box Quinn showed a profound consideration for its delicate construct. "I am glad you mustered up the courage to bring this to my attention. It's about time you took some responsibility, and stopped running from who you are."

"I'm not the one who avoided my responsibility." pouted Lou.

Quinn placing the cube down, pushing the magnifier to the side, sliding the letter toward him, as he pulled from his desk drawer a metal letter opener baring the crest of the city. Carefully cutting the seal he glanced at the writing then started to place the paper back on his desk.

Lou insisted. "Read it now, are you still afraid of the one thing you have forgotten. The truth!" Lou snatched the paper from Quinn. The guard moved forward, but Quinn motioned him to stop. Lou read the message out loud.

"Master Quinn, I hope I can reach you before this letter does. If I am delayed then things may have turned for the worse. We are fighting a grotesque looking foe from the forest above Gourd Lake, scaled men with paralyzing weapons that utilize unknown arcane properties. Even with what local militia I could assemble, we have been powerless to gain a victory. We are unable to track the enemy's movements until they make their presence known by striking another target. What men we send out, don't return, never more than a few dead bodies left on a field of battle. What dead we find, are mangled, deformed, and wear the face of our enemy.

Hundreds of people have been reported missing. These strange troupes move quickly and are gathering in strength. I am in Newhaven, where we found a woodsman who clams the untamed selvain's are organizing the attacks. I cannot see how. There's no proof to support these accusations.

We have also heard reports our enemy has established a post by the temple ruins in Avalon. It's possible this is where the creatures originated? There is concern Hanson and some of the smaller villages along the southern part of the main road are under their control already. If that's true, we may be surrounded. I believe Newhaven will be taken soon. They have no real defense. I am going to send this letter by land. I plan to travel by sea. My hope is that I reach you before this word. If you are reading this my plight may have turned fatal.

Gandelain.

"Most disturbing," Quinn mumbled to himself. Quinn kept his ground. "This means nothing, It does not prove you were right or the temple is involved.

Lou bounced back braking Quinn's condescending gaze, waiving the parchment above his head. "I warned you all."

We could tell Quinn was worried about the disturbing report we brought, no matter how much he tried to not show his emotions. He was not about to let Lou have the upper hand no matter how justified he was. Quinn had to much pride to admit he was wrong. Standing he exploding with anger, "Is that all you have too show me?"

The copper talisman was placed on the desk. Father, as cordially as possible said, "Have you seen this symbol before."

Quinn took a second to size father up without having to think he stated, "Are you sure the creatures were traveling under this banner?"

Father nodded.

Quinn continued smugly. "We have seen selvains carrying similar talismans; this symbol is part of their savage religion." Grunting, "This may be a local problem after all."

Lou just shook his head.

While they were distracted I pulled the ring off my finger, placing it under the large looking glass. "Why is this creature here?" Quinn screeched. The man behind him picked up the ring, holding it out as to place it back in my hand away from the desk.

Kat snatched it from him, turning to Quinn, smiling with all her charm. "What does your glass tell you about this Master Quinn?"

Irritated for a brief moment, snipping at Kat, "Never, call me that my sweet. Please, call me, Great Grandfather. My title is a formality for those not born of a noble bloodline. You have your Grandmother's eyes." Taking the ring in his hand, his voice growing warmer again, "Come closer dear, stand over here by me, on this side of the desk." Holding the ring under the glass, "Do you see the bands of light in the luminescent aura forming around the ring? The colors mean everything my child. The white outer glow shows the object to be of a balanced nature. The second ring of color identifies its spiritual qualities. See the rich green layer? The inner ring identifies the presence or the devotion in this case, pink, it contains some sort of healing abilities.

"The glass also identifies magical text and deciphers language", turning the ring upside down to see the writing on the inside band. Quinn took his time he was quite proud of his toy, "It says, Cleanse, It is written in . . ." Hesitating then hawing in a frustrated voice, "This language is unknown to . . ." Gawking across the room at me, erupting again in anger, "Where did you get this creature?"

That's when Lou pulled out the parchment, with the symbols he copied from the side of the boat, laying it under the glass, leaning over to read the word himself. It said, 'Sea Sprite.'

"What's that you have," Quinn butted in.

"If you will stop interrupting me" Lou stated, and then started to tell the story of the thieves we encountered outside of Nautica.

Quinn interrupted anyway. "You think the ring came from the ship in Nautica, with the weapons my men took from you at the door?"

Quinn crudely concluded any further discussion on the matter at hand. "That's enough! I will discuss this with the council immediately. We will examine the items more closely. I will send for you tomorrow." Lou took the ring shoving it in my pocket, repeating Quinn's last word, "Tomorrow."

Quinn, re-diverting the conversation changing the subject abruptly, "I trust you will be staying at your aunts?" insinuating yes to be Lou's only option.

Lou trying to get a word in edgewise, "She, does not know, we-"

Interrupted again, "She would be disappointed if you did not allow her to see Katinka in person." Quinn gave Lou, "The Look," not allowing any response before looking away. Reinforcing his position, "Your mother would not allow such selfish behavior!" I think Quinn knew the mention of Lou's mother would infuriate him. He still could not argue the point.

Frantically, Quinn started searching the shelf for something, before he changed the subject again. "One more thing, before you go," Pulling a tattered book from the shelf, "I have something for you my dearest, Katinka. It was your Grandmother's first spell book. Keep up your studies. Unlike your father, you have the potential to rise above those around you." Quinn turned to leave through one of the doors behind the desk, before Lou could react to his harsh words.

The second man re-entered the room. Both men just stood there glooming over us, silently waiting for us to just go away. We stepped back into the recession in the wall together, triggering the floor to glow. We started our descent to the lobby.

CHAPTER FIVE

Family Ties

The moment we walked out the etched silver doors of the Academy, we were cornered by a man in tall black hat, speaking in an elegant tongue. "Wickets party, ah there you are. You must be Katinka. You are as beautiful as she said!" Smiling, as he started walking around the group, squirting dust on the ground and making a yellow circle.

"I have taken a small liberty. Your things are already here." Our surrounding instantaneously changed. We found ourselves standing inside a beautiful home. The well dressed man transported with us, precariously standing with his hand out, giving us, The Look. Finishing the sentence he started on the steps of the Academy. "Your travel trunks are in your rooms, and your cart has been stabled with your horses. I trust this will be satisfactory to you?"

Flanking us from behind, talking as she was walking, making a B-line for Kat, and moving like she was late for dinner, was an older lady wearing a sequined evening dress and too much make-up. We were obviously under-dressed for the occasion and the eccentric looking lady was way too over-excited to make any sense. What made even less sense was her pink hair swirled around her head to look like a beehive. All I could think was, that definitely can't be her real hair!

Her voice reminded me of nails on a chalk board, from what I could tell she said "Thank you, Rudnick, that will be all," placing, a silver coin in the man's hand.

With a few graciously chosen words, "You're too generous, my lady!" the well mannered man immediately disappeared, leaving a small puff of multicolored smoke swirling in his wake.

The high pitched sound was deafening as the hellish creature continued its assault on our ears, "You don't write. You don't visit." Scorning Lou, turning to Kat, "The last time I spoke to your father, you were three." sighing to catch her breath.

"I am your Aunt Roz, dear. Come. Come, let me see you. Turn. Turn. Spin. Turn, dear let me see you. You so remind me of your Grandmother." A tear ran down her cheek, "When you're tired of living in the woods, sweetie, there's always a good home here for you." Aunt Roz seemed to not care what Lou or Julia thought. It was a hateful statement. Not only was she implying Kat was being raised inadequately, but she also made it sound as if Kat was the only one really welcome.

Changing the subject before Lou could do anything. "Who's hungry?" I was about to take back every malicious thought running through my head about the snooty old woman, until she looked down at me. "And what does your pet eat, dear? There is plenty of hay outside."

Kat giggled, really getting a kick out of the way I was being treated, badly. I don't know what's more insulting, the fact that her aunt offered to keep me in the stable or Kat's royal treatment. I could tell Aunt Roz was directly related to Quinn by the hair, and the attitude. I just silently cursed the vile wretch.

Lou was not looking very happy at all. I can see why he left. All the money in the world was not worth the way we were being treated. I felt completely humiliated. To make things worse, Kat ad-libbed at my expense, running her hand threw my long hair, "Can it eat with us. He does wonderful tricks." Sticking her tongue out at me, she was just throwing lamp oil on the fire. I will never be able to live this down.

My only real question was, when are we leaving and will this lady ever be quiet. I had never met anyone who was able to out talk Lou. "What's your favorite color, Katinka? Do you want to go shopping tomorrow for a dress, Katinka? What do you think of the city, Katinka?" On, and on, and on, I don't think she even noticed there was anyone else in the room. If it wasn't for the food on the table, meeting Roz would have been absolutely unbearable.

Her inappropriate behavior was easily excused by her hospitality. Platters of cookies and sweets, not to mention a full, eight-course meal, onion soup, fresh venison, mashed potatoes, gravy, green beans and carrots, fresh bread and butter, with cherry and lemon flavored drinks, followed by ice cream, chocolate cream pie, then more pie. If that lady would stop talking, I could die here!

I think she thought if our mouths were full, we would not be able to interrupt her. "What's your favorite food, Katinka? What spells do you know? Do you like hats, Katinka? Katinka!" Katinka, ahhh!

Katinka pulled out a tattered ad she had ripped out of one of Mister Kevil's newspapers. It was unfolded and folded so many times, the pretty girl had all but faded away and you could barely make out the large letters, "Always dress for success with Sparmoni."

Roz's eyes lit up like she had found the daughter she never had. Making her talk even faster! "We can start there dear-ie, then Mcbriys and of course Deor's." Katinka just sat there nodding and smiling, as Roz listed every store in the city.

At the far end of the table I was involved in a one-man cake-eating contest. Across the way was Aunt Roz's talk-a-thon. I hope it gets better than this. I would hate to have to agree with Lou about hating the undesirable deceitful people you meet when you travel to the big city's.

Aunt Roz's decorating style was as excessive, as the spread on her table. Excessive is not entirely a bad thing. The dining room was probable the fanciest room I had ever been in, let alone eaten in.

Vaulted ceilings with long windows covered with exquisite layers of expensive fabrics. There was a huge painting of two strawberry blonde twin girls wearing pink, in a lavishly textured gold frame. Centered under it was a half moon table with spiral metal legs. The small table matched the long table for twelve that extended the length of the room. Both tables had matching silver candelabras, all spaciously arranged with spots of color provided by bouquets of fresh flowers. Then of course the multi layered trays of sweets, and of course the stack of empty fine china plates stacking up at the southern end of the table, next to me!

Julia was amazed at how much food I could put away as she silently stood watching over me and Kat, making sure we did not break anything. Her attempts to offer help were ignored.

I would have to say the coolest thing at Roz's was Knick Knack. He was a floating swirl of air, with just enough colored smoke to keep him translucent. His face would become more animated each time he spoke. A conjured servant who ran the kitchen, answered the door, and cleaned the house. I overheard Roz tell Kat, "He also does windows."

For me I was happy with another piece of pie. Snapping my fingers loudly, "Knick Knack could you see if there is another slice of the, Mmmm, strawberry?" I said in the snootiest voice I could muster up.

A loud chime rung, Nathan Lightbender was at the door, the man with the bracelet from the Academy. Father and Lou were in a room Aunt Roz called the study, my guess hiding out, as far away from her as they could, with a bottle of fine apricot wine.

Lightbender was just what we needed to pull them out of seclusion, and peel Aunt Roz away from Kat. He walked up behind her placing his hands on her shoulders. "Roz you can't monopolize all her time. Be nice, and share Katinka with the rest of us. We are all thrilled to finally meet her. Don't be jealous, you know I will always love you."

Gently kissing Roz on the forehead in an endearing manor, he pulled his hands away from her neck slowly revealing a necklace with five sparkling diamonds the size of plump raspberries. Kat eyes lit up when she saw the shiny necklace. Aunt Roz excused herself dancing to the music she could only hear, as she exited down the hallway. Flaunting the expensive trinket, she knew would not last.

Lightbender was dressed for a night on the town and was still wearing the bracelet that had fascinated me earlier. I was able to get a closer look at the large rubies as he sat down with us at the table. It was not long before I again was captured by its brilliance. The bracelet seemed to call me out, I felt like it wanted to be admired. It took will power to stop myself from just staring at it.

He was taller than I remembered; clean cut short graying dark hair. His soothing voice demanded your attention. He mesmerized Kat with his words. "You have beautiful eyes like your Grandmother. I am glad we have found this time to chat. Please don't take me as too forward. I am an old friend of the family and though I am not truly related to you, I hope you would refer to me as your, Uncle."

Lightbender went on trying to justify this title and his connection to Kat's belated family. "I grew up with your Great Grandfather. I remember Quinn, when his hair was jet black and he was still fancied as a lady's man. I was there when your grandmother was born, rest her soul.

He paused seeking Kat's approval, "I guess Luscious has his own reasons for sheltering you from us. You are part of our family, no matter how much he wishes you were not. Some things can never be changed." He paused, "Know your father was happy here, once! When we first met he was about your age. I was there when Little Marium," stopping to re-think his choice of words, "your father found his first book. I helped guide him in his studies and stood beside him when things got rough. We fought beside each other in the Time Trials. He is like a brother to me."

There was a sadness in Lightbender's eyes as he changed the subject, "Let me see your hands child," Pulling Kat's right hand closer to him. He acted intrigued about what he saw. "I envy your youth. You have a long life line and courage in your heart; you will also find love and happiness. Your luck line is deep." Bending her fingers looking at her scuffed nails, shaking his head, "Oh no, my dear, this is implausible, Ah, nothing a good manicure won't fix, Be sure to tell Febe your Uncle Nate says hi, when Roz gets you to the salon."

Lightbender continued to examine Kat's hand particularly the configuration of groves in Kat's fingertips noting each finger had what he called a noticeable loop, "That's a sure way to identify a strong talent. It's not surprising you have an explosive nature, like your father, sassy, maybe a little stubborn, don't argue with everybody, too much, my dear." Nate smiled, amused by his connotation.

Shaking his head in approval, "All loops, very rare, very impressive." raising his voice, in hopes he could be heard form the other room. "Roz you were right. She is special."

"Show me what you can do." Kat started to rub her fingers together, opening her hand slowly. In her palm appeared a flame, with a hand gesture she flicked the fire onto an empty plate, were it started to dissipate. "That's just wonderful. Your Grandmother was a keeper of the flame too."

Lightbender waived his hand above the flame Kat had created stating "Entertain us." The fire started to burn bright again. He started shaking his hand in different directions as if he was holding a small marionette, below his fingers the fire reshaped itself into a tiny puppet made of fire, which started to dance. Kat thought that was cool. So did I, although not as cool as the jewelry dangling from his wrist I just wanted to reach out and touch it.

I rolled down to the other end of the table sitting next to Kat, who asked Nate if he could explain to her, how to do that trick, calling him Mr. Lightbender. He gave her, The Look." As if she made an inexcusable rude remark. "Please. Please. Every body calls me Nate." Rewording her question, "Nate, I mean, Uncle Nate, show me how."

Gleaming in approval, he wasted no time explaining to her that this incantation does not create the fire or manipulate it. "The spell affects those who watch the flame altering their perception of it. Once you understand the flame is not the target of the spell, the people in the room watching the flame are. You just need to subliminally suggest to your subjects what you want them to see. It is not a very productive spell and it does not last a long time, but it can add a dramatic effect to monotonous activities or emphasize the grandeur of the spells you already know. It makes things cool. Let me give you an example, Oh Knick Knack."

The floating aberration drifted into the room. "You see Knick Knack is a combination of spells. The manpower is supplied by summoning an invisible servant, but Knick Knacks' color and shape, and of course his personality, are the illusion created by your silly Aunt Roz for our entertainment."

Roz came back in the room the necklace was gone, "No. No. You are not going to tell her all my secrets." She said giving Nate a peck on the cheek. Kat was shaking her head as if she understood what Nate was teaching her.

Roz was mocking Lightbender using his own words. "Nate dear, you can't monopolize all her time. Be nice and share Katinka with the rest of us. We are all thrilled to finally meet her. Don't be jealous. You know, I will always love you, too."

"I have a treat for you my sweet." Aunt Roz raised her voice. "Come in dear, meet your cousin" What was this, another one of Lou's wacky relatives? A tall bony young man entered the room, he had short jet black hair punked out on the top, and thick side burns. He was wearing more eyeliner than Aunt Roz, sporting a large black and white checked suit jacket with a black shirt and pants. His leather shoes were pointy with metal tips and thick soles. His eyes sunk into his pale face highlighting his lips which still had a touch of rose color giving life to his inexpressive grin. Tilting his head up, flaunting a piercing just under his lower lip, an oddly bent silver wire curved out then down spiraling forward like a metal goatee.

He favored his disfigured hand. It looked like he was badly burned. The skin on his hand was coarse and leathery it was stretched so tightly you could see the shape of the bones beneath its greenish rough texture. His index finger looked like it never healed completely exposing tendons, and bones that seemed to twitch each time he moved his wrist. His nails had a green metallic sheen and on his pinkie was a ring with sharp points.

He spoke in a fast paced tempo with an attitude like he was trying to sell you something, "Hi ya toots, I'm Mordian. So you're the illusive cousin that's being raised as a farmhand." Nate looked up with disapproval, as Mordian winked back. He and Lightbender were not quite friends, more like playful rivals.

They were not at all alike. Nate was well liked and respected by all the members of city council. Mordian had an impulsive argumentative personality with strong family ties, namely Quinn, making him one of the town's untouchable reckless youths. He was also growing in strength and becoming a more formidable mage. He studied a School of Thought that questioned one's moral fiber. Choosing to research more aggressive spells that deal with the questions of life and death. He was powerful and unpredictable, a dangerous quality especially at his age when most seem to rebel against authority. Mordian and Nate both knew where they stood, particularly with Roz, who obviously had the hots for Nate.

Snickering, "I'm glad my mother has not talked you to death, yet."

No one answered until Roz chimed in, "Be nice."

Laughing inside, I wanted to say something, adding to Mordian's snide remark. I was probably glad Lou interrupted me, because it would have been sarcastic, and it's probably not good to insult your host, especially if she can turn you into a toad.

Kat pulled my hand onto the table. Smiling at Nate she said, "Will you read Riley's palm and show me how." Kat was fascinated that he could tell so much about someone by just looking at their palm.

Nate grabbed my hand placing the attention in the room back on him, telling Kat this will take you a lot longer to master than my last trick. He explained "Each hand has hundreds of subtle differences effecting the interpretation. The basics are easy if you know what details to look for." It tickled as he massaged my hand pointing out the individual characteristics, stating each wrinkle had a meaning.

Even this close I still couldn't get a good solid look at the wondrous object on his arm, but it was fashioned to resemble a screaming face with two red eyes, the mouth swallowing his hand.

Nate's disposition suddenly changed. At first he looked bewildered then spooked. He pushed my hand away immediately, claiming the stress lines must differ on Selvain hands. The expression on his worried face said he did not believe what he was saying or seeing?

Mordian snickered at Nate stating he was getting old, loosing his touch. Nate's ego was a little ruffled and he got into Mordian's face shouting, "You should know by now, to have respect for what you do not understand."

Mordian stood his ground, "Don't get testy. That bracelet you're wearing does not work on me anymore. The time of parlor tricks is over." The confrontation brought Lou and my father out of the study into the dining room.

Lou said, in a mellow voice, "What's all the hubbub."

Lightbender, answered, "Nothing Lou, his bark is bigger than his bite."

Mordian decided to give Nate a break, focusing on a new challenge, "Lou." Mordian took an educated guess, blurting out another sample of his boyish charm "One day back in town and he thinks he's in charge. You must be my infamous Cousin, Luscious. Keeper of the Fire, Victor in the Time Trials, now a pig farmer and the only one who aggravates my grandfather worse than me. It's nice, to finally meet you."

Lou was aware of Mordian and his rebellious reputation, smirking as he turned to look at Roz, rolling his eyes. Lou lunged forward grabbing Mordian giving him a manly hug taking advantage of his own naturally large stature, picking Mordian off the ground squeezing him as hard as he could then dropping him down, slightly winded, followed by a couple over zealous pats on the back. "You are a feisty little shit." Turning to compliment Roz who was comforting Nate. "He's strong, you have done well."

Mordian started to excuse himself "I would love to stay and play with the department of geriatrics but Certsey is meeting me at the club, Katinka would like to join us for a drink. The Funhouse is always a splash."

Lou answered for Kat. "No, thank you, maybe another time."

Aunt Roz stepped in "Nonsense she will go," Giving Lou, "The Look," "She will not be your little girl forever. Let the kids play. Mordian will not let anything happen, to my sweet, Katinka." Roz refocused her evil eye giving Mordian a light slap on the cheek, reminding him exactly, who is in charge, insinuating if anything goes wrong he would be answering directly to her.

Kat looked shocked, Lou, her dad, was being cornered by Roz. Lou spoke up still trying to hold his ground, hoping he could screw up the deal, "Only if Riley can go!"

Mordian stepped up to me, sizing me up. "Fine with me! Everybody is welcome at the funhouse. But these clothes absolutely, will not do. Mother, can you do something about this?"

Roz stepped up, then tapped me on the shoulders and spun me around, as I came to a stop, my wardrobe was seriously upgraded. I was wearing an oversized tailored suit with a light green silk shirt. These clothes felt so soft against my skin, and my shoes were fine black leather, pointed with metal tips, I was dressed to the nine's. The vote was still on the wall, whether I was going to love Aunt Roz or not.

Kat ran forward, "Aunt Roz, can you do me to? Please? Please?" She flashed the saddest puppy eyes I've ever seen Kat throw, as if she needed to waste her talent on Roz. Who was grinning from ear to ear, ecstatic she could do anything to put a smile on the face of her only niece.

With a similar spin, Kat was wearing a short leather skirt and a red corset with a thin white shawl, that was weaved like a spider web. Kat was enthralled, jumping up and down hugging Aunt Roz and modeling for her. Roz in the moment, "Turn. Turn. Spin. Turn."

"I love you Aunt Roz, can you teach me that trick," Kat exclaimed with glee as she added the colorful sash she had gotten from Alerick, wrapping it around her waist, and then tying it off.

Lou did not like any of this, being here in Suxen Falls, seeing his family, Kat going to a place called the Funhouse and especially that revealing little outfit. Giving us a, "New Look." I think he's going to pass out.

Anyhow, I was thanking my lucky stars he could not say "No" to her. Aunt Roz must have looked and sounded just like his mother, she should Roz was her twin sister.

Mordian had his own coach. It was black leather with pewter detail. The handles and hardware were formed to resemble human bone piles accented with skulls. It was pulled by two black stallions. Inside the seats were upholstered with a rich green fabric, the only color on the exterior was four dark green wheels and matching leather harnesses. It was parked inside Roz's coach house.

On second thought being one of Roz's pets may not be such a bad thing. Roz's coach house was bigger than my old barn. I could see our old cart in the corner, amongst several other much fancier coaches. Kat had brought Bauble out a piece of meat from the table, we found her with our horses in one of the stalls, in the stable across the way.

Mordian seemed to always have a smirk on his face, like he was up to something. Declaring, "Were all hooked up. All we need now is a driver, Riley, your it."

How was I to know he was kidding, there was no argument here, I was just ecstatic I was getting to go. Wasting no time jumping up top, as Mordian helped Kat into the Cab like a gentleman, hopping in behind her, shutting the door.

I was surprised to find an old gooey burlap bag that smelled like rotting food, stuck on the seat when I got there. I heard Mordian knock on the roof three times.

Suddenly something started to twitch. Once then twice, all of a sudden the bag started to expand, like a growing bubble. The thin cord that tied the bag closed began to unravel, as the contents started taking shape I jumped to the side of the bench where I could still see what was happening.

There was a small copper ring around the unraveling rope, still trying to hold the sack shut. Goop started to spit out from the seams of the bag, as the stitching gave way, covering the seat. The sticky mess was starting to form into a crude figure. The burlap sack stretched out, clothing the forming creature, as the head took shape so did a hood, hiding the creature's deformities. The rope was slithering around the side of the strange mass like a snake, encircling a large area that was starting to resemble a shoulder. Then the rope traveled down the arm weaving itself into a gloved hand that was already reaching out for the reigns. On that hand that was the ring that originally held the bag shut.

I tried to look at its face, but the creature had a bent spine and a hunchback, making his body lurch forward. Its legs never formed completely exposing patches of skin that looked like the back of a toad, greenish black with a, gritty, pocked and blistered texture. The unformed legs hung down like two melted candles in the sun, continuously dripping slimy liquid onto the top of the cab.

Pulling the reigns, it slowly turned its head toward me. Snarling, "To the club my liege."

Mordian yelled out confirming, "The usual." Pausing for effect, "Hold on to your hats boys and girls, tonight's going to be a wild ride!"

I almost lost my chair, and my dinner, as the sinister looking cab darted into the night. Each time the hoofs hit the ground there was a green electrical discharge.

The guards at the gate in the high quarter seemed to know when to hold their ground, and when to step aside. It was an exhilarating ride and I was in the front row. We wound through the city streets that were now lit up in a fascinating assortment of colors. I could not keep track of which way we were heading. As we gained speed, everything became a blur.

When the coach finally stopped I jumped down. Mordian shook me then smacked me on the back. "What do you think? Want to be my driver? I'm just kidding. Ha, Ha. You're a good sport Riley. If Kat likes you, you're in with me. Now! Let's have some real fun."

CHAPTER SIX

The Funhouse

The Funhouse was the hot spot for young adults. When we pulled up, there was a small line of dubious looking characters waiting to get in. I noticed Several Selvains in line as well. We did not have to wait ourselves. A large man at the door knew Mordian. With a nod and a bro-glance, he removed a small chain barricade letting us bypass the line, opening the door, letting us in!

Totally crazy! From outside we could hear the beat of the drums, inside the sound was defining. The music was emanating from down a dark crowded hallway where I could see lights flashing. The guys here looked rough in a dark fashionable way, muscles and tattoos. The girls here dressed so different from the girls in our little town. Here, they were practically naked, dresses so tight they left nothing to the imagination. A drunken girl fell into Mordian arms; he kissed her on the forehead, then asked her if she had seen Certsey. Giggling, she nodded yes.

Mordian was pointing toward us, as another large bouncer stamped the back of my hand. "First time in? Have a blast!" Mordian snickered leaving the inebriated girl in the hands of the doorman.

The club was filled with the aroma of tobacco. The smoke had an alluring effect on the shadows created by the dimmer lights. Seductively the seemingly effortless display of sporadic flashes of color, all in sync with the pulsating music, pulled us toward the funky scene. The hallway lead to a room filled with gyrating club goers with pompous spiky hairstyles, emphasized by the unnatural light that radiated from behind them. Strangely, the flickering light show placed an eerie black and white imprint in my mind, as the demented energetic group, for a moment in time, appeared to be dancing in slow motion.

When we got closer to the dance floor I could see the lamps had no fire. Like the lamps on the bridge, they were filled with glowing crystals, in-cased in boxes that mechanically opened and closed or spun on rotating poles behind pieces of colored glass. This created the appearance that they were flashing on and off, sporadically projecting irregular shapes, highlighting only small portions of the dance floor. The crowd dancing below the lights seemed unaware of the intricate mechanisms as they endlessly moved up and down to the hypnotic drum beat.

We slipped through the crowd, following Mordian, who found an empty table in one of the dimly lit corners. I waited for a light to shine in our direction then pulled a chair out for Kat. We were right there where the musicians were playing.

The music was very tribal, a low thudding bass drum provided a constant back-beat, while a variety of odd instruments was mixed in. Musicians bent elongated pieces of metal and tapped on an assortment of different colored glass bottles, ever-so-gently, to create a diverse assortment of high pitched sounds, compounded with multiple drummers who would join in, all with a different beat, adding to the intense tempo that drove the synchronized movements of the crowd.

Throughout the room there were beautiful young girwls, selvain and human. With bright flowers painted on them, they danced on raised stages, tapping and shaking their assets. The dance floor was jumping, the club was pumping. I had never imagined anything like this.

A girl sat down next to us with a round of drinks. Mordian introduced her as Certsey his girlfriend. Kat and I gave each other, "The Look." We knew we should not be drinking, as we both took a shot of light blue liquor from the tray without hesitation, holding them up to make a toast, silently condoning what we were about to do. Mordian smiled, joining in, as Certsey said, "To new friends."

Mordian looked at Kat. "You do know how special we are? Not everybody can do what we can. Just reading the books does not guarantee one will be able to twist reality. Most never get beyond card tricks. This town is filled with second rate magicians."

Mordian liked to bag on the old timers that run the city. He was constantly making fun at the Council's expense. He also liked talking about himself. Each time he put one of them down, he bolstered himself up, bragging that he is becoming one of strongest wizards in Suxen Falls, more advanced in his studies and half the age or some of the relics that rule over this town. Bravely claiming he would lead the council someday.

Overexcited he lashed out, "We control the city, we watch over the simpleton's, as they squabble over our change!" raising his hand signaling for another round.

Mordian could not have known what we had brought with us or had informed Quinn about, only mentioning we dropped a bomb on him. "Whatever it is, it has Quinn worried." Mocking Quinn's decrepit laugh as he congratulated us, "I thought I was the only one who could constipate my Grandfather like that." Mordian seemed happy about anything that caused Quinn anxiety, blurting out, "Especially when the incompetent fools need me for some kind of research!"

Then Mordian turned the subject to Lightbender. "He thinks he can control me because my mother likes him." Making another bold statement claiming he could take Lightbender in a fight on any given day, "Most of his strength comes from that cursed bangle he wears." Referring to Lightbender as a know nothing with no natural talent. "Not like those in our family," holding his glass up to Kat then taking a hefty swig. After which he placed both hands on the table and whispered, "The rumor is, Lightbender's bracelet in not really a bracelet at all. It was a dragon's ring. His father left the trinket to him. It had been handed down by his family for generations, and it is the only reason people like him at all. The enticing piece of jewelry has the ability to charm all caught in its gaze." Mordian believed it was the only way to explain how Lightbender became a hot shot in the actor's guild. "He is conning the high society snobs, who compete to watch him act like a clown in their fancy plays. If the crowd only knew, his talent is worn on his sleeve?"

Certsey was as skinny as a girl can get. She had more piercings than I could count. Above her eye, in her nose, on her lip, just to mention a few. She accessorized her skimpy little black outfit with the kind of boots that come up past the knee and a necklace made of small shards of glowing crystals. Certsey was happy to sit quietly, shaking her mop like head of jet black and pink hair to the music, listening to Mordian brag, as she snuggled up to him. Until she needed a refill, "Humm where's that girl." Certsey stood up, making it her duty to not let us run dry! "I'll be right back." In a blink of an eye she was gone.

The waitress finally walked up to our table with a fresh round, saying loudly, "Did you order the Bloody Fetus?" placing a glass in front of me filled with the nastiest drink I had ever seen. I shook my head no.

The flirty serving girl turned to me and winked, purposely trying to avoid eye contact with the other bar-maid who was rushing around trying to take care of everybody. I thought the two girls were twins for a second, until I realized it was Certsey, standing in front of us with another round. As the lights fluttered, her outfit slightly blurred, changing from the outfit the waitress was wearing, to the waitress wearing Certsey's cute little black outfit. When the lights flashed again we saw Certsey smiling at us in the right set of clothes. I was not crazy, Kat noticed it too.

"Showoff!" Mordian patted Certsey on the butt, complimenting her on how beautiful she was. "That's my girl, free drinks all night. So drink up."

The more I drank, the more I noticed the whole bar was filled with people who had profuse piercings, tattoos and bizarre body-altering modifications. Each time another light went on and off, it highlighted a new face with a different shiny metal attachment.

Here Mordian and Certsey looked just like any other face in the crowd.

Fascinated by the musicians, I watched, observing each time one drummer would stop; he was replaced by another, altering the tempo of the music ever so slightly. The hypnotic beat seemed to never end.

It was impossible not to notice one of the Selvain drummers on break, necking off to the side with a long legged light skinned blonde, wearing the skimpiest outfit in the whole place. Like most Selvain's he had deep greenish skin tone with dark hair and dark eyes. I was actually a little darker than most Selvain's with light eyes.

What caught my attention was not her dress, it was his face tattoo. I asked Kat if she recognized the pattern. We both nodded it was the same style as on the Lizard creature that attacked us.

I was a little tipsy and starting to feel the effects of the first couple of rounds. Kat did not take that into consideration when she pulled me to my feet. Informing me I was going to dance! Kat was looking so good, "Wow!" I never thought she would be able move like the regulars. Mordian and Certsey joined us too, as we all lost track of the time. Now I know why they call this place the Funhouse!

A few empty glasses later we ended up dancing by the sexy couple we noticed earlier. They were hidden away in a dark nook that had a large booth; there was lots of extra space. Kat asked if we could sit for a moment. They were too preoccupied to notice, this couple was ready for a room.

Kat pushed me into the seat, and then forced me to move down by practically sitting on me. The girl physically turned the drummers head to kiss him, as if he needed prodding. He fondled her briefly exposing her chest, putting her in several precarious positions. Still for some unknown reason he kept looking back over his shoulder.

We were all sitting together, but nobody was paying attention to each other. The girl was occupying her time by rubbing her tight little frame against the drummer. It seemed his eyes were focused on the back door. It was hard trying not to get caught up in the show his lady friend was putting on, but my mind was actually on

Kat. In lieu of the situation, anticipating anything else she might be thinking to do. Unfortunately for me, Kat's mind was on getting information. Sigh.

Kat tried to break the ice, but the guy acted indifferent, until he took notice that I was Selvain too. Once he realized Kat was with me, he started to acknowledge her, ignoring his girl, always keeping one eye on the exit.

Kat was interested in his tattoos. "Do they hurt? What do they mean? Where can I get one?" I could see what just one evening with Aunt Roz can do to an impressionable little girl. Kat asked five questions before he even got a chance to speak.

The Selvain introduced himself as Reein, saying, "They do not hurt, but the process might be painful, for a homely lass such as yourself."

He went on saying how he had to earn his tattoos. Those like him of the Badger clan must undergo specific ancestral rites of passage, "Tests of courage and strength must be endured to prove one's position and loyalty to the clan." He nodded at me, as if we had a brotherly connection.

Reein told us how his clan records their journey through life in what we call a tattoo. Reein referred to the design as his Grail. Those who bare the sacred marks are always looking to reach a higher level of enlightenment. As one gains the understanding of their path in life they become worthy of the right to add more ink and tell another piece of their story. Explaining there are different variations of the design, the intricate work denotes warrior, priest or worker, in the fine details are symbolic lists of ones individual achievements. "I have the mark of a warrior!" Reein said. "We believe our Grail protects us and makes us strong." Some of the elders in his clan are completely covered from head to toe, showing a living record of their accomplishments. They start their Grail as children and spend their lives trying to complete them.

We were interrupted by two figures that came through the back exit Reein had been fixated on since we sat down. They too bore the mark of Badger clan. They had with them a mysterious package, suspiciously similar to the leather case we had left with Quinn!

Reein excused himself abruptly, abandoning his girlfriend, leaving a disappointed look on her face. He did not explain what was so urgent only that he must go. He turned to me and said "Soon all will feel the conviction of the Badger Clan."

Oh, how right he was, Kat had to peel me out of the booth. I was reaping the rewards of my liquid diet. It gets kind of fuzzy for me here. Kat claims she had to hold me, to stop me from falling and walking into people. If Lou knew that she had to watch me, I would never live this down.

We found Mordian "Rollin the Bones" in one of the back rooms where there was a crowd gathered around him. He shook the dice above his head, screaming, "Time to dig up the bank." There was a let down in the volume of the roar and I heard a voice yell, "Next shooter. Who feels lucky?"

Certsey was enjoying the dance floor from above on a Go-Go pole. Sparks were shadowing every move she made, like she was holding shooting stars in her hands. Nothing was out of the ordinary in this crowd.

Mordian took one look at me and said "Looks like you had one too many, my little green friend."

Certsey slightly amused commented, "Both of you boys should have skipped that last shot."

We finally made it out of the maze of intoxicated night clubbers. The fresh cold air felt good, it helped me gather my wits. Outside we saw Reein across the way with his two friends. They waited till a forth person showed up then ducked down an alley. Kat mentioned to Mordian that they were up to something bad, possibly part of the bomb we dropped on Quinn. Mordian said this is the wrong part of town to be following people at night. We were on one of the piers in the harbor. I could hear the waves below us. Most of the buildings around the club were large empty warehouses.

Not listening as usual, Kat had already run to the edge of the building where the alley started. She was looking down into the darkness between the buildings. I looked at Mordian, "Lou will kill me if something happens to her."

Mordian chuckled, "Lou is tuff, but reluctant. Aunt Roz, mad, is unpredictable and our worst nightmare. She once turned my shoe lace into a snake because I left it untied. If something happens to Kat, dead might be a good thing!"

Without hesitation we crossed the street together, chasing after Kat, who was not waiting for anybody. The ally was connected to a small back street, with little light. The globe on the lamp post was broken and the crystal missing. When we finally caught up to Kat, She had lost sight of her quarry.

Kat picked up a stone or something hard from the ground, removing her colorful sash folding it into a makeshift sling, arming herself.

I tried to stop the insanity, asking Kat if she realized what she was getting us into. She called me a chicken making the appropriate sounds, letting go of the rock, breaking a window across the way. Mordian was impressed. "What else did they teach you on that farm?" Like everything else, he said it sarcastically.

The door on one of the garages across the way slid open a few inches. A head peaked out, the door slammed shut again. Certsey wanted to try something, she pulled a vile out of her little black studded purse, pouring the powder on her hand. Blowing the dust gently, she whispered, "Swoshe!"

There was a subtle change in the direction of the wind as a fog bank slowly moved in. Kat smiled at Certsey "That was cool girlfriend." Kat grabbed my arm pulling me across the way without being seen.

Shaking my head I was thinking, what are we doing here?

Mordian winked at Certsey, "I'll do you one better." We were right next to the door where we saw the lookout. Mordian waved his malformed hand swirling the fog around him. "Stink." He was pointing into the garage. Some of the fog became a greenish mist. Slowly it traveled threw the cracks around the door and under the windows.

Coughing and gagging was heard from the inside. Within a few seconds the door slid open, two men ran out. It was hard to keep track of them as they scattered into the fog. Kat said "Not them, we want the one with the satchel."

Kat looked inside then ran in, Mordian tried to stop her again but she slipped by, exposing herself to the toxic green cloud that permeated the small warehouse. Immediately she gripped her stomach starting to gag! I wanted to help her, but Mordian held me back, assuring me she would be alright, "A little green, but alright!"

By the time it was safe to enter the warehouse, Reein was gone! Nothing but a pile of junk and couple of lavishly painted delivery carts. One read, "Under the Udder Dairy," the other, "Sunny Brook Farms."

Mordian walked over to one of the carts, opening the back. Facetiously he asked, "Let's just see what there up to."

There was several empty small baskets made to carry two to three dozen eggs, one was still half full. Certsey said with a smirk, "All these guys are guilty of is delivering breakfast!"

I added, "At this time, their delivering more than breakfast."

"There is a lot of things they could be smuggling into the city." Mordian remarked.

Kat concluded the conversation, "How many would, how did you put it, constipate, the old man! I'm telling you they're up to no good."

Mordian called Kat closer, "Watch this!" sliding his hand across one of the egg crates, tapping his metallic nails twice, "Marten!" The eggs started to sparkle! Kat pulled one out, it was heavier than a regular egg and appeared to be made of solid metal. "Try one of those in your fancy little sling, that will do some damage." Kat shook her head smiling, as she grabbed a couple more, filling my pockets with her stash.

Sectioned off in the far corner was a small cluttered office. Invoices were scattered thought-out the room, on, in, and around a series of wood file cabinets that were lined up by a small desk. On the desk was a handwritten note with tonight's date, the Funhouse, one o'clock, and the name Reein underlined.

Under the note was an invoice from Sunny Brook Farms, number fourteen, Sunnybrook Road, Kelideco. It was dated earlier today for six hundred eggs. Someone had used the back of the receipt as a piece of scratch paper. One word scribbled in large letters then circled several times with a thick pen, "Friday!" Did it mean next Friday, that was only a couple days from now?

Mordian called out for us, he was flipping over a piece of wood fencing that was out of place on the floor, with a little help he exposed a hole in the ground. We all looked down into the void. It looked like someone had tunneled through the top of a huge pipe, creating an entrance to the sewer below.

Kat said, "Still think they're delivering just breakfast?"

I pointed out if anyone was there, they were long gone. The girls gave me, "The Look." In retrospect, maybe we should go home, was the wrong thing to say, "I would rather be a live chicken, than a chicken that smells like down there!" That didn't work either. Mordian volunteered to go first, but Kat had already started descending. Mordian followed, mumbling to himself about what would happen if Roz found out about this. Covering his nose, "Maybe the kid is right, this might be a bad idea."

Metal spikes were hammered into the side wall holding boards that created a slimy, slippery ladder. I helped Certsey get her grip then followed them down the hole. What was Lou thinking when he sent me to protect her? Who was going to protect me? The ground crawled with bugs and sludge. I could not believe Kat was even down there. She probably could not see well. I on the other hand, have very good eyes for seeing in the dark. Somehow I think it would be better to not know what I was standing in, this is the sewer!

Certsey pulled off her necklace, pushing the crystals in it closer together. As she did, the light they emitted intensified. There was a lot of trash in the tunnel, old cans, a shoe and a rusty little sledge hammer, probably used to dig the original hole and make the ladder, garbage too heavy to be easily washed away. In the distance, I could also see several pairs of tiny staring eyes, they were to close to each other to be Reein, hopefully just a happy family of rats.

There was about five inches of grimy water running down the moss covered center of the pipe, making it slippery and hard to keep your feet dry. A row of lights shinned down from above, dimly lighting up small sections of the cylindrical tunnel about every twenty to thirty paces. The evenly spaced rays of light shinned through grates in the sidewalks above us. I could hear voices coming from the streets above, people unaware we were listening below.

The tunnel carried sound very well. I could hear Kat saying "Come on were going to loose him!" So I picked up the small hammer griping it tightly and followed our group already moving down the pipe. Finally we could see what looked like Reein in the distance. He was standing there with the leather bag strapped to his back. He was opening a tin can. He poured the yellow contents into the dirty water.

I think I heard Mordian give one last quote. "That's not good."

The water started to bubble and a gelatinous orange blob started to grow filling the pipe. Quickly we were loosing sight of Reein who laughed out loud, "Have some fun with this." This did not look like fun. Why did we ever leave the party?

Certsey pulled out another bag of powder, frantically squirting it in a circle around us just like the man who teleported us to Roz's. She was to slow. Once the faceless creature was fully formed it started moving toward us fast, too fast, it destroyed the circle before she could finish.

Someone yelled "Run" as it pursued us I could see it collecting everything in its path, sucking the scattered debris into its body as soon as it made contact.

Certsey slipped, Mordian stopped to defend her. "Gamarey!" he unleashed some sort of green electrical discharge from his hand, it only quickened the faceless monster. In seconds, Certsey then Mordian were engulfed by the creature. I could see them suspended in the orange gel choking. They looked like pieces of fruit in a gelatin dessert. All we could do was retreat or suffer the same fate.

I wasn't proud, I ran like a chicken. It was not fast enough, even as I gained the lead on Kat. It did not matter, we were both still losing ground. Hmmm . . . I never realized it, not that it was important, but I also run faster than Kat.

Kat wailed out a war cry as she let go with a metal-egg bullet. It pierced the creature doing very little damage. Her fate was sealed, Kat was overcome and I was next. I didn't know what to do.

Ready to give up, I turned around and with all that I had I swung that old rusty hammer. In that brief moment, I was thinking of all the good things in my life, as the flat of the hammer came in contact with the flat front of the horror before me.

There was a loud smack. With a blue flash of brilliance, the creature popped like a puss filled blister. Kat, Certsey and Mordian fell to the ground, gasping for air, soaking wet with all the stuff the creature had retained.

I was somewhat dry till Kat hugged me. Mordian slapped me on the back, "Riley, you're officially my permanent driver!" Taking a minute to confirm one fact, "None of this gets back to Roz!"

We returned to where Reein was standing. On the floor was the can, it had a plain label. "Industrial Strength, Slime Aid, Your solution to squeaky clean pipes."

Directly above us was another makeshift opening. We came up in a tiny room filled with brooms, mops and buckets. Through large cracks in the wooden door, I could see people walking back and forth. Opening the door we found ourselves in a hallway. Some kind of kitchen on one end. In the other direction we could hear a lot of commotion just beyond two partial swinging doors.

Inside we found a very large posh lounge, with long embroidered tapestries depicting stylized dragons hanging on the walls. They had taken down one of the tapestries on the far side where a man on a ladder was painting a large mural of a five petal pink flower. It resembled the flower Alerick described. Like the one I smoked. No wonder these people were walking around without a care in the world, no one even noticed we were soaking wet and smelled awful.

There were three round sitting areas with groups of men gathering around a central hookah. Each of the large unique glass bongs had multiple extending mouth pieces that were being passed back and forth.

Two girls walked around with trays selling tobacco. Once sold it was given to an assigned individual whose job was to keep the pipes lit and packed, while the patrons continuously enjoyed smoking comfortably perched on piles of pillows of various sizes. The many pillows were handmade with an assortment of different colored fabrics and beaded fringes.

The combination of sweet smelling smoke and heavily muted lighting made it near impossible to make out anyone's face until you were standing right next to them. Some of the men had sashes like Alerick of the Sharkfin Clan, others had the mark of the Badger Clan, but Reein wasn't anywhere to be found. There was no way to even be sure this is where he really exited the sewer. There could be dozens of ways to go in and out of the underground tunnels.

No one even blinked as we cased the room. Everybody was totally engrossed in the gossip and smoke. In the corner was a crooked set of stairs leading up and out to the street where clusters of closed shops lined the road. The sign above the steps read, 'The Drag Inn.' Carved in the wood was a smoking dragon, its tail pointed down the stairs.

It did not take long for Mordian to get his bearing on where we were. We had come up in the merchant section of the city. Mordian snapped his fingers as his coach rounded the corner. "That ends our tour. I think we've had enough fun for the night."

Chapter Seven

Be Ready

My head felt like the pile of metal eggs I was lying on were rattling around inside my brain. Thank the heavens Clovis, Kas and Bauble were the only ones around. No one else would be able to resist the obvious jokes. Even they seemed to be dumbfounded as they nibbled on the pile of hay, I was perched upon. Life's sarcasms never cease to amaze me!

When I found Kat, she was looking at Aunt Roz in a daze. Needless to say Roz does not disappoint. They were sitting at the table in front of the kind of spread I have come to expect from her. As always, she was chattering away. "Katinka aren't you hungry? Can I get you something different to eat Katinka, Katinka, what is your favorite breakfast! Katinka eat, we will need to keep up our energy? We have a long day ahead, oh Knick Knack!"

I think Father was uncomfortable with the hocus-pocus at Roz's. Still I was willing to stay for the food! Nevertheless, father took and sold the extra horses in town. With the money we rented a room at a place called The Paw of the Bear Inn. In the lobby was a small pub called The Little Cub.

The inn was located on the busy streets of downtown Suxen Falls, surrounded by multiple taverns and a countless number of shops. Signs hung everywhere with colorful names like, The Turtles' Shell Hat Shop, The Horn of the Goat Tavern, Spots on the Mushroom Cafe, and The Windsong, where a large group of wind chimes hung out front, playing a song of their own. There was a sign shaped like a boot with the word leather carved in it. Some signs just simply stated occupation, Tailor, Metal Smith, Scribe, etcetera. No two signs were alike.

We spent the day perusing the onslaught of restaurants, gorging on exotic foods. At least they were exotic to us. I realized just how sheltered a life I've had.

One sign caught my eye, Celestial Earth. Inside there were lots of long shelves covered with weird beautiful things made from colorful rocks. They even sold glowing crystals! On one shelf was a group of rocks broken in half. They looked like the yolk of a hard-boiled egg had crystallized. Scribed on a piece of paper nailed to the shelf, "Dragon Farts." Father stretched his arms out then twisted his waist until he tooted. "That's a farmer fart."

The proprietor was not amused, but didn't say anything to Father, he was too busy keeping close tabs on me, always checking to see if I was filling my pockets.

People here in Suxen Fall were more tolerant of my kind than those in Nautica, but they still seemed to treat me different. It was like they thought I was guilty of something even if they just met me. Was I that different?

We stumbled upon a donut shop called, The Donuts' Hole, I don't think Father needed more fuel for the fire, but we sampled anyway. We had so much fun, spending the day forgetting our troubles. We even splurged buying new clothes for both of us, from a small shop called The Loose Button.

What was amazing to me was the abundance of carriages; we saw ten times as many as we would see in a month back home. There was also a lot of Selvain's driving the carriages. After awhile I noticed most of the Selvain's were servants, driving cabs, shining shoes, making deliveries or servers in the local shops and bars. Their green color made them easy to spot in a crowd; several had the mark of the Badger Clan.

I didn't keep a lot of secrets from my father, and I had no doubt anything I told him in confidence would never get back to Roz, so I spilled the beans about our wild antics last night. I excluded some of the fine details, but I told him about Reein, his Grail, and what we found at the warehouse. Each time I pointed out one of Reein's clan members, I could feel trouble staring back. Was I being maliciously prejudice toward them, as the townsfolk here are to me? How does one truly know your enemy when their faces are no more than a distorted reflection of yourself, the deceit in their eyes is concealed by a true darkness hidden in the heart. Could they all really be involved?

People rustled about, in one store out the other. I wondered if this is how it always is in the big city. What could they all be looking for? It was not hard to get lost in the hustle and bustle of the busy streetscape.

With all the confusion, we were surprised to stumble upon Kat with her Aunt. Hand painted red letters on the huge glass window read Sparmoni. Inside Kat was trying on several short dresses. Knick Knack was policing a pile of boxes with tags from many other shops. Over the whistles, yelling and the constant commotion we heard the piercing voice of Sweet Aunt Roz. It cut through the layers of city noise like a hot knife through butter.

We turned our heads and slipped away, hoping they did not see us. We could still hear Roz from a block away, "You look absolutely fabulous' in that Katinka, Try this on, it matches your hair Katinka, Your eyes shine when you're wearing that hat Katinka. Clerk we will take it all. Oh Knick Knack!"

We never saw Lou or Julia. The last we heard they were summoned to see Quinn at the Academy of Arcane Knowledge. As it darkened, a light fog rolled in, the streets became filled with an eerie glow. The crowds disappeared. The city was going to sleep. Most of the store fronts lit up. Many doorsteps had lighting in the archways. Even some of the words on some of the signs glowed, especially the few businesses that stayed open late into the night.

I noticed the streetlights were not as fancy here, as in the high quarter. Definitely nicer than the streetlights in the alley behind the Funhouse. I asked father if he believed they could really capture a ray of sunshine placing it in the stones. He was as bewildered as me, saying "If they can, there must be a sunny day missing somewhere."

It did not matter how they were made they reminded me of the great powers to be, Lou talked about. Was this fascinating new world always right in front of me?

Somehow we made it back to Little Cub. The sound from The Windsong served as a beacon on the now quiet streets. It was a much tamer night spot than the wild antics of the Funhouse. Most of the patrons here were older and the music was definitely more somber.

Father told me he overheard that guy Lightbender telling Lou why he was spooked last night. He was saying that my life line was broken, stopping and then starting again. Like dying, and then coming back from the dead. But that's was not all he sensed. He claimed my soul had been marked. Crazy talk! Lightbender said something about the eyes of a dragon, searching for me? He feared I would bring a terrible rage down upon us all. Father was flabbergasted, "That's just nonsense!"

That's when Lou caught up to us. He wanted to know what we wanted to do. Lou was frazzled making bold hand gestures as he talked. Lou was rattling on about how the council was already aware of some kind of black presence in Avalon. It hindered any form of magical communication, teleportation or even general Scrying, whether it be of arcane or spiritual in nature. All lines of communication south of Nautica were cut off weeks ago. This had the council worried, whatever it was it did not want anyone to know what it was up to, or want anyone dropping in unexpected. Some members of the Council had researched spells that could cause this effect. But have never heard of anything powerful enough to be able to block off an area so large and for this long.

Quinn had asked Lou, if he wanted to return to Nautica to study the dark ship, and Lou offered to take us with him. At first none of this made sense. Father said, "Calm down and just start from the beginning."

Lou took a large breath and relaxed for a moment. It seems when he got to the Academy of Arcane Knowledge several high level mages, priests, and council members were already assembled.

Quinn told Lou the Council suspected something sinister was brewing at the Temple. That's why Gandelain's party was sent on foot to find answers. He was supposed to report back to the council to explain this dark phenomenon. No word had been sent until they received the letter we carried. It was conclusive, first hand evidence that substantiated a true threat was gathering in Avalon!

What was confusing was the ship that had arrived in Nautica; it landed after the interference was already noticed. Still, it was too much of a coincidence for the ship not to be connected, and how exactly were the Selvain's involved, no one knew. Quinn noted that the Selvain's found on the ship had been somehow lobotomized making them permanently confused. It seemed pointless to continue interrogating them. He also noticed the characteristics of the local population of Selvain's are slightly different from those found aboard the ship. This group had a much darker skin, smaller, more fragile physiques, and light or blue eyes.

Quinn was infuriated with the whole ship, in general, and where it fit in the overall puzzle. The council could not be sure that the ship was even directly involved. The facts did point to one obvious conclusion. The ship had crossed the ocean, something no man had ever done.

Pride was a factor. Many disbelieved a bunch of uneducated dirty barbarian misfit Selvain's would be able to organize this much trouble, especially so quickly. Lou apologized to me for Quinn's choice of words as he described the day's events in detail. Quinn was uncomfortable to admit it, in front of me, but they also knew the boat, weapons and the ring we brought are of Selvain origin, Quinn was familiar with the magical language written on them.

Not only that, but the items we had were finely crafted as well as infused with magical qualities. The council does not think the Selvain's found in the Commonwealth are capable of that level of craftsmanship. The council is also aware the weapons are enchanted with a different type of magical essence than what is empowering the dark energy emanating down south. In fact whatever the dark force behind it is, they have never seen anything like it before.

The council fears whatever is coming has only one foreseeable objective, that is to take the knowledge we posses or to destroy it. It is logical the library is the city's most valuable resource. Regardless of cost the council has pledged to protect the library and will fight to the last man.

For the moment the counsel has no reason to believe there is any immediate threat, Nautica would have to be taken first, and compared to Newhaven, it is easily defendable. Plus it would take months of planning, and thousands of men to attack a city the size of Suxen Falls. Its tiered design was made to keep the unwanted out. Not that they were taking this threat lightly, they were doing everything possible to find out what they could.

Lou and the group of City Elders were escorted to another area; several robed figures were being detained in a small cell. Quinn pointed out they were the Selvain's from the ship. They did not look healthy at all, drooling, peaked, it was as if they were sedated, some incapable of speech. The one that Lou had seen close up had deep wounds on the back of his head. Lou asked what the Elders had done to them. Quinn shook his head, and stated, "That's how we found them."

Lou's expressions became more intense as he continued. One of the Selvain males was removed from the cage and strapped in a chair, with leather binds that held his hands, feet, head, and neck. In front of the chair was the lady with the long curly hair in the white robe, the one we had seen in the hallway when we first arrived at the Academy. Quinn introduced her as Sister Gazelle from the House of Sunfire!

The Selvain was indifferent to what was happening around him. His face was expressionless. Sister Gazelle reached out with her hands holding his head, saying only one word "Remember."

The man immediately jerked violently in fear as if he was being threatened. He started to rant in a different language. He kept saying, "Miond Flarer, Miond Flarer, Miond Flarer!"

Gazelle's head jerked to the left then the right. She cried out as if she could feel the man's agony. She pulled back as she collapsed to the ground, the Selvain laid limp in the chair. Quinn helped Gazelle up, she looked him in the eye. She sighed, "The same." Her head dropped in exhaustion as two men helped her walk away. I asked Quinn what she meant by such an odd statement.

Quinn in his natural cold cruel voice said, "Sister Gazelle has the ability to feel negative and positive energy. She also can see memories. She is a useful tool."

What Sister Gazelle meant by her brief statement was their memories are gone, their names, their childhood, their lives, erased, as if something had eaten their thoughts. Lou asked Quinn, "Something, what could do such a thing?" The thought terrified him; it would terrify any magic user. The only memory these men have left is the attack.

It seems the majority of them were huddled in the hull of the ship holding on, hiding! At first why was unclear. It was as if the entire ship was being shaken. They all remember watching as their comrades wigged out, waving their arms as if they were fighting something that was not there or invisible. They had no choice but to watch, as many ruthlessly took their own lives!

Some recall unexplained flashes of light. Most likely the ship was caught in a terrible electrical storm. During the brightest surges of electrical energy, some of them seemed to believe they were no longer on a ship, but floating in a dualistic world of strange lights and sounds, even though they were still aboard, there was a overwhelming feeling, it was as if they were thrown overboard, set adrift in the ocean, lost at sea.

There are several versions of the same story, but one of them recalled casting a spell designed to expose invisible creatures. Illuminating several translucent horrors, the largest was a bluish in color. Its body was that of a lion or great cat, only its brain was enlarged and exposed. It had tentacles that hung down like huge teeth that wrapped around the head of its victims. The back-end of the horrific creature was almost eel like allowing it to move through the air as if it was floating. The other creatures were smaller and slid through the air like fish, and latched on to the larger creature, once it was done feeding.

They could all see, the now visible foe attacking their friends. One by one it clawed at their heads eating their thoughts. Their hands and weapons went through the creature as if it lacked substance or was not there. There was no way to hide. They were helpless to fight or even defend. The eyeless creature could sense their fear chasing the men through walls, as if the physical obstructions did not exist in its own world. Those who survived are still reliving this nightmare. That was all they remembered. It was all they knew.

Just telling the story, Lou was in disbelief, and that was just the beginning of his day. The excitement started when his over opinionated unruly cousin showed up! Lou could tell Mordian was late by the dissatisfied expression on Quinn's face.

They were all taken to another room where the pieces of the creature Lou collected were laid out on large raised metal platform, positioned as if they were connected to a complete body. The hands and feet shackled as if still alive. Mordian stepped forward while the others stepped back to observe. First, he drew a crude outline of a body with a piece of pea green chalk, defining the missing parts of the beast.

Mordian had summoned a spectral creature, a life that had been lost. Some how trapping it in a glass jar of his own design, The jar was sealed with a waxed cork and there were strings holding etched metal coins on the sides. Mordian inscribed the same symbols on the walls of the room. He carefully placed the odd receptacle in the center of the missing torso drawn on the table. The bottle's contents swirled and momentarily Lou could see a lucid face in the mist. Its cries went unheard. Mordian gave his peers a final warning. "Be ready."

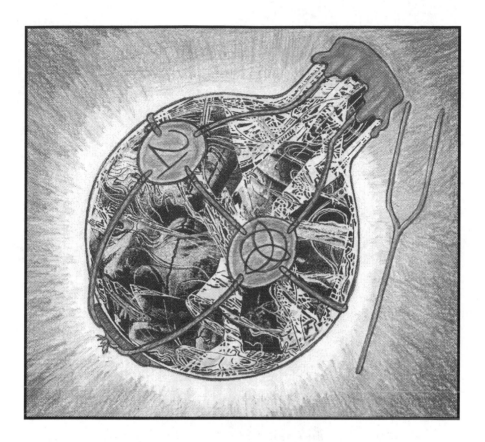

They all took another step back as Mordian shattered the glass with a metal tool shaped much like a fork that let off a high pitched sound. As the smoky spirit tried to escape the crude drawing of the body it was drawn into the limbs of the mutilated lizard looking figure. As the cloudy gas gained in density the spectral aberration filled out the absent shape of the creature.

As soon as it was fully formed the dead creature's eyes opened, immediately wrenching at the shackles, crying out in pain. Lou did not know what was more disturbing; the ghost like form wearing the bloody limbs as if they were a matching red mask, set of leather gloves and some rain boots, or Mordian's sick little laugh like a child who knowingly did something wrong, and got away with it.

Quinn joined the freak show, grabbing the writhing abomination by the neck slamming it down against the table with a loud echoing thud! Quinn yelled. "Who are you!

The monster hissed. "I am Kalian of the Badger Clan."

"What are you" Quinn argued in even a louder voice.

"We are Drazzi!" It snarled back.

Quinn pulled the brass talisman we gave him out, pushing it in the face of the reanimated being. "Who sent you?"

"That is the true mark of the leader of the Selvain realm." The agitated creature let out another horrid scream.

It was rare to see Quinn lose his casual disposition, spitting as he held one of the cubes. "What of this?"

The dragon faced corpse laughed out loud its teeth dripping with saliva and blood! "Rebirth! Redemption! Break it and see the truth old man."

Quinn knowing he was pressed for time. "What do you want?"

The creature started to dissipate. It seemed to almost smile as if it knew the torment was almost over. The body parts fell to the table with its last breath it whispered, "All of you," Ha hah.

Most of the members were shaken by this. Discussion broke out throughout the room. Quinn told Lou the clay boxes contained some sort of non-indigenous venomous bugs. Magically manipulated for some perverted purpose, he believed that their bite may cause mutations.

When it was over the council agreed on one thing, the main concern is the threat at the Temple, the ship having already been neutralized and abandoned.

It will take a few days, but they are going to rally and send all the troops they can to meet the oncoming threat before it grows too strong. The council made the offer to Lou, asking him if he wanted to check out the ship in Nautica. Quinn already made all the arrangements. Lou held up a piece of parchment "I have all the documentation I need to be able to claim the Selvain boat. "I'm going."

He told us we could stay here if we wanted to. He would be back in no less than a week. "Think it over, I and the girls will be leaving in the morning, we will swing by the inn. If you want to go, be ready?"

CHAPTER EIGHT

Truth Is On The Menu

The decision was easy. That morning we were packed and ready to go. We waited at the Little Cub by a long window with a view of the stores outside. We joined into what seemed to be a mourning ritual as patrons lined up for a quick bite to eat. On the street was an army of delivery carts, all with large words painted on the sides or back doors, describing what was on the dollies and in the crates being delivered.

We saw an ale cart, then a vegetable cart, and many other deliveries as one after another they dropped their packages, including one that read, Under the Udder Dairy. The cart was just like the one we saw in the warehouse. Father pointed it out saying. "See . . . They're just delivering milk!" Maybe he was right, maybe it was just a case of an over active imagination, we were talking about Kat. I really didn't see anything and a lot of Selvains shared that same tattoo. And like Mordian said there is numerous things they could be smuggling into the city. Father told me to "Stop worrying about it," he was sure Mordian would have mentioned it to Quinn, besides it was one of our rules, "Never let anything interfere with breakfast."

How sweet, there was even a pie cart, it smelled better than the hotcakes and sausage coming from the kitchen, decisions, decisions.

Another cart passed by "Suxen Times" It did not even slow down to drop its load, a man tossed bundles to several kids in the streets as it went by. One boy stood on the corner holding up a copy screaming out the day's big headlines. "Mystery Boat Crashes Into Nautica." "The City Council releases new design for the first horseless carriage, runs on hot water." "Celebration At The Temple Tonight, Greet The Gathering Priests." "Special, Fresh Spare Ribs, The Farmers Basket." "Get it all here."

It was like watching a sleeping giant wake up as the city came to life. Even though every thing looked fine to the naked eye, there was still an uneasy feeling in the air. I wondered what the papers said about the boat. It seemed Lou already knew more than the locals. Could it be true? Was it built by people like me? I bet that's not in the paper.

There was some kind of commotion as everybody's head turned. Nice! Who was this coming up the road. If I was anything, I was a good judge of carriage. Someone important was traveling in style. The fine carriage pulled up out front, followed by six mounted solders wearing leather armor bearing the silver crests of the private guard of the Suxen Falls City Council.

The finely polished cranberry red wooden cab had copper handles shaped like bouquets of flowers. It had all the extras, including permanently lit lamp-lights that hung delicately from curved arms that extended out at an angle. The metal accents were fashioned to look like grapevines entangling the entire top of the coach. The metal vines extended down the sides looping across the back creating elegant racks for packages or chests. In front, a raised bench for the driver who was wearing a top hat. The older Selvain man climbed down unhooking the fold out step, then he opened the door, to our surprise, inside was a familiar face.

Lou stepped out, his arms outstretched, looking at us as if he was seeking approval. "Isn't this great and the men are compliments of Quinn." He was quite proud of the ride he had finagled.

All this can't be just for us, no doubt it was provided by sweet Aunt Roz. My guess, there was no way she would let her precious little Katinka be loaded up like a sack of potatoes on a horse cart ever again. I should have guessed sooner, our new ride was elegantly being pulled by four white horses with flowers braided into their manes. All I could think was, I hope this doesn't go to Kat's head.

Inside the cab was nice, but nothing was as impressive as Kat's frown. There was a satisfying, sad look, on her face, make-up dribbling from her eyes, as she looked for solace in Bauble who patiently sat on her lap. She was all polished up, hair styled, nails painted, she was wearing fancy jewelry with a new dress from a designer store, sporting one of the nicest rides I had ever seen, and still, she was unhappy. Go figure?

Kat just could not understand how her mom and dad would want to take her away, now that she had become one of the important people. I wondered if she would ever forgive them.

I just giggled, mumbling to myself, "He does tricks." as I mounted Kas, who I had not noticed was trailing behind the carriage. Posing with a big smile, in my new silk shirt, blue breeches, short-cut vest and real riding boots with spurs and all, not to mention a jeweled sword by my side, I felt like I was ready for anything. I really just wanted to return home. I didn't know if that would happen any time soon, but at least we were heading in the right direction.

It took most of the day to clear the city. We stopped only briefly, to rest the horses by a stream, just pass the infamous Under the Utter Dairy. It looked like an ordinary farm with cows in an overgrazed field full of withering wildflowers. The workers rushed in and out of the barn. Either way it was peaceful enough, putting my suspicious mind finally to rest.

I really was not happy Kat was sad. While we were stopped, I looked down, noticing a perfect patch of wild flowers.

The mountain flowers reminded me of home, I missed the good times we spent playing under the old willow tree. Kat and I would run off to the safety of its branches whenever we were in trouble. It was not far from where we lived. One time Kat accidentally ruined her mom's favorite dress, playing house with me in the garden. Julia was pissed, yelling at us as we took off into the woods, laughing. We ran to our secret fort under the old willow tree in the small meadow where wild flowers grew. It was our favorite spot to make believe we were the important people, heroes on a quest to save the world. We always gathered flowers placing them at the base of the special tree that became our home away from home. It was the only willow tree around and its leaves were a bright shade of green, so it always stood out amongst the cottonwoods. The branches hung all the way to the ground making the walls of our pretend castle. We even made a hiding spot under one of the large roots of the aging willow. That's where we kept our stash of things we did not want anyone else to know about, pretending it was the royal treasury, but it was really just a bunch of useless trinkets, like our slings, just pieces of tattered material, nothing that held any real value.

We would arm ourselves with these crude slings, and a handful of colorful rocks, seeds or whatever was hard enough to toss, anything that could aid us in our battles. We had placed an old metal pie dish in one of the smaller cottonwood trees. It was the eye of the evil dragon. It made a satisfying thud whenever we hit it. As usual Kat had better aim than me.

The day Kat soiled the dress was the day we found Bauble. I should say "Saved her." She was almost dinner for a big black crow. The bird had carried Bauble high up to one of the branches in our willow. We were not going to let her be on the menu. Kat had scared the bird away with a pebble thrown with great accuracy from her sling, and I climbed up to retrieve her. There Bauble lay lifeless, underdeveloped covered with parasites, probably abandoned. She was so small, she must have been the runt of the litter.

Lou and father were waiting on the porch, when we got home, I don't really remember them being mad like we expected them to be. I think saving the helpless kitten, helped us to forget why we ran away in the first place.

Kat asked Lou why bugs had eaten Bauble's tale. We were too young to know the kitten was a lynx which is actually a tailless breed. The two old men laughed at our question anyway, never really explaining why.

Kat cared for her wild kitten, bottle feeding it day and night, till its eyes opened. Bauble is healthy now, but never grew bigger than an ordinary house cat. She was always smaller than other adult cats of her kind.

I reached down picking that perfect patch of wild flowers, and then tied Kas to the back of the carriage so I could ride inside. Hoping the wild flowers would cheer Kat up. Lou was staring at her as they gave each other the silent treatment. I could not believe they had been acting like this the whole day. Julia gave me, "The Look," like she had finally given up. I reached over placing a purple flower in Kat's hair. Saying "Smile, at least for a moment, you were one of the important people." Kat had to work to keep her frown. You know something is wrong when wild flowers can't bring a smile to Kat's face. She was just being stubborn.

The driver tapped the top of the coach easing the silent tension, speaking loud enough for us to hear, "I know of an inn with a tavern in Kelideco, it's not far. We could stop and rest the horses, maybe even spend the night. From here it's an easy ride to Nautica. We could be there by sundown tomorrow."

Lou remembered passing the inn that was near the home where he grew up, and darkness was creeping up on us, as we passed the sign that read "The Croaking Toad Inn and Tavern, Number Sixteen Sunnybrook Road."

The inn stood three stories high and had two balconies. The roof was red cedar shingle, large beams extended out from the side of the building holding huge planters with fresh mountain flowers of every color. I could smell them as we drew closer. The inn was situated just off the main path in a grove of trees, the inn appeared more than inviting. Lou motioned the driver to stop.

We were greeted by the timid little voice of a small Selvain boy my age. He was dressed in a brown coat and tails. As soon as we came to a stop, he reached down unfolding the stairs that were built into the carriage side. He then opened the door, offering his hand to the ladies, winking at me in a friendly manor as we exited the coach.

When the soldiers dismounted, he offered to take the horses around back to be brushed and fed. As the driver stepped down off the coach, the boy rattled "I can tend to your needs. Just call on me, ask for Travis."

"Ouch!" Kat exclaimed.

Lou, "What's wrong now." Giving her, The Look.

Pouting, Kat whined, "My dagger pinched me." The driver tossed a silver piece to the ground where the boy stood, then followed him around back.

As we got closer to the entrance the more I noticed most of the flowers hanging in the planters had wilted, but my mind was on food and the odor from the kitchen was luring me like a rat to a piece of cheese. I was dreaming of the stewed potatoes we had smelt when we passed the inn just a few days before, and I could almost taste the fresh biscuits with gravy as we stepped up on the raised wooden deck. Two heavy rustic doors were the only thing that separated us and dinner.

Inside, there were eight plank tables. Two sat by the front door. Four were situated under three windows along the far wall, where you could see the dried-out flowers outside. Another two tables were situated by a curved stairway, with a broken handrail. It probably led upstairs to a hallway where one could gain entrance to the individual rooms on the second floor. On the far wall was a painting of a summer meadow hanging between a hallway which had several doors, and an open area with a long sit down counter, where we could see into a kitchen. Above the counter hung a huge wooden menu, truthfully a selection to die for.

The place was empty other than a Selvain bar maid, who had a smile that lit up the room. Standing in the kitchen talking between themselves, were two chunky male Selvains wearing stained white smocks. They awaited our orders, tending to several large pots that smelled wonderful.

Ahhh! What a treat and we had choice of any seat in the house. Our group was able to spread out over three tables. Two of the soldiers excused themselves and went back outside. They were ordered to keep watch over the cab. Going out through the hallway by the kitchen they passed the driver who joined us at our table.

I don't get to meet many Selvains my age so I asked to be excused then stood up and went out front to find the boy who greeted us. That's when I heard two Selvain voices whispering from around the corner in front of me. I was standing on the far end of the deck, next to a large planter with a bush shaped to look like a toad. I never heard Selvains speak in their native tongue. I could not understand them. With only good intentions, pretending to be important, I grabbed the hilt of my sword and strutted forward like a peacock to introduce myself. Once I touched the hilt I immediately understood the voices! "Are they ready?"

"Almost. When Karen shuts the front door, that's our cue."

I let go of the sword handle. The voices returned to gibberish. I hid behind the amphibian shaped bush to see if I could hear more. Something was up!

Inside, the server was taking everyone's orders." I'm Karen. What can I get you all, to quench that traveler's thirst?" Kat tried to order a fancy drink she once drank with her Aunt Roz called a Purple Mimsey. "We do not serve those." Karen said, pointing to the menu. Kat, still pouting, still mad, having been forced to leave the big city. She was not about to accept any substitute her father suggested.

Lou finally just ordered her lemonade, to allow the waitress to move on. Adding, "Something sour, for a sour-puss."

Quickly, Karen brought out our drinks. Father pointed out to Lou that one of the cooks had the Badger clan tattoo, we were all familiar with the markings.

Karen shivered, thoughtfully she offered to shut the front door. "I don't want any of you to catch a draft now!" Closing the door as not to be noticed, smiling as the metal workings inside the door handle clanked shut. Kat flinched as the enchanted dagger she carried, gave her another shock!

Back outside, "That's our cue," the voices said, as the two tall Selvains I had heard talking, came around the corner. They snuck up to the door sliding a large metal latch to the locked position. Startled to see me, they turned around, the taller of the two Selvains asked. "Who are you?"

Already suspicious, I asked, "What are you doing?" both were members of the badger clan.

Inside, Kat pulled the dagger out placing it on the table showing it to Lou. "It keeps zapping me?"

Karen asked if everybody was alright, moving by them into the hallway, quietly locking the door behind her. By this time, two soldiers had laid their heads on the table, and a third had fallen to the floor.

Julia told Lou she was feeling sleepy. My father, who downed his first ale and already ordered another, was starting to slide out of his chair as well. The only two people who did not take a drink were Lou and Kat, who were still arguing over, why the inn did not have the trendy drink Kat wanted.

Lou realized something was wrong. He just could not put his finger on it. Staring at the dagger that seemed to zap him, each time Karen spoke. "If you folks need anything, I'm right here."

"Ouch" Lou exclaimed, handing the dagger back to Kat.

"Hope everybody is hungry, you are going to enjoy the food." Zap, "Ouch!" Kat pushed the dagger back at her dad.

Lou was puzzled as he watched Karen through the open area above the counter. Walking into the kitchen nonchalantly, she reached out pulling down a lever mounted on the wall. "Sorry folks."

Kat looked at Lou. "Something is going on!" Just as Lou rose up, Ka-blam! The large menu fell forward slamming down, blocking the serving counter, at the same time, bars fell across the windows sealing them in.

I heard the commotion from outside, "What was that?" I said. Both Selvains were blocking me from reaching the latch on the front door. I ran around back to get the soldiers I knew were watching the carriage, as I turned the corner, I tripped over their bodies. They both lay on the ground with their hands tied behind their backs, helpless, their throats were slit.

I could hear the young Selvain boy, Travis, looting the cab. Bauble was hissing at him. The two tall Selvains cornered me. "He will be alright. He is one of us. Don't worry about your masters, boy. They will be dealt with soon enough."

Inside from the stairs above, handfuls of the clay boxes, like the ones we had brought to Quinn, were being tossed down the stairwell shattering as they hit the stone floor in the tavern. In each cube, were scary looking centipedes, with attitude.

Their bodies were bright purple with hundreds of black spidery legs, they had fangs in front, and beetle-like pinchers on their back end. The tiny critters were about two to three inches long and moving fast. They headed in every direction, looking for warm bodies.

The bodies of the sedated were easy prey. Lou, thinking quickly, lifted Kat up on the table. The little creatures moved at lightning speed instantaneously reaching our guards lying on the floor, while others were already climbing the table legs heading for Kat. "What are they?" She screamed. Lou bashed the front door with his shoulder as a board slid over the opening in the stairwell.

Kat watched a bug enter the ear canal of the driver, he immediately started to shake. The limp bodies of the sleeping soldiers started convulsing. Lou felt something on his leg under his clothes. Stepping back from the door he looked at Kat and said "Don't worry baby, I'll get us out of here."

Outside, I could hear Kat's screams. I jumped to the cab swinging up top, landing on the driver's bench. Grabbing the reins, I yanked them hard, yelling out, "Go, Go."

The coach started to move. The two older Selvians started laughing as they watched the young boy climb up behind me. Pulling out a bloody dagger, Travis grabbed me from behind, placing his knife at my throat.

I could hear his friends cheering him on. I had to lean back to avoid being cut, forced to let go of the reins, as the cab raced away down the road. We both fell back landing on the roof of the speeding carriage.

I pulled my sword out taking a swipe at his hand holding the knife. Missing badly, my sword went through the roof, jamming itself tightly, off to the side of the wooden hull.

Meanwhile in the tavern, Kat looked down at a centipede climbing up her leg, she reached down creating a small flame burning it. It fell to the tabletop, as she stepped on another moving toward her.

Gawking in dismay, Kat saw my father and her mother's bodies start to shake profusely, knowing the infected soldiers were already starting to transform into lizard men right in front of her.

Tails, scales, clawed feet, and jagged tongues were sprouting. Lou grabbed a fork from the table and stuck it in his leg through his pants, just missing the squirming little creature. Pulling it out he tried again a little higher. This time successfully piercing the little bug and his leg! Lou didn't have time to yell, he could feel more tiny footsteps already moving up his body.

Outside, the Selvain kid jumped to his feet and with a stabbing thrust he planted his dagger in my shoulder pinning me to the roof. Visibly happy, he yanked the bloodstained blade out, readying himself for another blow.

Just like back home I flipped out, grabbing the straps that held Lou's chest to the luggage rack. Swinging off to one side, I was left grasping at the winding metal trim just above the spinning back wheel of the driver-less coach.

Travis lashed out, impulsively cutting at my hands. I reached up grabbing his shirt pulling him down. He plunged into the wheel well. Blood splattered across my face as his body twisted. His head was grinded off immediately, and I was next, barely holding on for my life as the horses raced down the road at top speed!

Then the cab hit a rut in the road making it jump. Travis's body was torn apart, his arm caught in the wheel. Pulled from its socket it broke several spokes, violently jerking the entire cab. I lost grip with one hand as the wheel came down hard spitting out the rest of Travis's corpse. Barely holding on with one hand, I was no longer able to hang on, I was about to fall.

Out of the corner of my eye, I saw an opportunity. My fumbled attack left my sword stuck in the roof just, below the metal rack. I lunged for it, using the hilt for leverage I was able climb back on top of the runaway cab. Taking hold of the reigns I turned the damaged carriage around, heading back to the tavern.

Inside, Lou now had three more forks and Kat's dagger stuck in his leg. Moving back from the door, he shouted to Kat "Cover your eyes!" Raising his hands he shouted, "Fiearo" and with a forward motion a huge fireball shot forward from his hands. The area around the front door exploded, bursting into flames. Bodies, bugs, tables, everything was on fire, even Lou. The doors themselves were a pile of burnt splinters. Lou ran to where Kat was thrown. "Are you alright? I'll never forgive myself if you're not all right." Kat started shaking her head rolling her eyes.

Gripping Kat by the waist, Lou threw her over his shoulder like a rag doll. He ran out the door, just as the Selvain men, still standing on the side of the inn, were forced to jump for their lives, dodging the oncoming carriage.

Driving like a madman, I skidded to a stop, parking the doors of the cab right in front of Lou and Kat, who climbed aboard immediately!

"Where's my father?" Again I screeched. "Where's my father? Now several adult Selvain's were coming out the burning inn, dragging out their unconscious victims. Some of which were already wearing the face of our enemy. They had been turned into the fearsome creatures we been fighting all along.

Quickly the inn was being engulfed in flames. Kat screamed, "I think he's dead. Go, I think he's dead. I think they're all dead or worse." Tears ran down her face, as Lou collapsed in the cab. An unlikely meat cleaver struck the door, just missing Kat's head. Pulling the reins of the disabled carriage we darted into the failing light.

Panicking, I didn't stop till the weakened wheel collapsed and the axle split. We almost paid for my carelessness with our lives. Having lost control of the spinning cab, the horses broke free and we dropped off the road into a large ravine, wedging us between a small group of trees and the rocky cliff.

I don't know who was watching over us, but we were saved from certain death. I took a minute to assess the situation, pulling down several low branches so the coach could not be seen from the road. Teetering on a small ledge, we were hidden from our enemies, safe for the moment. All we needed to do was hang on through the night.

Climbing down into the cab that was lying on its side, I held Kat close to me. She was shaking hysterically. Her father was hurt, her mother dead or worse. Lou called my name, half alive his body badly burned, and riddled with dinnerware. Bauble was licking at the blood, Lou's leg, looked like a pin cushion. Grunting in pain Lou said, "Riley are you wearing the ring." I nodded. Lou pleaded, "Try it."

I asked, "How?"

"Place you hand over my wounds and say the word."

With all my soul, I wanted him to be alright, "Cleanse." The blood dried, the wounds closed, and color returned to places burnt and blistered, I was speechless. Could I have really done that? In all the excitement, I had forgotten I was injured too, but my shoulder felt fine. I pulled back the red stained cloth where my shirt had been cut. My shoulder did not even have a scar, just an old birthmark that was shaped like a leaf. I did not complain, nor tell the others of my wounds.

Kat and I tried to console each other during the night, I don't think she ever stopped crying. Why was this happening? How could our lives be turned upside down so quickly?

In the morning we could finally see just how screwed we were. Julia and my Father, gone, Kas too! We were dangling on the side of a steep cliff, a hundred feet up, in a carriage tilted on its side, held only by a small cluster of trees. Things couldn't get worse.

That's when we first heard them. A sound we heard many times before, sitting on my porch waiting to see who was coming up the road. Only this was amplified a hundred times over. Something was moving toward us up on the road. Peaking out of the top of the cab I found our view was somewhat obstructed by the same branches that gave us cover.

Kat set Bauble gently outside. She was easily able to climb to the highest branch where she sat perched unnoticed. Kat stared and concentrated. Then she started to describe what she saw, through Baubles eyes.

First, there was a Drazzi scouting group. The sound of a few foot steps, the sound doubled then tripled, soon there was too many to count. The ground started to vibrate as they passed. There must have been thousands of reptilian looking humanoid soldiers. In tow, were several catapults and cartloads of those clay cubes. The weapons of war were pulled by exotic scaled creatures of all sizes. I think maybe at one time they were a simpler type beast of burden, now super-sized Drazzi monsters.

A huge lizard army of mutated humans was marching on Suxen Falls, in truth, brother against brother. We had no way to warn Quinn, to let them know they were fighting our own people.

All I could see peeking out a small broken window on the back of the coach was the tips of their sharpened weapons pointing up. Kat continued. "They're hideous!"

Most had the same characteristics as the one's that attacked our farm, but some were grossly deformed, abominations with three eyes or two tales. One had snakes for fingers and another, two heads, both with forked tongues. Some had gone insane and were chained or caged. Kat flinched, as they lashed out violently. There was a group with wings, and still others only partially changed. Just their head, arm, or leg was melted into a mess of red scales and twisted skin.

They were crudely divided into groups or ranks. Including a large bunch of mounted soldiers riding the beaked monstrosities we saw that fatal night back home. They must of been horses before they were . . . I tried to swallow as I thought of Kas. I didn't want to think about it.

At close inspection you could tell what roles the people played before they were drafted into this unholy army. There tattered clothes, jewelry and weapons, ruminants of there former lives. If they were carrying a pitch fork, odds are they were farmers. Those wearing the frayed uniforms of the Commonwealth's army were armed with the standard issue long swords. Then there were the townsfolk, carrying kitchen knives or whatever they could find to make a rudimentary club, not that it mattered. Many had formed natural defenses, venomous fangs, death dealing claws, sharp teeth, and spiked tales. Kat even saw several wearing the same color sashes as the thieves that attacked us.

Even women and children marched, not that she could tell by the leathery faces, but by their height, their elegant necklaces or what was left of the skirts they were wearing. The smallest details told their owner's story.

Listening to the demoralizing report, in my heart, I knew we were doomed. Kat no longer was able to use Bauble to see, her own eyes filled with tears, she started to cry again. It took hours for them to pass.

Attempting to make Kat feel better, I said, "Don't worry everything will be alright. They can't see us here." Kat flinched. "It's going to be okay, I don't want you to worry, Suxen Falls is too big to attack."

"Ouch!" Kat winced trying not to scream, "Riley don't lie to me"

Still I tried to comfort her. "It's not as bad as it looks."

"Ouch!" Kat recoiled in pain.

"Are you hurt?"

"No Riley it's not that, every time you lie, my dagger shocks me."

I guess I was really trying to convince myself, and I wasn't doing a very good job. I can see everything crumbling. That army seemed unstoppable. "We can't go home. We can't go back. We can't stay here. What was going to happen to us?"

Wiping my tears away, Kat shook me 'Riley don't worry, it will be alright."

Stuttering, I responded "I think I liked it better when I was lying to you."

Lou sat us down and put it all on the line. "Do you know what a nexus is? It's where we're at. It's when by your control or not, something or someone has started a change that will affect you and everything around you. Sometimes there is nothing you can do. Sometimes, it's not worth trying. But once in a while you are placed in a spot that can make you great. Even if you can't stop the change, you can tip the balance in your favor. Shape what your world changes into."

Pausing Lou gave us a moment to take in what he meant, "I don't know if we can stop what's happening. But we have to try. We may be the only people in the right place at the right time. For the people behind us, I do not know what's going to come of them, their immediate fate is in their own hands. Hopefully the council had enough time to rally troops to defend the city. Maybe your father and your mother, my Julia, are still alive. We may be their only hope!"

Lou, reminded us, "This all started at the ancient temple, we may be the only people on this side, of that army, able to do anything. We may be the Commonwealth's only chance to stop the evil that lies there. With a little luck, we could reach Avalon and get to the bottom of what's causing all our troubles. What happens next will be a turning point, a nexus for the world we know."

I was getting, what he was saying. I turned to Kat, "If we hide now and do nothing, there may be greater losses for everyone, if we don't try, there may be no place for us to call home."

Lowering his head Lou said, "This in not make believe, and I won't lie, life plays for keeps. You both learned that last night. Sometimes the best you can do is just stay positive. Never give up."

Kat held me tight, "I didn't actually see them die. They had changed into those," she hesitated in tears, "those things."

Reluctantly Lou finished by saying, "I cannot make this decision alone. This is your time to choose your own path. You can become the important people you always dreamed about!"

Lou told me to gather what useful items I could find. I did not see how we were going to get up the side of the cliff, let alone all this stuff. But I did what I was told and started to salvage what I could from the cab. There was no way to carry everything. I asked Lou what we should leave behind. Lou said we can place everything in his chest. I did not understand. There was no way everything would fit. Lou explained, reminding me of the small pouch, the tall men, put the swords in at the academy, when we first saw Quinn. Its similar magic to that.

Lou showed me how it worked. Opening the chest, Lou asked. "What do you see?" I was surprised to find it empty, lined with dark purple velvet. So dark a purple you could not define the corners or the bottom.

Lou asked, "Do you remember the staff I used against the thugs at the bridge."

I nodded, "The long one or the one with the gooey ropes on it."

"Either!" Then he instructed me to picture one of them in my head and reach into the chest, suggesting I close my eyes the first time. Not wanting goop all over my hands I pictured the long staff. When I opened my eyes I was pulling it out of the box.

I asked, "How much would the chest hold?"

He answered, "The inside of this box was equivalent to the storage area of a large room."

So we placed in the chest my father's tool box, a rope, a tarp, two of the finely crafted directional lanterns that hung from the carriage, a small barrel of oil and anything else that was not nailed down including my fancy mirrored box. Lou noticed the locking mechanism that was shaped like a cat. He said it was not just any cat, it was a lion. He had only ever seen pictures of them in the library. They were considered to be the king of all cats.

Now that we had gathered everything, I looked up at the cliff-side, with doubt in my eyes. Lou took a rope and tossed it in the air. "Ropadeop!" The end seemed to clime the steep embankment tying itself off to the rocks high above. Lou yanked the rope making sure it was sturdy. Handing the rope to me he said. "Have no doubts, we are the right people."

I climbed up and then helped the others. As soon as we all reached the top, Lou grabbed one side of his chest and I grabbed the other. It was lighter than I expected. Lou nodded in approval, "See Riley, We did it together."

Still out of breath we moved away from the road. Kat let us carry our burden till Lou was winded, which was not very far at all. "Now set it down." We gave each other, The Look, taking her advice.

Kat pulled out a tiny set of shackles and said "Aunt Roz taught me this. She said a lady should always have someone to fetch things for her." Laughing, "Actually she said a lady shouldn't have a dirty creature as a servant." Shaking the shackles like a bell, "Ling Ling!" A small cloud of smoke gathered around the bottom of the chest as it rose off the ground. "Shall we?" As it floated away Bauble jumped on top for a free ride!

CHAPTER NINE

Finding Your Faith
Losing Your Innocence

"Which way boys?" We planned to travel till Kat's invisible servant spell petered out, but we noticed a nice place by a particularly memorable bridge to camp.

There was a low spot dug into the ground, behind a small hill set in a thick group of trees. The spot was perfect, so perfect it had obviously been used before, probably by the thieves that attacked us. I understood why they chose here. From the tree line we could stay hidden as well as see travelers coming in both directions. We had circumvented another large convoy and two smaller Drazzi groups along the road today. I was glad to have found this spot. It was getting harder and harder to remain unnoticed.

One of the trees had several pieces of wood nailed to its trunk, another wider board up high concealed in the branches. Making it easy to climb and sit giving one a bird's eye view of the road. There was two make shift beds made out of leaves, and a small area covered with stones hidden in-between the roots of the tree, just large enough to keep a small fire hidden. I also found a concealed hole under a rock it was probably dug by a small animal. It looked like a good place to hide something. The thieves must have thought the same. In the hole was a pipe with a pouch of tobacco that smelled like the flower petals Alerick was smoking. Also a shinny piece of twisted metal, rolled up in a hand crafted silk flag. Kat was excited when I pulled out the treasure trove.

145

Lou smiled, "It's about time something turned in our favor." taking the smoking tackle away from me immediately, pretending to dump it out. In reality he stashed it away in his chest the first chance he got. Not that it mattered, the other things were much more interesting.

The flag defiantly grabbed my attention. It had the same design as my pendant and the stained glass window on the balcony doors in my dream, the tree with the sun behind it, divided into twelve. There was a line of unreadable text across the bottom. The letter style was the same as the writing on the ships bow, Selvain.

Lou pulled out a magnifying glass, it was given to him by the council to help him complete his task. It was kind of like the one on Quinn's desk, only smaller. Two hands held the glass lens and the arms entwined forming an angled handle. We held the viewer over the word, together we read it out loud, "Etlanthia?" Lou shrugged his shoulders as if to say, just because we can read it doesn't mean we can understand it.

Next, we all looked at the odd piece of metal, what made it peculiar was the sensation I got from holding it, I could feel energy from within, it made the hairs on the back of my neck tickle. Lou or Kat did not get the same stimulating sensation I felt when I held the piece. We thought it might be the sextant Alerick spoke of, Lou having grown up in a town of sailors was sure of one thing; it was not a tool for navigation.

Later, Lou helped Kat learn one of the spells from the spell book Quinn had given her. I overheard him say, "Not all spells have flash and pi-zazz, the simplest of incantations can be the most helpful. The first thing any young mage must learn is to detect and identify magic." They sat mulling over the strange piece of metal trying to divine its properties. Frustrated because it radiated no magic, Lou moved on showing Kat how to cast another spell. I was listening to them talk as I sat watching the road nested up in the tree.

"Pronunciation, combined with the fluid motion of one's hand gestures, are as important as using the proper spell component. It's all in the hands! Meditation can be crucial. Focus, place your spells wisely. You have a natural ability, trust your instinct." Lou went on with the lesson, he looked so happy spending time with his daughter, I can only imagine what it was like to keep his secret for so many years.

Tears came to his eyes, "Do you remember when I taught you to start the fires. Picture in your mind 'One,' it is the idea, a single point. 'Two,' you have a second point it creates a line, a symbol, a word. 'Three,' is the third point it makes a shape, an image, a surface in which to build on. 'Four,' points, now your idea has taken form."

"Five" Kat interrupted snapping her fingers! A bright flash then a stream of fire shot forth from her hands, searing the leaves above. Lou stepped back. "Concentrate, control, breath, then chose your target." Lou sighed. "Three's so much more, but you must master the basics."

He told Kat she will come across thousands of spells. No one can know them all. She would need to choose the spells she learns wisely. He used as an example the rope spell he cast to get us off the cliff. It merely controlled the direction the ends of the rope traveled. A conjurer would be able to create a new rope already fastened to the rock. Someone who specializes in summoning might call forth a tree with long vines. A mage must understand how to make any effect their own! All methods produce a similar end. The difference is the school of thought that produced the manifestation. Lou grinned at Kat, "You will always be strongest in those spells that manipulate the flame." Kat just giggled as she absorbed the information like a sponge-cake!

Lou touched Kat on the nose in an endearing way. Warning her that magic can be dangerous, cautioning her that the spells she masters will eventually mark her.

Lou showed Kat his biceps, there was a tattoo, an arm band of flames. I never remembered seeing that before. His explanation was, since he had been casting again they started returning. Lou asked Kat if she noticed Mordian's hand, pointing out he's is a necromancer, specializing in dark magic. He can summon the undead, ghosts or even worse to do his bidding. Flexing his arm again, to make the point, "The energy in the spells we use changes us all differently!" They talked through out the night. Lulled by bauble's purring I eventually fell to sleep.

Early that mourning before the sun even came up Lou had spotted a small Drazzi caravan coming our way. It did not take me too long to figure out what Lou and Kat had planned. I was shocked to hear Lou order Kat to move the log the thieves used on us, it was twice as big as her, and took two horses to drag it to where it was. Kat simply shook her shackles, summoning her invisible servant, "Ling Ling," placing the log setting the trap. Cat smiled, "Reading books, understanding the text is not enough. Casting spells in the field especially under pressure is the best training."

Bauble sat watch from the lookout, as Kat refocused rattling off details about the small party. "There are six soldiers marching in front of the cart with two soldiers on the cart, four more mounted Drazzi warriors positioned, two in front and two in back. They're riding those nasty two-legged beaked monsters."

The two mounted men, if you can still call them that, being that they were half-human half-Drazzi abominations, reached the top of the hill, motioning for the caravan to stop. Then they rode down the hill to the bridge to evaluate the tree limb on the road, wasting no time they directed the six Drazzi grunts forward to move the log. Lou was nodding to Kat as if everything was going as planned. I felt as useful as garnish on a fancy plate, so I did what I could, I stood and watched.

Kat was bursting with glee as she singled me with her hand to stay down. Then she dipped her finger into a small glass jar, rubbing her fingers together, "Greasalo!" The soldiers started to slip and fall in a clear slimy substance, tumbling down the hill making a lizard pile at the bottom. Lou whispered "Kabilsilk." casting his clingy rope-spell cementing the group at the top of the hill together. Mounts, cart, soldiers were a struggling mess. Then Lou in a little louder voice, with a hand gesture and a single word, "Fiearo!" unleashed a fireball, shot from the tree line where he stood. Aimed directly at the entrance to the bridge, where the last two solders not incapacitated had stopped.

The fireball nearly demolished the bridge. The explosive force caused one of the men to be blown off his mount and over the rail. While the second figure was thrown down when his mount, overwhelmed by the flames, jumped backwards over the log, fleeing down the road with its backside on fire.

The Drazzi soldier on the ground had fallen on his pouch crushing its contents. A green smoke rose up around him engulfing the area. Lou screamed. "Get back!"

As soon as the scuffed lizard-creature started to rise, he fell to the ground passing out.

Lou clapped his hands as if he was proud of his student, walking over to the creatures immobilized on the ground. Rubbing the compound Kat created between his fingers. "Kat, what is this, it's not grease its clear and it's, sticky."

Kat defended herself, "Dad you told me to make the spells my own! I used hair gel. Its slippery at first, when it dries it gets, sticky."

Lou sighed. Thinking, both compounds are similar in nature, and it worked! Realizing she was right. With a quirky smile he gave Kat 'The Look' and a thumb's up. Complimenting her on that green gas effect that made the last creature pass out!

Kat looked puzzled? "I thought that was you."

These Drazzi delinquents all had pouches that held four round clay spheres, Similar in construct to the square cubes, but with only two symbols and no small hole. I threw one as far as I could, it exploded, and a small area was filled with green smoke. It took about five minutes to disperse. Lou noted they must be some kind of sleep bomb. These could be handy some day.

Lou carefully put quite a few of the pouches containing the spheres in his chest. I saved one for me, placing the case over my shoulder. One by one we dropped the gelled and the roped lizards down the drink, the same way we disposed of our would-be thieves just a few days ago. We left the one soldier sleeping in the road, hoping he could tell us something helpful when he came too.

We still had to deal with the lizard-like-bird-beaked creatures the soldiers used as pack animals. Two were attached to the cart and two more were entangled in the sticky ropes.

Kicking off on the large scaly thigh of the one of the frightened beasts, I climbed on its back, settling into the saddle. Just before the ropes disappeared, I grabbed the reins. The creature fought at first. Within a few minutes I was riding it as easily as Kas.

The other creature tried to take a bite out of Lou, unable to grab him it ran down the path taking a chunk out of the helpless fallen rider, still sleeping on the ground. The vicious animal ripped a leg off the slightly charred body before running into the woods. In retrospect it would have been better to have dropped him over the edge with the others.

The cart was filled with cubes and spheres. Kat used the spell she practiced last night and tried to burn them. That did not seem to work. We realized plugging the air holes was the most effective way to destroy them. Eventually the bugs inside would just stop moving. We decided to throw the shipment in the river with all the other rift-raft.

Even though the last two lizard like mounts were already attached to the cart, they were still intimidating. I had already watched these animals rip apart two people as easily as biting into an apple, and I was riding one, how cool was that!

Once everyone was settled on the cart, Lou grabbed the reins. With wheels under our feet again, we were quickly on our way. Bauble made herself comfortable next to Kat, who was studying one of her books. With luck we would be in Nautica by noon.

It was not long before we came upon the hill that overlooked the harbor city. We stood there less than a week ago. From a distance we could see the morning sky, it was as beautiful as the sunset the evening before we had left. The cloudy horizon rippled with so many shades of red, I closed my eyes so I could recall the city noise, the way the streets were teaming full of life and how the ocean breeze smelled so good.

Approaching the cliff side I tried to remembered the song I heard that little girl from the market sing, The melody was stuck in my head. "Red sky humm . . . night humm . . . delight, . . ." I just could not recall all the words.

I don't think anything could have fully prepared me for what I was about to see. When I reached the edge I was in shock, I stood shaking in the cold air. looking at the horror that had unfolded below. I could smell the burnt buildings over the chilling sea breeze. It was a saddening sight to see. Other than the marina, the town was burnt to a crisp. Not one building stood tall. I think Lou had expected this. I don't think I could have imagined such devastation.

Small boats were either sunk or on fire. There were still buildings burning throughout the city. Leaving plumes of smoke that looked like giant arm's reaching into the sky. I felt sadness in my heart, I missed my Father. I realized the pain I was feeling, must be felt by many, with such apparent widespread destruction. Lou was right, our world was changing right in front of us.

From this vantage point we could not see any troops and we also noticed the dark ship was gone. The road we were traveling upon ran right threw the burned out city. We had little choice but to trudge forward, if we tried to circumvent the city we would have to cut through the thick forest, and cross over the river. We had to stay on the road to continue on.

As we descended from the mesa, we passed farms that once produced food. Crops were harvested or burned to the ground. Farmhouses themselves looked like piles of burnt toothpicks. Rolling into the inner city, the buildings and the ground were covered with soot, black footsteps lead in every direction. Glowing embers were scattered throughout the smoky madness.

To think a week ago, these streets were busy with townsfolk. We went shopping here, in the farmers market while Father was getting drunk in the tavern just ahead. Now, the town was deserted, devastated, destroyed.

I could imagine where the shopkeepers stood by the docks. Their carts flattened. If that wasn't horrible enough! Piles of dead mutilated people, half-turned monstrosities littered the road. Men killed during the transformation or the change produced an unsuitable soldier, unable to fight because of their disfigurement. Did it matter why? The failed experiments were just pushed aside or burned in the road. No longer could I smell the fishy smell of the marina, the town smelled like death.

On the corner hung the sign for, The Belly of the Whale Inn, now it hung by only one chain link, twisting and turning in the wind, making a high pitched sound each time the wind blew and the metal grinded.

Turning the corner we expected to see a clear road all the way to the bridge, instead we were met by twenty or so Drazzi troops resting within the burnt out tavern. I think we were as shocked to see them, as they were to see us. Several creatures attempted to run in front of the cart. But Kat's quick thinking and a well placed hair gel spell. "Greasalo." They slid, falling on each other into the street, as they tried to rush out the hole in the wall where the front door once was.

Lou tried to make the cart go faster! I threw one of the clay spheres over one of the burnt walls, where several of the creatures were gathered, still they poured out of the crispy rubble behind us.

Getting by those soldiers made no difference. There was another larger group of mutated lizard men rushing out the buildings right in front of us, exiting what was left of the shops on the main road. Lou took advantage of them being in a cluster, and launched his fireball into the group. "Fiearo." The initial blast shot flames and body parts through the air. Solving one problem only created another. Now dead bodies in the road could give us trouble.

To make matters worse the bulk of the Drazzi fighters did not seem to be harmed by the fire. Their newly acquired, naturally scaly armor did not burn as easily as human skin. Drawing my sword I made an attempt to lead a mounted charge on what was left of the hostile crowd, hoping to make a clear path for the cart using the inherently lethal advantages of my recently stolen mount.

One soldier was trampled below me, sliced down by the talons on the large feet of the wild beast. When I came out on the other side of the group, there was an arm hanging in its beak. Like a bird of pray it paused trying to gulp the piece of flesh, whole. I turned around for another pass.

On the fringe of my perception, I could see another muscle bound man charging. He was not altered like the others but his oversized posture made him stick out in the crowd of uglys.

This was not good. His face was as black as the soot on the buildings and he was screaming at the top of his lungs, swinging two swords as big as me, one in each hand. He was cutting threw the crowd heading straight for us.

The wheel of the cart popped up as it caught one of the bodies in the road, almost pitching Kat from the cart. It was all happening so fast, what was left of the small army was, starting to block us in.

Lou threw his net spell where he thought it would do the most damage. "Kabilsilk." The ropes encased a small group of Drazzi, barely scratching the surface of the oncoming threat. At least twenty or more red faced monstrosities were still blocking the wagon.

They were throwing round clay spheres. Several broke in front of the cart. One shattered on the seat. Lou dropped the reins as he fell limp in a cloud of green powder. The cart swerved hitting a body, flipping the cart on its side. Lou's was flung into the air along with Kat, Bauble and the rest our cargo. While the scariest fighter, the big guy charged them from the front.

I rushed in leaping from the creature I was riding, landing by Kat who was trying to get to her feet. My mount, blindly engaged a cluster of creatures before taking off down the street. Other than taking a random chunk of meat out of an unlucky Drazzi shoulder, its futile attack was of no consequence. We were surrounded.

The brawny hind legs of the animals attached to the wagon struggled, pulling the upended cart slowly away, dragging it on its side, removing any shield we could have had from the multiple creatures cashing in on their prize. Us!

Kat pulled her dagger out as I waived my sword. Back to back with Lou out cold on the ground between us. We readied ourselves for the last stand. I put myself between Kat and the dark enemy who towered over me and everyone else in the crowd.

I mustered up what courage I had left taking first blood. Putting a good size slash in the forearm of the large dark man. He was not so hard to hit. I just needed to swing; he was so big he was hard to miss. At least that's what I kept telling myself! He swung at me missing my head by inches. His overextended clumsy attack beheaded two of his own men. He tried to stick me again, but I evaded him easily!

Flames shot from Kat's hands, until her spell was disrupted by one of the creatures that was in her face. Magic is not always useful in hand to hand combat. My second attack did no better. It was foiled as I was pushed to the side by the awkward fighter's massive leg. His indecisive unwieldy thrust, impaled one of his own, stopping the attack on Kat and luckily for him, knocking my sword to the ground, nipping his toe. He was definitely gonna lose that nail! Before I could reach for my weapon, he had accidentally sliced off the arm of another enemy.

Then the huge man tapped his swords together sliding them apart above his head, making a terrible scraping metal sound. He extended his arms cutting two more Drazzi misfits completely in half, at the waist, with a single blow.

He jumped up on the pile of bodies now stacking up below his feet and belting out a battle cry, routing what was left of the frazzled foes, leaving only one! He chased the others down before the head of his last victim hit the ground. Slicing the legs of the runners clean off. Their torso's spun in the air landing on the ground creating several blood fountains.

Those stuck in the hardening gel or the sticky ropes were quickly dispatched, sometimes two at a time. Many of the incapacitated put their hands up trying to surrender, as they lay helpless on the ground. I could hear, "No. Augggg." They had barely enough time to hiss before the frightening man without, emotion, impaled them.

I reacquired my weapon, whispering, "Can your servant spell lift your father?" motioning to Kat, it's time to go. She stood there motionless jaw on the ground. She must have been thinking the same thing I was. How far would we really get?

The evil looking warrior moved back toward us, as if he was walking through a park on Sunday, without a care in the world, planting his sword in what was left of the wounded. When he was done, he waived his swords giving a final victory cry. I raised my sword and shook. He grinned and placed his weapons in their sheaths, then started to laugh. In the raspiest voice one could imagine, "Hello my friends! Have no fear." As if that was possible!

Stammering as I defended my actions, "I didn't mean to cut you so baldly, but you jumped in the way of my deadly swing."

"Ha Ha. You are brave if anything," he said, patting me on the head, laughing. "I'm going to like you." Amusing himself. "You are blessed! No one living can claim they have cut me in battle . . . and lived!"

I'm pretty sure I had stopped shaking before offering to bandage his arm. Bending down, he showed me where I cut him. His constant need to laugh at me was getting to be annoying. There was nothing more than a tiny scratch. I looked down at his foot his toe was already scabbed over. "I will be fine," He boasted.

Kat introduced us. Then pointed to the ground, "This is Lou, and who exactly would you be."

As sinister as he could make it sound, "I am known by many names, but you may call me Eyiyo."

Kat asked "Are you from here."

He grinned, "I am today." His laugh was so deep it hurt . . . me.

It took about twenty minutes, but Lou finally came to. Not quite understanding what happened, even after we told him twice.

We found Bauble licking a fresh blood pool around one of the body's. Kat gave Bauble, The Look, She was smart enough to know what Kat was saying, she quickly scampered off.

Eyiyo was straight forward laying it all out, bluntly. He wished to travel with us offering his services, referencing his sheer strength and unique fighting skills. Walking over to the cart he flipped it upright, all by himself. Picking up Lou's chest, he placed it onto the bed of the wobbly cart.

This set well with no one, except Bauble who was purring as she rubbed up against his thickset leg, then seated herself back on the chest. It was quickly becoming her favorite place to roost.

We were not in a position to say no. He did save us. Not wanting to stick around we made a hasty decision. With out a word Eyiyo cleared the way of bodies, and we were on the road again.

We made it as far as Three-Keys before stopping. Like Nautica, nothing was left but the sign in the middle of the road. Stashing our cart in a nearby burnt out farmhouse, we set up camp. We did not dare light a fire, someone was bound to find our dirty work in Nautica and come looking for us.

More tired than hungry, we made due with what was left of a box of cookies Aunt Roz sent with Kat. The farther away I was from that lady, the easier it was to love her. She had the best taste for sweet treats.

Lou pulled Kat aside and I was left with our new friend, Eyiyo, who did not eat much, he just sat and stared off into space. Don't know what he was staring at. He was very quiet and did not seem to be very happy. Not that any of us were. Maybe he lost friends or family in Nautica. He seemed to be happier when he was fighting, killing all those things, whatever they are.

It was making me sad just to think of it. It was just senseless death. Justifying our actions, we had to defend ourselves. Could they really of been people we once knew? Those repulsive things killed my father and burnt the only home I ever knew to the ground.

Because of them my carefree life would never be the same. I did not want to think of it, the whole mess was making me sad.

Eyiyo looked over and told me not to be sad, as if afraid was an easier emotion, there was nothing reassuring about the desolate feeling one got just sitting next to him. Even when Eyiyo was smiling he was intimidating. His presence embodied everything that was wrong. I was shivering in the uncomfortable silence while Lou and Kat enjoyed another heart to heart just outside ears reach.

Lou was gloating "Kat, I was so proud of you today. Your reflexes to cast are as sharp as any trained young mage. You are a natural." Lou's voice lowered, "Maybe Quinn and Aunt Roz were right. I may be more stubborn than wise. I should not have kept you from who you could be, what you are." With regret he went on. "I can see you will be a great battle mage. It's in your blood. I should have taught you more, before something like this happened. We all knew it was coming. I ran from it while they ignored it."

Lou became more serious, "If I fall again like today, know you have the strength to take my place. You will be more powerful than I ever was."

Lou was rambling on how he wanted Kat to start using his spell books for research. He vowed to show her everything he knew. Lou pulled a ring from his pinkie. "I want you to wear this ring it bestows our family crest. It will allow you to learn more efficiently." It was loose, but Kat placed the ring on her thumb anyway.

Lou made Kat a promise. "I want you to know I will never keep secrets from you again. You are old enough now to make your own decisions. I trust you and will always love you."

Kat replied, "Where you may feel you fell short as a teacher you did double time as a father. You gave me a heart, instead of the hatred I see in Quinn and Aunt Roz. Their negativity blinds them from the truth. If they would have seen Riley for who he is they would of never of treated him so badly. If they could have seen him defend me today, when the bravest of men would have run, they would never doubt him again. I trust Riley with my life." A tear ran down Kat's cheek. "I need not be afraid. Maybe your stubbornness put us in the right place, with the right people, at the right time. It may end up being the single wisest decision you ever made, whatever those reasons may have been. Don't regret any thing for me. We are going to be fine. I love you Dad!"

Before tears started to fall from his eyes Lou said, "Now let me, show you . . . a spell I liked to cast when I was your age."

Meanwhile, I was still practically alone, sitting on a log under the night sky with the mountain of muscle. Eyiyo was defiantly not a talker. So I had to be, "Still Hungry?"

Eyiyo, "Nope."

"Did you have friends or family in Nautica?"

Eyiyo, "Nope."

"You grow up around here?"

Eyiyo, "Nope."

It was obvious this was going to be a one sided conversation, Eyiyo was quickly becoming famous for his clever one word response.

"Kat and I grew up just down this road. She has an apple tree on her farm. Do you like apples?"

"Nope."

"Kat makes the best apple pie, everybody likes apple pie." There was a silence, "You must like apple pie?"

"Nope."

"You sure know how to fight good."

Eyiyo, "Yep."

I was finally making headway, "Are you ever scared?"

"Nope."

Maybe not, "Can I trust you?"

Eyiyo turned his head and made eye contact, "I cannot let you die my reluctant friend. Someday I will need you to fight by my side."

I got him to talk now I just need for him to make sense. Not that his words were not sincere, they just lacked rational thought.

Then his head returned to its original position and his empty stare. I think its better that way. Looking directly into his eyes one could only feel darkness. Solid black pupils made the whites of his eyes so bright they looked like they glowed, especially against the jet black skin of his face. If I would have looked into those eyes when he came at me in the battle I think I would of fainted. But now that we have had this little talk, I was starting to feel a little less uneasy.

"I'm sorry I cut you. You know I wasn't gonna hurt you.

"Eyiyo, "Yep."

"Tired?"

"Nope."

"Well I am gonna get some sleep." I pulled out some blankets. "Are you cold?"

"Nope."

Setting one of my blankets aside for him, I put my head down. I guess it was safe to sleep. In a funny way it felt like he was laying guard over me, if he wanted us dead, he could kill us, anytime he wanted.

I still could not stop thinking of how he cut threw so many of those creatures in just a few minutes. Thinking back, we were just in the way. I looked again at Eyiyo who was just sitting there staring out into nowhere. It was unsettling the way he sat, like he was waiting for something to happen. Standing, I picking up my blankets and said, "I'm gonna sleep over there." mumbling under my breath, "Way over there."

Not far from the camp, I found a running stream with a pool of water big enough to jump into. I knelt down to wash my face and oddly enough the water seemed warm. Warm enough to take a dip. So I swam for a minute washing off the dirt that covered my body. I even washed my clothes hanging them, on a conveniently low branch nearby.

The water felt relaxing. I was in my own little world. But no mater how nice the moment was I could not put out of my mind my sorrows. I missed Father, could he really be alive, one of them? How many other families have been destroyed? Could Lou be right, could I make a difference? What did Eyiyo mean by someday I would fight beside him? What is to be my destiny.

I looked up at the stars. Focusing on one that sort of twinkled, as I spoke out loud to myself.

"I just witnessed the most gruesome disrespect for life, actions taken by a true madman. The darkest soul I have ever felt. I am forced to cling to this warrior for protection, because I do not have the physical strength myself to fight those who have brought such chaos upon this world.

I Know I have the courage to do what is right. If my death is required to bring tranquility back to this world, then so be it! If it is truly fate that has placed me in the right place at the right time, grant me the power to fight for the side of truth, and give me the understanding to know the truth when I see it. This is my peace."

After making my peace I was left in a euphoric state, I drifted asleep. I dreamed a great hand lifted me into the sky. I did not understand why I truly felt safe in the blue talons that held me, but I did.

Night turned into day as I lay in the huge hand that cradled me, a dragon's eye stared at me, and I stared back into the eye of a dragon.

On her head extending out was a jagged edge similar to the top fin of a fish. It resembled a crown drizzled with a rainbow of colors giving her a majestic look. The uneven knife like tendon continued down her neck, and across her back, stretching the entire length of her tail, turning into clusters of ample sized spikes. Her massive wings curled back around her body as she lay motionless suspended in the clouds.

It was hard not to feel insignificant in the immense creatures' presence. The scales from her belly were bigger than the table that sat on my father's porch.

Most of her body was covered with coral blue scales making her almost disappear against the extensive blue background of the morning sky. The only contrast to the soft color was her claws, underside and expansive areas under her wings, they could only be seen when she raised her head or shifted her wing, these areas were a midnight blue, so dark a color, it could easily be mistaken for black.

Black as the pupil of her eye that reflected like a mirror, allowing me to look back into myself.

In the eyes of the majestic creature I found serenity. There was a new understanding in my heart, as if a fire was ignited in my soul. Water gathered in the dragon's tear duct and in it my reflection, she shed a tear. I watched the droplet fall to the ground as if I was falling myself, passing through the clouds, I fell toward the earth.

On the ground below I could see a knight planting a seed in a forest, covering the seed with fresh dirt. The tear found its home watering the seed. A tiny seedling immediately sprouted. And there I was standing on the ground next to the warrior.

I looked up to see if the dragon was gone. Only to see vaulted ceilings painted like the sky. When I looked back down, I was in a large room with marble walls, decorated with old tapestries depicting armies battling. The hall was filled with rows of statues of elegantly dressed men and women. On the floor etched in marble was that round symbol split into twelve but there was no tree.

What did it have to do with me?

There was a huge stairway with a curved stone handrail leading to a balcony full of people. The great warrior knelt on the ground. His full plate armor was gleaming in an angelic fashion.

He removed his belt, holding it up offering it to me. Then he removed his helmet placing it under his arm. He looked me straight in the eye. "Save us" he muttered, as he bowed his head. I caught the reflection of a pink flower in his somehow familiar gaze.

Slowly one by one the people from the balcony descended, they were of different races. Some so foreign to me, I would be at a loss of words to describe them separately. They all joined the humbled fighter kneeling before me. The symbol I stood on cracked.

Suddenly, I awoke from my dream!

Morning had already come. I was completely refreshed like I've not felt since I was back on father's farm.

Somehow Kat had found me in the night and slept by my side. She hugged me, whispering in my ear, "I hope you do not mind me lying by you, I always feel safe when I'm with you," She felt so warm snuggling against me in the cold morning air.

As we lay in each others arms I tried to explain to Kat how I felt. I was invigorated. I was no longer afraid.

I looked in her eyes, "I will never fail you." thinking to myself how wonderful a feeling it was to hold her in my arms.

We cuddled for a minute. Maybe more than a minute, then Kat gave me a real kiss, the kiss I had so long waited for.

Chapter Ten

I Believe, That's Not True

I stood up, gathering my unsoiled clothes calling out to Lou, "Fresh water over here."

Lou, looking around, "What water?"

Defending what I believed true. "It was here last night."

Lou hollered back "This is not the time to be funny." We were all thirsty and hungry, except maybe Eyiyo, who had the same empty stare on his face.

I was not crazy, my clothes were clean. Kat nudged me, "I believe you."

Baffled, Lou put an end to the discussion he could not believe he was losing. "We are close to Neval we can be at the Shivan River before midday, if we quit this horsing around."

Kat, Lou and I had to ride upfront on the bench, while Eyiyo sat on the back end, he took up most of the cart. He was big and heavy. Bauble had taken a liking to our new friend and chose to keep him company while we passed the time listening to Lou. He was talking about the intricacies of casting spells and stuff with Kat. I concentrated on driving we had been making good time and since we left Nautica there had been no sign of any other travelers in either direction. I was thinking if we did not waste a lot of time at the river, we might be able to make it to Lou's house in Maguire by tonight.

By the wooden bridge there was a dirt path that led down to the water and a clearing large enough for us to turn the cart around. Our mounts were thirsty and needed to rest as much as we did. It was sad to think the last time I stood here I was with my father. I had to remind myself that this road we were on, may lead me back to him someday. I wanted to believe he was still alive. I had to believe. By taking this road it would help change things for the better. I looked down. By the shore were more wild flowers, they always lightened any weight on my heart.

Eyiyo knelt to wash his face in the river. He was covered in so much soot it turned the water around him black. We were all shocked, we could see for the first time there was someone human under there. He was a little blue no more blue than someone who ate something bad. Kat shouted at him. "Don't stop there, if you're going to ride with me, your going to need to smell better too." Ordering him to relinquish his clothes, she offered up some of Lou's stuff to wear.

Eyiyo sure was big, and his new outfit was two times too small. Kat shook her head deviously commenting, "It's not the best ensemble I've put together, but it will have to do." Then she took Eyiyo's clothes and washed them down stream. I didn't care if I dreamed water or not, my clothes were already clean.

Lou was preoccupied, pulling a rod and reel from his chest. He was hoping to catch some fish. We all were in need of a little nourishment. I tried to help by looking for some wild berries. I was not as successful as Lou, who did not have very good luck at all!

We lit a fire to quicken the drying of Eyiyo's clothes and attempted to make lunch out of the two little fish Lou caught. There was not enough to make us full, but no one complained. I decided not to eat at all, giving my portion to Kat.

Lou would not let my good deed go by, refusing to eat as well. I explained to him I was not hungry. Kat jumped with a buzz of her dagger, "That's not true!" she placed her portion of fish back on the plate by the fire.

Lou explained "I owe it to your father to see that you kids are taken care of. Then he claimed this whole road-trip was his idea and I should be home, safe in my barn. I argued back. "That's not true either!" Lou did not send that fateful cart crashing down the road that night. Leaving was the only choice we had. "you saved us!"

Eyiyo stepped between in. "This is not the way it happens. We must work together!"

We all looked at him puzzled, realizing in an odd way he was right. We should not be arguing with each other.

I reached down taking a small piece of fish to eat, "If I eat will both of you?" Wishing to myself, there was more food to share.

What was this? I noticed a basket of fresh picked fruit, with biscuits, and honey floating in the water. It anchored itself by the shore in the wild flowers I was admiring earlier, making it easy to retrieve.

I picked up a piece of bread splitting it in half, handing a piece to Lou.

Lou thanked Eyiyo for the basket of plenty, Eyiyo shook his head. "I did nothing, it simple appeared when you were arguing."

Lou did not believe him, "No really, thank you." Eyiyo stood his ground claiming it was not him. Lou and I looked at Kat, wondering if Aunt Roz taught her another little do-da. She denied having anything to do with it as well.

Lou reached down tapping Kat's dagger looking back at Eyiyo. Kat shook her head signaling the fact Eyiyo was telling the truth.

Lightheartedly, I stated, "Maybe it was sent down the river by the dragons in the mountains." I was thinking of the story father told us last time we came past here.

I did not know exactly what I said that was so wrong, but Eyiyo became enraged by my words. Protesting, "Dragons, Its not dragons. They do not protect anyone. They are selfish, backstabbing, petty, vicious vile creatures, whose smell alone is enough to sicken your stomach and turn men running!"

Eyiyo did not speak much but when he did, he did!

I quickly tried to change the subject because Eyiyo was getting emotionally distressed by his own words, increasing his rage. "Certainly not dragons! It is possible the basket was forgotten by a careless passerby. Many people stop here to draw water from the river."

Kat knew I was lying, we all knew, we had not seen anyone on the road. Eyiyo looked down at me. "Do not mock me. I like you Riley. What is happening here will affect a lot of lives. More lives than you would believe. I would suspect there are many eyes watching us. Like me, some may be willing to aid you on your journey. Be wary, there may be others who will try to hinder."

Lou shook his head in agreement, adding, "There are many ways to watch from afar."

Lou's eyes lit up as if he had an epiphany. For some odd reason he did not seem to want to share it with us, but his demeanor changed, apologizing for questioning our good fortune, with a smile and a healthy bite from the bread I had given him, he said, "Let's eat, and be on our way!"

It was hard staying positive, especially the closer we came to home. Sorrow entered my heart as the night took over. We were starting to pass through Airwindale. The few stores that made up the meager town by our home were destroyed. Nobody was insight. We had seen this gruesome scene before. They had fallen to the same fate as the other towns we passed.

But this was different. I did not want to think it true. These were our friends, our neighbors.

Our caravan was forced to stop, when the mounts that pulled the cart started to make a meal out of a half cooked corpse, I jumped out of the cart, hoping to pull them away somehow. Eyiyo stopped me. "All creatures need substance. These lost souls are in Eden now."

I did not need to be told everything was lost. I could see the burnt corpses. It was too late to help them. I was trying not to blame myself for their misfortune. Would they have even believed us, if we had tried to warn them?

I wondered if the people I had known were changed or did they lie in the ashes at my feet? I wished I knew exactly what happened.

My head started to spin as the area was filled with an eerie glow. All around me the people I knew reappeared. There voices were distorted, but I could still hear them calling out. It was as if they were ghosts trapped in time, somehow forced to reenact their demise. Kat's classmates came running out of the school house that once again had walls. They were panicking, grabbing at their clothes, and then they fell to the ground.

Old man Kevil was sitting outside his shop on one of the rocking chairs Father had made, until the screaming caught his attention. Mrs. Fullwilley was throwing pies at a group of Drazzi underlings who were tossing cubes off the back of a wagon as it traveled through the town. I yelled out to warn them, but my voice could not be heard. When I looked down I could see Kelso and his father, lying at my feet in front of their cart that was still half filled with fresh vegetables. Above them was a green cloud that was being dispersed by the wind.

Now I could see larger groups of Drazzi solders marching forward throwing spheres and cubes. Store clerks and farmers did not stand a chance against the advancing threat. The defenseless villagers fell to the ground uncontrollably jerking. I was forced to relive their slaughter. Watching the wicked little cubes do their damage, their twitching victims dotting the road. Some were caged as their mutations took longer. Those that were grossly deformed were burned. Not only were the humans affected but also horses and dogs started to change. Horses were turning into the strange mounts we had been seeing. Dogs were mutating into scaled attack animals, ruthless forest lizards with sharp claws and big fangs. Even Mrs. Fullwilley's cow was changing into an exotic snarling horror. The grunts started to burn the buildings as the Drazzi leaders started to shout orders at the newly formed creatures, which mindlessly joined the ranks with the old. It was all very methodical.

Frozen helpless, all I could do was listen to their screams. The illusion suddenly came to an end as I found myself being shaken by Lou. "Snap out of it Riley!" he said as he grabbed at my arms. The hazy light lifted, the night sky was restored, the buildings returned to rubble as the condemned people and the Drazzi soldiers disappeared. "Lets go, there is nothing for us here!"

Sometimes knowing the truth can be a burden. I know now, what Kat had seen. I understood my Fathers fate, and for once in my life I realized I had chosen the right path.

It was not long before we came upon Kat's house. We pulled down the drive. The Drazzi were very efficient in making sure not to leave any structure standing. Lou thought maybe we could salvage some vegetables or apples, but nothing was left behind.

Kat was in tears, heartbroken. The apple tree we played under looked like twisted black spikes reaching for the sky. She came to me in the garden that once sat below her window. There we promised each other we would stop whatever or whomever was behind this.

We passed my home without hesitation. I did not need to look I knew. My barn, the porch and even the old table, everything including the trees that overhung the house, were no more. It felt awful, but I had already left my sorrows behind me, I was looking for hope.

I knew one place in the forest we would be safe. The place we played as children by the old willow. I suggested we spend the night there. I thought it might make Kat feel better. I hoped it would do the same for me.

We were far enough from the main road to light a fire. As usual, Kat and Lou took off so not be disturbed. Lou had so much he wanted to teach her.

I hoped Eyiyo would be more talkative tonight. But his litany of one word responses continued.

"You cold?"

"Nope."

"Nice fire?"

"Nope."

"You like fires, everybody likes fires."

"Nope."

This wasn't working. There was one subject I knew he could not refuse. All I had to say was one word, drawing it out slowly pronouncing each syllable I said, "Dra-gon-sss."

A little angry Eyiyo snapped back asking if I knew that dragons were born out of fire. Not just any fire, he explained, it takes the heat equal to that of an erupting volcano. Only constant extreme heat and pressure will release the whelp from its egg. "Anything born of a red flame will never be trustworthy. "That's why I don't like fire!"

"Oh." I muttered quietly.

Eyiyo continued, "An adult is more than a large ferocious creature with the strength of a hundred men, flashing big teeth and bad breath. Those attributes are no match compared to the devastation they bring to the table with their devious minds."

I just sat and listened as he vented. "It is also true they fly but the older and larger they grow the less they are likely to do so naturally. They are never defenseless and always dangerous, from the minute they are hatched. Even as small whelps they are brutal hunters breathing corrosive fire with no concept of what is good or bad, they destroy indiscriminately burning every thing they don't eat. They enjoy fresh meat but can survive on coal."

I just kept nodding, "There is no more reasoning with a young whelp, than with an angry selfish child. They only seek chaos leaving a path of ash in their wake.

Eventually they will learn to manipulate their breath weapon. Not only can they burn their victims, they can also concentrate that force into a beam of pure energy accurate enough to cut a tree in half without setting the surrounding forest on fire.

That is only the beginning, once they discover their innate ability, to be able to pull magical energy from the plane of fire they are born of, there is little that can stop them."

After taking a moment to breath and curse he went on. "This ability allows communication with other dragons. They will be taught wicked ways to weave their webs of despair. Of course, nothing is free. This knowledge is in exchange for their compliance, creating a hierarchy amongst themselves. They become avid magic users, with no idea of morality, with a natural connection to spells that aid in their treachery, or cause misfortune.

When they mature which can take hundreds of years, they only get more malicious, callous, and cruel. They continuously grow in intelligence and size making them even more dangerous, never to be underestimated.

Even with all their powers, they are not invincible. There was once a specially trained skilled group of fighters that was able to take on and kill dragons.

This skill requires not only great strength but also cunning and a non-wavering confidence in one's self and each other. To be victorious each dragon hunter must know all the dragons' weaknesses."

Eyiyo tapped his chest twice with his fist, "All off my kind strive to rid this world of red dragons. So do not just merrily mention dragons in my presence. They are to always be taken seriously."

Eyiyo looked me in the eye, "Riley to fight a dragon you must understand how they think. Only by realizing this will you understand who you are fighting."

Eyiyo paused and I felt like I should say something. His tone gave the impression his words weighed heavy on his heart. I just gave the nod and replied in a way I thought he could relate to, "Yep"

"Dragons do not play well with each other, even though they will work together. They will turn on each other. Teaching one to sow the seeds of distrust has its downsides, paranoia, greed, the constant need to have influence over each other. They will ruthlessly try to dominate each other, as they do with any sentient creatures in their sphere of influence.

The strongest dragon will govern the others with ruthless might, creating a coven. Although retaining supreme authority, the leader will divide the land, and will give those who prove themselves loyal, rule over their own territories.

Their is no end to the treachery. Once a coven is established, absolutely dominating the land, they will find a way to lash out into new worlds if they can.

They do this by making slaves of weaker, more vulnerable races. Praying on the weak, they love to manipulate the truth creating leverage with lies. Offering individuals power in exchange for their allegiance. They love unscrupulous people who will turn their backs on their own kind willingly."

Eyiyo's voice grew louder. "They want us to fight amongst our own, and amongst the other races in their domain. It makes us weak, easier to control."

Taking a moment to reflect, "A hard lesson well learned." Nodding to himself, "They too must be divided to be easily conquered."

Quieting back down he went on, "These foul retches will resort to any sort of tom-trickery, blackmail, simple addictions, fear tactics, offering protection from themselves, anything to achieve their devious goals. When their dark promises are not enough they will resort to magical energy, which there is no shortage of. These winged demons are armed with an arsenal of fiendish spells. They find despicable ways to dominate and control."

Eyiyo shook his head in disgust. "We fight for their entertainment as they reap the spoils of war. Demanding tribute in return for their treachery, there is no limit to their greed. Cherishing fancy cloth, precious gems, gold and silver, they gather immense treasure hordes, but they value books most of all. They love to gather extensive libraries.

Like any bad karma eventually, they too will be controlled, but only by their own paranoia, afraid to be exposed to those who may try to defy them or try to take their wealth. They will be forced to dictate their misery from their places of power, unable to leave, they keep tabs on the misfortunate with an endless supply of underlings to do their bidding, always watching with magical eyes, as all their needs are fulfilled by their indentured servants.

The damned who live in the shadow of a dragon are forced to spend their lifetimes mindlessly producing what their ruler demands, offering all they have, down to their last breath, hoping to avoid whatever nightmare their oppressor has dreamed up if they do not comply. When their control is complete, there is little chance anyone will escape a dragon's grasp."

Eyiyo must have been told many tall tales when he was young to know so much about dragons. I wondered what made him hate them so bad? Hoping to learn more I asked "Do you know any stories about real dragons."

Eyiyo made a pact with me, if I promised to never trust any red dragons, or as he referred to them, the crimson deliverers of deceit, he would tell me a true story about where dragons come from and when they first came to this world.

I did not have to even think about it. I promised!

Eyiyo kept his part of the bargain, "A long time ago, before the Commonwealth existed, this world was inhabited by a single dominant race, humans. In the height of their existence, they mastered a magic called Technology, they learned to fly, heal, and even feed the masses. They had bio-engineered servants and an endless supply of energy. They were able speak and see each other across far distances. There were vast markets, filled with anything one could desire from the different ends of the world.

They had built cities of light with buildings as big as mountains. Filled with millions of people, their empire stretched to every corner of the land. There were thousands of these cities, all connected by an intricate web of roads. There was no part of this world they had not explored.

Their only fault was they could not make peace with each other. Distracted by their leaders, the rich sowed the ideals of distrust and prejudice for profit, dividing the populace. Those with power could then easily alienate the smaller groups, taking advantage.

They pitted the people against each other using their wealth or lack of. When that did not work they used deep seeded beliefs. The trusting people allowed their mentors to argue over the distant past, instead of concentrating on a future together. Each group was told they were different, superior, the chosen.

Most factions were directly or indirectly controlled by their religious leaders, who were in turn influenced by the wealthy. Instead of helping each other, they chose to horde their riches, and to protect their riches, they made weapons of war. Labeling themselves with flags and symbols, referring to themselves as the United Nations. United was an understatement!

Preaching solidarity, these leaders pressured each other, to allow themselves to assert what force they believed necessary for the rich to remain in control. Year after year they attacked their own, and each other, pointing fingers across the room, for the atrocities they committed behind closed doors. Charming the naive with diplomacy, paying their debts with secrets, keeping the populace divided with their own trivial disputes.

One attack led to a relentless chain of retaliation, anger spiraled out of control. Eventually, there was a whirlwind of massive explosions. No one really could remember who started it. In the end, it did not matter.

The most powerful group of men had perfected a new weapon, beyond the others capabilities. It was able to destroy any target by emitting a beam of energy that could be fired from high above the sky. There was literally no protection from the men who controlled this weapon. It was designed to cut through any type of force field or barrier. This weapon these men created with their science-magic burned so hot, it ripped an opening in the time field that normally separates the alternate planes of existence, the planes of fire, water, air, and earth.

These men unwittingly created a common doorway to this world and a battlefield where ancient elementals could move without one having the disadvantage of time over the other. This drew the attention of these primordial enemies, exposing this world to their will. Too large to physically battle for control over this new domain, they broke off small pieces of their being, to battle for them. This devastating raw power unleashed on this fragile land literally erased the civilization that set them free.

Being the quickest, fire elementals came first. Creatures whose lifeblood was lava, their bodies made entirely of flames. Their natural instinct to seek out anything that would combust, they needed to feed to survive. The more fuel they found the larger and stronger they became. They were drawn to the destructive power of the bombs set off by the self-absorbed race engaged in their insignificant quarrels.

Once set loose these flaming entities of fire moved freely through the cities, smoke stacks poured from their brows as they jumped from one building to another. At first they went unnoticed, drawing power from the heat of the already burning high-rises, fueling uncontrollable firestorms. Above, huge rain clouds started forming in the blackened skies, as towns disappeared in flames.

The living storm systems voiced their presence with a thundering sound, raining down lightning blasts that became electrical fiends. Surges of power sprang from their fingertips, destroying all the flying weapons of war the soon to be lost civilization could supply.

Placid rivers started to gush backwards as water flowed into humanoid shapes forming giant liquid warriors. Settlements adjacent to these waterways were flooded or buried by huge mud slides that entombed the tiny inhabitants by the thousands.

Then the forests came alive, as the spirit of life rejuvenated the silent wooden warriors who had stood frozen for years. They immediately engaged in battle against the onslaught of energized denizens, as the first wave of living elements placed a foothold in this world.

Winds blew into tornadoes bigger than anyone had ever seen, as larger elemental forces established their presence. The swirling forms entwined, forming colossal bodies standing with the clouds. Their rotating appendages quickly filled up with debris from the disappearing world below. Entire cities vanished, as buildings were uprooted, jagged glass, sharp rock, and bodies of the young and old, churned in their inner cores, along with hundreds of small colorful metal vehicles made by the doomed witnesses who watched in disbelief. All the shinny surfaces glimmered in the flashing light display of the night sky, as the pieces of this lost land dashed in and out of the heavy black smoke, highlighting the menacing silhouettes of the gigantic air elementals.

Oceans rose up creating massive waves, enveloping the burning cityscape, wiping away what was left of the seaside communities. When the water retreated, the only thing left standing on the shores, were enormous water elementals. Fleets of sea vessels were trapped in the living waves and were used as ammunition, as these giants engaged each other. Memories of the shattered people became an endless supply of projectile weapons to fuel the elemental war.

Mountains became living walls, as the earth elementals were drawn from the ground. These colossal creatures were covered from head to toe with the occupied dwellings of the local residents that had made their homes on the cliff-sides. Many of the minuscule people jumped to their deaths, as the arms and legs of the colossal creatures became animated. The land was literally ripped apart as the descending armies gathered in strength. Cities that took centuries to build fell in minutes.

Volcanoes erupted, spitting out clouds of glowing ash, lighting up the faces of their elemental enemies. The enraged storm clouds showed their prowess, pouring their cache of rain on the warriors of fire rising out of the rivers of molten lava.

Finally, the volcanoes themselves stood with faces of fiery fury, molten rock sluing from their mouths. These armies of titans fought each other, carving out paths of utter chaos, leaving nothing less than total mayhem. The angry men were like fleas on an animal being slaughtered, the hunter truly unaware of the teeny pest's existence.

These elemental beings had no tangible dispute, no reasonable justification for their rampage, only naturally opposing natures. The war spiraled out of control.

Earth's elementals were bent on restoring order, by separating and controlling the other elements. They split the great land masses apart creating massive fissures miles long to stop the advance of water and the flow of lava that was reshaping this world.

Slowly their rage weakened, the skies cleared, the fires burned out, the ground settled, the seas calmed. The elemental warriors had lost their stamina, disconnected from their own worlds and the power that fueled their hostility. Temporarily, peace was restored to the blighted land.

What was left of the doomed race crawled out of the holes that sheltered them, only to watch as strange races poured out of these alternate dimensions, into their ravished world.

Groups of bizarre creatures, from the Realm of Air floated in on living airships, larger than any flying machine they had ever known. These vessels had no moving parts. They were living beings that seemed to be pushed around by the mercy of the winds. On their backs were entire cities filled with generations of intelligent beings, little people who lived in a sort of symbiosis on the fantastic herds.

Out of the Earth Realm grew a gigantic Sequoia, a piece of the great earth elemental. Moving like a snake carrying its cargo of seeds in the loose gravel wedged in-between its massive root system. Riding the growing branches were more hitch hikers with various woodland eyes, including your kind.

Thrown into the sea, came underwater armies from the Realm of Water. They rode massive sea creatures, taking them to the deepest parts of the oceans. The races of creatures that lived in these dimensions were all willing to leave everything behind."

Eyiyo paused, saying one word in a long drawn out way. "Dra-gon-sss . . ." then he spit on the ground as if it was needed to continue his story, ". . . left the plane of fire!"

Fully disgusted, he shook his head. "Can you believe, once they too were considered small insignificant creatures, in their own homeland?" Amazed he looked at me seeking conformation, mesmerized, I silently waited for him to continue.

"They saw this new world as a place to exploit, allowing them to break their bonds, becoming masters themselves. These filthy creatures were the most aggressive of the unwanted refugees. Bent on conquest and destruction, they learned to dominate.

First, they destroyed any ruminants left of the previous civilization's claim to this land. This once proud race crippled, relegated, now simply used as a source of food.

Then the Red Dragons attempted to seize authority over this world's new residents. Individually they attacked the floating cities but were turned back by the giant floating animals and those who protected them. Next, they tried to burn the trunk of the great tree, the strongest of the earth elementals. Again they were turned away by those woodland creatures that inhabited her branches. But with each attack there were great losses.

Eventually the red dragons learned to work together attacking in groups signaling out specific targets. With each attack the red dragons gained the advantage, eventually killing the great air creatures. One by one they fell from the sky crashing to the earth. The cities on their backs left in flames.

With their natural breath weapons, they ignited the great Sequoia. Many of the smaller creatures of these distant worlds had innate magical abilities. They too banned together pulling energy from the elemental plains for protection. Drawing the last of the dormant energy from within the heart of the living tree where they sought refuge, together they were able to call forth two stone warriors that mimicked the shape of their enemies, and were able to defend the pious life-force.

In the end the Dragons were just too powerful eventually they were able to place their hold on this world. Very few were able to resist the dragons clutches.

The Red Dragons united calling forth the destructive powers of the elemental plane of fire. This flux of power was breaking down the intangible walls that separated the dimensions themselves. The Red Dragons were willing to destroy everything to further their conquest.

Avenu, the mother of all, watched. She could not allow the destruction to continue. It is her love that binds all worlds together. Our failure would have torn this universe apart. The ancient element of eternal fire would expand indefinitely, if fully freed from its cage. It would destroy the harmony Avenu had created.

The reign of the Red dragons lasted almost a thousand years, but with the help of the new inhabitants of this world, Avenu was able to reseal the dimensions, by separating this world into sections and dividing the biggest threat, the group of red dragons.

This was done with great sacrifice. Pieces of the ancient elemental beings were permanently trapped here. Their power dissipated or was absorbed into the natural elements of this world. The remaining

Earth elementals were reshaped into mountains. Water elementals returned to the seas and rivers. Air elementals absorbed back into the clouds and the Fire elementals retreated to the hearts of the dormant volcanoes. This is why such a strong magical connection remains between the elemental planes and this world."

Riley interrupted, "But what became of the red dragons?"

Eyiyo finished, "A man known as Kodas Foehammer came forward and healed the great Sequoia, the mother of all trees. Because of his gentle heart and bravery in battle, Avenu granted Kodas the ability to control the blue flame. With that power he hunted down and killed almost all of the Red Dragons. For this his people made him king. To this day, the last of the Red Dragons still seek revenge on those who helped defeat them, and their families."

I had to ask, "Was that really a true story? Mountains don't really rise up. Fire does not come alive."

Eyiyo, "Don't you believe in the living elements? The ramification of their war is apparent each time you see something happen that is not physically possible. You grew up near here, surrounded by elementals. You just chose not to see them.

Riley, with disbelief in his tone, "Where?"

Eyiyo, "Have you never seen a storm cloud pouring rain on a sunny day. Have you never seen dusters on your farm, wind traveling in a circle picking at the ground? Have you never touched a doorknob and been shocked or listened to the voices in a crackling fire as it sends sparks up into the air reaching out for more fuel. Rivers of water carve caverns through mountains. Lightning strikes and you still do not believe? This is strange to me."

I looked Eyiyo in the eye, "Friends!" He just smiled back, and with that I climbed off to bed.

Chapter Eleven

Watching Eyes

There on a branch I had carved a heart long ago. Inside I had written our names, Katinka and Riley. Kat always wanted to scratch her name out, but she could not climb that high. Always worried she said, "Do you want everybody to gossip about us?"

I don't know why, but on summer days it was always easy for me to fall asleep here. It felt like I was being cradled by the old willow, held like a baby in a basket, and rocked as the tree swayed in the wind. This place would always be considered home.

I climbed up to where long ago I placed our names. The lulling sound of crickets helped me fall asleep in the tree top. Just being here made me feel better. After what I had seen earlier today, I could not understand how. I kept thinking about the story Eyiyo told. It made my mind wander, as I slipped under.

I knew I was dreaming because the tree seemed to be more than just holding me. I could clearly see a face in the bark on the trunk. It was looking down, smiling. Even if its oversized half open eyes gave the impression the creature was sad. Everything was moving in slow motion. The tree seemed to ooze a drop of el. El is the sap from the willow; it dripped from her eyes like a tear, taking forever to fall onto my lips. It was as sweet as honey.

That wasn't the strangest thing. The tree was humming a sweet lullaby. Like a mother singing to a child, causing a soothing transcendent feeling.

"Sleep noble child, fear your heart shall never keep, do not fall to deceit, let me guide the way, draw your strength from me." The voice seemed to come from the wind passing through the leaves.

"Riley, Riley, wake up. Let me see you with these eyes one more time. I must leave soon, they are coming for me. I have been waiting so long to deliver this message to you. I am so glad you made it, in time."

I will admit, lately my dreams have been more than vivid, definitely entertaining. I asked the tree if she was real. She said, "I am as real as yesterday's sunset or tomorrow's sunrise. I don't know an easy way to explain. I am of your world but of another time, occupying a similar space. What happens in your world affects everyone, even my kind, like ripples in a pond plundered by a stone. The waves will eventually shape the far away shore.

I know you will not fully understand. You don't have to. I have heard your heart calling out to me, since you were born. All you need to know is your innocence is a beacon of light, which can be seen in my world.

Here time is immeasurable. I do not live, I exist. It takes years of meditation, standing in one spot to see into your dimension, for even a brief period of time. These eyes have been here watching over you, your entire life. Fond my memories will be of watching you play with your mate in my embrace."

"What do you want of me?" I wondered.

"I need you to do something for me. You must take a piece of this body and shape it into a staff."

"Why me?"

"Do you think it was simple fate that placed you here, at this place, in this time? You are the sign we have been waiting for. Your Grandfather was a great healer. His acts of kindness and bravery will be revered for all time! It is his song that sings in your heart. In you I feel his memory, his love, and his courage. We believe you will make the right choice, at the right place, in the right time."

"What do I do with the staff?" I asked.

"Give it to her, and if you are ever in need, just call out, have faith, we will always be there."

"Wait, I don't know who you are. Who is she, I don't understand."

The tree just started to sing again. "Sleep noble child, fear your heart shall never keep, do not fall to deceit, let me guide the way, draw your strength from me."

That morning I found Kat crying. She believed somehow we would never see this place again. I told her, "It will always be here in our memories."

Kat put her hands around my waist, she was gripping at a belt. Looking down I realized it was the belt I dreamed the knight had given to me, the night before last.

The silver belt was finely crafted and fit like it was made for me. The front tapered to an oval area. The top and bottom edge was crafted to look like a loosely braided rope. In the center was an intricate pattern, made with a single line that continually fed back onto itself. On the back there were groves giving the impression it was mechanical in nature. Like a box with multiple compartments that did not open.

I showed the belt to Lou, and told him about my dreams. Lou looked at the belt, and the worry that had been in his face since we first left home, was forgotten. "I know this belt. Every man, woman, and child in Suxen Falls knows this belt. It is worn by the figure in the waterfall. It is the belt of Race Bliss. I remembered the statue, finally realizing where I had seen the Knights face. The huge temple guardian was a statue of him.

Lou sang a jolly, Ho, Ho! "I've had my suspicions, ever since that basket of food showed up. That ring you're wearing is a healer's ring. You should not have been able to use it. It's of a spiritual nature. The dreams it all makes sense. I was afraid of pulling you kids into this mess, especially you Riley. There is no doubt you have all the courage in the world, but you're not a fighter. You have always been clever, but you are not a mage. Now, I can see you have the heart of a healer. This belt is a sign for you. It is the beginning of your spiritual road. All you need to do now is have faith."

I was ecstatic, "Are you saying . . . I made the food!"

Lou smiled, "It's so much more than that."

That's when I noticed a symbol on my belt that was not visible before. It was glowing and appeared as if the symbol was entangled in the engraving on the front. I touched the belt and instinctively turned my palms to the sky, and before us appeared a large apple pie. "My favorite!"

Lou Laughed . . . "and so it begins."

I returned to the tree to do what was asked of me. I noticed a branch had split open just above the main crotch of the tree, inside I could see an impression of my belt. The tree had grown around it. How long had it been here? How could they have known?

Before we left I found a large root that could be easily cut away. Even though it was gnarled and twisted there was a straight line to it. It was angled at the top and felt good in my hand. I packed it in the chest. That and with our bellies full of pie we started to move again.

This was the longest part of our journey, passing the burned out farms of many we called "neighbor." Even the trees that had been an everyday part of our life looked ravaged, their over grown limbs seemed to reach down almost into the cart, as if they were reaching out for help. The narrowing path seemed to grow smaller as we passed through the forest we use to call home.

The farther we got the more the road became a stranger to us. We noticed some of the trees had some kind of infestation growing on them, Lou stopped to take a sample. The berries on the strange vines had a luminescent glow and the stalks had reddish veins, giving the appearance that they were more animal than plant. The root systems of these parasitic plants seemed to be able to cut through the tough outer layer of the trees, securely attaching themselves with thousands of tiny tendons.

The farther we went, the more we could see several varieties of flora we were not familiar with. They were sucking the life out of the trees native to this area. Many large cottonwoods lay on their side or were barren of leaves. Others had died, but had not fallen. They were completely covered with the bloodthirsty plants, like a constricting snake killing its victim, wrapped from the lowest parts of the trunk to the ends of the smallest branches by the encumbering vines.

Slowly the thick stalks, riddled with the red veins, were replacing the defenseless trees that once lined the road. This aggressive breed of plant had a much thicker canopy and blocked out the sun completely. Giving us an uneasy feeling, the less cottonwood's we saw.

Lou pointed out the root system of some of the thicker plants were crossing into the road, making our ride bumpy. Voicing his concern to show some caution he said, "Slow down."

Silently, what was like a giant green hand, reached down picking Eyiyo up and right out of the cart? We would have never noticed, except the cart gained speed once Eyiyo's weight was removed. It happened so fast the cart traveled fifty feet before we were able to react to what happened.

By then another enormous green pod came down swallowing one of the mounts, lifting it into the air, still attached to the cart. We came to a jagged stop. The front of the cart was raised off the ground as our mount was fully enclosed in its jaws. Then the cart was abruptly yanked sideways, pulled out from under us, slamming Kat, Lou and me to the ground. Bauble, who somehow managed to hang on by digging her claws into the wood, jumped down gracefully, running under the cart as it dangled above us.

The pods looked shiny, like a cabbage, split at the top. Around the mouth were thick purple veins that led back to a stalk where they became a much deeper red. The large stalks were as wide as any cottonwood, the pods the size of two small row boats. Above us we could see the pod had completely encased the beaked monster, as it took the shape of the struggling creature inside.

The cart could be only lifted so high, until the leather restraints snapped and the cart came crashing down. Kat pulled me aside in the nick of time, I would have been smashed like a pancake. On the ground I could see the mangled harnesses were not cut, they were dissolving in what looked like acid.

Two more pods dropped down through the canopy of trees. They swayed like snakes sizing up their prey. I yelled at Kat, "Stand still I think they are attracted to movement." pointing down at the road.

We all stood still as the creatures honed in on the second mount that was struggling to free itself from its predicament. It was like a fish on a hook and it was not long before one of the massive mouths took the bait.

Lou whispered, "Did anyone see what happened to Eyiyo." We were not sure, but under the circumstances his chances were looking slim.

Even with daylight, there was not much light coming through the canopy of heavy leaves. Kat said "I can't see the ground it's to dark."

Feeling a serge from my waist, I touched the belt, it made a screeching sound. From in between my hands a star of energy rose up lighting up the surrounding area. It shined like the sun on a clear day in an open field.

I have said this before, sometimes its better not to know. Thousands of sporadically scattered roots overwhelmed the road, leaving few places to step, and three bright green, acid dripping, salivating mouths, with dark purple veined stalks hovering around us, waiting for the slightest movement. Two of which were occupied with our animals. Make that one. The pod that took the first mount opened its mouth, letting out a yellow sticky mixture of puss and the partially dissolved bones of the beaked creature. It looked like a banana cream pie exploded, but smelled like the barrel of body parts we had brought to Quinn.

Lou was standing motionless with a pod not far from where he was standing. Kat yelled to him, "Don't move!" as she cast a spell. "Fietballi."

Her spell started to create a small floating ball of fire. Lou was coaching her "Concentrate, control."

Turning slowly and moving back, her foot slid slightly, tapping a purplish green root. As soon as she touched it, she was snatched up in one gulp. The huge jaws clamped around her sealing shut!

Once her concentration was broken her spell fizzled out. Lou waived his hand, screaming, "No!" as a steady flow of flames shot from his hand. At first he tried burning the pod that held Kat. Then he focused on the closest largest root near her pod. The tree it was wrapped around burst into flames, the root itself was only singed. It crackled like a wet log, secreting bubbles of sticky liquid mixture; still it did not weaken or give up its hold.

My belt was glowing. The word, "Wither." came from my mouth, I bent down touching one of the roots. It was as if a disease left my hand, affecting all that was part of that root. I watched the disease travel from the smallest fibers to the thickest heavy green stalks. Moving like a multitude of fuses. Up around the trees it coiled, killing the wicked vines. Smaller vines shriveled first. Eventually affecting the large pods, that turned brown before crashing down. The pod Kat was trapped in, bellied up on the cart turning it to lumber, as if a huge fist came out of the sky. Bauble darted to the trees.

I ran to Kat's aid, as the cryptic pod's outside leaves lost their luster then withered away. Kat was struggling inside kicking to get out. I pulled my sword and slit the side open.

Kat literally poured out. She was lying in a pool of thick clear liquid her body covered in a jelly like substance. Her hair was a mess as if someone took scissors to her and her dress was almost dissolved. There were large areas of her skin with bruises that looked like road rash with blisters. Kat was gasping for air trying to get the strange goop off her yelling, "It stings. It stings."

I took off my shirt, trying to wipe her face clean, the material corroded away in my hand. "We need water!" I shouted. My belt lit up emitting a series of bleeps! A running stream sprung forth from my hands. It flowed until we were standing in a puddle of mud. Kat was rubbing the mud on her skin while I panicked!

Lou came over and put his hand on my shoulder. "Riley calm down, breathe. Search inside yourself."

I placed my hands on Kat and I believed, "Cleanse." The scars on her hands and legs started to disappear. "I did it, I really did it." I exclaimed.

In all the commotion we had forgotten Eyiyo. We all looked back down the path, he was eaten first. Could he be still alive? We ran down the road, to where he disappeared. There was one pod on the ground shaking.

I readied my sword as the pod exploded in my face. Eyiyo had finally cut his way free, shredding the mouth that imprisoned him. He was not badly burned, like Kat was. He stood up covered in nothing but the slimy yellow liquid, his clothes completely dissolved.

Kat relieved he was alright, chuckled as she said, "Well, I guess you didn't look that bad, in my father's clothes!"

Taking a moment to regroup, looking at the cart, thankful it was not us sitting in pieces, we prepared ourselves to travel by foot. Kat redressed pulling another new outfit from the chest, and then made a pouch for Bauble she could strap over her shoulder. Lou gave Eyiyo two of his shirts, one to wipe himself clean as best he could, the other to wear. It was tight to say the least. Kat laughed wiggling her nose, trying to help adjust the material by pulling at it, commenting, "You were so clean. If boys can't find a mess, the mess will find the boys."

We realized the entire terrain had changed, and we were strangers in this jungle. There were all kinds of interesting new greenery. Were they all as lethal as the plants dried up at our feet? Lou pulled a box out of his chest, it was filled with empty jars, he took samples of the yellow and clear liquids and several plant species, placing them back in the box, which in turn was placed back in the chest.

Before we left I looked at Eyiyo's wounds. They had disappeared. He shrugged it off, claiming he had a much tougher hide than us pesky little Selvains. Eyiyo picked up the chest reassuring me he was all right, balancing it on his shoulder, holding it by one of the two heavy handles. With a sword in the other hand he suggested we move, while we still had some natural light.

We had not traveled that far when we found that our path was starting to break up. The road was no longer identifiable. The plants had completely overtaken the scene. I was amazed at the exotic plant life. Mushrooms the size of a houses, strange leaves so big they could be used as sails on a ship, flowers the size of Eyiyo's head, with bugs to match.

I don't think we realized we would be fighting through miles of hostile plants. For hours we fought pods of different sizes. It was a battle to just clear the way. I was not as effective as Eyiyo. His swords sliced through thick vines and sharp branches as easily as chopping vegetables for dinner. Plants seemed to move around him, slapping me in the face. Soon, Lou and I were carrying the chest, officially Eyiyo took lead.

Kat's new spell was useful. "Fietballi" the small ball of fire that fizzled out the last time she tried to cast it, now turned into a sphere of flames the size of our old table back home. She could roll it in any direction, clearing a path. This was especially helpful when we were confronted by a bunch of ankle biters, smaller pods that had not grown to full size.

We started moving a lot faster, but not a lot farther, when we found a small clearing. We decided to camp. I was in charge of dinner as Lou lit the campfire. Tonight we all sat around the fire together. As the sky darkened, the jungle took on a bizarre glow.

The deep red veins of the plants gave off enough color to be seen from afar and some of the flowers gave off a purple haze reflecting in the moonlight. There were large areas infested with the plant we identified earlier. We could tell by the clusters of bright berries. It reminded me of fireflies on a summer night. Kat said it gave the appearance that thousands of eyes were watching us in the distance. It was as spooky as it was breathtaking.

Eyiyo and Lou were talking about the stars, pointing out some of the larger ones. Eyiyo was saying they were planets. He said their names, Neptune, Mars, Venus, Saturn. He was explaining to Lou how each one had a connection to the elements, fire, water, air, earth, and that this connection, links our destinies with theirs.

I asked Eyiyo if he really believed you could tell what is going to happen by the stars. He paused choosing his words wisely. "For some their deeds are legendary, their tabloids are permanently encrypted in the sky."

I gazed out into the night, joining the conversation. Eyiyo pointed up. "Riley, do you see that star there, shining so bright." I nodded. It was the one that I had focused on when I made my peace.

"Look at the group of stars around it" Eyiyo twirled his finger at a tight knit section of twinkling stairs. Specific groups of stars form what he called a constellation. Eyiyo continued my schooling, "The brightest one is Eden. She is the eye of the constellation Avenu." He went on to say, "With a little imagination you can see Avenu is pouring fire from a clay jar made of the earth, she kneels cradling the pot in her arms. She pours that fire into a pool of water below, stirring the air around her. She is creating new worlds with her love, out of the four elements. She watches over the universe like a mother tending over her child. Avenu is always there watching over us, even if she is not visible in the night sky. You must never have doubts, have faith she is always there." Who would have thought Eyiyo would be as good a story teller as Lou.

I woke to the sounds of grown men screaming, not far from our camp. From a distance I could not tell what was wrong, until I saw what looked like a tree being pulled out of the ground, revealing the sharp black talons of a bird of prey.

The men were gathered in a clearing by a river not far from our camp. If that was the Scoal River that feeds Gourd Lake, we made better time yesterday than I thought, but we were going in the wrong direction. Any forest can be disorienting without a road to follow or a guide to show you the way.

Breaking the tree line, I could see the dilemma the men were in, but I was helpless to do anything. They were too far away. A giant egret was hunting for breakfast and found the group of weary travelers. It was like the birds I used to watch when Father and I would go fishing, only bigger. Its long pointed beak was as sharp as a woodman's spear and as long as a canoe. It stood several stories high, walking on two awkward looking legs. With ease, like pulling small pests from the mud, it plucked the men from the ground.

When I first spotted the other party, there were only five men still alive, that I could see, but that number was dwindling rapidly. Hesitating, the egret bobbed its head zeroing in on its next victim, pulling another man from the ground, flicking him in the air like a crushed bug and gulping him whole.

One of the massive legs slowly lifted, then came down with precision, pinning down another as he tried to run away. Repositioning itself for the final attack, using its razor sharp vision, the egret took its time acquiring the location where each man was hiding. When it was ready, the beak went down pecking rapidly at the ground. Before it lifted its head, there were three more men impaled on its beak.

One man was speared by the shoulder, the next through the groin, and the third was already pinned to the ground. The egret beak went into his back; the beak had pierced its way through his torso exiting his stomach, splattering blood all over the rocks. He went limp instantly as the other two men called out in pain.

The huge bird halted its attack and started to move away, its gullet full. It strutted by us, as if we were no threat to it, probably planning to return for another meal, leaving us and only one other well hidden man behind.

Was he crazy? The survivor immediately started following the huge bird. When he noticed me, he yelled loud, "The bag! The bag! We must get the bag." His screams woke everybody else up, except Eyiyo who never seemed to get much sleep.

Luckily, the plant growth was not as dense by the rivers edge. Following the large bird to its nest was not a problem. Its footprints were as big as the table on my old porch. We could also hear the egret's final destination. Honing in on the piercing sound of its young, eager chicks waiting to be fed, was easy. 'Chick,' seems to be the wrong word for a baby bird twice the size of a healthy horse, ready to be fed a full grown man. Yet still, a very accurate description.

There was a tall healthy tree near the water where the giant egret found a place to build a nest for its young. What were we going to do, now that we found the big bird was the question, just having witnessed it rip through almost ten men just trying to feed its young breakfast? We stopped close enough to the nest to get a glimpse of what was happening, hopefully still far enough away not to be seen by the egret's watchful eye.

Our resourceful new addition to the group pulled out a rope with a grappling hook on it. Whirling it in the air before tossing it up into a tree, he shimmied his way up to get a better view.

I could only imagine the nightmare, first the feathered nursemaid would feed the smaller chicks by regurgitating the men in its gullet. Then the large bird will shake its head and the men on its beak will fall into the nest. Our lookout yelled down "They're still alive." We did not need the play by play, we could tell by their cries. Our scout turned his head. All he could do was stand there, his friends dying, watching nature happen, a loyal mother feeding its young.

I pulled out one of the clay spheres holding it up, grabbing the hilt of my sword for reassurance in the other hand. "Maybe we can use these."

Before I could finish my sentence, a large beaded black leg stabilized itself right next to me. I looked up in time to see the sharp beak it was attached to, come out of nowhere, piercing my thigh. Eyiyo started whacking at its leg, it sounded like he was hitting a hardwood tree, as I was taken for a ride high above the forest canopy.

I whacked the bird with my weapon, but the sword vibrated free of my hand once I made contact with the hard beak. Already having a clay sphere in my other hand I held my breath, slamming it against the beak that impaled me, aiming for the hole near its huge lifeless eye. Green powder went everywhere.

The huge bird legs buckled, all I could do was hug the beak that I was attached to. The long neck of the bird got caught up on the branch of a tree as it fell, breaking my fall. The head jerked, sliding me off the beak abruptly. I dropped to the ground not ten feet away from where I stood five minutes before. It happened so fast, everybody just gawked. Ruining my moment, the new guy said. "That worked great got any more of those."

There was a brief silence as the mother bird walked away from the nest, focusing on us and its mate that had fallen. Pulling another sphere from my bag, I handed it to the woodsman saying. "That's how. Now it's your turn. Make it count."

Lou was rattling off 'Come to papa," "Ropadeop!" casting a spell on the rope still hanging from above. Powered with magical influence it snapped tight between two trees. Entangling the bird's legs, it fell forward toward us, its beak smashing down in the middle of our group. The man took the sphere in his hand effortlessly crimsoning the egrets beak. The area around him was engulfed in the green powder. His last words were, "That was easy enough." Just as the giant bird closed its eye, he blacked out falling over the deadly beak that took so many of his friends.

Eyiyo pulled out his blades, "We will eat well tonight," dispatching the dangerous animals before they could awaken.

Kat asked us to stay quiet. She could hear one man still calling out. Suspecting the mother bird placed the injured men by the largest chicks, so they could practice killing live pray. Everyone refocused on the man screaming for help. Preoccupied, I don't think anyone noticed my leg was healing itself. I stood up, following the group toward the nest.

As we got closer we could see the nest was twenty feet wide and thirty feet up. The lower branches of the tree were broken off, making the possibility of climbing it slim, even if we could get close enough, most of the area around the tree was muddy and littered with broken branches or covered by bird dung filled with the bones of bears, deer and the unfortunate.

My belt started to sound off again in several high pitched tones. Oddly enough I understood what it was saying. It was as if the belt was teaching me.

I remembered the young acolytes working on the road just outside Suxen Falls. Reaching down touching the ground, "Dig."

Where the mighty tree was firmly rooted into the ground, a hole started to form. Soon the roots were exposed, the hole grew deeper. The river water rushed in eroding the dirt even quicker, loosening the roots even more. The weight of the nest was helping, the tree started to topple. The huge nest came crashing down, spilling its contents. The gigantic chicks fell into the water and were washed away in the current. The man was thrown a life line and pulled to safety by Lou. The ground beneath us was starting to give, as the gushing water continued to sweep the tree, the nest, and the rest of our problem away.

I healed the injured man who introduced himself as Eian. Shortly after his friend awoke, we found out his name was Gavin. After thanking us for our troubles, Eian told us their party was headed for Suxen Falls to deliver a relic to Cornelius, one of the head priests at the Temple. They were relieved the item was safe, tightly wrapped away in Eian's backpack, pulling it out briefly, double checking to make sure it was not damaged.

Surprised to see the relic they mentioned was just a twisted piece of metal. I looked at Lou, it looked very familiar. Lou reached into the chest pulling out the twisted piece of metal we found. They were similar, a slightly different configuration, but they defiantly were made of the same metal and the same design.

Now that the pieces were brought together, we could tell they were part of something larger. I asked if I could hold them. Just touching them made my fingers tingle, holding both pieces the sensation doubled. I held them together at different angles like a three dimensional puzzle. Kat was standing over my shoulder. "No put them together like . . ." In the middle of her sentence, something moved and they locked becoming one! No more were there two pieces. They were one, seamless where they connected. As soon as the connection was made, I felt a serge of power pass through me.

Together they made my favorite shape they looked like a piece of pie with a line through it. Could this be part of the symbol I keep seeing in my dreams?

No one had noticed till they were upon me. I was intensely lost in my new toy. Three floating lighted spheres had somehow crossed the lake. They hovered above me, and then randomly darted in odd directions, checking out everybody else. Finally returning to me and the item I held.

Eyiyo took a swing at one. His blade went right through it. We were all alarmed. The lights seem to be alive or even more so, dead. Like a spirit, no form, pure celestial light only. We could not touch them. As fast as they appeared, they flew up and over the trees into the jungle flying in a group, but without a formation. Independent of each other, like a group of children playing tag. I wondered how long had they been watching us? I placed the metal part in my bag.

We told Eian what we knew. Soldiers, man-eating plants and massive snake eyed armies descending on Suxen falls. He said he was aware of the soldiers and shocked they moved so far up the coast. They were also aware of the strange plants that were popping up in the forest. He asked us if we wanted to go back to his village. He believed his elders may be able to give us some insight into what is causing these changes. His elders would also want to see what happened to that metal relic he was entrusted with.

The woodsman asked if we would help take some of the meat back to their village. There were many hungry mouths to feed. Eian hoped Telib would not be so disappointed, if they didn't return empty handed.

Gavin chimed in, "It would be an insult to Avenu to let this bounty go to waste."

Eian and Gavin were very resourceful. With a couple pieces of cloth and a few logs they created two stretchers, cutting off as much meat as we could carry.

Before we left Lou grabbed a bunch of the long black feathers, and a handful of smaller white ones. Bauble was sitting guard back at camp when we returned to retrieve our chest. Lou and I carried one stretcher. Eian and Gavin carried the other. Eyiyo picked up the chest and Kat lead the way.

Chapter Twelve

Control

The woodsmen camp was not too far, it was in a dense part of the forest not yet infected by the ravaging plants. At first all I could see were several smaller huts, temporary storage, for tools, weapons, and food; all strategically placed to not allow a direct line of sight till we were close. There was one central fire in a cleared area, here the people gathered. Together, they engaged in cooking, weaving, anything that needed to be done for the survival of the group.

Gavin said the Drazzi scouts would not waste their time for only a few people, so the majority of the huts are hidden high up in the trees. Looking up I saw hundreds of small enclosures, built with rope, and logs. Larger, straight logs were used to make the floors and basic frames, while the thin misshaped branches were dedicated to the roofs. The side-walls were made of weaved reeds, that grow on the riverbanks. Eian acknowledged the necessity for camouflage, it is better to remain unseen for many reasons.

We were greeted by many children eager to see different faces. They relieved us of our burden. Stretchers of breast meat were taken to several workers who sat by the fire, they immediately started cutting and preparing the meat. We were made more than welcome.

One little girl named Mia, who had big brown round eyes like most Selvains, gave Kat a necklace made of reeds and a shiny river rock. The center stone had two halves spiraled with different colors. Mia laughed as she told Kat, "The River has brought the two elements together, making one."

The elders were more concerned with questions than cordial greetings. Eian was quickly ushered into a private meeting to explain why he had returned so quickly and where the missing members of his party were.

We gathered with the others around the campfire. Gavin explained a lot of things, describing his clan as forest folk who have forsaken the big cities. Many of them called outlaw by the Commonwealth, all of them unwanted for one reason or another.

Because of their village's neutral status they had befriended the Selvain leaders, and had begun regular trade in the past. They learned to share the forest together. Many had adopted Selvain ways and beliefs, their religion a mixture of the two cultures. Some men had even taken Selvain brides, having half-bred children. Outcasts welcome nowhere but here.

He went on to tell us what he knew about the strange happenings. The Selvain's believed a goddess had come from the temple in Avalon. She promised to show their leaders a magical land, where castles are built in the arms of the Sacred Tree, where rooms are filled with riches beyond their belief. She was able to organize several of the Selvain villages into her own personal militia. The more she showed them new weapons and powerful spells, the less they made contact with Gavin's village. Eventually all trade stopped!

At the Queen's command the Selvain leaders were forced to move their villages to the deserted areas by the old temple. The people of Gavin's village knew they were not welcome, but never thought they would be attacked. Their natural distrust of others allowed many of them to escape to the woods. But not everybody made it out. Some were taken and used as test subjects. The self-proclaimed Queen was perfecting her method to alter people into the abominations she uses as soldiers. Without warning or provocation, she waged war upon the citizens of the Commonwealth. Newhaven fell in days.

Gavin claimed she draws strength from the crystal she wears around her neck. It provides her with a connection to the evil spirits that help guide her.

Eyiyo interrupted as if someone finally said something that had interest to him. "Is the crystal jet black, so dark it stares back at you?"

Gavin sighed, "Yeah that's it."

Eyiyo bolstered, "It must be destroyed."

Continuing his tale of woe, Gavin said those who escaped her initial attacks eventually hid here in the forest. As the Queen set her sights on more populated areas, systematically moving up the road taking Hanson and Maguire, she had traveled all the way to Nautica. There she acquired a large ship to transfer the troops, back and forth between Newhaven and Nautica. Gavin had no information on were she was headed from there. We were able to confirm his suspicions that she had moved her forces as far up as Kelideco and believed her sights were set on Suxen Falls.

He went on to say the priests chant day and night in the old town square by the temple. Since they started deadly plants and animals have been uprooting the forest, making travel along the main road unbearable. That is why she left the high road deserted. We could attest to that part of Gavin's story, as we rehashed what we had seen in the last couple days.

Eyiyo asked Gavin, "Where is the Queen now."

He answered, "She is gathering troops by the temple."

Lou clarified "The troops come off the ship in Newhaven? Not leaving on the ship?"

"No, the soldiers are gathering at the temple. They are building a small keep there."

We were led into one of the larger huts. It was filled with those who were injured. Many had severe burns. I stopped and asked one man what happened. Gavin interrupted, "He was burned when they attempted to rescue those that were captured." Pointing out the severity of Shabeir's wounds, there was little hope for recovery.

Far in the back, behind a woven divider, was a disfigured man. Scales covered half his face, they ran down his back ending at his tail bone, which was enlarged creating a partially formed tail. It forced him to arch his back. He looked painfully contorted. He was mostly covered by scales but still had patches of human skin and one arm with an oversized claw. Even though his legs still showed some human characteristics they were twisted making it impossible for him to walk. Telib was a failed experiment the only one to make it out alive. He looked at us with one reptile like eye. His forked tongue, jagged sharp teeth, and mangled half human jaw made his speech barely recognizable.

Lou asked if he could hear us. The creature answered "Yes-sss!"

When he saw Lou, his face lit up. "I know of yo-ou, your name is-ss not Lou, its-ss Luscious, Luscious Wicket. My name is Te-lib I am the las-st of the Temple Guardians. I was there when Marcel your fa-father first vis-sited the temple many years-s ago. Before I die I must confess-ss to sa-someone what I know."

In a sloppy slurred raspy voice he continued. "We-ee were aware the council in Sa-Suxen Falls was s-sending down a group to s-study at our t-temple. We removed what we be-e-lieved to be the temple's key, stashing it in the woods, we feared the council-l would f-find it, and take it back to S-Suxen Falls to exploit its power."

Telib was hard to understand but we got the picture. He was talking about the twisted piece of metal. It was written that the metal shard be only entrusted to a true Temple Guardian, to all others it will bring misfortune.

Telib was ranting a little but from what I could make out, it was also written that to control the shard you must let go. Not everything he said made sense.

Now, Telib feared the holy item could fall into the wrong hands if it remained here. Damming himself, "If-ff only we-ee would have listened to the s-scripture literally." Realizing their dire mistake, he cursed the day the Guardians decided to hide it from the council. He believed it may be too late to discover what true power it possesses, if any at all.

Lou was glued to each word Telib said, especially as he described the day his father came to Avalon. When Marcel arrived he was accompanied by two other mages, Finwell and Bolotar, graduates of the arcane. Three priests came as well each representing a different spiritual house, Kayal Tanzir, and Cornelius. The six men represented the Council and were sent to learn what they could about the temple's energy. Telib said they followed their daily rituals and prayed as always, in the fashion described in the Holy Book of Time.

It was written on each full moon they were to make an offering in the temple. Gold would bring prosperity. Silver will send good fortune. Wine or ale bestows happiness. Wheat and grains entrust a strong harvest, while fruits or vegetables brought the promise of fertility. The offerings were made freely by those who wished to bring these blessings into their lives.

Telib did mention, that those who do not make an offering of goodwill, brought bad luck upon themselves and those around them. It was also said less than ample sacrifice would cause the wretched to return to feed upon our very souls. The Temple Guardians lived by the scripture in their Holy Book, adhering to these words literally, their duties a gesture of good will and a responsibility that came with a dire warning. The group sent by the council did not think the same.

Marcel and the other acolytes studied the priest's rituals, discovering a word they thought was a verbal catalyst that activated the temple. Lou's father believed the temple was a teleport device. The group wanted to place themselves in the offering area, and activate the mechanism. This did not stand well with the guardians.

Telib grew restless. "There were warnings-s!" Clearly it was written, no man shall enter the area of offering. Telib and the others were determined not to allow them to misuse their rituals. There would be terrible consequences if they desecrated the temple. The curse of the dragon would return.

The council's men would not listen. The one called Finwell cast a spell on several of the Temple Guardians making their minds meander. They lost their focus and wandered off. Telib writhed in agony as he moved suddenly. "Agains-st our wishes-ss, the coun-cil's lackeys, conducted their ex-s-periment, that is what brought this aff-fliction. upon us-ss all."

The mages Bolotar and Marcel with Priests Kayal and Tanzir were to step in the circle. Cornelius and Finwell were to activate the temple, then report back to the council in Suxen Falls, whether or not things went awry. Telib bowed his head as he continued, recalling how they were taken in a flash of light, disappearing in the same manner as their offerings.

Two weeks later just before harvest moon, Lou's father came back through the temple. It was late night, the surrounding streets were deserted. As always two Temple Guardians were present and preparing for the next offering with meditation and prayer. Telib was one of those men. He paused as a tear ran down his human cheek. He reflected back on the night thousands of people lost their lives. We all heard the stories growing up about the night everything turned to fire.

Telib said it all started with a couple of quick silent flashes, and then someone appeared. It was Marcel, Lou's father. He ran out of the temple, down the steps, and into the street at the edge of the court yard below. There was another series of flashes, and two Selvain's dressed in blue and green robes came running out of the temple after him. One final flash and a third Selvain appeared. He wore a black robe with highly detailed gold embroidery across the back and curved silver spikes on his arms and shoulders. The first two were already in the street in pursuit of Lou's father.

Marcel stood his ground and cast what looked like a circle of protection. A double lined glowing symbol appeared under his feet. The Selvains down in the street summoned what sounded like a small version of what Eyiyo had described as an earth elemental, a large creature made of mud and rocks that rose from the ground, cutting through the stone pavement as it moved.

It approached Lou's father with its arms wailing, but could not invade the invisible barrier Marcel had created. The Selvain in the dark robe moved to the bottom of the steps and lifted his arms. Emanating from the spikes in his outfit and surging from his fingertips shot a bolt of lightning. The bright beam of energy shot toward Lou's father, but he cleverly pulled out a glass prism reflecting the bolt at the rocky crusader who burst into a pile of rubble. The beams arcing currant continued randomly hitting the Selvains in the blue and green robes. One of them was badly hurt.

Lou's father threw a stream of fire at the dark wizard who had tried to electrocute him. The robed figure waived his hand, somehow drawing the energy of the spell into the spikes on his shoulders. They turned red hot before bursting into flames. The Selvain that was not hurt and was still standing nearby Marcel, banged his staff on the ground, opening up a crack in the road splitting the circle of protection. Lou's father was thrown.

Telib paused, "What happened next-t was h-horrible."

The Selvain in the dark robe called on some kind of dark creature. The flames coming from the spikes on his shoulders turned purple letting off a thick smoke that transformed into a floating mass. The spikes lost their glow as the eyes of the apparition opened. It looked like he used the energy he had harnessed from Marcel's spell to summon some kind of evil specter. All Telib could make out was the dark silhouette of a black cloak. It floated across the way toward Lou's father.

He pulled a talisman from his cloak, tossing it on the floor under the creature. The small trinket sparkled and emitted different colors. Then it started to hover and spin in the air creating some kind of vortex, sucking the hideous creature into the tiny amulet, before falling to the ground.

The Selvain that had knocked Marcel to the ground had now somehow transported himself right next to him, throwing a net over him. As the net hit the ground the edges dug in, pinning Lou's father down. Marcel started to glow like a piece of hot metal, Telib thought Lou's father had created some sort of fire armor. It was burning the ropes away.

Telib looked Lou in the face, "Your f-father fought brilliantly, there were ju-st too many of them." The Selvain mage by this time was right on top of Marcel. He held his hand in his face and a blinding light shot forward from it. Marcel tried to cover his eyes but it was too late. He started waiving his hands as if he could not see. The dark figure took control shackling Marcel magically with ropes that seemed to grow around his wrists, while the other healed his friend.

With all the commotion, quite a crowd had gathered, some recognized your father and were advancing to his aide. The three Selvain's stood in a circle and harnessed their energy in a way Telib had never seen. The skies started to glow red. Balls of destruction rained from the sky. Thousands of exploding meteorites of all sizes showered the town with flames. Those responsible for casting the spell ran back into the temple.

Telib took refuge in the only safe place. He did nothing as the Selvain's took their prize, escaping the same way they came. He was the only surviving witness that knew the truth.

Telib became distraught, ashamed of his actions. The guilt he had held for so many years finally broke him down. "I deserve this-ss wretched fate, that has-s been be-stowed upon me."

Even I knew the rest. The people outside were incinerated in minutes but the fire storm lasted for hours. The devastation encompassed the entire city.

In the morning the city was destroyed. The rectory where Telib's brothers slept was burned to the ground, along with his salvation and all who he called brother.

Everyone, except the dead, left the city. Telib's world had fallen apart. He did not know what to do, taking refuge in the forest where the priests had hidden the twisted piece of metal, the sacred shard from the temple. He started a new life where he could still keep his honor. He took a vow to uphold his duty and protect the shard, always watching over the temple from afar. He founded the village, its laws, and their creed.

We showed Telib the merged pieces of metal. "What-t, did you do-oo to make it grow?"

Lou dumbfounded, "It merged with a similar piece we had in our possession."

Telib struggled to hold up his hand. "We-ee were wrong. We ss-should have given the piece-ss to your father. I can no longer pro-tect it myself. I will entrus-st it to you, Luscious-ss. I know you will put it in the right-t hands. Promise me you will put it in the right-t hands." Lou nodded.

I tried to heal Telib but he was not truly injured. His mutations were caused by something unnatural, beyond my abilities. But, I was able to heal many of the others including Shabeir, the brave man who risked everything to save Telib. Grabbing my arm, thanking me for his life, he pulled a tattered book from under his bunk, giving it to me he said, "We took it from her!"

Later that evening, I reached in Lou's chest, picturing his magic magnifying glass in my mind. The one used to decipher the silk flag. Holding it in my hand, I opened the book. It was a diary. Her diary! I started to read, out loud.

"The last few days of being in Etlanthia are still blurry to me. I remember informing the high council of changes to expect after my inauguration in the spring. I was turning twenty five. The council knew I was the rightful heir to the throne. I am the only living bloodline to the ancient kings.

Odell the Regent, stood as head of the high council long enough, having had control over my kingdom since my family was murdered. I was only seven when the regent was placed in charge to help make decisions until I became of age. They all were realizing, the day they thought would never come was almost here. I had every intention of reclaiming the throne. I guess they figured I was just a young girl they could control and bully. They never thought I would stand up against Odell and his council. How could they be so ignorant, to believe I would not take my place as their Queen? As if a mundane, would be left to rule the Elvin kingdom forever.

Phineous, and Bentlodin, who also sat on the council, both turned their backs, while Odell ordered my private guard Myles to subdue me. They all took part in my assassination. Myles disappointed me the worst. He had watched over me like a father, raised me as if I was his own. He was a friend to my family, and my mentor, until he restrained me with five of his best men, under the direct order of the Regent.

They sewed my lips shut, then I was hogtied and placed in a bag, dumped out where my people conducted trade, and collected tribute, from the indigent races that plague our world. I had been to the temple in Brentwood many times as a girl to watch and learn. Later to overlook the accounting of Cronin Thistlefoot, who probably earned his seat on the council with this act of lunacy.

Their method was cruel, but they were wise to have silenced me, I was privy to the intricate workings and the different commands that teleported whatever or whomever lay in the circle at the temple's center. Through the years I had met many of the dignitaries from the races we did trade with, Gnomes, Pelkins, Centori. I had visited the different realms on many occasions.

There I lay at the mercy of all who would benefit from my disappearance, or stood to lose out when I gained control of my father's empire. Even that weasel Cronin was present. I swear I will make them all pay.

They were arguing over exactly what to do when Phineous struck the first blow. Then all of them started kicking me. Yelling "We will do what must be done, she can't be left alive." Bound and gagged, I was given no chance to defend myself. I remember feeling one rib break, then another, as my leg was snapped in two places. The piercing pain of a small dagger thrust into my back, was nothing compared to the betrayal I felt in my heart. Then a boot came down on my head, and I blacked out.

It has been 35 days since I arrived here. I am writing this memoir at the request of my keeper, Emi. But also to remind myself of exactly who will be accountable, for the indignities I have suffered, when I return home.

I was left for dead, alone, unable to call out, lying in a pool of my own blood, on a cold hard floor, paralyzed! I passed out over and over, each time my eyes focused and I gained consciousness, I realized I was far from home beyond the reach of any help. The walls of this temple were not the same as the temple walls that lay in the heart of the Elvin city of Brentwood. It was overgrown with vines that grew through the doors and into the staging area. This temple was not controlled by any allies of Etlanthia I had known.

There is no way to know how long I lay there making blood bubbles, gasping for air. I wondered, was this how I was going to die? Left to rot in a strange land in a deserted temple?

I was found by a race of creatures I had never seen before. I could only describe them as elf size insects. They looked like giant praying mantises. I thought what now, was I going to be bug food? But I was left untouched.

They must have brought my saviors, the humanoids that collected me, Noble beings, I have come to know as Dross. These creatures were similar in stature to the lizard men who inhabit the cliffs where the seals gather by the shores in the southern tip of my kingdom. Their heads were larger and more defined, still bony, scaled faces. I do not know how long I laid there waiting for death to come, as they stood meditating, standing in judgment over me, and at the time I did not understand why these miraculous creatures chose to spare my life.

Some bandaged me while others prayed. Spreading strange jells over my bruises, placing some sort of larva in the deep wounds, I could not see them, but I could feel them crawling under my skin inside the bandages. What still sticks in my mind, was when they re-broke the bones in my legs and left arm placing them in splints, just so I could be laid flat. When your own bones break there is a popping sound, I could here it over the roar of voices, when my legs were broke. It was even louder in the silence, as my bones were reset to heal straight.

I had to be pealed from the floor, my dried blood was like an adhesive, pulling at my face. Finally they cut the stitches that held my lips shut, my shattered jaw was pulled open to release the clump of mucus and blood that had filled my mouth. I was placed on a stretcher and carried out of the temple.

Outside, I could see this temple lay in the heart of a bizarre jungle, filled with ominous looking plants and animals. It was a day's journey before we finally reached our destination. The farther we traveled the more I came to realize this was not a bad dream. Those I truly trusted had turned against me.

A giant set of doors built into the side of a mountain was pulled open, by several large pack animals. I did not think any place could be as uncomfortable as the hot and humid jungle, until I was brought inside where the temperature was compounded by the stale air and confined spaces. My senses were overwhelmed by a musky smell that kept me alert as I was carried through a maze of mildew covered catacombs, passing what looked like thousands of unnamed tombs set into the walls.

Finally the endless supply of hallways broke into a huge cavern with an underground lake. In the center there was a small island. I was carried over a rickety bridge made out of the skeleton of a gigantic snake. Face up, all I could see was the tips of the rib bones as I was carried across to the other side. Did those impaled on the bony spikes, deserve their ill fated end? I lay hoping to avoid the same demise as those I was paraded by.

The island was not a real island at all. The ground was made entirely out of metal, not one piece, but thousands of coins, goblets, candlesticks, rings, gems, swords of all sizes, plate mail, ring mail, all types of metal valuables, a true treasure horde. Not many of the items were usable. Most had been trampled, or fused together with great heat. I was flabbergasted. There was more treasure dumped here than in my whole kingdom, and I could only imagine how many more riches lay beneath the water. I was finally laid to rest on the gleaming shore, abandoned once again.

As I waited there drifting in and out, in agonizing pain, my mind began to wander. I had heard of treasure troves like this, but only in stories. Tales told to me by Myles and the other nannies as a child, Most of the time they were associated with tragic endings, great warriors who had fallen in battle. They were always guarded by . . .

First I heard the jangling of metal crushing together as she approached. Her massive feet dug into the mounds of riches, as she pulled her talons from the ground scattering piles of metal in every direction. As the beat of footsteps came closer, it reminded me of the gentle sound rain makes.

Standing above me was what only could be described as a red dragon. I had seen paintings and pictures in books, but there is nothing that can prepare one's self for its true grandeur. Its teeth were longer than my arm; its mouth could easily swallow me whole. Starting at it's looming nostrils, were rows of horns, trailing over its calculating eyes, they connected to a large bony plate that resembled a raised crown on the back of it's head.

In my heart I wanted to run as fear overtook my body. But I was paralyzed, strapped to a stretcher, and presented like an offering to the mammoth beast. Not at all what I expected happened next. It spoke to me in a soothing intelligent voice, in my own native tongue.

Whispering she said "You are an elf."

Even if I wasn't held down, I was not physically able to move. I was only able to look straight up.

Terror engraved each word she spoke into my every thought. She said to me, "My name is Coro'anathio'lese'ruso'tralapanthan'k elso'de'emi,

Surveyor of time, Keeper of the Fire's of Kobol, Controller of Treachery, and Creator of Misery. But you may call me Emi, for short. I have waited your life time to meet you Mytoka! Rightful heir to the throne of the mighty Elvin Empire, Daughter of Angus Foehammer Keeper of Time, first born son of Kodas the Sequoyan Tree Healer and once the mighty King of the Elvin Realm. I am here to answer your prayers. Do not fear me. I can heal you, I can help you thwart those who have wronged you, and I can return you to your rightful place among the elves. Together we can tackle any task set before you to accomplish these goals. If this is what you wish."

She went on to say, "I will show you how to create an army. I will give you the weapons you need to reclaim what is rightfully yours. And for this favor you ask of me, all I would humbly accept in return would be a small gesture of your appreciation."

Emi held up a clawed finger to her massive mouth, like an adult shushing a child, "You don't have to say anything, just blink your eyes. If this is what you wish. If not, I can let you die right here."

I woke healed but vary weak. I was clothed, fed and bathed and given all the necessities to survive in this brutal world. I was granted access to a library of books and a laboratory while my wounds healed and I regained my strength.

The Dross that tended to my needs stayed silent, obeying Emi's orders in detail without question. The only sound her servants made was the sound of song, as they gathered in daily prayer or private meditation.

The library was filled with manuscripts written by races I had never heard of. I was allowed to study ancient arcane texts, reading passages out of books so big it took three servants to turn the pages without damaging the brittle documents. My gracious host Emi has allowed me to take possession of one weapon, and one piece of armor from the substantial fortune she had accumulated. I hope I will be able to repay her she has not only given me my life, but hope as well.

Day 39. It took days to cover the small metallic island she created, but I found a magical breast plate made entirely out of gold. As well as a staff made by a wizard long dead from a culture time had forgotten. The staff's construction is brilliant. It allows multiple spell components to be placed in its many modular sections. Once the component is held to the staff it is immediately taken in and preserved, suspended in a dark piece of amber along the shaft.

Day 63. In the last few weeks I have been shown Emi's realm. The land I am in consists of a volcanic mountain range. A group of Islands many with active volcanoes. All that is left of the biggest volcano is a huge crater with water in the center. It looks like a submerged dark red eggshell cut in half then filled with water. Emi lives on the second largest island. Through the years the Dross carved many corridors connecting a cluster of natural caverns building her lair.

My generous host cast teleportation spells taking us to places impossible to reach by foot. This allowed us to cover more ground in less time. I was gathering a list given to me by Emi of rocks containing strange properties, rare plants, and other living specimens to use as spell components for the task ahead of me.

On one of our trips outside the underground city, I was sent to gather a large clear crystal. I was taken to a cavern that had fascinating mineral formations. As we plundered the cave for specific list of essential items, we found groups of stalactites, stalagmites, all covered in algae that grew in a rainbow of colors, bright enough to illuminate the caves. There were also many hot springs turning some of the smaller caverns into blistering hot saunas or deadly gas chambers. The Dross priests cast spells that protected us from the searing noxious fumes.

I think the entire continent had thermal activity. After extracting the rare crystal we also gathered samples of the abundant array of fungi from the oddly shaped rock configurations.

Any time we left the safety of the secluded compound we were under constant threat. The island was inhabited with treacherous life forms. Back home in the Library of Etlanthia were reconstructed bones of similar creatures our scholars pulled from the bedrock of this planet. Here they roamed as kings in this bizarre jungle.

The Dross keep the giant animals at bay by using the spores from a particular type of mushroom that commonly grow on the island. I found I was immune to the mushrooms drowsy affects. Any dangerous creature that caught our party in their gaze was dosed quickly putting them to sleep.

Even the plants here were lethal. Whether it was the three inch thorns or poisonous leaves, everything had an unfriendly touch. Nothing in this alien terrain was completely defenseless. Many were deadly some plants just came alive their attacks were as ferocious as any animal. The dross called them Snapdragons, growing as large as the local supply of prey would allow. They were usually found along game trails, digesting large animals caught in their jaws.

It was ironic to find some of the smallest organisms more dangerous than some of the largest wild beasts. We crossed this inhospitable terrain to an especially hazardous part of the island to find a live specimen, a rare centipede, described in one of the ancient texts. That morning before we left, I was invited to take part in a Dross ceremony to honor their dead. They sang a dark tale and drank a sweet tea made of a pink flower.

This specific pest we were hunting had a similar hierarchy one finds in an ant colony or a bee hive. I needed to collect the bug queen, which was no easy task. This bug was known to be aggressive and extremely hostile.

The soldier centipedes excreted a toxin that gave control over their victims to the queen. Typically the easily subdued would return to the queen's nest which was usually a small cave, hollow tree or an abandoned burrow of a previous victim.

The lucky would become the food supply for the colony. Others suffered a different fate. The Queen used them as a receptacle to lay her eggs. Still under her mental influence she simply had them return to their herds, flocks or packs carrying her foul brood. Once the eggs hatched inside the unwary carrier, the infectious centipedes would eat there way out of the victim, only to bring its siblings home.

One bug queen could control a large territory, a vicious little creature able to rule at the top of any food chain.

There was an old text written in Dross I found in Emi's library. The fall of their civilization was caused by one such infestation. They were almost completely wiped out.

The script referred to the tiny monsters as Gratsed, meaning mind devil. The creatures mainly thrive on mindless, wild animals that inhabit the jungles, but do not discriminate against intelligent beings. The Gratsed were able to annihilate entire colonies of Dross. They never imagined their worse nightmare was unwittingly carried to the next town by the same people trying to escape the swarms.

It was by luck, the Dross found a lifesaving plant, ingesting the pink flower petals made them immune to the Gratsed Queen's control. Those who are left owe their lives to a monastery in a small town where the priests used the flower in their religious rituals. Many of the locals used the flower petals as a spice for everyday cooking. They were untouched by the Gratsed advances. By the time they realized the plant's redeeming qualities, it was too late. The devastation was complete. Their numbers have never returned. This bug is now harvested as a food source, a delicacy for Emi.

We were finally finished with Emi's demented shopping list; I wondered what would be next?

Day 71. I find Emi to be an excellent teacher; she has been so patient with me. She has taught me several spells from her collection of old tomes and she has asked me to research several more. With all the spells that allowed mental control of their victims made available to me by use of these magical texts, I wonder why I was not the focal point of this brand of manipulation. It was as if a willing cohort whose actions are chosen freely is needed to perform the favor that will be asked of me.

I do not care! My quest is righteous. My vengeance is noble. No matter what it takes or whoever has to fall for my glory, I will take the position I was born too, Queen of Etlanthia, Ruler of the Elvin Realm.

Day 74. Today, I was taken to a stadium that was no more than a large cavern. There were scorch marks on the walls as if great battles had been fought there. Some sort of luminous rock was embedded in the floor, creating several glowing symbols and a center ring permanently lighting up the arena.

The day before I was shown and told to study a specific spell. This was done at the request of my mentor, Emi, who was focusing me on what I needed to know, to prepare me for today.

I knew what was expected of me, I held the clear crystal we had gathered above my head. Emi smiled as she oversaw the entertainment from the comfort of a private balcony. She sat smoking a large water pipe, as a group of robed Dross placed a massive book on a metal stand, opening it to the right page.

There were two other sizable roosts. One was empty. In the other, I thought I could see another dragon, not as large as Emi, but the whites in its eyes leering in the shadow gave its presence away.

Many Dross had gathered, gawking down from even smaller raised balconies scattered throughout the cave. They were cheering me on. Emi started reading from the huge ancient books, causing the illuminated stones under my feet to turn different colors, ultimately changing to a red hue. As the light they projected intensified, I set the crystal on the ground in front of me, just outside the main circle where I stood. The crowd went wild!

Emi was summoning a being from a dimension so void of light that ice ran through its veins. Its eyes looked like blue sapphires, clear, empty, reflecting the tiniest amount of light back at you. His gaze was so cold it chilled my bones. He towered over me standing at least thirty feet tall. When the creature spoke he exhaled a cold fog, immediately dropping the temperature on the showground floor. In an angry masculine voice that shook the ground I heard "Why have I been summoned here." A large roar of anticipation came from the balconies high above the battlefield.

I held my staff above my head and started my incantation. Areas of the staff lit up, highlighting the spell components encased inside its shaft that were needed to imprison the enraged fiend. Sparks flew as a funnel of light appeared. The creature tried to strike me with its tail as his dark wings rose up, he became even more enraged as he realized he was confined to the area within the round symbol on the ground.

The spell was trapping his life energy. His rage was being drawn into the crystal that lay at my feet. The crystal was no longer clear it was turning midnight blue, like someone was injecting a dark liquid into the transparent stone. Emi watched, as her wicked laughter was almost drowned out by the sound of the spectators echoing applause. The creature tried to use its freezing breath to stop me. Its frenzied attack was thwarted by the invisible barrier around him. He was caged like an animal, allowing me to finish my work, capturing his soul. The crystal was now almost jet black as his very essence was pulled into it. The hideous creature shrank until only a shell of a man was left.

My final task was to send what was left of him back to the realm from which he was summoned. I picked the dark crystal up, holding it for all to see. My actions were awarded with grand review. I did not know why, only that I would need this magical item to achieve my goals.

Later Emi congratulated me on a performance well done. She said I was almost ready to be shown specifically how my exploits were to help me accomplish the task ahead. I hope I won't have to wait too long.

Day 78. Another piece of the puzzle was unveiled to me earlier this evening. With some of the unique plant specimens we gathered, Emi showed me how to make a permanent poly-morph potion. Giving me a vile of her own blood to complete her insidious recipe, she sighed with content gazing at the ingenious concoction, "This will transform even the feeblest farmer into a physically powerful more agile fighter." she roared.

I was shown how to inject the strange brew into the venom sacks of the centipedes.

As we worked she told me there were many things the dark crystal would empower its possessor to do. She said it gave me the ability to conjure a magical flame from the dark creature's realm that was cold to the touch. With this blue flame I could encase live creatures like the Gratsed in a ceramic shell without burning them in the process.

I was starting to understand what I signed up for. If I could somehow control the Gratsed Queen, all I would need would be an ample supply of warm bodies? I am sure that will be my next lesson.

Day 89. That was not the lesson I expected. Emi whose size always allowed her to loom over me, asked me to kneel before her. I did as she asked.

Placing the end of her long razor sharp talon on the back of my head she said, "This may sting a little."

She tapped down penetrating my skull. Lifting me off the ground, I felt like a puppet on the tip of her finger. My body seemed to go limp. She placed me face down on a table with lights suspended above it. My arms, legs, and head, were strapped down allowing me no motion. I could feel the cold tip of her razor sharp nail peeling away the skin and bone from my brain. It felt like a thousand pins walking in my mind. Needless to say the pain I was in was not Emi's concern.

I could taste my own warm blood in my mouth again, as the red liquid dripped down my face pooling on the table. Somewhere between the excruciating pain and the loss of blood I let go.

To no surprise I awoke with a headache. I was told seven days had passed. Reaching back to feel what she had done I found most of my hair was gone, and it felt like I was wearing a hat with grooves. It was the body of the Gratsed Queen. Somehow she had grafted it to my head.

I did not remember signing up for this. Did I really know what I signed up for, having never read the small print? No matter, there is no turning back, I am indebted to Emi no matter what was in store for me.

Day 94. It was not the coronation I always dreamed of but yesterday I had been truly crowned a Queen. A metal guard was attached to my forehead to protect Emi's handy work. I feel good, the headaches have passed It is a strange feeling. I can feel the presence of others in my head all the time. I know somehow I am in control of them, it is a powerful feeling. I don't know what will be asked next of me, but I must remind myself I owe everything to her. For all I have suffered, I will have my revenge.

Day 125. It's been over a month since my last notation in this journal, the day had come for me to leave. Emi had done as she promised I have been armed with the weapons I needed to gather my army. Emi had chosen a temple that reeked of humans, suggesting to me that they would make an easy target. Low intelligence not much resistance. There was also a small colony of feral elves that may be willing to help, without the use of magic.

Finally I was told what was expected of me, for making this unnatural deal with Emi the horned devil. I was given a box with three urns of which laid the remains of deceased Dross holy men. They were to be laid to rest using a specific ritual I was to perform during the burial. I was also given one large crate to care for as well, to be delivered into the heart of Mount Helos.

Day 126. This will probable be my last entry in this journal. Yesterday I was escorted back to the forest temple. The Dross started to chant and then they were gone. Or should I say I was transported to a land I had never been to before. Just like Emi had said. I had found a group of my kind and they have accepted me into their clan. Other than a slight accent we have been able to communicate just fine. The rest is up to me."

CHAPTER THIRTEEN

The Jokes On Who!

The diary was quite a bit of information to take in. One thing was clear we needed to stop Queen Mytoka.

That night, Lou took me aside, he told me how proud Alester would be of me, if he was here with us. Just in the last few days Lou could see my mindset was changing, I was being led down a spiritual path and with that came the burden of responsibility.

He went on to say, Kat has him to use as a guide, to help in her studies. But I was carrying the torch alone. He wanted me to know I could come to him, if I had questions. He didn't promise he could always help, only that he might be able to point me in the right direction. He did not claim to know a lot about the road life was steering me down, but he knew a few of the basics.

"At night most priests pray."

I told him, "I had never prayed before."

He reminded me of my dream, when I made my peace. "That's all you need to do, each night, before you sleep."

He also thought I would be better off with a different weapon. That sword had failed me for the last time. He pulled my father's toolbox from his chest, reaching in, making several clanking sounds before he found the right object, ultimately pulling out my father's old hammer. "Most tree hugging priests fight with a blunt weapon like a mace, this will do just fine."

In the morning I was surprised to see Kat up so early. She had been studying late as usual.

This mourning there were lots of little girls gathered around her, she had taken pieces of several of her outfits and was playing dress up. Putting their hair up with flowers, faces full of makeup, all wrapped in fancy scarves that clashed with their everyday plain clothes and bare feet. Even Bauble was dolled up, fit with a new collar weaved by the kids.

Kat walked up to me with a leather loop I could attach to my belt to hold my trusty hammer, making fun of me, "Are you going to protect me, or fix my wagon with that darling?" I just gave her, The Look, as I started to chase her, promising, I was gonna fix her wagon.

We were all cleaned up and ready to go, especially Eyiyo. Some of the women had taken his tight shirt and placed weaved reed panels in the shoulders, waist, and forearms, giving his clothes a much better fit. Kat was wearing tight black short pants and a red shirt that had pockets on the arms for spell components. Braided in her hair were beads, flowers, and one large black feather. Eian and Gavin elected to be our guides. They were dressed in clothes that made them hard to see in the forest.

I had one more thing to do before we left. I stood in front of the almost bare huts where the food was stored, touching my belt and raising my hands to the sun, filling the empty storerooms with rice and grain. Lou nodded his head in approval as our group gathered to head out.

We had walked for a few hours before we realized we had picked up another guide. Eyiyo noticed her following us, I don't think he even saw her. Grunting, he took in a large breath of fresh air. "I can smell someone behind us."

Gavin finally realized who it might be, calling out, "Ari, we know your there, come out and show yourself."

Her name was Ariana; they called her Ari for short. The scrawniest little half-Selvain mix lowered herself from a tree. I could not see her till she moved into plain view. She was equipped with a longbow. It was almost as big as her. Other than the glare from the three daggers she kept on her thigh, she could easily disappear into the landscape.

Ari had long brown hair a little unruly like mine. her eyes were a little large like most selvains but her skin was more human with a slight olive coloring. Gavin vouched for her, "She don't talk much, and she's the best shot we got." She held up two rabbits she had caught while following us, "We will also eat better while she's around."

We marched to the shore line, and then followed the riverbank. The far side was desolate, with almost no vegetation, only reeds and a few clusters of small trees grew on the water's edge. In some places the cliffs extend straight up from the waterline the entire length of the river. The few places where it might be possible to land a boat are plagued by jagged rocks.

Scoal Mountain's slate rock cliffs are home to several types of birds, scores of nests litter the rock face. The smoky mountain overshadowing the ridge is Mount Helos. We could smell its hazy emissions when the wind was blowing from that direction.

The side of the river we are on is plush by comparison. Some of the treetops rival the cliff sides. The size of trees was amazing they put the largest Cottonwoods back home to shame.

This is where the Shivan Forest starts it stretches over most of the lower half of the Commonwealth,. It is surrounded by the second of the two mythical dragons father talked about. To the south-east is Mount Helos, the head. The river flows out of the Shivan Mountain Range, the dragon's body. The forest extends far to the north, past Maguire and Airwindale, all the way to the Shivan Lake which is held by the dragons tail.

Once I got my barrings I could tell we were traveling in the wrong direction, away from Mount Helos. Sometimes you must take two steps back to make one step forward.

The day was uneventful, until Lou started limping. He had stepped on something sharp he did not see on the ground. A large thorn went through the bottom of his boot.

Unlucky I guess, we were unable to find the plant it came from, or any other prickly plants in the area. Gavin said it was not much farther, so we pushed on. Nothing to stop us but a gentle breeze, that for a moment sounded like chuckling children, as the wind blew through the river reeds.

The deserted village we were going to was set next to the Scoal River as it funneled out of the mountains. It is where Eian and Gavin lived, before they were run off when the Selvain's first attacked. We returned here, hoping to find a seaworthy boat that could take us back down the river and across Gourde Lake. There was an abandoned pier on the back side of Avalon at the small end of the lake. Gavin feared crossing the bridge in Newhaven might be impossible, as it was controlled by the Drazzi. A stealthy approach seemed to be the wise choice.

Unlike the towns and villages we have been to, this place was constructed much different than anything I had ever seen. There was a lot of fire damage, but I could picture this place in its glory, if you could imagine a small twig covered with salmon eggs. The huge trees looked like that, only the eggs are the homes of those who lived here. Eian told us the villagers had adopted many of the building techniques of their Selvain brothers.

The hard shells of the oval looking huts were made of red resin and river grass. The doorways, windows, small walls, areas with handrails, roofs, or any place needing a little extra shade, were made of weaved reeds, just like in the smaller village. To connect the spherical structures to the trees they used a flexible material, so resilient it allowed the trees to continue to grow, griping tight even if new limbs sprung forward. To acquire the sticky substance, the Selvains would boil the sap of a particularly resilient tree, which grows only up river, on the eastern slopes in the Shivan Mountains.

At night the oval huts must have lit up like oversized lanterns, illuminating the well manicured forest paths below. Where there were large clusters of huts, remnants of stairways still wrapped around the colossal trees. I could still see parts of an unconventional series of rope and log bridges that extended from tree to tree, there were many ways to get back and forth, up and down.

Also many vines hung from the forest canopy to the ground. Some were altered, used as pulleys, to carry up heavy objects to their homes, the same way I used the pulley in my father's barn to pull up hay bales to my loft.

The winding pathways all lead to one large cleared area, where there were three communal fire pits, a large clay oven and a raised stage.

Near the water was what remained of a dock that probably housed several dozen small canoes? The dock was made of multiple floating sections. The top was finished with heavy logs laid out in rows. Underneath were some type of oversized plant pods that looked like big string beans, all glued together with the same elastic substance used to connect the huts to the trees.

The joke was on us, the boats were gone, probably set adrift or sunk. Eian suggested a plan. If we could salvage some rope from the bridges that did not burn completely, he thought we could probably make a raft with what pieces were left of the dock.

Something had Eyiyo on the edge. He asked Eian if Ari had brought any other little friends. He kept smelling the air, with a dissatisfied expression on his face, as if something was eluding him.

We split up to gather rope, Ari was a very good climber and this was her home turf. She used the vines to climb up to the lowest branches, as soon as she cleared the bottom level; she used stairways, if they were intact. Most of the damage was confined to the areas closer to the ground. Once the highest levels were reached, she was able to use vines to swing from tree to tree. I followed in her path. It was not too different from swinging on the ropes in my barn back home.

Ari and I were working together to take the knots out of a rope that was part of one of the longer bridges. We were about sixty paces up. Eian and Gavin were working on a bridge that had fallen to the ground while Eyiyo dismantled the dock. As usual Lou sat down by his chest, petting bauble as he took off his shoe to rub his sore foot.

Kat wanted to climb up to us. I told her it was too dangerous. To get up here required climbing one of the smaller trees, then swinging to the larger tree. I thought Kat would turn around when she got too high, but she finally climbed to where she had to swing from. She shouted at me, smiling, "You're gonna catch me."

Her father looked over yelling "You be careful, focus," Even Eyiyo turned to watch the spectacle.

Asking her to turn back one more time, I stood there, slightly annoyed, ready to catch her. She jumped grabbing the vine. As she swung, she was distracted, mumbling to herself. I don't know what happened. Somehow she let go of the rope too soon. I reached out as far as I could. She started to fall! I jumped to one of the vines crying out as I slid down trying to reach her, but I was too late to stop her descent. There was no way for me to stop her fall.

At first I thought their might be tears in my eyes. The air seemed to be visibly swirling around Kat, stopping her in mid-air.

She suddenly started floating up chuckling. Lou must have known. Everybody but me was laughing and Kat was somehow flying. Rubbing it in, doing somersaults in the air. She flew over and tried to give me a kiss on the cheek. She knew, The Look, was coming. Not amused, ignoring her, I started to climb back up to fetch more rope.

I don't know what it was, our screaming, Eyiyo hacking the dock into pieces or movement in the vines above, but we started to hear a humming sound. At first it was drowned out by the river, as it grew louder. Out of several of the huts flew what looked like wasps, only larger and a lot scarier. Some were as big as apple creates, with stingers as long as any dagger, only sharper.

'Brrrrrbbbbrrrrr!' one flew by me. Ari had it in her cross-hairs and fired before I knew what was happening. 'Ssssswhhooo.' I don't know what worried me more, the arrow passing inches from my head, or the bug that was now plummeting from the sky.

Eyiyo was quickly overwhelmed. Twenty or so of the giant insects gathered around him. They were dropping as fast as he could swing. It was like confetti was falling all around him.

The whole area was swarming with the flying nuisances. They must have found the burned out huts, made big comfortable hives.

Reaching into his chest Lou cast his spell, "Kebisilk," The sticky nets shot out of his wand draping down like cobwebs spun by giant spiders, it was working, the gooey ropes ensnared the flying menaces.

I slid back down the vine I was on. As I did I could hear my belt beeping and screeching. With my signature move I flipped out, jumping to the forest floor, picking up my father's hammer.

I left the hammer on the ground at the base of the tree because earlier it had come free from its belt loop, and fell on my foot.

To my amazement as soon as I held it in my hand, it started to glow and the hammerhead burst into a blue flames. Then my skin started to feel tight, it was hardening taking on a bark like pattern.

One of the humongous wasps landed on my back. I pulverized another as it flew in my face. Lou was right I was more adept at using the Hammer. I could feel the bug clinging to my back trying to sting me. Its stinger was tapping my new skin like a woodpecker, but was unable to penetrate the hard shell that had formed.

More of the flying pests landed on my posterior. I was getting swarmed. I slammed myself backwards, up against a tree, smashing the creatures, still swatting those in front of me with my hammer. They burst into flames as they were dismembered by my new weapon, just like Eyiyo, a small pile of dead bugs was starting to grow at my feet.

Ari was well hidden. All one could see was the occasional arrow and another winged invader drop from the sky. Lou had waded into the water, occasionally bobbing up for air. Eian and Gavin ran into the large oven, covering the flu with their shirts, leaving Eyiyo to tend to the masses down by the shore.

Kat was flying at full speed with a bakers dozen in tow, she would fly in close to the tree limbs, losing one or two to midair collisions. I motioned her to fly by me, but I could only take a few out with each pass.

Arrogantly Kat yelled, "Watch this sugar." as she flew toward one of the larger nets, as fast as she could, stopping abruptly, and turning down. The group of wasps chasing her flew into her trap. With a cocky smile, Kat lit the ropes on fire like the wicks on a lantern, in a flash there was ash and bugs, falling to the ground. The few wasps that were left started to disperse.

Gavin was yelling for help, down below. Somehow when they hid in the oven, the door got wedged so tightly they were unable to open it. Eyiyo had to brake through the side of the oven to get them out.

When the side of the oven finally crumbled, an odd gust of wind blew the ash all over Lou, Eyiyo, Eian and Gavin. They moved out of the dust cloud, covered from head to toe in filth. I bet they did not think that was funny.

I could hear Kat and Ari chuckling in the distance. It sounded like the whole forest was laughing at them.

To make matters worse with ash covering their eyes, Gavan tripped and fell into Lou, then they both fell into a mud puddle. We all watched the comedy unfold.

Maybe that was comical but the girls didn't have to laugh. I ran over to help. Angered and a little embarrassed at himself, Lou shrugged me off.

I just was not amused with our misfortune and still the little tiffed at the little prank Kat had pulled, as soon as all the commotion was over, I felt I had to say something. "Katinka this is not a game. Those bugs were dangerous and tricking me was not funny."

Sarcastically, she knocked on my shoulder, like she was knocking on a door as my skin slowly returned to normal, then blew on my hammer making the fire go out, she smiled "Pretty neat stuff. I thought your tricks were cool too," Smiling she changed the subject. "Where's Bauble. Here kitty, kitty, kitty.

"I saw bauble in that tall tree." Kat flinched as her dagger shocked her, I smiled, "No, there she is over there." Zap!

Kat Giving me, The Look "That's not fair!" I think she knew not to say another word, pouting as she floated away.

I really thought she had fallen, I don't think she understands how important she is to me. Every day she went off to school, she came home with a quirky story of a new friend she met that day, she knew everybody. I was lucky to even see the other kids, Father and I only went into town a few times a month to pick up supplies. Even if I met other kids, I would rarely get a chance to play with them. Some kids weren't even allowed to talk to me, except Kat who was always there for me. She is more than my best friend, she is everything to me.

I can heal her if she is hurt, but I don't think anyone could help her, if she really fell from that height. I would have never forgiven myself for dropping her.

Eyiyo walked over, patting me on the back, "Nice job, at first I was not sure if you were really the one I was looking for."

In all the excitement I don't think I even realized I was actually facing my enemy and winning. Smiling as I realized it was really me fighting by his side, and my skin, the blue flame. I did all that. I knelt on the ground taking a moment to reassure my newly found faith. I did not know what I was doing. Somehow It felt right to just believe.

Getting back to making our raft. Ari and I climbed back up into the trees to finish gathering rope. Ari and I enjoyed swinging on the vines and playing in the tree tops. We were trying to see who could climb higher. I noticed Kat was starting to get very competitive with Ari for my attention. Kat kept flying above us bragging that she could get higher. Ari and I did not care we were enjoying the climb and each other.

Kat flew up and whispered in my ear "Anything she can do, I can do better."

I could see Kat was a little jealous. Ari and I hit it off so well. I was still a little mad, so I kept flirting with her anyway. Enjoying the fact it did not set well with Kat.

The girls and I were dropping rope down to Eian and Gavin. A snake must have dropped from one of the tree limbs above, falling onto Eian. He thought we dropped it on him as a joke. But none of us ever saw the snake until Lou and Gavin had to pull it off him.

The whole day was full of Hi-jinx's. Just after that Eyiyo lost one of his swords. He pulled a fish out of his sheath to cut a length of rope, expecting his sword and finding dinner.

It must have come loose from its sheath when he and Lou were forced to take an unexpected swim in the river. They were chasing one of the sections of dock that floated free while they were working on the other pieces. It was the second time Lou had been in the river that day.

Eyiyo Preoccupied with looking for his weapon, got his foot stuck in an old basket he accidentally stepped in. How do you not see a basket? Eian and Gavin had to pull together to get it off. All of them fell to the ground as the basket came loose from his foot. Needless to say everybody was frustrated. Nothing was easy about creating that raft.

Somehow Kat always found the humor. "Daddy that's the cleanest I've ever seen you." She got, The Look.

Kat had to remind us all a little laughter might be helpful. We were all stressed out. It's probable why we were making so many little mistakes. She smiled at me saying "Your not gonna stay mad at me forever. Are you?"

I considered her proposition, I just did not answer.

My favorite funny of the day was when Kat and I were gathering fire wood. She found a piece of wood not knowing it was covered in tree sap. By the time she noticed, she already had sap all over her hair and her snazzy little outfit. She had to take a dip in the cold river water to wash it off. I had to say it, "That's karma for tricking me." I got The Look. Twice! Lou watched feeling redeemed, adding. "How's the water!"

With all the shenanigans that delayed us from getting our work done in a timely fashion, I was surprised we even finished. Somehow we persevered. It was quite an accomplishment. By the end of the day we had fashioned a raft, it was easily twice as big as the old table back home and seemed sturdy enough, except for maybe the flat stick mounted on a crude swivel Lou had rigged to help steer.

Eyiyo was placing the finishing touches on the raft while Eian and Gavin started a nice fire, Ari was preparing to cook a smorgasbord of animals, rabbit, snake and of course, Eyiyo's fish. Lou reached in his miracle chest, pulling out a small barrel of apple wine he'd been saving, "This is for tonight and a job well done." placing it next to one of the large fire pits.

I reached in to his chest and retrieved the gnarled piece of wood I took from the willow. Kat and I studied it. I reminded her that in my dream I was told to make a staff out of it. I really didn't know where to start.

Kat removed the necklace the little girl from the village gave her, wondering if somehow I could use the multi colored stone. I pressed the stone into a knot in the base of the shank, right at the top just before the handle arched. It was like my hands were wood working tools. The small staff gripped the stone, while the braided reed chain entwined itself around the top, defining the handle. The fine details continued to surface, until the whole piece became a finely polished petite little stick. It was too short to be used as a walking staff. It was more the size of a cane. Kat's eyes lit up, "For me!"

I nodded, "You don't deserve it."

Our meal smelled done I had never eaten snake, Ari assured me, "It is good eating," taking a bite herself.

During dinner we discussed the particulars of our plan. The decision to leave tomorrow was easy, Eyiyo said in the day we were highly visible. Lou replied. "Then we will leave at dusk tomorrow and let the moonlight guide us."

Even with all the mishaps, it turned out to be one of the most enjoyable nights I've had in a long time. Kat and I never really drank before. Sure we had a few sips here and there, oh, and then there was the funhouse, but this was different. Tonight we weren't sneaking a sip, we were drinking with Lou! He did not stop us, he filled our glasses.

After we ate the delicious meal, I had to make a toast. "To Ari our chef! That was absolutely delicious!" Gavin set the mood for the rest of the evening playing a cheerful tune on his flute for us.

I don't know what came over me maybe I was still a little mad about earlier. I leaned over whispering in Kat's ear. "You think you can cook better than that." I thought she was going to slap me right there, I probably deserved it. I knew Kat was a good cook, she made the best pies. Still I grinned like the cat that ate the canary as she pretended not to hear my comment, elbowing me in the ribs.

In the middle of our conversation, Lou accidentally sat on Kat's dagger, jumping to his feet with a yelp. "Kat did not know how it got there. Lou laid on his belly for the rest of the night. I don't think he wanted me to touch his butt to heal him. One must be thankful for little things.

The six of us told jokes and funny stories, getting to know each other, while Eyiyo mostly nodded keeping his distance from the fire. Throughout the night Kat kept making small sparks by snapping her fingers. The coolest thing happened when she held the cane I made in her other hand. The sparks came out blue. And when Kat tapped the small staff on the fire pit the reddish orange flames intensified and changed to blue as well. I looked over and for a moment I think even Eyiyo was enjoying himself. Until Kat realized the flame was no longer warm. Oddly it was almost cold to the touch. Tapping the pit again, the flames returned to normal.

I never had many friends other than Kat. Since we met up with Eian and Gavin I've finally met people that respect me; a whole village of people who treated me as an equal, especially this girl Ari who is my age and part Selvain. Tonight I felt like I was camping with a group of old friends.

I have to admit sometimes Kat is right. It was like the universe knew we all needed to laugh.

I did not drink that much, I was enjoying myself too much. Regardless I must of been drunk, because when I came back from the little Selvains' room, I tripped into Kat, spilling both of our glasses of wine, onto her. I think she was too exhausted to be mad. It was the third time today she had to change. She didn't seem to mind, she came out in a pair of comfy baggy pants, carrying a blanket, snuggling up beside me, grabbing my arm, taking one last look at Ari, before pulling me a little closer, falling asleep. Staying mad at Kat was always hard.

After a while we forgot about all today's little accidents. Most of us fell asleep where we sat, except Eyiyo, who didn't drink. He stared up at nothing, with a puzzled look on his face. Something just wasn't right. He just couldn't put his finger on it.

That morning Eyiyo woke us up at the crack of dawn. He was banging two pans together. Something had him spooked. Gavin was already up and arguing with Eian, fed up with the jokes. He was saying Eian had tied his shoes together, while he was sleeping.

Gavin was denying it. They both looked at Ari who slept through everything.

Kat looked at me, still holding me tight from the night before. "I'm sorry I tried to trick you. Promise me you will never stay mad at me. I don't want you to ever distrust me. I don't want to fight with you like that." Holding me tightly, we listened to the woodsmen arguing.

Ari was up now placing the blame for the shoe prank back at Eian, claiming she was on the other side of the fire pit the whole night.

Eyiyo was rushing everybody. Not that I claim to know him well, but it just was not in his character. He was constantly looking around. Double checking the knots on the raft, making sure the chest was tied down and the sections were still tightly connected. He kept saying, "There is something not right here."

Lou asked him, "What do you mean."

Eyiyo could not attribute it to any one thing, he just pointed to the woodsman shaking his head. He just wanted to go. Now!

Lou said "I thought we were going to cross at night."

Eyiyo calmly asked Lou, "How many daggers have you accidentally sat on," emphasizing, "in your life!"

Now Ari, Eian and Gavin were getting loud. Someone had taken Ari's daggers leaving flowers behind. Lou was starting to agree with Eyiyo in a forceful voice. "Arguing or not, everybody onboard"

Eyiyo took out his last sword and hacked the rope connecting the raft to the shore. We started to drift. It seemed like the village was happy to see us leave. The reeds and the wind gave the same eerie chuckle we heard coming into the unlucky city.

Gavin grabbed the pole that steered the makeshift vessel, pointing the raft to the opposite shore where the current picked up. We floated down the river toward Gourd Lake and our destiny.

One of the ropes holding the sections together must have been cut underneath by a rock. Lou said not to worry we doubled up on every knot. As he finished his sentence another rope snapped. We were in open water. There's no rocks here, Gavin pointed out.

Lou tried his magic rope trick to reattach the sections, but as quickly as it fixed the problems. New sections were breaking free. Scratching his mustache he reached in his chest pulling out an old pouch. Tearing it open clapping his hands together ensuring the bag's contents 'A fine powder' covered the raft and everything onboard, as the white cloud dispersed, more than we expected was exposed.

Three Little flying people maybe the size of a melon were coughing as they inhaled the dust. Their heads looked too big for their miniature bodies, emphasized by their long dragonfly wings, which kept them suspended in the air like hummingbirds. One was by the front of the raft, gnawing on the ropes that held our dinghy together, severing another piece of twine. She seemed proud of her mischievous deed.

The only male in the group took a final slash at the ropes by him as they started to shred, quickly flying away before Lou could grab him.

Ari pulled out an arrow to fire at the small creatures, realizing she was duped again, holding the long wooden spoon she misplaced last night.

Eyiyo successfully grabbed the last one. It screamed in pain, badly acting as she put on a show for her friends, who enjoyed the slapstick comedy. Then she bit Eyiyo's hand. She spit as if he tasted awful, disappearing in an instance, reappearing next to her male counterpart just out of our reach, leaving Eyiyo's missing sword in his clenched hand.

The one with the sharp teeth flew down, and with a wave of her hand shrank several of the pods that held the raft afloat, loosening the rest of the ropes. The wood logs still kept us adrift, but we lost a lot of buoyancy, the raft started breaking up.

The malicious misfits met up together and flew off back toward the forest city, giggling and laughing with the reeds. You could hear them talking over the wind purposely loud enough in a language we could understand, "Did you here the bald one scream when he sat on the knife? Ha ah-aha aha ha ha. And the other two, slipping in the mud? They were fun."

Chapter Fourteen

Learning To Sea

The raft was starting to break up and I was standing where the pieces split. Into the water I fell. I was never a strong swimmer, but I was not afraid of the water. For now, it did not matter. I was at the mercy of the river, unable to swim in any direction, slammed into one rock after another.

Tossed and turned, then pulled under, I hit my head on an underwater rock formation. I grabbed onto it, and then I pushed off the river floor, shooting myself up to the surface, gulping for air as the current pulled me down again.

My ears were ringing as I struggled to find something above the waterline to anchor myself to. Somewhere downstream, I was finally pushed aside from the heavy torrent landing on an outcropping of rocks that was inundated by reeds. The reeds allowed me to grab hold of the slick moss covered slopes. I was thankful to be close enough to the river's edge to climb onto the shore. Unfortunately I ended up on the far shore.

It took me a moment to catch my breath. I was gasping for air, having drunk half the river. Scanning the horizon, my friends were gone. The only thing I found was a goose egg on my forehead.

The rocky shore ended abruptly at a sheer rock face. The black shale cliffs were hard to navigate. Climbing on small ledges and slippery rocks, I followed the water's edge.

Suddenly I fell through a stone wall. I had stumbled upon a secret door to a hidden cave. Inside the roof was very low, even for me. As I crawled further in, several rocks above me illuminated, revealing a good size room that had been roughly carved out of the rock.

What I mean by that is there was an area, however small, that resembled a fire place with chairs. Off to the side was a raised rocky platform that could easily be mistaken for a small bed. Also there were stools and a counter in the corner. The only thing that was not stone was two tall mirrors. Oddly enough their decorative frames seemed familiar to me. I don't know why, We never had fancy mirrors like that back home. They looked like something you would see at Roz's house in the High Quarter.

I crawled toward the rocks that resembled a sitting area. The stone began to define itself with color. The chairs became a brilliant striped green and were soft to the touch. No longer made of rock they were upholstered with a plush fabric. A white bear skin rug appeared on the floor, and the mantel of the fireplace formed a finely crafted carved detail, covered with small trinkets including a picture of a very short elderly gentleman with big ears. Then the fireplace lit itself. I was rendered speechless, as I made myself comfortable on the inviting chair in front of the warm fire.

Something shifted beneath my seat. Out of an opening on the side of the chair came a long metallic arm, attached to the end was some kind of organic roll. The object was forced into my mouth. I thought it was my belt that was clicking, but the sound came from the end of the hand like extension. I reared back as a small flame appeared. Before I could sit up straight and realize what was happening, the arm disappeared and I was smoking a tiny cigar. I coughed and immediately threw it in the fire.

Getting up, I stumbled toward the kitchen area. It too was magically altered. More metallic arms came out of the wall, placing a pan on what looked like a grill built into the polished rock countertop. An unconventional configuration of metal sticks bent and swirled turning into several hands. One was holding a tiny spatula. A different door in the ceiling opened and down dropped a tray with a basket of tiny blue spotted eggs, a couple of pieces of some sort of fruit, assorted muffins, and several tiny sausages!

The little metal hands cracked three eggs into the pan throwing the shells into a container that lowered into the countertop. The fruit was cut up, the sausage was cooked, and the toast was made. The extra hands neatly folded away as they were not needed. I could smell breakfast as the contents of the pan were flipped up onto a plate and slid out on the counter. It was just like father would make, only smaller.

I moved forward to survey the free meal. Another tray slid out of a panel in the wall with silverware, napkins and a small glass of what my best guess was milk.

Feeling a little dizzy, I slid over to the bed area which had a slightly taller ceiling to compensate for the two large mirrors that seemed out of place in this miniature home. Then I realized why they seemed so out of place. They were just like the mirror I saw in my dream, the one the cloaked figure went through. Both were identical in every detail, from the elaborate swirls in the silver frame, to the tiny keyhole held by two hands at the bottom.

It was no surprise that by the time I reached the bed it was made up with fine linens and several comfy pillows. There was a stand by the bed. When I was close the top opened up, a mechanical device holding a circular spinning object started to talk, or better yet play music.

Unlike my first impression, the cave was a cozy place to relax. The longer I was there the more little details became apparent. Artwork, plants, the floors, even the walls were finely finished. Warm and comfortable I rolled onto my back to stretch, spending a minute lying flat listening to the rhythmic sounds, with my feet hanging over the end of the bed.

Looking up, I noticed a shelf with a hand mirror on it. It was easy for me to reach, but probably high for those who lived here. I held it to the one of the mirrors the same way the man in my dream did, and just like I had seen, there appeared a small key. This couldn't be real.

I slid the key in slowly! The mirror that reflected the ornate little cave with the small bed, now revealed an alternate view. I saw the sun coming through a window, a balcony, and a closed door. Slowly I reached out feeling the glass, it was cold. I pushed my hand through anyway. Pausing for a second to make sure no one was there, I stepped into the other room. I could hear noise outside. Walking out onto the balcony, I saw people were strolling about in the streets below. I was in Suxen falls in the private home of someone who lives across the way from the inn where we stayed.

There was a ruckus inside the Little Cub. Through the window I could hear the waitress was frantic. It sounded like someone dropped and broke a lot of dishes. Whatever shattered caused quite a stir. The regular brew of morning folk spilled out of the door, disrupting the usual hustle and bustle of the city streets. Other than that, it looked like business as usual, as the squadrons of delivery wagons descended. Barrels of ale for the tavern, fresh vegetables and supplies for the restaurants, and pies for the pie shop. Two names stuck out, 'From Under the Udder Dairy, and the nefarious, Sunny Brook Farms.

This was not shaping up to be a typical day, I could hear more yelling down the street, and I could see a few young kids throwing stones, breaking windows. When the driver of the Sunny Brook Farms cart pulled away, a box of eggs fell out. He must have forgotten to shut the back doors. As he passed below me, I could see they had swung open. What was he thinking?

Now a second box had shaken free. I tried to motion to the driver. He looked up at me with a sinister smile. I noticed he belonged to the Badger clan. In the other direction there was even further chaos. A newspaper cart had turned over losing its load.

Something was wrong with this picture. It took a moment for me to realize what was happening. There were no bundles of papers or boxes of eggs. hundreads of cubes were being smashed below me in the streets. What was looking like a couple unfortunate mishaps was turning to total mayhem. Someone ran out of the tavern falling to the ground, he immediately started convulsing. Now I could hear random cries above the regular traffic coming from every direction, as pandemonium rang out.

Off the back of a speeding wagon, a Drazzi soldier was throwing bottles of flaming oil, lighting many of the surrounding buildings on fire forcing people to come outside. A haze started moving across the city. Out of the smoke walked groups of scaly red warriors, all with leather pouches, throwing round spheres at the groups of bewildered people jumping up and down trying to get away from the bugs.

The children breaking windows were closer now. They were throwing cubes in the windows, and on the doorsteps. One looked up at me with his snake eyes and forked tongue. The tiny insects were the perfect weapon. They could easily infiltrate the minutest crack crawling under the doors and into the homes of the townfolk.

From my perch I could see other carts moving up the road. On one was an enormous catapult. It had set up position just outside the wall of the high quarter. The great gates were closing. The standing army was hustling to get inside. Their giant walls and oversized doors would be no match for the agile little pests.

Hundreds of cubes were released into the air. They kept their shape like geese flying in formation. The first shot had fallen short, hitting the very top of the wall. Thousands of eager enemies crawled out of the explosion. The Drazzi soldiers rapidly reloaded, recalibrating the huge machine to fire higher, over the wall into the high quarter.

Out of the corner of my eye I noticed several winged creature canvassing the rooftops. I moved back inside closing the balcony doors.

Glass and wood was scattered in the air, as an enraged, snarling nemesis, crashed through the doors landing right in front of me.

I took a good close look at him, he sure was ugly. His head was half burnt, and his scaled neck was stretched extending out like a reptile. His wings folded onto his back but still towered over his body. He had more than one leather pouch strapped over his shoulder.

Then it caught my eye. The torn boots that wrapped around his ankles might possibly be my fathers. On second glance there was no denying, that was our pie knife from the farm, stuck in his heel. Could this monstrosity really be him? I pulled my weapon but hesitated to use it. "Father is that you?"

The creature lunged at me grabbing at my skull. I had no choice. I clocked him in the side of his face. He started bleeding as he held me up by the neck. Throwing me down he stepped on my head, forcing me to look forward. All I could see was the balcony, and the curtains igniting, as the room started to catch on fire.

To make things worse, now there was a pile of half shattered cubes in front of me. Whoever he was, he was going to be my downfall. His tale came thrashing down, breaking up the few cubes that had not already busted open. Several of the creepy crawlers were heading straight for me. One climbed on my face I did the only thing I could do. I bit it in half.

My hammer head burst into Blue flames as my belt sounded off. I slammed the winged beasts other foot as hard as I could and the abomination stumbled. I hooked the pronged half of the hammer around the back of his shin and yanked, pulling his leg out from under him. I scrambled for the mirror as he regained his balance.

Diving into the little room from which I came, I turned to see the creature in the mirror staring back at me. I reached for the key that was still in the keyhole, as the relentless monster tried to follow me. As soon as I turned the key the reflective surface returned and his face disappeared. His clawed hand amputated, it slid down the smooth surface, falling to the ground.

Spooked, I dropped the key and crawled back outside where I could see the rivers edge. The farther I got from the cave entrance the harder it was to recognize the door. It did not matter. I was not planning to return! At this point I did not have a choice. There were no distinguishing tool marks anywhere in the rock face, the opening had literally disappeared.

I scaled the cliff side till I could go no farther, choosing to rest on a flat rock near the water that was nestled in the private secluded cove.

Looking across the river at the opposite shore filled with an overabundant amount of life, I was reminded of the brutal contrast of the desolate shore I sat upon. There was nothing here but rocks. The closer I looked the more I became aware there was life even here.

Two small turtles were perched on the rocks trying to catch a little sun. It was strange I could almost feel their enjoyment, as I stood and stared at my new acquaintances. One of the turtles crawled right up next to me. I guess I made a new friend. It rubbed up against me, arching and twisting its neck, like bauble does when she wants attention. It allowed me to pet his little head.

I was really thinking of how I could get to the other side without throwing myself into the current. If only my little friend was bigger, he could take me where I wanted to go.

Caressing his head, I did not notice my belt was glowing, and the turtle was growing. The enlarged creature carefully climbed down the rock and took to the water. Somehow, I knew it was safe to climb on its back. At first he moved slowly on top of the water, I held on tight, taking a large gulp of air as it dove for the deeper water.

Under the water was another world I did not realize was there, even when I was looking right at it. I could see the fish along the river bottom hiding in the river reeds, several fish swam next to us as we took to the open water.

Resurfacing, I looked back at the rocky shore I thought imprisoned me. Across the way I could see the fertile shore that seemed impossible to reach. I was learning. Things are not always as bleak as they seem. I remembered the words in my dream. If you are ever in need, just call out, have faith, we will always be there. I do not think I will ever feel truly alone.

I held my breath again. The turtle dove deeper. I touched my belt and I was able to inhale under the water, choking at first, then I just breathed in the life-giving liquid. Letting go of the last bubbles of air I still held in my mouth, as gills formed under my chin.

It was amazing. I never realized just how alive a river is, so many large fish, and the ground was teaming with crabs, snails, and other slimy critters all fighting for their own piece of real-estate, plus all the plants growing along the bottom, with their long leaves reaching for light from the world above. The snails were eating the plants, the crabs eating the snails, the fish eating the crabs, the turtle eating the fish, everyone trying to stay off tonight's menu. I saw an endless circle of life and death. I gained a renewed respect for the living and the dead. In an eerie way I began to understand how all things are connected to each other. Eyiyo's words came to mind, "All creatures need substance. These lost souls are in Eden now."

The sunlight shined down, becoming muted as it transcended through the murky water. As it passed through the leaves of the large underwater plants it made ribbons of light, creating a geometric obstacle course of shadows. I was surprised by a school of fish that darted in sync. Everything around me seemed to be reacting to each other, I felt my connection to this world in a way I never felt before.

As we broke into the mouth of the river, the river bottom changed. There was a huge plant invading the normal vegetation growing into the water from the far shore. The roots were sunk deep in the ground pushing up abnormally shaped rocks.

These rocks must have lain buried, under the surface of the river bottom for many years. Now exposed, the rushing water was clearing away the years of muck, hollowing them out.

They were not natural formations at all and they were rusting as if they were made of metal. Some had broken glass windows, centered around the top of the shell like structures. All had two glass lamps on the front corners or holes where the lamps were missing. It made them appear as if they were staring at you, like they had a story to tell. Lying in different degrees of decay, they made an unnatural playground for the fish that swam in and out of them. Once I identified a couple of these mysterious frames, cleaned off, I realized there were thousands scattered across the river bottom, covered by years of small animals making homes out of the metal shells. Could these be pieces of our distant past? No matter how much we see there is so much more we never notice.

After crossing what seemed like miles of river bottom we reached my final destination. As we approached the shore the turtle slowed and my head rose out of the water. I was choking on the air as I dismounted my ride.

I was forced to kneel in water deep enough to be able to put my head easily back under to catch my breath. My body had become comfortable breathing liquid. It took a while for my transformation back to normal to be complete.

Stumbling out of the water, I fell, hitting my head hard on another rock, in the same place I had hit my head when I first fell into the water hours ago. Lightheaded, blood trickling down my forehead, I pulled myself onto the grassy shore, to the world I was born too, the world where I was fed by air.

My fair-weather friend had gone long before I reached the shore. Cold, soaking wet, and still spitting out river water I sat gasping for each breath. Exhausted, I found a tree momentarily passing out under it.

Chapter Fifteen

Easy As One, Two, Three

Ari was whistling, while Kat shook me. Hysterical, raving, worried about everyone's safety, Kat was trying to clue me in on what happened after I was separated from the group.

I was struggling to focus, on which Kat was the real one. Still water logged the last thing I remembered was watching the raft start to break into two pieces. That, and the nefarious laugh of those wretched little nymphs, a sound that would be etched into my mind forever. Everything else, including Kat, was a blur. Could I truly believe I hit my head, 'twice' in the same spot? The cave, the turtle, the mirrors, it all seemed to be so unreal, was it all another dream?

One could only guess, what was to blame for my throbbing skull, the goose egg I could feel disappearing as I rubbed my head, or the senseless dribble spewing from Kat's mouth. All I was hearing was bla, bla, bla, as Kat just rattled away. I swear she was sounding more and more like her Aunt Roz, everyday.

As my eyes focused, Kat was going on about Eyiyo. It seems he ended up on the smaller half of the raft. He was too big to balance himself. When he shuffled his weight the small piece of dock he was on, flipped completely over. That was the last time she saw him. Crying and stuttering, her words slowed, "He never resurfaced."

There was a much needed moment of silence as Kat took a breath. Ahh, much better, now there was only two of her! Then that earsplitting sound started up again, as she told me how Ari grabbed on to one of the large dock pods that popped up when she fell into the water.

Ari interjected herself into the conversation, in a thundering voice. I mean a double helping of thunder, as she exclaimed. "Kat took to the air like a bird."

I wondered if they realized that I was unable to understand anything in my condition. Where do girls learn to speak, "Fingernails across the chalk board?"

They both remembered hearing Lou cursing at the mischievous little monsters when I disappeared. Kat couldn't recall the last time she saw her father so frazzled. From what I could piece together, Lou's quick thinking and a well placed net spell, saved what was left of the raft, by wrapping the dock, the chest, Lou, Eian, and Gavin, as well as everything else together, including Bauble who was clawing the top of Lou's head for dear life. I think I would have smiled if it didn't hurt so badly.

What sounded like a sticky comical mass of confusion was sea worthy, but out of control. Ari on the other hand was struggling just to stay afloat. They all were at the mercy of the current, which sent them twisting off in different directions.

Each time Kat or Ari interrupted each other, their voices got louder, and louder, thunder, then lightning, lightning, then thunder. What I could retain through the thumping in my head and all the screaming was that Kat decided to help Ari. The current was too strong. She could not pull her back to the others. Eventually Kat decided to pull Ari to shore. By the time she was safe, they could no longer see where Lou and the others ended up.

During a small dizzy spell, Kat grabbed me to see if I was still listening. I think it's an inherent trait that young Selvain's get. Instinctively I knew to shake my head up and down and give her, The Look, saying, "Yes dear I heard everything."

Then Kat changed from a shrieking banshee to a hopeless sobbing mess in my arms. "It's all my fault, I should not have left them, they were helpless."

I held Kat close for a moment, with her warm skin against my cold wet body. "Calm down. I'm here. Now tell me how, that, was your fault . . . Quietly!"

She could sense Bauble was in trouble, if she concentrated hard enough she could see everything through Bauble's Eyes. They didn't have a chance, the Queen's army was waiting for them, Lou, Eian and Gavin were taken prisoner as soon as they reached the shore. Bauble scattered as soon as she could get to dry ground, finding refuge in a group of pylons, part of the old marina. By the time Kat got there the others were gone, all she could do was save Bauble.

I could see Kat was scared as she went back to ranting. How I was right. "This is not a game; we are in over our heads." She was only saying what we were all feeling. What are we doing here? Can we do this without her father? If we even make it to the temple, are we supposed to fight the whole army, with only three people?

Pulling Kat tighter to me, I whispered in her ear. "We are going to be all right. A week ago I was ready to run. Today is different! I have found strength from within me. My eyes have been opened to an unbelievable world. As each day passes, I realize how much I am an important part of this world. I don't know how, but I will make a difference, I have become a tool for a force greater than me, with you by my side there is nothing we can't do.

The Queen is no more than a scared girl with darkness in her heart. Her name is Mytoka. If she draws her power from within the crystal we must destroy it, she must be stopped. What happens here in the next few days will change the lives of more people than we can imagine. We can not give up.

I am alive, maybe Eyiyo is alright too, he never told us his whole story, but he believed his destiny lies along the same path as mine. He will catch up with us, if he can. I don't know why, but I think he's been here before, I don't think he would miss this, he will find us when the time is right."

Calm, came over me, as I looked into Kat's eyes. I told her that I had another vision and I think my father is still alive. "We can save him and your father too. Remember what Lou told us about the nexus. I understand now. If I have learned one thing, it is that we are not alone. We are all connected. It's the only way to explain why we can do the things we do. If you can only believe in one thing, believe in me. Know I will not abandon that which has given me the strength and the direction to make a difference. I will never abandon you.

Kat, you have taught me the most important lesson of all, it is to believe in the impossible. If there is such a thing as destiny, then my destiny is entwined with yours. I have and always will, love you."

Ari stood quiet for a moment, then erupted, "Enough with the romance boys and girls, we have things to see and places to be."

In the last two days we had drifted, flown, and rode farther up the coast than I thought, almost all the way to the big end of Gourd Lake, where water flows over the Shivan falls into Gull Bay. It was not feasible to double back to the marina, and the cliffs here are too steep to climb. The only way to get to Avalon from here is to ride the lifts in Newhaven.

You have to ride the lifts to reach the main road from any of the lower levels. Large wooden platforms that dangle by four thick ropes, each lift is manually controlled from a pulley room that is located on the level above.

With one more day of traveling we had moved as far as we could, without being seen we positioned ourselves at the top of the falls, from here we could see most of the city was intact. The fact the city still needed to serve a purpose was probably the only reason it was not burnt to the ground.

There was a truly incredible view from our vantage point. Looking out, I could see the two bridge levels and the floating city below contrasting the ocean sky.

Below us was Gull Bay, where rows of huge supports loomed hundreds of feet up, suspending the two massive ancient stone structures. The harbor was compiled of several floating mini villages, completely encircling these large supports.

We were actually eye level with the middle tier, the lower of the two bridges. It extends out of a cliff side cave, a dead end road that curves out toward the ocean before ending abruptly. It must have collapsed into the ocean long ago. At the end of this short road, amongst a chaotic maze of decrepit buildings sits the pulley room and the main lift area.

Above us, where we needed to go, was the main bridge. An extension of the main road, from end to end it stretched across a massive ravine, standing almost five hundred feet high. At its center was another control room. This was the tallest bridge in the Commonwealth, and our last obstacle in getting to the Temple.

We stood and watched as another day passed. During the evening the missing dark ship had pulled into the natural harbor, nestling along a make-shift dock in the bay. They were using one of the wooden bridges that connected two of the smaller city sections together, to accommodate the oversized vessel.

For two days the lifts stayed in motion as the Drazzi Soldiers that debarked the ship were lifted up to the top. In the mourning the ship was gone. I guess headed back to Nautica to load up again.

Kat and Ari had an 'Easy Plan!' Step One. All we really needed to do was scale the cliffs to reach the second tier, and secure the lift undetected. Step Two. Kat would have to fly up to the main bridge and take out anyone in the pulley room. She could then lower the platform, and bring us up. Step Three. Once there, we could make a dash across the bridge to the forest.

"Easy!" I cried out sarcastically. Kat patted her dagger nodding, with an energized smirk on her face.

That night we noticed a storm was gathering off the coast. The thick cloud cover made it appear much darker early on. We spotted fires within the maze like corridors where groups of solders were gathering. Judging by the lanterns and fires, most of the action was in the city below. Most important, the lifts were no longer running and the second level appeared to be deserted with only a few red menaces positioned in the pulley room.

Wanting to take advantage of the calm and the darkness, we decided this would be the night. Ari had already scoped out a passable route along the cliff side. With a little bit of effort, we hoped to reach the lower bridge without having to set foot on the bottom tier. Our biggest problem was we could not see what troupes still waited for us up top, on the main bridge. From where we sat our view was obstructed.

There was one other small detail, limited supplies. I had four spheres, but only two had survived the river. Ari had eight arrows and three daggers. Kat only had one piece of the large feather on her, the spell component needed to fly. Optimistically Kat added as she waived her cane in the air, "I can always whack em with my stick, and don't forget your hammer."

I guess that was it, "We're ready."

Getting to the path was more intimidating than the path itself and by the time we reached the cliffs it was drizzling, making the stone wet and our climb tedious. Ari climbed, we just followed. It wasn't long before we reached the top of the cave entrance.

Below us were crudely built wooden houses lined up like books on a shelf, literally stacked one on top of another, some only accessible by staircase or ladder. They reached deep inside the mountain and extended out the entire length of the old bridge. I don't know what was more unsafe the decaying wooden buildings or the crumbling stone structure they rested upon. From here it was a small drop onto the highest rooftop.

The shingled roofs gave off a rotting musky smell as the damp air turned into a steady pour of rain. We did not hesitate, taking advantage of the thick cloud cover and the sound of heavy rainfall. We swiftly moved unnoticed, jumping from roof top to roof top, circumventing the catacombs of wood shacks and deserted streets. Round One of our plan was working.

I had been here once before and remembered the area up top was laid out the same. A rectangular portion of the bridge was broken away, around which a raised stage was built. This was the base for four large pulley wheels. These pulleys guided ropes as thick as my arm, up and around, then out of sight under the raised area. The ropes were connected to a chain of gears and sizable counterweights that hung below the bridge. This gear system allowed heavy loads to be raised and lowered with the minimum of effort, by one very strong or two average sized men, using a large but simple hand crank.

Next to each staging area was the control room. There were only a few levers that needed to be adjusted for weight and direction, and the big hand crank set the lifts in motion. The only difference between this pulley room and the one up top was a second staging area for the descending lift.

The crude mechanized contraptions were ingenious. Still it was hard to believe the same people could have constructed the original stone goliaths they were connected to. Who knows how long they have stood here. Could Lou's and Eyiyo's stories have been true! Were these bridges proof of a lost civilization? Are they the same people who wrote the books in the library?

I concentrated for a moment I wanted to know the truth. I wished I knew exactly what happened.

Just like in Airwindale, my head started to spin as the area was filled with an eerie glow. The building I was on disappeared and I fell to the hard stone top of the bridge, which was no longer old, it was like new. The horizon had also changed the ocean was gone. The bridge I was on was no longer broken it extended out pointing to a city of lights that stretched on forever. It was just like Lou had described.

Above me I could see two bridges not just one. And below, there was no floating city, now there were multiple roads reaching out in every direction. The roads were lit up by thousands of well lit colorful metal coaches filled with people speeding along the way. These coaches did not need horses to move. It took me a moment to make the connection, but the horseless carriages were shaped like the strange hollow metal shells I had seen in the river bed.

I heard a loud horn. One of the four wheeled contraptions was headed right for me. I rolled to the side as it dashed by. But I had rolled into the path of another machine coming in the other direction. There was nothing I could do the bright lamps on its corners were in my face.

I put my hands up to shield my head. It passed right through me, like I wasn't even there. It all happened in a flash and then I was back, the old wooden buildings below me had returned and Kat was waiving her hand saying, "Keep up." A little shaken I nodded and moved forward. I did not say a word. I knew they could not have seen what I saw.

I wondered what the single turning point was for all those people, what could have happened differently that would have saved them. It did not matter now, they were gone and I needed to focus on our plan.

By the time we caught up with Ari she had found a sheltered area with a raised porch toward the end of the bridge, right next to the control room. From here we had a clear shot to the landing area for the platform.

Kat Pulled out the piece of feather she had, as she cast her spell it dissolved in her hand. She took Bauble then flew up and out of sight. She came back down alone leaving her kitty on the windowsill of the control room high above.

I asked if there were a lot of those scaly faced things up there. Kat avoided answering the question directly, saying she thought she could easily take the solders up top out with one of my clay spheres.

Round Two started with giving Kat the sphere she requested. Kat had figured out a whole scenario, telling us exactly how it was going to go down. Using Bauble as a distraction, she presumed the bumbling Drazzi stooges would open the window, thinking perhaps her bait may make a nice snack. When they did she would just toss the clay sphere in. She would then climb through the window and release the levers, setting the group of four pulleys into motion, lowering the platform.

I had to ask how she was going to crank us up alone. Kat laughed "I'm never alone silly, Ling Ling will help." again she flew up and out of sight.

There was no way to find out what was happening up top. What if something went wrong? Not knowing was the worst. If you could squeeze a day into a short period of time, that's how long it took, before the lift slowly came into view. For the first time, I was really beginning to think, we could really pull this off.

But we weren't the only one's watching and waiting. The guards inside noticed the lift coming to rest in the staging area as well. One of the creatures wandered out of the control room.

Ari looked at me and said, "Now comes the hard part!"

"Signaling Kat?"

Ari gave me a puzzled look, "No silly, commandeering that lift! Kat said Bauble would know when we are ready."

Ari swiftly repositioned herself dashing across the street while the Drazzi sentry walked over to see what was sent down. Stealthily, Ari leaped between two close buildings, landing on the roof of the control room, she readied her bow.

There was nothing on the platform except several empty crates. The nosy attendant stumbled threw them finding nothing but a stowaway named Bauble, making a confused gesture. He motioned to his friends in the booth. As soon as he did, I could hear the gears below us engage. The crank made a clucking sound. Clic. Clic. Clic. Clic, the pulleys started to turn, they were bringing more men up on the other lift.

Instinctively I grabbed my hammer, overlooking the fact it might burst into blue flames when an enemy is near. Immediately his eyes turned to me. Sooner than I could react, Ari took him to the ground silently, with an arrow.

I rushed down toward the entrance hoping we could move the body before the others noticed. As I drew closer I could see there were a lot more figures moving inside. Too many to deal with all at once, but how could I seal them in? I wondered, if I could straighten a crooked piece of wood to make Kat's cane. It's just possible I could warp the wood door to seal it shut.

Before I could do anything three more Drazzi warriors shuffled out into the rain. I slammed the door closed behind them holding it shut with my body. The tips of my fingers were tingling as I thought about what I wanted to do to the door. My belt agreed. As it lit up with a song of dashes and dings, the planks in the door turned and twisted, pushing out, wedging themselves into the molding. Immediately I could hear banging from the inside. The door was sealed!

I turned around swinging my hammer blindly. All my enemies took one step back. The sound of my hammer crackled as it whipped through the air, raindrops sizzled as they came in contact with the blue flame.

Ari jumped from the rooftop, sinking her dagger into one of their backs, then she engaged another. I swung with all my might aiming for the largest jaw. The blue flame shimmered as I made contact, dropping my enemy to the ground in one swing.

Turning around I saw Ari was in trouble. She was being over powered. Like a mighty war hammer, my weapon chose its target for maximum devastation, and the blue flame was doing extra damage. When we were done all three Drazzi soldiers were laid out cold.

We both ran to the lift. I looked at Ari; we both looked at Bauble, who just stared up into the sky. We didn't have much time. The fighters trapped inside were restless, and starting to brake out the windows.

Suddenly, crashing threw the glass as if he was thrown by the others. One large warrior came flying out, charging at full speed, tackling me! We rolled off the edge of the platform into the staging area.

Ari screamed, "We only have one shot at this!" As the lift gained weightlessness, the platform screeched as it detached from the tier.

I could not get free. My captor just had to hold on. Bashing my head as I kicked him in the side, we wrestled trying to subdue each other. I could hear more of them coming through the windows. There was nothing I could do. He was on me, and I was pinned to the floor. Behind him I could see the lift rising without me.

Spitting blood on my face, an arrow from Ari's trusty bow ripped threw his chest and almost into me! I brushed him aside, leaping for the platform, missing the edge, catching Ari's hand. I was hanging just out of reach of the Drazzi mob as they piled out of the pulley room.

A particularly ugly one catapulted himself off the back of another. I felt him grab my wet leg, but he slipped away, falling into the others as Ari pulled me to safety.

Safety was a poor choice of words, as soon as I no longer felt solid ground beneath my feet. I realized just how bad this whole idea was. We were trapped on this small rectangle stage with nothing but a couple of empty crates to hide behind, and a single hand rail to hold onto.

For the first time in my life I knew what it was like to be the fish on the hook, dangling in the darkness, as the heavy platform swayed in the wind.

It was dark and there was no moon or stars to be seen. I held my hand up creating light, but no light could shine bright enough to help us. We could no longer see the ground; we looked up at four ropes extending into obscurity.

We could hear screeching, I thought it was the animals below, but something wasn't right. The sound was coming from above. Ari asked, "You did say some of them could fly?" I shook my head as a dark shadow passed over us. Other than the noise rain makes when it comes down in a steady flow there was an uncomfortable pause as we awaited our fate.

I did not see what Ari took aim upon but she launched her arrow with deadly accuracy. I heard a creature cry out, before it came down, crashing onto the deck, damaging the floorboards. Ari rolled the horned winged creature over, stepping on its red scaly chest, reacquiring her arrow, prepping her bow to fire another shot, she turned slowly looking out into the nothingness.

The heavy platform was rocked back and forth in the wind, keeping our footing was becoming an issue. Concentrating on our balance, we could feel something peculiar. One of the four ropes was intentionally being shaken. The vibration continued for a few minutes. Finally we could see the rope falling toward us, briefly hitting the deck before going over the side. It was there long enough for us to see, it was cut! Another rope started to shake. Ari fired along the line of the wobbly rope. Nothing!

Ari shook her head then placed her bow in its sheath, sticking a dagger between her teeth, she started to climb. It wasn't long before I could hear her cursing at the winged monster, which was clawing at the rope.

Just then, my first class ride was downgraded when an overstuffed horned Drazzi demon landed beside me, it jeered at me with its forked tongue. He was a lot bigger than his buddies who were cheering him on from below, and strong enough to pick up the body of his dead comrade, and hurl him toward me busting the railing before it fell over the edge.

Lousing my footing on the slippery deck, I fell back. I was almost impaled. Under my arm a sharp piece of splintered railing jutted out catching me. Bauble came to my defense hissing with her hair on end, distracting the menacing beast long enough for me to regain my balance.

One way or another, this ride was ending. I could hear the ratcheting sound of the wench above a good sign we were getting close to the top. My hammer was screaming for battle, and it did not look like I was going to disappoint. The smiling menace swung at me his claws shredding my shirt, when he became overextended. I struck him in the shoulder severely damaging his left wing. As he shifted his weight to the wrong corner of the lift the whole platform started to spin. I was flung into the air. I fell back, landing on what was left of the now horizontal hand rail, catching Bauble.

The creature scratched and kicked to stay aboard. Unfortunately for him, the boxes slid across the deck offering the final blow, knocking my adversary over the side. He tried to fly but his broken wing could not catch the air, he spiraled down out of control.

Without the heavy misplaced weight of the creature, the platform leveled out, tossing me back across the deck, I grabbed onto the edge and was left hanging over the other side. Bauble was safe, her claws anchored her to the ground, but she could not help me.

What now! For a moment I thought the situation was going to improve. But as each second ticked by I started to realize I had bigger problems than just dangling on this edge struggling just to get a better hold. Above me I could see the landing area. There was not enough room for me and the platform. If I am unable to get aboard quick, I will be cut in half when the lift docks!

I turned, only to see another creature headed directly for me. It came barreling down, hitting the edge of the deck, then bouncing off leaving a blood soaked stain were it cracked his head. Ari slid down the rope behind him, landing on the platform next to me. "Quit lying around on the job, we're almost there." helping me up, and back to my feet in the nick-of-time.

The clicking sound was getting a lot louder now. Tic. Tic. Tic, the lift came to a stop. All I could think was, did I ask her how many there were? I sure of it, I asked her specifically if there were a lot of those scaly faced things up there!

There was not just a few, there was a whole army of scaly faced, hissing and spitting, bug eyed creatures. Kat was locked in the control room, which was partially on fire, probably due to her specialty, and she was screaming at the top of her lungs. "It's about time you got here."

The creatures were breaking through the windows, but Kat was not completely defenseless. Each time one popped in, it got a face full of flames. Ari unloaded a barrage of arrows clearing the way to the door. What she did not knock down I knocked out.

Kat opened the door letting one of the creatures fall forward tumbling into the flaming deathtrap, as she stepped out. I was having de-ja vu, only last time we were surrounded, Eyiyo saved us, at least Ari was not passed out on the ground like Lou.

The crowd was advancing. Ari spouted out "I'm out of arrows," throwing a dagger onto the forehead of a Drazzi henchman hoping to cash in on her disadvantage.

Kat was keeping them at bay with a spell that created a shower of sparks and flame, but the creatures were somewhat resistant; their scaly skin did not burn easily.

I asked her if she had tried the blue flame. She pulled her staff out tapping it on the floor, reciting her incantation over. A burst of blue flame coiled out from her fist. With the blue flame, came an added blast of energy, knocking a large portion of the approaching denizens down.

It helped, but there were so many of them still in front of us. In all the excitement, it took a second for me to realize my belt was bleeping like crazy. Sometimes I think it actually is trying to communicate with me. I listened to the little voice in my head, slamming my hammer down with conviction on the pavement. Everybody was thrown back as a small crack appeared, it split the ground, and then split again.

The ground under us started to shake and the bridge started to break. An entire section of the bridge crumbled, collapsing under the advancing army. Then the whole bridge started to destabilize. Ari said, "Now is that time we talked about. Run!"

Everybody ran, us, them, jumping from section to section as the bridge broke up under our feet, I never looked back, I did not need to, I could hear the destruction as the upper level came crashing down, smashing into the lower levels, before plundering into the bay. By the time we stopped running. The damage was done. The entire city was destroyed. Ari collapsed. "Ya see, Round Three, no problem!"

Chapter Sixteen

Past Aggressions

A bone chilling wind blew and the temperature dropped, making the hairs on my neck stand on end. This old city was a desolate area, where the living did not travel anymore. If anything was truly cursed, it was here. One could not help but feel an intense overwhelming sense of despair.

It was like walking into a world picked clean by time. Many of the buildings here were made of mixture of cut shale from the nearby cliffs and brown clay from the river bed. Few buildings had the amenities seen in the architecture in Nautica or Suxen Falls. You could tell even in its hay-day it had a gloomy feel. Still for its time it was a thriving metropolis, home to thousands of people and our capital city. Not that one could tell by standing here. The devastation was complete. All that was left were the stone footings of the larger buildings. Cobwebs and an occasional beetle are the only indication of permanent residents. Not even weeds grow here.

Even with last night's downpour the place was void of water. A dust bowl, everything was coated in a reddish gray film. What resembled streets looked like dried up river beds pitted with craters, some ten foot wide with scorch marks still around them. Telib's story of fireballs raining from the sky, the day of fire Lou and Father always talked about, I don't know what else could have done this. How does, someone fully described devastation? You would have to be here, to truly understand.

It takes something horrific to make people get up and abandon their homes, without a thought of ever turning back. I did not truly realize how quickly people had fled, until I saw the dead. Most were left where they died, a virtual graveyard without headstones. No epitaph. The only evidence of their existence was their dusty skeleton's, wearing the tattered remnants of their scorched clothes. If you listened you could almost here them whispering, almost.

The smell of the corpses was long gone. Oddly enough the place still smelled like it was burning. That and rotten eggs. Kat said the awful smell is sulfur. It's a combustible element, and probably was what made this place burn so long and hot. When she was young Lou had taught her how to recognize different elements, especially those that caused fire. Ari pointed toward the mountain in the distance, Mount Helos looked menacing as it continued its quest to darken the sky. A fitting mantle to this unwelcoming scene.

I was miserable, my mouth was dry, and my clothes were wet. I was on the verge of collapsing. We never stopped moving, avoiding troops throughout the night, sooner or later we had to find a spot to rest. What we found had at least two standing walls. It was not much, but it blocked the constant wind, and allowed us to conceal ourselves if needed. I just wished I could get warm.

Kat had perched herself on an anvil that was in the center of the theoretical room, while Ari tried to find anything that we could burn. The only thing she found was twisted rusted tools, all missing their wooden handles, indiscriminately scattered on the ground around the area. From what I could tell this must have been the blacksmith's shop. If only we could burn metal.

My belt was hooting like an owl. It's been more than helpful but it seems to have a mind of its own lately. It was as if it was trying to tell me something.

Kat jumped up rubbing her ass, "That's not funny." pointing at the anvil. I put my hands to it. It was getting hot, and eventually we could not even touch it. Soon the metal had become so hot it glowed. It was like having a fire. Within a few minutes, I was no longer cold; all we needed now was . . . "Walla," lunch! I was becoming quite the homemaker.

I had never noticed it before but Ari had a partial tattoo. It was not finished, but what I could see looked very familiar. Ari explained that her mother was of the Badger clan. The clan was not a society like that of the Commonwealth. There were priests for spiritual guidance, warriors to hunt and protect, while workers make children and care for the tribe. Ari's grail was that of the worker class.

Ari started to explain. "In our clan we did not have a monetary system where one is measured by wealth. We all did our part for the clan's survival. We had to earn our position over another. No one was born into nobility. The wisest and strongest were placed on pedestals. We were a proud people.

No matter what opportunities our tribe offered, some of our youth had rejected our ways, choosing to live in servitude rather than with our own people, in exchange for the many vices the big city had to offer. The elders feared the comforts of the human cities would tear apart the values of our clan.

Mytoka arrived in our moment of weakness. With her she brought hope. The legends once told by our elders came alive again, stories about Selvain city's, grander than any city in the Commonwealth, Etlanthia where she was Queen. She claimed the lineage of the Badger Clan belonged among the legacy of this distant mighty empire. She offered the elders the best of both worlds. Wealth and status, with the promise of a destiny never to be forgotten, a world under her rule, rid of savages that lack the tradition and the ideals of the Badger Clan. All they had to do was vow to help her."

Ari continued telling her story. "The first task assigned to the elders was to bury three urns in the woods. It sounded innocent enough. Six of our most revered shamans took the decorative jars as she requested down river, far from our home. They were to plant them like seeds, then watch and pray over them for seven days. Only one of the shamans returned.

At first he refused to talk about what he had seen. We thought it was out of loyalty. Later we learned it was out of fear. Slowly he let details slip, calling Mytoka the weaver of despair, warning the tribe that her promises are laced with treachery. His story was that of horror. They had found a place on the lake shore, to plant her evil brood. On the third day several unknown types of seedlings sprouted up where they had placed her dead. By the fifth day the area was inundated with aggressive plants that had overpowered the indigenous growth. The Queen insisted the priests stay and finish the ritual or bring shame upon their clan. By the sixth day there was no evidence of the original habitat. Even the wild animals were gone. Not a bird in the sky or sound of beasts in the night.

The last evening, where they had buried the urns, three lights rose out of the ground. As they pulled free of the earth there was an unwholesome sound unlike any they had ever heard, similar to the echoing cry of a child being born in pain. Fearing they had done something wrong they tried to rebury the urns that had been unearthed. During the process, their efforts brought about their own demise. The bodies of three priests shriveled up and dried out, as their essence was some how drawn into the vessels, before they sank back into the ground. The others tried to return to the village, all but one fell victim to the carnivorous plants they had unleashed into the wild.

Before this tale was told, Mytoka had already struck out with twelve of our mightiest warriors. It would take five days to climb to the peak of Mount Helos and one more to walk down to the mouth of the living mountain. They were given the task of delivering her precious cargo, to the edge of the pools of flowing lava.

The survivors said, within the first couple of days, three floating lights appeared in the sky. With them came bad karma. Two men were lost to landslides that day. Another the next, he lost his footing, plunging to his death on the steep cliffs. Despite the perilous journey the men completed their duty.

Upon arrival, Mytoka uncrated a spotted egg the size of a full grown bear. The three unearthly spectral aberrations emitted a humming sound calling forth a creature conceived of fire and charcoal from the one of the pools of lava. When it rose up out of the fiery liquid many of the men were badly burned. Deceived with good intentions, their only fault, was agreeing to help in this sinister pact.

The being of fire took the egg into the heart of the volcano, but before they could get away, there was a small eruption. Only three men made it back to the village, the others were victims of the lava as it boiled up and was spit into the air. They were crushed by flaming projectiles and burned alive. Those who survived did not last, only living long enough to tell their stories, before succumbing to heat exhaustion and fatal burns. The volcano has been actively smoking ever since. Somehow each time the false Queen of deceit survived unscathed.

As the rumors surfaced, the elders started to believe they had dammed us all. The forked tongue of Mytoka explained their defeats as the lack of faith, calling those who had fallen, True Heroes of the Selvain Realm.

That is when I was turned away for having mixed blood, exiled from my own village! That was the last time I saw my mother, my family, alive. For the longest time I was bitter for being made an outcast, now I see it was for the best. Their selfishness saved me.

After I had left, Mytoka uncrated the rotting body of a large animal. It was too degraded to tell what kind of beast it was. I do know it was crawling with the vile insects you described in the attacks.

Those of the Badger Clan, who continued to speak out, did not for long. We had no idea they were being controlled, those originally infected were not transformed. My clan was used to attack the local villages. I realize now they had no choice in the matter, they were merely pawns. Telib and the others were taken, and that was when the first experiments with the contents of the last of the crates started. She was still learning then, perfecting the cubes.

My clansmen were the first victims, deceived by her lies, later mutated into the wretched beasts that form her army. Some took the liquid willingly, drinking straight from the barrels Mytoka provided. If they survived the change they were larger more powerful that those infected by the bugs, if they remained coherent they were given rank in the Drazzi horde. Those who lost the game of chance became unspeakable horrors.

Kat interrupted, "You mean you have seen her?" Ari nodded. "What does she look like?"

Ari blushed, she did not want to be mean, trying to lighten the mood, wiping the tears from her eyes, she said "Mytoka kind of reminds me of Riley."

What Ari meant was her facial features, the color of her skin and eyes. I, was skinny and much darker skinned than the Selvain's in her clan. They are typically lighter skinned, taller, and more, stout. Ari was having a hard time reiterating what she meant without Kat laughing.

Ari apologetically added "What I wanted to say was Mytoka is lanky and dark skinned and has, Riley's blue eyes. But that's not all; she has a decorative metal head piece embedded under her skin, above her ears and around the front of her head. It's held in place by two rows if spikes no bigger then warts, protruding through her skin. The golden metal guard is exquisitely crafted and resembles fiery horns in artistic relief along the sides. It's similar in shape to a large overextended tiara that curves upward like a crown toward the back of her head.

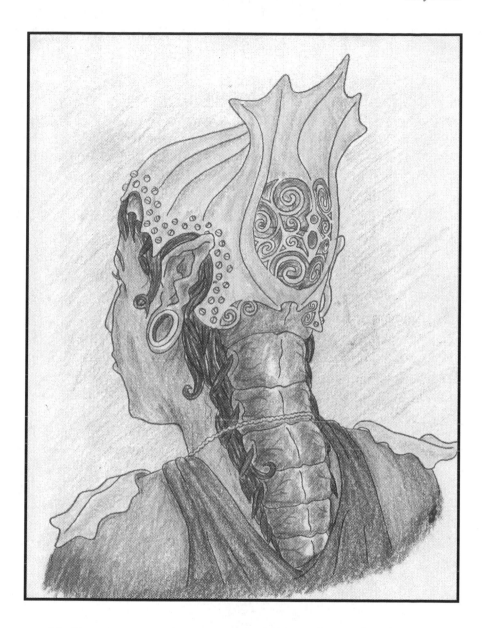

I believe it was made to protect what's underneath. Through the intricate metal guard, you can see fixed to the back of her head, the carcass of a centipede like creature, it is a larger version of the bugs she uses in her attacks. The many legs have been weaved around what is left of her hair as they dig into her skin. The ridged sections of the bug start at her forehead, and follow the curvature of her skull and spine ending at her lower back. If you can get close enough you can see the blood vessels pumping, it still breathes."

Our meal was interrupted by the pitter-patter of little feet, a patrol of four mounted solders. They stayed to the road and did not go far into the buildings, which made staying out of sight fairly easy. That and our clothes were starting to get permeated with the red dust that covered everything else in this miserable town. Ari was somewhat familiar with the layout of the city, telling us we were not far from the temple and should expect to see more solders more often.

Ari ended her story by saying "If Mytoka was not bad when she was born, she is evil now. I have just as much at stake in this as anyone. I will follow you into battle; rely on my bow, and no matter what happens, I hope we will always be friends."

The deserted war zone offered plenty of dilapidated dwellings, giving us plenty of cover as we moved forward. Ari told us to follow her, to duck where she ducks, run when she runs, she was very good at being unseen. We disappeared into the cityscape.

CHAPTER SEVENTEEN

All you need is the right tools

Our guide was surprised to see a large square fortification being built across part of the burnt out city, closing off the ancient temple. The troops were concentrating on finishing the main entrance. We had finally reached our destination, the beginning of the main road.

Much of the compound was still under production. They were using whatever building blocks they could find readily available, to erect the outer walls. Most of the rock came from disassembling stone work from the older incomplete structures, but nothing was wasted. They even used the skulls and bones they found. Mixing the unwilling in with the mortar, as if the lifeless residents of this city had not suffered enough indignities, their resting place desecrated, duped into being part of this fortress of the dammed.

We circled around the complex to figure out the easiest way in. The builders of this atrocity had barely broken ground on the south wall. Rows of tents started there, and ended up around front, making a small Drazzi city encircling the construction area, too many eyes to easily sneak in. On the north side there was little commotion. Would scaling the finished wall and dropping into an open courtyard be any easier? The main keep was a dark windowless extension of the back wall, and we could see armored sentry's with longbows on the roof. Needless to say regular patrols made their rounds around the entire structure. Getting in would not be hard. Sneaking in unseen, unlikely!

We held up on the back side of the compound. Other than the sentries on the roof, this area having been completed was patrolled less. Other than deciding to wait out the sun, we did not have an exact plan. Ari wanted to risk sneaking in. Kat thought up and over was the way. I had another Idea.

With a little bit of timing we moved forward to the back wall of the keep. We could hear the creatures lurking up top. Ari made it clear, "If we stay out here much longer we will all be detected." Looking at me she said. "Choose! There are two ways to go."

I whispered to her, "If I have come to believe anything on this adventure, it is there are always other choices. Just open your mind and believe in yourself."

I located a place next to a pile of rubble big enough to crouch behind, standing up close I inspected the ominous wall. I thought about what I had learned in the last couple days and reached down making contact with the ground. I was starting to understand, what the belt was doing. It was teaching me about the tools I posses. Now, it was time to figure things out for myself. I said one word. "Dig!" What I hoped would happen, did. A hole by the base of the wall started forming, soon the foundation was exposed. The ditch started getting quite deep. It was not long before it was deeper than the foundation.

Ari was getting nervous, "How much longer is this going to take." She could hear a patrol coming around the far corner.

"Get in" I trusted the hole would be deep enough to conceal us. Not only was it big enough, but when the earth was removed one of the bulkier stones shifted, and an opening into a dark room appeared.

I went in first, coming up through a crack in the stone floor, entering into a small pitch black room. There was no light other than what little starlight followed us from outside. Ari and I could see well. Kat stumbled, then held Bauble's head saying, "You will be my eyes."

The room was ten by ten, with stone walls. There were two cots, one on either side, divided by a small wooden table with an unlit lantern set on it. On the opposite wall next to a couple of hooks where a dirty robe hung, was a heavy wooden door with black metal hinges and a bone handle.

Kat cracked the door, setting Bauble on the ground. Kat shivered as Bauble's feet hit the cold stone floor. Bauble looked back at me, glancing around the corner, before she walked forward. Kat told us what she saw.

Bauble was in a hallway with a lot of similar doors. The room was lit by light fixtures made with human skulls, illuminated with crystals held within their jaws. Across the hall one of the doors was ajar.

Bauble peeked inside, where she saw four figures in dirty smocks and white masks, they were working at a table in the center of the room that had glass sides, above the table was a directional light brightly illuminating their workspace. Bauble also noticed two other tables; one had a low shelf and was butted up against the side wall. Kat thought Bauble could easily conceal herself, scampering into the room she quickly found a spot to hide.

The men were still engrossed in their work, too busy to notice Bauble enter the room. Inside she had even a better view, off to one side there were several different size stacked cages, there was too much stuff in the way to identify what was in the cages, but she could see things moving in them. There were also two cells, bars extending from the roof, to the floor. In the largest cell was a disfigured horse that had not turned completely, from the smaller cell, all Bauble could hear was something, or someone moaning as it lay on the ground.

The figures stopped working and started walking around the room, one of them closed the door cutting off Bauble's escape to the long hallway, while another walked through a second door into another room, leaving the door ajar. Those left in the room slowly approached the table Bauble was under, with a view of only their feet she could not see what the figures were up to, only that they were occupied by what was on the table, she was hiding under.

A metal tool dropped, startling Bauble. It rang like a bell when it dropped to the floor. Kat could feel her heartbeat quicken. Bauble was very nervous being so close to the strangers, practically standing under their feet. The metal tool that had fallen was a clamp holding a centipede, just like the ones they put inside the cubes. Kat shook as the purple little creature wiggled free from the device, landing upside-down next to the table leg. The hostile little thing flipped over and started to scurry toward Bauble, who backed up as far as she could. Bauble's natural reaction was to arch her back and hiss, showing her claws. She was pinned beneath the table, the wall, the bug, and a whole lot of feet.

One of the masked figures jerked down, briefly glancing under the table. With a gloved hand, He picked up the clamp and reached under the table. The small creature's advance was abruptly thwarted, as the masked man grabbed the squirming little insect.

The men continued to work directly above Bauble, as if they did not see her hiding there. Kat hoped she went unnoticed. She was not liking the fact the door to the hallway was still closed.

Bauble watched as a set of legs walked over to the stack of cages at the far end of the room, picking out a small empty carrier, bringing it over to the table. Suddenly two arms reached for Bauble. She sprinted for the other room. They all tried to stop her. One man put his foot down while another shut the other door, Bauble had no where to run. She jumped up on the table, where there were several centipedes stretched out on metal pans. The table top slid beneath her feet, it was moving her, toward a window in the wall that led to the other room. All Bauble could see beyond the wall was blue flames!

Kat was no longer able to tell us what was happening. She was lost in a trance as Bauble emotions went wild. "We have to get in there," Clutching my hammer and saying the words that I knew would prepare me. "If it is my destiny, protect me and make me strong." My skin hardened thick like wood, my hammer flamed on.

Ari shook Kat as I rushed into the hallway kicking the door open to the strange laboratory. The masked men were caught off guard. Ari threw her dagger silencing the man standing closest to us, piercing his Adam's apple. Blood spurted on the wall behind him as the knife stopped a few inches past his spine. Grabbing his throat he started to slump forward. Taking his last gasp of air he fell, overturning the center table they were working on. If he was not already dead by the time the table hit the floor, his end came when he landed abruptly, breaking the glass sides of the table, slicing him almost in half. He made no sound sliding down the sharp edges of the broken container.

The glass was shattered! The contents of the table dumped onto the ground at our feet, hundreds of tiny caterpillars started to scatter out of a rotting cadaver. With a word, "Greasalo" Kat gelled the crawling mess in a flash, stopping the progression of the tiny creatures.

In all the commotion the masked figures split, one ran into the other room while the other moved toward the cages. He was releasing the disfigured horse, locking himself inside the cell. The scared creature reared toward us, opening its bulky beak attempting to scream, its forked tongue made it gag as the maimed creature let out a stifled high pitched squeal that echoed through the halls of the dungeon.

The creature's huge head was partially transformed like one of the beaked mounts. However it still had the body of a horse, except for the right hind leg, it was oversized and scaled, with a webbed clawed foot, making the excited scared creature off balance as it raised up trying to stand on its hind legs. Ari stood tall holding her last dagger as it backed up staggering sideways into some of the smaller cages, killing or setting free the creatures inside. Unable to balance itself on its large disfigured leg it spring forward, lunging threw the air. I stepped up clocking the clumsy beast on the beak before it could do any damage. Its head jerked sideways, pointing the creature in the direction of the door, and into the hallway. With a crashing sound and another blood curdling scream it smashed into the wall in the hall, eventually righting it self before escaping.

I could see there were several smaller, half lizard, half dog, creatures in the room growling. Let lose by the graceless actions of the uncoordinated experiment that got away.

The smaller more agile experiments easily slipped through the larger bars of the cell door. Justly they engaged the man who had chose his fate by locking himself behind the bars. He tried in-vain to avoid the well deserved retribution from the miserable un-caged animals he had created.

One of the other disfigured dogs was snapping at my heels, its teeth, deadly weapons. My readied hammer brought down retaliation, as the hammer hit its head, and its head hit the floor. Its skull exploded splattering brain all over my feet, putting the crazed mutation to rest.

The man in the cage was still screaming, as he fed his victims, one last time. Kat had magically lifted the last of the failed experiments in the air with Ling Ling. The snarling beasts little legs still tried to gain traction, frantically kicking and squirming to attack. Even if it yelped like a dog, it was no longer cute or cuddly.

Across the room the door sprang open, two masked men entered the room, one of them was brandishing two sharp knives; his friend had picked up a small shovel and was holding it like a bat.

None of us realized that still moving in the gel were two bugs that were immobilized by Kat's spell, but not defenseless. They were the same purplish color of their smaller relatives, only a lot larger, about the size of a loaf of bread with larger fatter sections that seemed to be separating. Out of the gaps an onslaught of spikes was released, flying through the air in all directions.

Two spikes stuck in the forehead of one if the masked man. His friend was able to block the assault with his shovel. The shards made a knocking sound when they hit hard surfaces. Plink, Plink. Plink, on the shovel. Dink. Dink. Dink on the stone walls. Tink. Tink. One sharp missile lodged in the handle of my hammer the other stuck in my back of my hand. At close inspection there was a small poison sack on the end of the projectile, much as on a bee stinger that still throbs, pumping its toxin even after it's pulled out of the bee.

Those spikes we did not hear found a home in flesh. One masked man was spiked in the head, he dropped to the floor. His friend with the shovel was aware of the effects of these animals' fatal defenses. With a desperate crazed look in his eye he hysterically tried to drag his comrade back into the far room.

I looked down not realizing Ari had fallen to the ground as well. Kat let the creature she had suspended in the air fall onto the treacherous monstrosities stuck in the goop. Then she pulled Ari through the door into the hallway, as the wicked little pests prepared to fire another barrage of spikes.

The venom was unable to penetrate my skin or the handle of my hammer, Sticky reddish brown liquid oozed from the tip of the pin like projectile, unable to penetrate the hard surfaces, it dripped down the side of my hand and the handle of my hammer. Ari on the other hand was already out cold, foaming at the mouth and breathing heavy. I pulled the still pulsing stinger from her neck

"If this is Ari's destiny then let it be, but if I can draw the poison from her." I could hear my belt singing my song, placing my hand on her. I said the word, "Cleanse." I could see the poison pushing itself out the tiny pinprick. Ari grabbed my arm as she took a gulp of fresh air.

In the hall I could see the disfigured horse left a trail of destruction. It had broken through the door on the very end of the hallway. Confiscating a piece of the door still attached to the handle I used it as a shield for my only soft spot, the eyes.

I peeked back into the room, where I could see Kat had dropped the bizarre animal she was holding up onto the resourceful creatures, with the sharp personalities. The half breed was looking up contently, he was no longer trying to move; he just chewed on what was left of the large bugs, their gelatinous innards covering its face.

I could see Kat was attending to Ari, she was sitting up and was starting to breathe a lot better, so I cautiously checked around the corner where I saw the masked man looking up at me. I could not understand him. He was sadly ranting in the same language as the Selvain's at the inn. I grabbed the hilt of my sword, the words became clear. The man was shouting at me saying, "You're not supposed to be down here, it is dangerous work preparing the cubes."

He held his Selvain buddy, who was no longer moving, close to him. I tried to help but he was already dead. I reached down exposing his face. I was not surprised to see the markings of the Badger Clan.

Refocusing I looked up and there was Bauble. "Kat" I called out, she had to see this for herself. Kat walked into the room, and started to laugh too. Bauble was standing on some kind of mechanical device, staring at me with a crushed centipede in her mouth.

This room was half the size of the laboratory. The only thing in it was some sort of mechanical device, a dingy dark metal box, large enough to cover a full wall. There were several bent chutes leading up into the ceiling, as well as several square pipes protruding from the top of the metal contraption. Out of its side was a rolling counter that stretched out a small window, into the other room, where the Selvains were feeding the injected bugs into the machine. Through a glass window on a large metal door in the front of the contraption we could see a blue flame inside. This was how they were making the cubes. I reached inside and extinguished the flame.

Ari staggered in, still a little wobbly. She stopped to thank me, giving me a friendly peck on the cheek. Kat reminded us the importance of leaving quickly. Her gel spell wasn't going to last forever, and we didn't want to be here when the rest of the miniature army was released. Kat suggested we tie the Selvain man up. Ari didn't think it was necessary, I think she knew him. She was right he wasn't going to leave his friend.

We all walked back through the other room, carefully looking down for any other little surprises. They were all still caught in the goop. There was hundreds of struggling little insects, at the mercy of the forked tongue of the mutated dog, who was frantically licking them up. In the cell were two lizard tails, wagging in the air. The malnourished creatures really made a meal of the barely recognizable Selvain man, laid out in a pool of his own blood.

Kat asked Ari to scoop up some of the odd items from the table Bauble hid under. There was a small barrel with a tiny spigot, several glass tubes corked at the top filled with red liquid, as well as several spikes from the larger centipedes, modified with glass bladders, attached where the poison sacks were. There was also a book that was left open to a page showing a diagram of one of the large centipedes. Everything was scooped up into a sack. Finally, Ari slid a couple of the thin metal sharp knives into the empty sheath on her thigh.

We tiptoed out of the room into the hall before Kat's spell started to fail, taking one last look at the bizarre scene, before shutting the door behind us. I walked over to one of the skulls on the wall and took the glowing crystal out of it, handing it to Kat grabbing another for Ari and myself, stating. "This is not a job for Bauble."

I checked one of the other closed doors in the hallway; it was sleeping quarters much like the other room. Before I could look in the last two doors, Ari shouted. "Check this out." Ari was standing in a pile of splinters, they were on the floor where a door once stood at the end of the hallway. Coming out of the room was a strange type of smoke, or fog that seemed to cling to the floor, swirling as it poured into the hallway, covering the floor like a liquid, carrying with it the overwhelming stench of spoiled milk.

Reluctantly I peaked into the room. There were spooky shadows everywhere, the room was not shaped like your average space, at glance the walls appeared to be made of pebbles in a range of different sizes, there were thousands of little round spheres everywhere. I told the girls to wait here while I checked it out. The room was large enough to give the deformity that had crashed through the door a great place to hide.

Holding the light up I was amazed at what I saw. The walls were completely covered with mushrooms, from small to enormous, making the walls only appear to be misshaped, and there were no pebbles, just mushrooms on mushrooms. I looked down and there were even small mushrooms growing on the ground, reaching out of the murky yellowish fog. Looking up I realized I was under a giant mushroom almost four times my size. The mammoth mushroom was covered with smaller mushrooms, growing on top of it, under it, and off of its steam.

I tripped on something in what resembled a path. I held my crystal down into the swirling mass, there was a body ripped apart. Surprised, I almost cried out, I had to hold back my instinct to scream. The girls came up behind me. I pulled out my hammer still holding the crystal in my other hand. Ari held her dagger to the neck of the corpse, double checking the specimen was dead. Kat held up a second light giving us a better look at the massive room.

We all stood back to back. The doorway we came from was no longer lit up, the mushrooms were disorienting, every direction looked the same. Except in the far corner we could see another metal machine similar to the one in the laboratory. We walked over to check it out. There was a large cleared area with lots of baskets. Some contained a green powder others had larger green flat wafers. Another bloody victim laid on the ground next to some kind of grinder, this must be where they made the round spheres.

The metal machine was set up like in the other room with chutes from above and pipes leading up into the ceiling, only this one's metal doors were encrusted with the green powder. Out of the side came a funnel where the powder was fed into the metallic monstrosity.

Something in the room shifted. One of the mushrooms I was under started to shed. The green spores dropped to the ground, flipping in the air as they came down, slowly descending like falling leaves. I held out my hand collecting the little wafers as they drifted, almost hovering in the air. It was kind of peaceful to watch as a chain reaction was started, one then another, soon the whole room was filled with different size spores, some tiny like powder, others the size of my hand. We slowly started to walk back to center of the room where the path split in several directions. Suddenly I realized Kat was missing.

Turning back I mindlessly searched the dense fog. I found Kat's glowing crystal on the floor. It illuminated the reeking mist, but she was gone.

Ari called out, "Over here." She had found our fair-weather friend its oversized leg stretching out of the eerie looking fog, the crazed halp-horse was passed out, lying in the path with a dismembered Selvain still in its beak. Ari pointed out that it was still breathing. I shook my head. These mushrooms are the ingredient that makes the round spheres potent.

We found Kat's limp body by a winding stone staircase covered with mushrooms. In her arms was Bauble who was also not immune to the incapacitating effects. At the top of the steps was a stone archway, we had to get Kat out of here. With a little help from Ari we carried Kat up the stairs, to a small landing not inundated with mushroom caps.

The corridor turned sharply. Only a couple more steps lead up to another hallway, oddly, above the steps, were two rods protruding from the wall, pointing at the door at the far end. Unlike most doors in this dungeon maze, The door at the end of the hall had a good size diamond shaped iron cutout, making it easy to hear voices from the other side.

There were two other regular doors, but they were locked. Ari pulled out a couple of small bent pieces of metal, and then started fiddling with one of the keyholes. Because of the cutout we were vulnerable, it would not be hard to notice us, if someone walked close enough to that door.

I lightly slapped Kat's cheek then pretended to bang my head. I thought to myself, we should have figured it out sooner, if one room was where they made the cubes; the lab for the sleepy spheres had to be close. We can't afford to make any more mistakes, and we need to find a safe spot to wait till this wears off.

It was not long before Ari looked up smiling, twisting one of the metal sticks until a clicking sound came from the lock. Opening the door we found a four poster bed draped with sheer fabrics in the middle of the room. Being used as a nightstand was Lou's chest, there's no mistaking it, there are not many hand crafted boxes with the initials, M.W. engraved on the side.

Laying Kat down on the lavish bedspread to make her more comfortable, I hoped she would come around soon. Ari placed Bauble beside her. Unlike the drab blank stone look the rest of this place was done up in, this part of the domicile was quite homey. The walls here were draped with fabric, on the ground a thick fancy rug. It was not quite Aunt Roz's house, however it would suffice in a pinch.

Ari kept watch, cracking the door just enough to see outside. Then she left, saying, "I will be right back." It wasn't long before Kat started to wake, she wondered what happened, stating, "I'm never gonna eat another mushroom again."

Bauble was still snoozing in her arms. Kat was happy to see the chest, grabbing out some of the components she needed to cast spells, including a few more snips of the large feathers her father had collected.

I placed the bag of stuff from the other room inside it, taking out a jug filled with water for Kat. At least I hoped it was, it's what I pictured when I closed my eyes. I saw Lou fill it at the Shivan River when we stopped there.

When Ari came back, she wanted us to check something out in the hall, but all she was doing was staring at the floor. Kat asked her, "What's up."

Ari was absolutely fascinated, as she tried to explain, pointing at the individual stones in the walkway. They had the same texture as the other stones, just slightly smaller, and rounded on the edges. She asked if we had seen any stones like these on the floor downstairs, I don't think I would have even noticed. They all looked identical. Kat didn't understand what all the concern was about, Ari thought they might be levers, for what she did not know? She strongly suggested we avoid the misplaced stones motioning to us where to step.

Kat said, "That's too confusing. Lets make it easy." casting her Fly spell. She hovered slightly above the ground.

I on the other hand, once shown could see the smaller stones for what they were, in my mind they glowed. Stepping forward avoiding the uniquely placed smaller stones we moved down the short hallway, to the door with the cutout.

We could see the room was filled with stacks of edged weapons, bows, arrows, shields and miscellaneous armor. We had stumbled into the armory. There was a stairwell on the far wall of the long room leading up, it looked clear.

Ari fiddled with the lock then opened the door pointing out a couple more bad spots to avoid. As soon as she entered the room, she realized she was not alone. Pulling one of her new knives from her leg, she threw it in one direction backing up in the other.

Seeing she was in trouble I pulled out my hammer, as it burst into flames. Calling for the necessary protections I leaped out into the room side stepping the trapped stones. None of us saw the large armored lizard men standing on each side of the hall entrance with their backs against the wall.

One was grabbing its head as blood spewed out between it claws, Ari's weapon logged in its eye, the latter of the two had cornered her and was yelling out making an alarming clatter.

Down the stairs came six other Drazzi solders, all fully armored with swords. Ari rolled away from the troupes, into a pile of smaller bladed weapons, then started throwing them as fast as she could. I engaged the one attacking Ari allowing her to continue her assault holding the other men back temporarily.

The Drazzi warrior caught my side. His sword was not fashioned to cut into a block of wood, it did little damage, but the force of the blow threw me to the ground. I came crashing down onto a small pile of shields making a rattling sound that went on forever, alerting anyone else that did not hear the first call for help! Stepping on my chest, the guard put his sword to my eye. Ari stopped her assault, as the guard demanded my full attention.

Kat came lunging out of the hall flying at full speed curling into a ball, she body checked the creature sending him flying into a pile of axes, getting in the final strike he swung his tail batting Kat into the corner by Ari.

Before he got up, I hit his helmet with my hammer as hard as I could, it sounded like a gong reverberating as the helmet flew free. One down, too many to go, Ari dropped someone else with a well placed short sword, but no matter how many we could take, more men funneled into the room.

These Drazzi fighters were tough, well armed, and trained in using their shields. They were slowly advancing on us. I position myself in front of the girls.

All of a sudden a blaze of energy shot from one side of the room to another, out of the rods above the staircase, through the iron cutout, and into anyone located in the center of the room. All the solders were wearing lots of metal. It caused a chain reaction as the serge went in threw one shield, and out threw the sword, then down the line.

They all stood there staggering as the wall shot out a second electrical blast, with a similar reaction. Only this time the glare in their eyes went out as the blinding current concluded. Simultaneously they dropped to the ground, smoldering.

That gave a new meaning to the word 'stench', it was awful. We all looked at each other wondering who did it, but none of us knew. We opened the door to look down the hallway. Bauble was standing there on one of the stone levers still dazed from the mushrooms.

Kat kneeled, and in a little girl voice she called Bauble to her, patting the ground. Bauble unaware at what she had done ran forward, stepping on another small stone lever. Ari and I looked at each other, jumping back as another charge shot out of the wall, and down the hallway almost missing Kat completely. Almost!

Ari and I burst into laughter! Kat stood up and turned around her lovely long hair burnt to a crisp across the top of her head, like a reverse Mohawk. Feeling her hair, Kat screamed.

"It's not that bad." Ari said as Kat flinched.

Trying to hold back the smirk on my face, "You can barely tell."

Kat pouted, "Stop that, I can tell when you are lying."

"It was funny," May have been the wrong thing to say, it caused Kat to give me, The Look. Cowering I recanted," But not that funny!"

Kat twitched, as she was shocked again by her knife, sometimes I forget she has that dagger.

Kat walked up to a pile of helms, "It just means I have to wear a hat, Aunt Roz says hats are always in!" Trying to convince herself she was alright, Kat placed a metal shoulder guard onto her head. It seemed to be a better fit than a full plate helm. Walking away from us, she gestured by placing her finger to her lips, "Not another word!"

Without thinking Kat walked down the long room and up the steps, Ari and I looked at each other then giggled, looking back at the steps hoping nothing would happen. There was a silence, then

Kat came running back down the steps, "Hey guys aren't you gonna come and check this out too."

Ari picked up a few new daggers and filled her empty sheath with arrows then fitted a chain link arm around her shoulder. I found a real war hammer, hanging my spare on my belt, I followed her up.

Chapter Eighteen

Help

We found ourselves on a balcony under the starlight. How could so much calm watch so much confusion? Beyond a sturdy block handrail riddled with the bones of the dead, we finally caught a glimpse of the ancient temple. Considering all the trouble it has caused, it sure was a lot smaller than I expected.

On the balcony next to the door, to my left was a stairway leading to the roof of the keep, another led down to a staging area. The keep was designed with a mirror image of the steps on the far side of the building, both sides having equal access to upper and lower level.

Down below, where the steps meet, is the center platform. We could see in this area, stacks of cubes were being stockpiled. From this center platform the queen had built a bridge giving her direct access to ancient temple. It was as if the new building was an extension of the old. The only way to gain access to where we are is to use the original temple steps, then cross the bridge to the platform.

Before we could go any farther we had to secure the rooftop and the balcony across the way. We could see at least two Drazzi armored sentries on the other balcony. Ari walked on her hands and knees to stay low, taking a gander up top, she was happy to report, only two more.

We had to take them out without incident or fireworks. We did not want to lose the advantage of surprise. Kat flew up around the side of the building distracting the guard. When he turned around I clocked him with more blue sparks than he could handle. Ari took out the second soldier at the far end with an arrow, throat shots are her specialty. We crossed the rooftop dropping down onto the other balcony. They did not know what hit them.

From the top, with the help of Lou's spyglass, after turning the glass disks just right to focus, not only did we have a nice view of the old temple, we could see behind it where most of the action was.

The style of the old temple, dubbed The Time Temple, was quite simple, a basic square base, with maybe twenty wide steps on all four sides, leading up to a raised area, at least until Mytoka blocked the steps on this side.

The undefined square building at the top had a raised roof made of flat polished white marble, but the center was dome shaped. The dome was rough, not perfectly symmetrical, and pitted as if it was dug up out of the ground, a much darker rock than the rest of the structure, it looked like a natural formation, set into a formally structured setting.

At the top of each stairway was an entrance into what could only be big enough for one good size room under the dome.

On the far side of the temple rests an old garden, now just rows of empty planters making a maze to the middle of the courtyard where a stone sundial was placed. Nothing grew in the garden except stumps; the only thing that remained was a huge dried up dead tree trunk. One of the main branches had been cut off and the other was burned reaching out in a jagged curve, a morbid reminder of hopelessness, a fitting trophy for this dead city. I could not tell you what kind of tree it was; only that it was once large enough to shade the small arena that sat at the end of the garden.

The arena was simply a round raised stone stage surrounded by curved stone bleachers, currently filled with a Drazzi cheering section.

On the right against the north wall was an area where several large pens sat, deep pits dug into the ground encased on top. This is where the Queen kept her larger experiments, some so wild they had to be kept in chains, behind the bars that held them in. Larger, stronger, unpredictable, Drazzi goliaths, that could only be let loose, their bodies distorted, their minds ravaged by an overdose of dragon's blood, a smorgasbord of muscle claws, wings and teeth!

The whole area was being enclosed within the walls the Queen was constructing. Where the walls were unfinished stood the rows of tents we saw from the outside and a standing army of soldiers, they poured out of the compound and into the deserted city. She was up to something and everybody was here to watch.

Queen Mytoka stood on the center stage, with eight Selvains wearing long embroidered robes. Priest's of the badger clan. They were chanting as they stood on the round glowing glyph that covered the entire stone stage.

We knew it was her, who else could fit Ari's description so accurately. The female stood tall for a Selvain. She was dressed in a golden breast plate which she wore over a black robe that draped to the ground. Her breast plate was engraved with the symbols of the four elements, the over all composition was a skull that did not seem quite human. The brilliant golden breastplate did not fit her properly as if it was designed for a different race, beings with a protruding torso. The loose fit made her seem very well endowed.

In her hand was a scepter with a dark modular shaft. Gold rings separated the tubular sections, one of which was a leather covered handle. Set into the top was a piece of light amber. It was held by a gold casting that resembled an artistically stylized flame, shaped like the scabbard of a sword missing the handle. Protruding out of the bottom was a sharp serrated hooked blade.

Around her neck hung many talismans, the largest was a dark crystal pendant.

Queen Mytoka held her staff by the center as she pointed at a wooden cage on the stage, inside was Lou, Gavin and Eian! She was boasting, making a spectacle out of their misfortune, the crowd edged her on.

Gavin was pulled from the cage. We were too far away to hear her boosts, but her laughter was carried on the wind. The roar of the crowd intensified as he was carried off to one of the large pens. I told Kat to look away as he was thrown into one of the pits. It was like wolves fighting over a small piece of meat. A roar came from the crowd, who started chanting her name, "My-to-ka, My-to-ka,"

The strangest thing, my senses seemed more attuned as I stood above the battle field. I could see what looked like aura's surrounding the figures below. Just like under the glass in Quinn's office. I could see the true nature of the people I was looking at. Lou, Kat, and Ari were all basically good in nature.

Even Queen Mytoka I sensed was not completely evil. Her aura was still vary dark, but the darkest aura I sensed was in a burnt out building just out side the unfinished south wall. Whoever it was he was hiding from thousands of soldiers that sat adjacent to him. He was like a tiny ship in a sea of Drazzi warriors.

I was shocked to see Eyiyo, but not surprised when I realized he was the one with the truly dark aura. I did not know how he fit into this crazy picture. I did think we needed him to turn the tide in this battle. Help had arrived.

Ari shot her bow arching the arrow high landing it right next to Eyiyo's head, gaining his attention and giving him our position. He nodded to us, then reluctantly, he smiled, his teeth and eyes were all we could really make out. Eyiyo was right, it was happening just like he said.

I took time to ready myself for battle. Ari asked if I would give my blessing to a large cluster of arrows she had taken from the armory. I had never been asked to bless something, I wasn't sure I knew how. My skin turned hard as I clutched my flaming war hammer. Ari patted me on the shoulder, "All you have to do is get me close enough for one good shot!" For that, she had my blessing.

This was it, we could not wait any longer Mytoka poked Lou with the sharp end of her staff, signaling him out, as another roar came from the crowd.

I winked at Kat "One last thing" Reaching down to Bauble I touched her on the nose. "Maybe I can help you too." Scrawny little Bauble started to grow and grow and grow. Her claws were the size of a bears. Large teeth, big ears, nothing you want to meet in a dark ally.

Kat nodded in approval, "Nice." as she launched herself into the air.

The rest of us walked down the steps quickly moving to the lower platform. In-between the rows of stacked cubes we encountered a couple more guards, Ari took one down with a dagger as I engaged the other. He swung at me putting up his shield, I swiped at his legs, knocking him down then out, with the blunt end of my hammer. Stealing his shield we continued not letting anything or anybody stop our momentum.

Eyiyo was not shy; he had already breached the wall through one of the partially constructed areas, and was moving forward dispatching all in his way. The commotion called the attention too him and away from us, as we silently weaved between piles of cubes and spheres stacked on the bridge.

Ari jumped up onto a stack of spheres, flipping up onto the roof of the old temple. Stepping out around the dome she found a perch where she could be most effective, right above the show. Ari set down her bundle of arrows, then patiently waited for the right moment.

For me it looked clear all the way to the steps on the far side of the temple. The guards were being distracted. Adjacent to me on the other side of the temple at the bottom of the steps was Eyiyo. He was making a strong impression, cutting through Drazzi like a hot knife through butter. I wondered if he could take them all on.

Ari let the first barrage of arrows go. The first two stuck in a head of a Drazzi guard who came out of the temple, killing him instantly, before he could attack me from behind. Bauble who had my back tackled another who thought he had the upper hand as we made our way down the front steps and into the garden.

Launched over me, Ari's second two arrows were a direct hit on the golden chest plate. Somehow, they were absorbed doing no damage. Out of the same place the arrows hit, two magical projectiles fired back at their source. Ari put her arm up to shield herself, but as soon as the magic missiles crossed over the roof of the temple they fizzled out.

The Queen was now privy to our ploy. Shouting out "Get them."

Most of the crowd seated in the arena had risen to meet Eyiyo's advance, while others moved in on Ari's position. They were drawing in the crowd, as Bauble and I moved forward unnoticed, crouching in the shadow of the planters then the huge decomposing tree.

Kat flew down attempting to free Lou and Eian. She was startled when the face of a Drazzi monster turned around in the cage wearing Lou's clothes. It was too late, he was already starting to change! The Drazzi creature we once knew as Lou picked up Eian, using him as a pummel to bust apart the cage. Tossing the mangled body aside he grabbed Kat holding her so she could not fly away.

My guess the tip of the Queens staff is more than just sharp, the tip must be laced with poisonous venom and dragons blood.

One of the Selvain Priests pointed at Bauble and me, who were now standing at the top of the stone bleachers. I tapped my war hammer on the stone steps, as several Drazzi warriors still seated in the stands turned around.

A different priest on the stage clapped his hands and a small rift appeared in front of me. The rift widened as the land vibrated. I recoiled back to avoid falling in. The priest had opened up a fissure in the ground that stretched from one end of the compound to another. It started in one of the large pits, then ripped the theater seating apart, enveloping part of the south wall as it lead out into the dead city. Splitting the battlefield in two separating us from her, it did not matter how close I was, there was no way to reach her now. The void was deep enough to bury you alive. I stood at the edge watching those caught too close to the rim fall needlessly into the endless ravine.

Holding Kat with one hand, Lou looked me in the eye and I found out what it was like to stare down a fireball, as he squealed out the word Fiearo!

I dropped to my knees holding up the flimsy metal shield, banging the end of my hammer on the ground. "Protect me." A blue circle appeared on the ground around me. The fire ball exploded right in front of me. I was surrounded by flames. Bauble and I were shielded by my beliefs. Several of the solders advancing on me were not so lucky. Those not badly burned, plummeted into the void.

Eyiyo who was not far from me used the body of one of his victims to protect himself from the blast, still he and those around him were thrown back by the wave of flames while I stood my ground. The shield became to hot for my hand. It was smoking I had to throw it away. We were sitting ducks on this ledge.

I opened my leather pouch and took out a couple clay spheres, throwing them both at Lou. Exploding on stage releasing the mushroom powder, Lou went limp, allowing Kat to fly away.

Not to my surprise the powder had no effect on the Selvain priests. I had suspected our kind may be immune to the sleepy effects. It was the only way to explain why Ari and I weren't affected inside.

I wondered if I was able to dig a hole, possibly, I could fill one as well. Touching the ground at the foot of the fissure, I made my peace, but nothing seemed to happen.

Kat flew in waiving the staff I had given her, letting go a stream of blue flame, it was like the queen and her entire entourage was protected behind an invisible barrier. The blue energy was drawn into the lines of the glyph at their feet.

The Queen shouted out a variety of orders. One of the robed Selvains created a wind that made Kat's aerial acrobatics hard to control. With a rough landing she tumbled down by the sundial in the garden.

I felt a rumbling beneath my feet. I hoped this was my doing, but this was something else, four earth elementals spewed from the stone planters. Twice as tall as Eyiyo and made out of animated masses of rock and mud, their angry expressions showed they meant business. Leaving a path of destruction, their cumbersome legs violently ripping into the earth with each step, as they headed toward us.

This was not going as good as I hoped. I stepped back as far as I could, overwhelmed by the creature that towered over me.

With a heavy blow a rocky fist came down pulverizing the stone bench I was standing on, turning it into a pile of rubble. Even with my bark skin to protect me, an attack like that would have turned me into a pile of splinters. I was luckily able to side step its cumbersome assault. Jumping down, I pounded my hammer, crumbling the foot of the stone elemental. He staggered back and forth but could not balance, collapsing in front of me, with a second swing I shattered its head.

Eyiyo's sharp blades did nil against the uncut-able adversaries. He was crushed into the ground, then picked up and thrown like a pebble into a crowd of angry solders.

The creature attacking Ari walked to the bottom of the temple steps, but for some reason could not pass. Ari's projectiles shattered on its chest, as it attempted to reach for her. Each time it extended itself over the sacred ground it showed signs of weakening.

Kat had formed a ball of fire, rolling it at the creature attacking her. It did not even blink. Stone does not burn, the creature stood tall as the fiery ball exploded around it.

We had to get across the fissure. I looked at the old tree. Thinking this old boy might be of service one more time. I remembered how I toppled the tree near the river, using what I know, I started to dig. The dried soil spilled into the void. But the roots ran deep into the earth. It was not enough.

I yelled at the creature grabbing at Ari. It turned around slowly, obviously frustrated. I stood behind the tree jeering him on, he lumbered forward placing his hand on the trunk to search behind it, the tree was almost ready to topple, and it only needed a little tap.

Sometimes moderation is a good thing. This would have been one of those times. The whole ledge gave way. We started to fall into the abyss. The stone monster went head first. I reached out for anything, clutching at air. My oversized enemy broke any branches that might stop our fall.

Bauble charged across the tree but it was not tall enough to reach the other side. Using her powerful hind legs she jumped the rest of the way. My favorite ferocious feline attacked the priest making trouble for Kat, hoping it would allow her to fly away.

Ari noticed what Bauble was trying to do. She pulled back her bow string, concentrating on the ring of priests, looking for the one whose attention was focused on the earth elementals.

She whispered to herself. "The Queen may be protected by her fancy armor, but you my friend are wearing a robe." Letting go her arrow, as the stone demons continued their deadly game of Kat and mouse.

I had problems myself, I was holding on for my life hanging by a brittle root and the stony creature that was attacking Eyiyo had turned its watchful eye to me. I looked up and saw Kat. She was helplessly knocked to the ground trying to fly away. She was defenseless against another attack.

Suddenly, Kat and I found ourselves in a matching predicament. We were both in the way of a speeding block of pain that was promising bone splitting results. There was no where to go, Kat was pinned down and I was literally out on a limb or to be more precise out on a root.

Ari's shot was true, cocking back the head of the priest that conjured this mess. Foiling the deadly swings of our enemies as the two remaining creatures disintegrated into a flowing cloud of dust. The Selvain priest's blood was the only testament the deadly creatures ever existed.

I climbed up, flipping myself out, landing on the trunk of the decaying tree that was awkwardly balancing itself over the expansive cavern. It was holding on by only a few gnarled roots I could feel it giving way with each step I took.

Kat needed a moment to regroup, flying back to the temple, not realizing her spell would give out. It was becoming apparent that the temple seemed to suck up any magical energy. She came crashing down next to Ari, who was firing arrows at the red army that was now scaling the wall below her.

Kat was useless, unable to cast anything from the rooftop. The girls were surrounded, and it would not be long before Ari runs out of arrows.

I no longer could hear the distinctive sound of Eyiyo fighting. He was overwhelmed. I could see several of the larger monstrosities in the Queen's care had knocked his weapons away pinning him to the ground. He was screaming to me, but I could not hear what he was saying.

My enemies were advancing on me as I made my way across the crevasse. Quickly I realized there were too many people on the tree. Its stability was failing as I ran. I was thinking if bauble could do it, so could I.

Leaping with all my might as the unstable bridge gave way falling into the depths, taking with it those who dared to follow me. I landed in the middle of the stage. The group of old Selvain priests neatly stepped aside, as I tumbled forward flailing my weapon.

I was finally head to head with her highness. Bauble was at my side, already in the ring mauling one of the priests, they were having a rough time with Bauble disrupting their spells. I believed the glyph, like the temple, protected all in its area of effect from the meddlesome mishaps of magic, not allowing them to cast on those already in the circle!

So I swung at Mytoka with all my might. She stopped my swing meeting my hammer with her staff. She looked at me, "Who are you."

Bauble jumped on her back tearing at the chains around her neck. She hooked her staff on my leg causing me to fall back on the ground, my war hammer flew threw the air.

One of the priests pulled out a sphere. By the time the green fog lifted I was on my back surrounded by Drazzi solders and angry priests, while Bauble lay asleep at my feet.

Queen Mytoka stood glaring down at me, pointing the bladed end of her staff at my neck. She smiled, and then pounded it down. But my skin was hard as a tree trunk.

Out of the corner of my eye I saw the crystal on the ground. Bauble must have broken the chain. I reached to my side were my fathers hammer still hung from my belt, smiling back, "I'm Riley Moon!"

Mytoka's eyes met my gaze as I swung down. "No" she cried out.

The Hammer came down on the crystal shattering it. It was as if by breaking the stone time slowed. The shards scattered rotating so slow you could see every angle of each piece of the clear rock. The darkness trapped inside the crystal was now free; it formed into a floating mass that looked like a cloud of fruit flies. It rose up then moved toward Eyiyo in a twirling action.

I could see the men struggling to hold him down, as Eyiyo inhaled the black cloud. His black eyes sparkled as they became animated with new life. Changing to the color of blue sapphires!

His skin grew purple almost black, slick like a dark plum, his facial features sharpened as his brow became more prominent, and he grew three times his already abnormal size. Bat type wings sprouted from his back, his hands deformed, his nails became claws, his legs took the shape of a beast, as spikes grew from his ankles. Then a tail slowly sprouted tapering at end, then shooting out barbs, it was shaped like a jagged arrowhead, its tip glinting as if it was made of a shiny dark blue metal. Finally he grabbed at his forehead and horns stretched over his ears coiling back.

The Queen yelled. "You fool you're ruining my plan, why do you fight for them. Those who treat you like an animal at best, a slave at worst. Your kingdom lies with me."

The now docile creatures that once held Eyiyo down, were tossed like toys as he flexed his arms.

Eyiyo spoke in a thunderous voice, "Ethereal Dore." Next to him under his clawed disfigured hand, an area became distorted. It was like looking threw Lou's scope before it was focused on an object. When the area came back into focus, a highlighted figure stood unlike anything I've had ever seen. The best description would be a man sized grasshopper brandishing a pitchfork. The head was shaped like a burnt piece of popcorn with eyes. One by one a row formed as Eyiyo summoned his minions.

Mytoka ordered her soldiers to attack. Drazzi warriors fled into the compound through the unfinished south wall. Eyiyo answered her call blowing ice cold air out of his mouth, a frozen wall started to form cutting off the soldiers advance. The men who were too close were encased in the hardening clear liquid, captured in motion, never finishing their war cries, they became a permanent part of the wave of forming ice that unexpectedly accomplished the task of completing the south wall, sealing off the compound.

Eyiyo was too large to be impeded by what to him was now a small crack in the ground. He lunged forward then glided down attempting to smash Queen Mytoka and the priests around her, with his bare fists. His assault was stopped by the same barrier that foiled Kat's attack; it was like he was hitting an invisible turtle shell. The glyph would not let him physically pass through its sphere of influence.

Mytoka held her staff up between her and Eyiyo, a cone of light shot forth from the center. Eyiyo recoiled in agony. I could here her shout, "Your soul will always belong to me!" The shattered crystal reformed at her feet, only now it was completely clear.

Eyiyo used his legs as leverage pushing against the invisible shield that would not allow him to hurt those inside. He fought hard to get away. There was nothing he could do. He was being pulled back into the crystal.

A vast amount of energy was being channeled through Mytoka, with a jerking motion she raised her arm directing her rage at the ice wall. "Bliskrege" a red electrical serge was released, arching up and down as it destroyed the cold barricade Eyiyo had created, dismembering the unfortunate already caught in the grip of the wall as the ice shattered into pieces. For a brief second when she cast that spell her control on Eyiyo temporarily weakened. Eyiyo relentlessly struggled to get away. It did no good, she was easily able to regain her composure and refocus.

In a stern voice Mytoka said, "Release the Goliaths!" Then with disgust she ordered, "And kill him." pointing down at me.

I could no longer see her, I was surrounded by six Drazzi warriors in plate mail, all carrying axes. The plate was tough stuff, if only I could use it against them. I held my open hand out and said "Warmth!" Just maybe, I could heat things up.

I rolled out of the way picking up my fathers hammer as one of the red faced sentries barely missed my head. The jagged edge of his weapon scored the ground sending out sparks, as again my hammer burst into blue flame.

The Drazzi armor starting to glow as another warriors shield bashed me from behind. There were just two many of them. Even out of balance I was able to bang one in the chin knocking him out cold, but another scale face filled his place. I paced off as many of them as was possible, watching their armor as it started to turn a little red.

Next, all I heard was the connecting sound of an axe, a critical hit that rendered me helpless, as I became a marionette. My skin the consistency of a log, an ax now wedged in my back.

As I was swung around I could see colorful tracers emitting sparks, flying in every direction, Eyiyo's minion's had set off a series of magical spells in an attempt to destroy the glyph, the only thing stopping Eyiyo from reaching the Queen. The energy from their spells seemed to only make her circle of protection stronger.

Slightly blinded by the bursts of light I turned my head away, allowing the soldiers to push me to the ground, face down. They stepped on my arms and legs pinning me down. I heard one of them say, "Our Queen wants him cut up like cord-wood."

The sound of an axe cutting into a tree, times three, as the solders started a free for all chopping at my arms and legs. The spell that protected me, made my skin as hard as a piece of wood. It was going to take several healthy whacks to dismember me. But the Drazzi metal armor was beginning to glow with each cracking sound.

Now I could smell burning flesh, it was a race against time. The first creature's armor that had turned red hot, was now almost white hot as the metal began to sear his skin.

They had already cut deep into my legs, and my arm was almost cut clean through, but one at a time they stopped the relentless assault as their chest plate's became to hot to handle.

The Drazzi tried to wiggle out of their blistering gear, attempting to cut the hardened leather straps that held the burning metal to their bodies, it was two late, the searing hot metal was burning into their skin, cooking them where they stood.

Unable to move I looked over at the pens, as groups of Drazzi cranked the chains that held the Goliaths. An array of bizarre nastys crawled out of the cages, but the one that required immediate attention was a giant craw worm. It was like a giant red lizard had been crossed with a centipede. It was hard to believe this was once a human, possibly a horse or something larger like a bear, its legs as thick as a tree and large enough to smash me to a pulp, as if that was not horrifying enough, it immediately started attacking. Spitting out a highly corrosive acid at those assigned the task of setting it free, dissolving them where they stood.

Eyiyo's minions communicated in a clicking sound as the craw worm reared up engaging them. Magical missiles of energy shot from their pitchforks leaving a trail of iridescent colors. When the craw worm stood on its hind legs it was as tall as the temple. When it came down it had wiped out Eyiyo's forces. They went out in a blaze of glory, their futile fireworks shimmered crashing into the beast's backside in an another amazing display of useless firepower.

As I blinked my eyes tried to focus, hoping I would not pass out. I just could not see how this could get any worse. I was lying in a pool of my own blood, that was trickling slowly out of my extremities like sap. Watching the last of Eyiyo's essence being drawn from him. How could he hold on any longer? Bauble unconscious, the girls weaponless surrounded by Drazzi Soldiers, pinned down on the roof of the temple. They were sure to be captured. Who knows what fate the Queen would chose for them, horribly mutated or brutally killed?

How could I be so wrong, it was possible for the situation to get worse? Top all that with, Mytoka's priests summoning even more creatures around me. I felt the air pushing back as the foreground became distorted, I could only imagine what kind of horrific beast was coming next.

I could not believe it. Were my weary eyes deceiving me? It was Mordian and Lightbender. Mordian looked down at me, boldly stating "Everything is going to be all right, my friend, help has arrived!"

I could see other groups phasing in, groups of three. Quinn's trio came in with a bang. They were near the temple steps fighting the Craw Worm Goliath.

The stage lit up as pandemonium broke out around me, Drazzi solders were everywhere. Before we could be surrounded again Mordian touched the ground, ranting about how this was his kind of town, calling for the dead to come to his aide, animated skeletons crawled out of the ground as he commanded them to battle. The weary residents were given a chance for retribution against those who had desecrated their place of rest.

Light bender waived his wrist as the eyes on his bangle lit up. He was disenchanting the glyph protecting the Queen. She barked out more demands "Into the temple". The soldiers started a mass exodus as the priests closed the fissure to make there escape.

The glyph protecting the Queen was starting to loose its brilliance. She turned to us venting any stored up energy she had in her, unleashing another immense red discharge of power. It struck Lightbender, then racked into Mordian, throwing them back like rag dolls.

Eyiyo briefly regained some of his strength, he could not wait any longer, he had one chance to break the hold the Queen had on him. "I'll be back you have not heard the last of me." With those parting words and his last bit of freewill, just like the creatures he phased in, Eyiyo phased out.

The dome of the temple did not shine brightly but you could see lights flashing inside the rocky shape each time the temple was activated. Outnumbered and uninformed Quinn and the others were to busy battling to realize she was getting away.

I tried to move my arm far enough to heal myself so I could help the others, but my wounds were too deep, in the time it took me to recover 'dinner was over' Queen Mytoka had escaped.

Chapter Nineteen

Temple

Kat flew over to where Mordian had fallen, and with the help of Ari, I stumbled over to Kat, I could hear crying as I reached down to help him. There was some sort of invisible force between him and me.

I poked at it, then something started to materialize, draped over Mordian's body was Certsey. She was holding him. It was her tears that I had heard. Then a raspy cough, Mordian was alive. It was too late for Lightbender he was gone, his body charred, and his remains barely identifiable.

As soon as the Queen was gone what was left of her henchmen forgot about us. It was as if they only knew their last order. Activate the temple and leave. Hours passed and slowly the ratio between them and us turned, eventually the situation was brought under control.

By that time Quinn had wandered over, helping Mordian to his feet. In his recognizable slow scratchy voice he said "My boy, you were exceptional." Pausing, "All of you were, brilliant," staring down at me. "Even you, it is Riley, if my memory stands correct. The council would commend you all, for the roles you have played, today."

Quinn was quite amused by us, or at least Kat, he gave her most of the credit, "Against all odds, my little Katinka, has saved the day! You make proud the Wickets name."

Something was wrong with Mordian's left eye. It was as if part of the energy he was hit with, was trapped in his pupil, crystallizing it. He tried to focus, through the clear red stone, but to no avail, he was permanently blinded. However Mordian could still focus with his good eye, if he squinted and cocked his head at an angle.

No one really knew the extent of my injuries. With the ring I wore came the power of regeneration, something I preferred to keep to myself.

Efficiently as I could I attended to those who were injured, starting with Certsey, whose arm had been badly burned. Even though I did not see her, she had partially deflected Mytoka's energy bolt before it has reached Mordian, she probably saved his life. Her wounds were not as bad as his. When I was done they both were as good as new. I was becoming quite adept in speeding up the healing process.

Mordian patted me on the back, "Who's buying the first round," whispering to the side, "We're even for that little bit of business in the sewer . . . right!"

We exchanged stories as we recouped from the battle. Mordian told us "We did not know it but when the crystal was smashed the city's seers were able to see the battle and what was happening at the temple. It was only logical we no longer were blocked from other magical means of support. The Council sent every battle-mage we were able to teleport. We knew Mytoka was the key, until then we just had no way to reach her."

Quinn acted relieved the ordeal was over. He stared at the temple. I think he knew this was only the beginning. Quinn proclaimed "I promise the council will not underestimate the ramifications of this doorway again." He took charge of the situation ordering a constant guard be established at the temple.

I stood center stage where the battle had begun. On the ground was the crystal. It was clear, except for a deep streak of purple color fanned throughout the multifaceted stone. I picked it up wondering if we would ever see Eyiyo again. I held the crystal in my hand as

Kat came over and leaned on me. I looked her in the eyes and kissed her.

She told me, "You were right, I don't know how we did it, but we did what we had set out to do."

Disappointed I said, "But we lost everything."

Kat held me tight, "Not everything."

With the help of a couple mages courtesy of Quinn, we were all teleported back to Suxen Falls. We stayed at Roz's. There was a somber mood about the place, but Roz never lost her talent for talking, as long as Nate was not mentioned. The girls had a lot to catch up on, and they both needed new wardrobes. Shopping would have to wait. Much of the city was burned or looted even here in the high quarter.

I spent most of my time helping Knick Knack clean up. For some odd reason, I suspect Roz will be up and running before the rest of Suxen Falls. For now, we would suffer with the bare essentials, only four choices of pie and simple three course meals.

Aunt Roz gave me a long collared leather jacket with pockets inside and out. It fit like a robe almost touching the ground. I lousily stitched the Flag we had found onto its back, the one with the word Etlanthia. Somehow it just felt right. I knew somehow I was connected to this symbol. I would have to find this place even if it meant I had to use the temple to cross over to the other side.

Most importantly my new look covered my new belt. I remembered what Lou had said about everybody in town being able to recognize it. Sometimes it is better not to be seen. Like a lot of things I still did not know what the belt really meant, only that it could help me complete whatever tasks I might find along my journey.

As soon as was possible an open council meeting was called. It was to be held where the gates of the high quarter once stood. Kat was summoned. Ari and I went with her for support.

A good turnout of enraged citizens had showed. I was shocked to see Drazzi faces mixed in with the townsfolk. They wanted to know what the council was going to do. It seemed since the Queen had gone the hold on her victims slowly diminished. She no longer controlled those she had affected and was forced to leave behind.

This still left the majority of the populace disfigured by the curse of the dragon. The council leaders vowed to find a way to help those who were transformed. It was said, without knowing the entire process, the hope of turning them back to their former selves was not promising. This did not sit well with the restless audience.

Then there were those in the crowd who had not been changed. They were demanding restitution. Most had lost everything when their cities were burned. What seemed like a good idea was becoming a free-for-all, as heated arguments turned to several fist fights.

Kandir from the School of Enchantment stepped forward, reminding everyone of the losses we all have endured, making note of the tragic passing away of Nathan Lightbender, his faction was concerned for the loss of the artifact he possessed.

Kat was called out. For a time there was silence. She told the onlookers what we knew about Mytoka, how she unleashed the monstrous plants in the forest, the egg she carried to the volcano's edge, how we came across the diary, and the subject of its contents. Many were skeptical. It was asked, "What proof did she have?" As if they needed to read it for themselves. With all that had conspired, what reason did they have to doubt her? Kat explained anyway. We had last seen her father's chest containing the items in question, in the keep during the battle, Mytoka soldiers must have returned to the room before she left, and taken it with them.

What really stirred the pot was when Kat told the story of Telib and the truth of what happened when the fire reigned down in Avalon. The implications that the council had a hand in it, was a touchy subject swept under the rug long ago.

Many faces in the crowd were not willing to accept this information third party. Those with pasts to hide yelled out slurs making Kat sound incompetent. I stepped in to defend her, but was met with even more hostility. An argument erupted on the floor. Many demanded to know why this Selvain should be allowed to talk.

Many of the people had resentment for my kind before anything had happened. The mob knew the Selvain's were involved from the start, even if the Selvain tribes were not the controlling factor. This intensified the already bad situation.

A man named Cornelius, wearing the face of a Drazzi, stepped forward shouting, "This is not the time for more lies!"

Whispering traveled through the crowd. Many remembered him as a highly esteemed priest from The House of Sunfire and a respected member of the council for many years. He remembered Telib and tried to add validity to Kat's story, informing the restless group of spectators, "Many on the council have come to believe the Selvain's from the boat tried to help. The shipment of Pink Lotus Flowers was sent with great cost, especially for those who delivered the message."

It was also known to many in the city that those who had smoked the flower or ingested tea made from the leaves, were immune to the Queen's control. Even if they still felt the sting of the poisons metamorphic qualities. This was most beneficial during the siege on the city, and helped turn the tide of battle.

Cornelius lashed out at the somber crowd, "Without the Lotus flower, the temple would have been lost early on. Without it we would not be having this conversation today. It was no coincidence that the boat came to our shores when it did, delivered by our Selvain brothers."

Cornelius stated if the council would have received the message in tack, Nautica would have never been taken. He gave a special thanks to the Shark Fin Clan, who had played a crucial part is bringing the contents of the ship to councils attention. Applause with nods of approval came from the common people. "The council realizes we may have allies on the other side, Selvain allies." Cornelius stepped down, "Quiet now, let the Selvain boy speak."

I reconfirmed Kat's story as accurate, refocusing on the true problem at hand reminding everybody, "This was not a victory. Mytoka had gotten what she had come for, an army to fight her war on the other side of the portal. The council was wrong our most valuable resource was not a bunch of old books; it was you, us, the people. Look around we would be hard pressed to find someone who had not lost anybody, to the unscrupulous recruitment of the Queen. There are thousands of people unaccounted for. Over half the population of the entire Commonwealth is gone. We had chased her off, but the damage is done." We must pursue her. We must save our families and friends.

They listened but did not hear, acting indifferent to what I was trying to say. It was like the crowd ignored what they wanted to, as talk of more trivial problems arose. What about my farm? What about the road? What is the city going to do for them today? They didn't want to hear about the possibility of danger tomorrow.

I never understood what politics meant until now. I could see what made fairly simple decisions so hard, as many of the inconsequential details were brought into question. But when it was said and done, there was one vote that was unanimous. The council decided to use the temple to send a group after Queen Mytoka to investigate. Realizing it may be a one way trip, they asked for volunteers.

We all had our own reasons for stepping up. Kat believed our parents may still be alive. I had so many unanswered questions that were beyond the scope of the council. The most important. Who am I?

Mordian liked the idea of adventure and Quinn was happy to have someone he could truly trust aboard. Certsey would never leave Mordian's side. Ari volunteered as well, keeping her vows to always fight beside us. The house of Bliss wanted representation and elected a younger priest named Zelron. There were several others, including Cornelius, but in the end the decision was up to the council. Another meeting was set. The council would make a final selection, tomorrow.

That night Mordian, Certsey, Ari, Kat, and I, oh and don't forget Bauble were all at the house, having a toast between friends. With all the excitement I forgot it was my birthday. Kat made a special toast to me. All I could think was I would rather be here with my true friends than with a whole town full of the obnoxious, unreasonable, untrustworthy, deceitful, people that fill the walls of this big city.

I raised my glass again "To Lou," he had taught me so much. Kat added "and Alester." Ari, "Eian and Gavin," The toast continued around the room three times as we all added the names of the people that were not there. "Julia, Kas." It was easy to see through Mordian's tough exterior, he really is kind hearted as he ended the endearing proposal with a few kindly words about Nathan Lightbender.

We herd a heavy handed knock at the door. It was loud enough to hear over the clanging of glasses and the constant chatter from Roz who was talking to herself in a nearby room, she was staying busy, pointing out to Knick Knack what to do next, as she magically fixed a vase that was broken before greeting the man with a low scratchy voice at the door.

Quinn entered then kissed Roz on the cheek, apologizing for her loss. "Nate will be missed. If there is anything you need?" Roz hugged him, then returned to the chore of setting her home back in place before she started to cry.

Quinn walked into the room were we had gathered around the large glass table with the spiral metal legs. He nodded at each one of us.

I never know what to expect, but he even acknowledged me, without using his typical condescending way.

Inside I knew Quinn and Mordian truly cared for each other, but like everything else they are involved with, it was complicated. Quinn's opening line was an insult as he singled out Mordian, "Wasting precious time again? You should have been there when the council reconvened in private."

Mordian didn't take harsh words well. "You and your friends, lying to each other, is not my type of fun."

After a few more rounds of paltry innuendos, Quinn's attention turned to Kat, "You should take example of the company you keep. How is my sweet Katinka this evening?"

I don't know what Quinn did to make people feel like they were under the attention of their schoolmaster? Kat sat motionless shifting her eyes back and forth giggling, then she whispered," Fine. just fine . . . Grandfather.

Then Quinn turned to me. "Riley that was quite the speech today. You are a shrewd one to watch. There is wisdom in you, but you were wrong about one thing. We may not have won the war, but we were victorious.

I am surprised you are not wise enough to realize the extent of your actions. It is true we could not stop Queen Mytoka from leaving or taking our citizens. We suspect she had sent thousands of her Drazzi solders through the portal before you even reached Avalon. But she would have taken thousands more, if you had done nothing."

I said to Quinn, "The council knew the importance of the temple. You personally knew it was a portal. Why did you not listen to Lou years ago? Why did you choose to ignore Avalon?"

Quinn, irritated by my question responded, "I can see you are not prudent enough to take a compliment."

Mordian stepped in "Don't be so hard on the old man. That's my job." Quinn left the room unresponsive nose-up to talk to Roz, purposely forgetting to say goodbye before he snuck out.

Mordian got a kick out of the whole thing. "Not many people tell Quinn what their really thinking. Its refreshing, but there was too many things in that loaded question."

"The truth is Lou knew the real truth. He was the real hero." Kat seconded my statement.

Mordian shook his head, you have a lot to learn about the real world my friend, the truth is rarely part of it. Nobody but us will ever know that little bit of information.

I wouldn't doubt it, if those sidewinders on the council spend all night trying to figuring out how to spin this entire story around to their side. When its all done and said, they probably won't even admit that it was you, Riley, a Selvain, whose single action saved Suxen Falls and the Commonwealth."

"But what else could they say."

"The hard reality is very few people know about what really happened in Avalon. They were here in Suxen Falls. Some will say those who realized the importance of the Pink Lotus Flowers, made the difference."

Certsey butted in, "I was there, They were too late to make any real difference. We were no longer able to hold the line. It was not until Mytoka had given her final order to withdraw that the fighting in Suxen Falls stopped and the siege finally ended. If you had not broken that crystal when you did, Suxen Falls would be no more and the Temple Library and the Academy of Arcane Knowledge would have been ransacked."

Mordian butted back. "I'm afraid Riley, that's as close as you will ever get to a thank you from dear old Quinn or the council, but I will tip my glass. Another toast, to Riley Moon!"

By noon the next day the masses had reformed and rumors carried through the crowd like wildfire. Mordian was right, every time I heard the story told of our adventure, it had changed. Rumor was that Quinn had planned the attack. The claim was the council had sent Quinn's Granddaughter Katinka, and her faithful side kick Ari to investigate. Katinka saved the day, Mordian saved Katinka and Quinn captured a giant craw worm with the help of Master Wizard Terintino.

The fact that the council was moving the massive creature by boat to Newhaven was proof of their heroics. From there it only got better; my favorite story was how the Shark Fin Clan provided safe passage for Kat and her band of heroes. At that point I had heard enough. I just stopped listening.

When everybody had arrived the meeting commenced. A scroll was read out loud. It listed the names of those chosen for the task at hand.

"Hear ye, Here ye, a group of eight has been elected to rise to the needs of the Commonwealth. They are to be sent out upon a heroic quest. It is their bravery that all shall fashion themselves to strive for. It is our duty to make all their needs met. It is their duty to dispatch

Queen Mytoka, make first contact with those who aided us, and find a cure to reverse the effects of the Dragon's Curse."

The man who was reading paused as a cheer came from the people. One after another he listed the chosen and their accolades.

"Zelron, of the House of Bliss," was called first.

Then, "Certsey Shiloh, representing the School of Enchantment."

Mordian Zelts, representing the Academy of Arcane Knowledge and the School of Necromancy." As each name was read, a cheer came from the crowd.

"Katinka Wickets, consultant to the city council." With each cheer the crowd grew louder.

"Fenwick and Liege Edgewater, of the Suxen Falls Elite Guard." Apparently they were brothers and high ranking officers, one of which had been given a permanent set of scales.

"Ariana Sheaf, interpreter of the Selvain language." It was true Ari was bilingual. Did anyone notice she was the only one who had remained silent this whole time? I don't think that is even her real name.

Finally, "Cornelius representing the House of Sunfire." was called. He was also named leader of the group.

I waited for my name but the statement was concluded with, "By the order of the Suxen Falls City Council." Then the scroll was rolled up.

I was shocked that the council did not want me to go along. No matter what was said they knew the truth. In the end I played a crucial part in saving the day. I stepped out to set these fickle rumors right. I was not afraid to make the record straight for once and for all, even if I had to demand that I be included.

Taking center stage I started to scream at the top of my lungs. Quinn quickly interrupted, verbally adding me to the list. "There is one other, Riley . . . Katinka's special helper." I think he just wanted me to remain silent, and adding me to the list seemed to do the job of taking the wind out of my sails. Later when I asked him why, he replied. "Did you not go into the temple?"

Six days had passed before we returned to the battlefield. I was not surprised to see a large group of the Suxen Falls Elite Guard stationed at the keep Mytoka had constructed.

I stood on the steps of the Time Temple wondering if this would be the last time I would see my home. I took a moment to remember the good days, spending time on the porch, picking wild flowers by the old willow, watching the passerby's . . . Dreaming. Who would of thought the wildest fantasies of two over imaginative children could come true.

Kneeling down I patted Bauble on the head. Kat had weaved flowers in her hair and she was impatiently scratching behind her ears trying to get them out. What a odd wonderful world it is. She must of somehow knew I was thinking of her because right then Kat came out of the temple and held me tight, "Come on silly, your holding everybody up."

She cupped my hands as we held each other face to face. "Kat, are you sure you want to do this"

Kat looked me in the eyes, "I don't know how. But I will make a difference."

I finished her sentence, "with you by my side there is nothing we can't do."

"You told me that not but a week ago, has anything really changed."

We turned around and entered the temple. The entrance on the west side led to a single room. There were eight walls pitched at an angle to give the room an octagonal shape. There were three other identical good size doorways, one on every other wall. At glance the walls and floor were plain, made of white marble, with an almost seamless workmanship, as if the entire temple including the stairs outside was cut from a single piece of stone. There were no visible tool marks in the polished rock anywhere.

Covering most of the floor, in the center, in-between four pillars was a circular symbol, evenly split into twelve. It was like the symbol I saw broken in my dream. I realized it can't be just a coincidence that the same configuration is part of the jeweled pendant I wear.

But where does the tree become part of the equation. What could it all mean? Where do I fit in?

The grand symbol was inlaid in dark green jade, within its pie shaped pieces cut crystal. Like the rock in Kat's cane with the elements fused together by the river, so were the different elements joined here, seamlessly.

Everybody was gathering on the symbol where several crates, were stacked, needed supplies for our departure.

Above the circular shaped symbol in the center of the room was the inside of the irregularly curved dome we saw from outside. It measured about twenty five paces across and was filled with crystal formations. It was the largest dragon fart you could imagine, just like the ones we saw in the little shop in Suxen falls.

Some of the individual crystals were as wide as my foot and longer than me, beautifully projecting a multi colored inner source of power, gently lighting up the room casting hundreds of little rainbows on the ground.

The walls without doors had decorated round shapes on them embellished in green, like the floor. They were not divided into twelve pieces. They had clear crystal centers that were cut of such clean pieces of crystal it looked as if the stones reached into eternity. Inside them thousands of iridescent colors met, it made you dizzy to just stare into them. When you were close enough, the blur of colors began to form into images. The longer you stared, the more the images took shape. Figures would form, and entire scenes would appear on the screens.

For a moment, I swear I saw myself on what looked like a horse leading an army. It was like watching a moving picture, my face was blurred but who I believed to be me was engaged in an intense battle. The more I stared into the image the more detailed it became; it was still hard to make out individual faces.

I turned to Kat to show her but she was lost in her own thought, staring into another part of the wall. I asked Kat if she had seen what I saw. She shook her head, telling me she saw an unnatural looking landscape with books as big as she.

When I looked back I could no longer revisit the same sequence of events. Now I saw a cart driving past my old house. My father was there, he looked very young. He watched as a wheel broke off a passing cart stranding a young couple. A small little pixie, like those who attacked us on the river, flew away.

That's when I felt someone pulling at my shoulder. Quinn was aware of the mesmerizing effects. He was also bewildered he told us not everyone can see the visions. Nobody knows for sure why, he suspected this ability is more prevalent in those with a strong connection to the temple.

Quinn warned us not to stare into the walls too deeply, they can trap you with their tawdry displays of the past or puzzling prophecies of the future. Pulling us together he whispered, "Let me give you two a little advice about predictions. Sometimes if you know the future, you can make it happen, even if you do so by trying to stop it."

Then Quinn turned to me saying, "In some strange way, your destiny is tied to the history of this temple. The truth is I don't think I could have stopped you from coming."

With that parting thought. The nine of us stepped into the center circle. Quinn hesitated. "Something is wrong, there should be one more." Through the doorway stepped another Drazzi look alike. "You all aren't gonna forget me."

He talked with a slur, but his voice was familiar, I just couldn't place him. Kat and I noticed it at the same time, dangling from his ear was a shark tooth earring. It was Alerick! We immediately protested asking why we should take him with us.

He reached into his shirt "Because I have the map." He held up several charts he had taken from the ship, laughing.

We all gave him, "The Look." Quinn broke the silence "Alright everybody's here."

Have you ever felt the air turn heavy, just as something really bad was going to happen? Something was terribly wrong. I just could not explain it. Was I having second thoughts?

The ground started to rumble. A shriek echoed through the land. It was as if the earth itself was against us. Mount Helos was erupting. It was no longer content to loom in the distance quietly smoking. Now it was verbally venting its opinion.

Then something massive landed on the roof outside. A huge red claw reached through the door of the temple grabbing Kat.

"Reon-day-vous." She screamed!

The Crystals above my head and all the crystals in the floor flashed.

The giant hand dropped to the ground releasing her. It was separated from its owner at the wrist, right where it crossed over the edge of the round green symbol. Blood squirted out all over the floor. I could see the weather outside had turned to the worst. I don't think we are in Maguire anymore . . .

The End!

Look for *Riley Moon©* and his friends in their next adventure . . .

Riley Moon, Kings of Etlanthia©